The Beheading Game

The Beheading Game

REBECCA LEHMANN

HARVILL

1 3 5 7 9 10 8 6 4 2

Harvill, an imprint of Vintage, is part of the Penguin
Random House group of companies

Vintage, Penguin Random House UK, One Embassy Gardens,
8 Viaduct Gardens, London SW11 7BW

penguin.co.uk/vintage
global.penguinrandomhouse.com

First published in Great Britain by Harvill in 2026
First published in the United States of America by Crown, an imprint of Crown
Publishing Group, a division of Penguin Random House LLC in 2026

Copyright © Rebecca Lehmann 2026

The moral right of the author has been asserted

Penguin Random House values and supports copyright. Copyright fuels creativity, encourages diverse voices, promotes freedom of expression and supports a vibrant culture. Thank you for purchasing an authorised edition of this book and for respecting intellectual property laws by not reproducing, scanning or distributing any part of it by any means without permission. You are supporting authors and enabling Penguin Random House to continue to publish books for everyone. No part of this book may be used or reproduced in any manner for the purpose of training artificial intelligence technologies or systems. In accordance with Article 4(3) of the DSM Directive 2019/790, Penguin Random House expressly reserves this work from the text and data mining exception.

Printed and bound in Great Britain by Clays Ltd, Elcograf S.p.A.

The authorised representative in the EEA is Penguin Random House Ireland,
Morrison Chambers, 32 Nassau Street, Dublin D02 YH68

A CIP catalogue record for this book is available from the British Library

HB ISBN 9781787305687
TPB ISBN 9781787305694

Penguin Random House is committed to a sustainable future
for our business, our readers and our planet. This book is made
from Forest Stewardship Council® certified paper.

For my daughter, Zephyr Adrienne

If any knight is brave enough to test my word,
Run up to me right now and take hold of this weapon.
I give it up for good, he can keep it as his own,
And I shall take a stroke from him on this floor, without flinching.
Then you must grant me the right to give him one in return.

— *Sir Gawain and the Green Knight*, trans. W. S. Merwin

Le temps viendra
Je anne boleyn
[The time will come / I anne boleyn]

— inscription in Anne Boleyn's Book of Hours, Hever Castle, Kent

Prologue

On 19 May 1536, Anne Boleyn, King Henry VIII's second wife, was executed by beheading at the Tower of London for the alleged crimes of adultery, incest and high treason. Five men, accused of being her lovers, had been executed two days earlier: Sir Henry Norris, Sir Francis Weston, William Brereton, the court musician Mark Smeaton, and Anne's own brother, George Boleyn.

Anne and Henry courted for seven years as he negotiated an annulment from his first wife, Katherine of Aragon, with whom he had one surviving child, the Princess Mary. The conflict over the 'great matter' of Henry's annulment ultimately led to England's break with the Catholic Church in Rome, setting the nation on a path towards Protestantism.

After their long courtship, Anne and Henry were married for only three years, during which time Anne was almost constantly pregnant, as Henry grew increasingly desperate for a male heir. Anne gave birth to one daughter, the Princess Elizabeth; her other pregnancies ended in miscarriage, including the late miscarriage of a baby boy in January 1536. Less than four months later, Anne Boleyn was beheaded. At the time of Anne's execution, Henry had been openly involved in a months-long affair with her lady-in-waiting Jane Seymour. Anne was the first, though not the last, English queen to be executed.

At her execution, she delivered the following speech:

Good Christian people, I am come hither to die, for according to the law, and by the law I am judged to die, and therefore I will speak nothing against it. I am come hither to accuse no man, nor to speak anything of that, whereof I am accused and condemned to die, but I pray God save the king and send him long to reign over you, for a gentler nor a more merciful prince was there never: and to me he was ever a good, a gentle and sovereign lord. And if any person will meddle of my cause, I require them to judge the best. And thus I take my leave of the world and of you all, and I heartily desire you all to pray for me. O Lord have mercy on me, to God I commend my soul.

The day after Anne's execution, Henry VIII became betrothed to his mistress, Jane Seymour. Most historians today agree that Anne was innocent of all charges.

PART ONE

Death and Resurrection

I

The Arrow Chest

Anne opened her eyes to darkness. And wood. Her face was pressed into the wood. And the left side of her body. She realised fabric as well. A thin fabric that covered her. Linen, she thought, from the smell of it – like wet grass – and the way the air moved through it. Just slightly, for the air here was very still. The linen was wet and sticky. She remembered once wrapping linen around the neck of a stag, whose flank she'd pierced with an arrow, whose throat she'd slit with an ivory-hilted dagger. When the beast had stopped convulsing, she'd draped the gash with linen and played at dressing Christ's wounds. That had been before, when she was young. Her brother, George, had stood beside her, laughing at her joke. She did and didn't remember the two men, servants, who held the dying hart by its horns while she cut its throat. They could have been any men, low class, assigned to serve her.

She understood she could move her hands. Movement came to her fingers slowly, in twitches, one finger, then another. She curled them in and out, made fists. She understood now that her arm could move too. Her left arm was pinned beneath her, but her right arm was free. She moved it so her hand, through the linen covering, touched the wood. She felt around, up, down. Wood below, wood before, wood above. Perhaps the wood before her extended to a height of three feet, joined at the corners to the wood above and the wood below. A box, then. She must be in a box. She rapped against the wood once, twice, three times, but no one answered. She rapped the wood above and the wood below. Little hollow knocks.

The back of her head was pressed into flesh. Whose flesh? Was someone else in the wooden box? She blinked her eyes open again, tried to open them wider. Her lids were hard to part. Something crusted their corners shut. Probably the same sticky wetness that she felt on the linen. In front of one eye, a piece of straw. And the linen, wrapped around her, right over her mouth. Its tightness, like being trapped in a bedsheet, made her want to scream. She didn't like it. She tried to scream but could draw no air. Or, rather, she could draw air; she could feel her chest rising and falling, but the air was not coming through her nose or mouth. She understood her mouth was shut. She understood her nose was clogged. She opened her mouth, which was dry, and pushed her dry tongue out to touch the sticky linen. It tasted like metal. Her fingers were light. No jewels. Perhaps she had been robbed. Perhaps she had been struck over the head and wrapped in fabric and thrown in a crate, to be ransomed.

She used her free hand to feel her body. All around her, linen, encasing her, like a caul. Through the linen, she felt something round and hard. It was at her knees. And large. Her hand went to her stomach, to feel for the roundness that had been there. Her baby. No. She'd lost the baby months ago. She remembered Henry's face when he confronted her in her chambers, in her sickbed. In her birthing bed? No, the child had come early and still. A boy, it had been a boy. The hatred then, in Henry's face. 'I see God will not give me male children,' he'd said. And his eyes, cold with retribution. No more sympathy. No more love. No more most-cherished one. No more consort. He'd limped around her chamber, stopping before the window, his injured leg bulky with the physician's dressing.

To dress a wound was to show care, after all. Who had shown Anne care? She remembered stepping to the stage. The stage was draped in black. And the straw, strewn underfoot, for absorption. No, she remembered being helped to the stage by her ladies, who stood behind her. They must have brought the linen with them. She remembered the good blue of the sky, the blue like a baby boy's eyes. *Good Christian people*, she'd declared. She'd wanted to say *my*. *My good Christian people*. No. They weren't her people any more. *Good Christian people. I am come hither.* That one lock of hair that kept slipping out of her cap, that she kept tucking in. Who had shown Anne care? The executioner, dressed so finely she mistook him for a gentleman, who'd let her finish her prayers, who'd danced behind her, moving so quietly from one side of her blindfolded and kneeling form to the other. Who'd misdirected: 'Boy, fetch me my sword.' She'd turned her head to the sound of his voice, searching for him. *Je vous cherche*; I look for you. But he'd already danced, silent-footed, to her other side; he already held his sword. As he swung, she searched, unseeing, unaware, in the other direction, no time to flinch, to botch the stroke. And then. And then a terrible pain. And then darkness.

How had he moved so quietly on the scaffold? He must have cushioned his shoes, or slipped out of them. So there had been care there. But then what? The good blue of the sky and the dancing swordsman, and now she was here. She understood she was in a box. She understood, then, that the flesh at the back of her head was her own knees. She understood that the round, hard object at her knees was her own head. She felt the back of her head with her free hand as well as she could, because her body was wrapped in one shroud of the linen, and her head in another. How carefully her ladies must have wrapped her body. 'Let no man touch me,' she'd instructed them. *Noli me tangere*, she thought, *touch me not*, recalling the love poem Thomas Wyatt had written for her. For wasn't Thomas Wyatt in some other chamber of the Tower, accused, like the others, of lying with her? *Whoso list to hunt, I know where is an hind,* he'd written, like so many men who'd wanted to conquer her, or any woman, who'd viewed her as a trinket, a trophy, a deer to master and slay, a mount.

So she was awake. Was she alive? Was she a ghost? Was this perdition? She understood her first task was to undo the linen, to untangle herself from the tidy work of her ladies. She shifted her body's weight off her left side so that she could shimmy her left arm out from under herself. She shimmied and wiggled until her arm was free, until she could press her left hand over her right hand, against her stomach, above her head. *Good Christian people, I am come hither to die.* She felt for a gap in the linen. There must be a place where the fabric ended, where it had been gathered and tucked in. She felt in front of her. Smooth. She did not want to feel above, at her neck. She did not want to know the loss there. She moved her right hand behind herself. There, at her back, a small bulge of tucked fabric, running the length of her body. With her right hand she grabbed a fistful of linen and pulled. It loosened. She pulled again. She wiggled. The linen came loose from around her back. She pulled the sheet of it over and, with small kicks, uncovered her legs, then wiggled her arms and torso free from the shroud.

There was the matter, then, of her head. First, next, then, last. She remembered the lesson in sequencing from her childhood. For example, to bake a pie: first, gather the ingredients. Next, make the crust. Then, cook the filling. Last, bake the pie. (Though she'd never baked a pie. She had servants for that.) To grow a garden: first, till the earth. Next, plant seeds. Then, tend the plants. Last, harvest the crop. (She'd never tended plants either.) To become and stay queen: first, go to court. Next, catch the king's eye. Then, marry him (this step took a while). Last, bear a son. She had been so determined, so confident that she'd bear a son. Henry was a virile man in his early forties when they finally consummated their long courtship. How could the child he fathered not have been a boy? But there instead was wee Elizabeth, squalling in her arms. She knew the names people called Elizabeth. *The bastard. The brat. The little pig.* Her Elizabeth, though she hadn't got to keep her long before she was taken, sent off to her own household, to be raised by noble ladies and maids. That was the way of things. *Ma chère. Mon coeur.* Elizabeth.

First, next, then, last. First, learn you are in your own grave. Next, unwrap your headless body from its shroud. Then, unwrap your head. Easy enough. She had two hands free now. She felt the back of her head. She could feel her cap, which had come askew, through the linen. She could feel the place, under the left side of her head, where the linen fabric was tucked. She pulled gently. She could feel the fabric sliding out beneath her cheek, beneath her ear, ruffling her loose strands of hair, knocking her cap off entirely. She could feel the fabric sticking at the nape of her neck, congealed there by her own blood. Panicking, she yanked. The fabric came free, peeling with it the scabbed blood, a bit of the skin beneath. She winced. She understood then that she could still feel pain. 'Why the delay?' she'd said to Kingston, the Tower constable, when her execution had been forestalled a day. 'He is a good swordsman and I have but little neck.' She certainly had but little neck now. She pushed the linen down so that her face was uncovered. She felt the features of her face. All there, all intact. It must have been one blow, then. Swift. Clean.

First, learn you are in your own grave. Next, unwrap your headless body from its shroud. Then, unwrap your head. Done. Last, get out of the box. How to get out of the box? She rapped against its side again with her fist. The knock was hollow. A good sign that she was not already buried. That would be more difficult. Unwrapping herself had already strained her. She was sweating. So she could still sweat. With her hands she turned her head to look up at the lid of the box. A faint light shone along one side of the box's lid. On the other side, a hinge. A set of hinges. A box with its lid on hinges. A chest? What if all it took was a push? She shifted on to her back in the box. She put her head on her stomach, looking upward. With both hands, she pushed against the lid of the box, of the chest. The lid moved. The gap of light along the edge grew wider.

She pushed again, sitting up as she did so, and opened the lid. Her head rolled into her lap, face down. She couldn't see. But she could feel the air on her collarbones. She picked her head up, held it at chest level. With her hands, she moved her head to the left, then to the right, to take in her surroundings. She was in a stone church. She recognised its modest interior. St Peter ad Vincula, the Tower chapel. The light that filtered in must be moonlight, because through the windows she could see the night sky. In front of her stood the altar. She tucked her head under her left arm and stepped, carefully, out of the box. She breathed heavily from the work of it. Could you call it breathing? She leaned against the altar to steady herself.

Holding her head in both hands, she turned it to look back at the box. She recognised the carvings on its side, ivy and acorns. She remembered it from her hunts with Henry. It was an arrow chest. An arrow chest? They had placed her body in an arrow chest. Were they going to bury her in this arrow chest? She tucked her head back under her left arm and, with her right, swung the lid of the chest closed. It slammed loudly. She hoped there was no one around to hear it.

First, discover you are the living dead in your own grave, which is an arrow chest. He didn't even have the decency to plan for a coffin. Next, get out of the box, the chest, your grave, with your head. Then, realise you are still conscious, you can still feel pain, you are still capable of thought. Of anger? Yes, of anger. Last, leave. Leave? Yes, leave. She needed to leave, to flee.

With her head tucked under her arm, she hurried down the

aisle of the church. At the door, she turned to look back at the box, the chest, her grave. She would leave it there. She was nobody's quarry now.

Anne pushed the chapel door open and stepped into the cool May night, into the Tower of London's Inner Ward. She could see the Tower's royal apartments, where she'd spent her last weeks. She could see the White Tower, the old palace in the centre of the Inner Ward. And the scaffold, still erected, in Tower Green. She didn't want to look at it. She could hear the lioness, that nocturnal beast, padding in her pen in the Tower menagerie. She ran across the open yard, past the scaffold, past the White Tower, past the royal apartments, through the gate of the Bloody Tower, towards River Gate. She hoped it was late enough that the guards wouldn't see her. She hoped the gate would still be open.

It was. Frog song from the riverbank filled the air as she passed through the gate's stone arch, beneath the raised iron portcullis, and out on to the dock, where the jailer's boat was tied. She stepped into it. It sank a little with her weight. She put her head down on its bottom. She could see each finely fitted wooden plank forming the vessel's small hull. Without sight, she turned and felt for the rope tying the boat to the dock and slipped it off the piling. The small vessel drifted away into the current of the Thames. She was free. She lay on her back in the bottom of the boat, bringing her head to rest on her stomach, so that she could see the stars above her, moving slowly past.

2

Needle and Thread

When Anne woke – for she must have fallen asleep drifting in the little boat – she was curled around her head. The boat was still. The first light of dawn dappled its hull. She rolled on to her back, turning her head to face upward. Above her, the new spring leaves of a stand of saplings. She must have run ashore in the night. She sat up and held her head to her chest so she could see. Before her, the pebbly bank of the river, sloping up to a low stone wall. She turned. To the north, on the other side of the river, the Tower, from which she'd escaped. She hadn't made it far. To the west, London Bridge with its big stone legs, with its collection of shops and houses, all quiet, the people who lived there asleep. In the bridge's centre, the Chapel of St Thomas, too, stood quiet, its bells unrung. In late spring the sun rose early. Anne knew it must scarcely be five in the morning. She knew, too, that the pikes on the bridge's southern gate would be adorned with five heads, each belonging to one of her accused lovers. Lovers? She laughed. Her laugh was a wheeze. She knew her brother's head would be there. She didn't know why hers wasn't.

She must be in Southwark, then. What she needed to do, since she had apparently survived her execution, since she was apparently still sentient, still capable of movement, not extinguished yet, was get her head back on. It was heavy and awkward to hold and carry, and she was lucky she hadn't dropped it in the Thames last night. She turned back to the riverbank. If she could get out of the boat and up the bank, into Southwark, surely she could find a needle and thread at a tailor's shop, a cobbler's, even in some middling wife's sewing basket.

Warblers had begun to trill in the scraggly trees along the river. Terns darted in and out of the mudflats searching for insects. It was low tide. This would work in Anne's favour. Cautiously, clutching her head under one arm, she stood and stepped out of the boat. Her fine velvet slippers squelched into the mud, and when she raised her feet to step, the sucking sound the mud made was like a last breath leaving the body. *Squelch, suck. Squelch, suck.* She curled her toes inside her slippers to keep them on her feet.

When Anne reached the weedy slope leading up from the riverbank, she held her free hand out to brace herself against the low stone wall separating Southwark from the Thames. In the distance stood houses and taverns, businesses and hostels. What whoring and revelry had happened here last night? Anne wondered. What whoring and revelry happened every night in Southwark? Anne hoisted herself over the wall and walked towards the town, her gait lurching at first, then evening out as the mud fell from her slippers in clods.

Where was Henry now? she wondered as she walked, hesitantly, into the streets of Southwark. Harry, she had sometimes called him. 'Harry, oh, Harry!' whispered in his ear at that crucial moment, her voice breathy, to make him shudder and groan and come inside her. 'Harry! Oh! Harry!' again and again. And when he had finished and gone back to his own chambers, her ladies would come to clean her up, even snivelling Jane Seymour. Jane, Jane, Jane. Jane, with her moony eyes, her pious religiosity, her Englishness. Jane, who looked away when regarded. Jane, who never spoke a word out of turn, who held her tongue.

Jane, twenty-eight-year-old flat-footed virgin who had somehow seduced her husband.

She supposed Henry was with Jane now; perhaps they were sleeping chastely on two sides of a shared wall, two chambers separated by a meagre partition, so that they could preserve her virginity for their wedding night – for Anne was sure that he would marry her – so that any children born would be legitimate, so that he could convince himself that he was holy, he was pure, he was the hand of God. How odd to be a man, Anne thought, to father children but to carry none of them in your body; to be able to convince yourself that you could begin again, start afresh, new wife, new life; to have no ghosts of lost babies haunting your womb; to have no womb at all. To have, instead, rooms. A whole host of rooms to fill with men and women, furniture and servants and portraits and fresh-cut flowers and lumpy English puddings and spiced meats, a whole feast, a morality play where all the actors speak with one voice to say that you are right. You are right, my king, my lord. Right. You are right.

The smell of Southwark overwhelmed Anne. It stank of piss and shit, to be sure, though many places outside the palace walls did. What street corner or alleyway wasn't a latrine? What window wouldn't a woman stick her head out of in the morning to dump a pot of waste into the dirty street? There was the smell of ale, as well. And vomit. Outside a tavern she walked past, three men lay passed out, sleeping off last night's celebrations. 'The great whore has been beheaded!' Anne imagined them jeering. 'The concubine is dead!' Some of the revellers would have gone off with actual whores to celebrate. Though not these men, curled up together like cold children. She stopped and stood over them, nudged one of them with her foot. He moaned. So she could touch others, she understood, so she could be felt. She hurried along. The early morning was getting brighter, and she needed to fix herself, for if she could be felt, it was likely she could be seen, and though the streets were empty now, they would soon be filled with Southwarkers.

By the side of the tavern, Anne found a narrow alley. She ducked into it. She had to hold her head in front of her to fit through. She was looking for a side door, a back door, living quarters. At the end of the alley, she found a door and pushed it open, taking care to do so slowly, quietly. There, a set of steep stairs. Anne used one hand to hold the wall as she ascended them. At the top, she found a corridor off which opened two doors. Behind the first door, half-closed, the tavern keeper snored in his bed. Behind the second, in a single bed in a smaller room, slept his wife and children. A little girl and boy. The girl, probably Elizabeth's age, two or three; the boy a few years older. Their mother, young and pale between them. She couldn't be more than twenty-five. In the corner, a baby mewled in a cradle, making its morning noises, kicking its small feet in the air. Anne caught her breath, which is to say she gasped and the air shot through her hollow neck, like wind through a reed. At the foot of the bed, she spied the fair woman's sewing basket. Cautiously, she crept into the room.

How many times had she crept stealthily around Hampton Court Palace? How many times before she married Henry, creeping into or out of his chambers? How many times after? Anne of the green sleeves. Anne with the sixth finger. Anne with the wen on her neck that she hid with a wide collar. Anne the Lutheran. Anne the prick-tease. Anne who wore a dress covered in human tongues to her coronation, to show the people what happened to those who spoke ill of her. Of course, none of that was true, though she'd loved the absurdity of the tongue dress, when one of her ladies had told her of the wild rumour. In reality, she'd worn a white gown to her coronation; she'd been heavy with child, and the gown was tailored to show off her round belly. She'd spent the eve in the queen's chambers at the Tower, feeling the babe's elbows and feet scrape across her belly. Little Elizabeth: even in the womb she'd been active, agitated, a fire sparked inside her. Imagine having no womb, Anne thought. Imagine having no ghosts.

At the bedside, a board creaked under Anne's foot and she stopped, tense, turning her eyes to the little ones in the bed, to the mother's placid face. All slept on. Only the baby in the cradle stirred, and it was busy making happy coos, entertained by the shadows, by the headless woman tiptoeing through the room, now hooking her fingers in her own mouth to better grasp her head as she leaned down and nabbed the sewing basket with her other hand. There, Anne had it. She crept back out of the room, pausing for just a moment to steal the woman's headkerchief, which was set on a small table beside the bed, and put it in the basket, for she'd lost her cap and would be conspicuous without a head covering. Then she moved silently down the stairs. She needed a quiet place, and private.

In the alley the sun had brightened. A few people wandered up and down the street, preparing the neighbourhood for another day. Anne followed the alley to the back of the tavern, which faced the weedy riverbank. She could hear the calls of dockworkers in the distance, loading the ships that left London with wool, that returned with spices and silk, maybe a fine fabric from Calais, maybe a proper dressmaker. And whatever else could be smuggled in the crates and barrels, between other objects. A flask of port. A stone phallus. A few pages of scripture, written in English, the people's tongue.

Anne crouched against the tavern's wall. She placed the sewing basket at her feet and put her head between her knees. She squeezed her legs to hold it there, angled down so she could see the basket. There were a few spools of thread; a big needle and a small needle, both in cases; a thimble; a case of pins; a swatch of felt and a set of shears. Anne uncased the larger needle and stuck it in the felt swatch, so that its eye pointed upward. She unspooled an arm's length of a cream-coloured thread, cut it with the shears, and poked its end through the needle's eye. She had just knotted the thread when a rustling startled her and she jerked, dropping her head in the dirt. What had that been? Probably just an animal in the trees, a squirrel or shrew. She felt with her hands and picked her head back up, dusting the dirt off her face and tongue. Luckily, the needle remained threaded.

Anne didn't want to touch the top of her neck. She didn't want to touch the bottom of her head, to acknowledge the separation, the violence. Nevertheless, she grabbed the threaded needle between her thumb and forefinger; then, holding the needle, raised and gingerly arranged her head atop her neck till it felt aligned and in place. It felt good to have it there, to see from the correct height the world around her. She took in a breath through her open mouth, and felt her lungs fill with air. She pushed out a little cough. Her throat was dry.

She held her head in place with her left hand and, with her right, pierced the needle through the flesh of her lower neck, just below her right ear, under the gap in her skin, into the flesh of her upper neck, and pulled it through, until the knot at the end of the thread caught against her skin, tugged, but did not give. Doing her best to ignore the pain and pinch of the needle piercing and pulling, she repeated the stitch, working her way to the front of her neck, beneath her chin, before changing hands and continuing with her left, around the side of her neck, below her left ear, around the back of her neck, where she felt the needle for a moment scrape her knobby spine, shuddered, then switched the thread back to her right hand, to finish where she had started, below her right ear. As she sewed, she felt the skin prickle where it rejoined, as though the wound were healing through some magic. She felt the bones inside her neck prickle, too, her windpipe, her gullet. She felt the pulse return to her neck with a flicker; she felt her heart, which she realised now had been still, quicken and strengthen into steady beats. When she was finished, she looped the thread into a knot, squatted down, careful not to lean too far forward, lest her head break its new stitching and fall off, and grabbed the shears. She held the blades close to her neck and snipped the loose thread.

Anne hadn't expected the thread to hold her head in place, but it did, or it did well enough. Her head felt wobbly, but connected. She turned it to the left, to the right, took a deep breath, felt the air travel down her mended throat, cold for a moment when it passed the healing wound, then warmer, each breath more normal, until she felt no difference, until her breath felt as it had before her execution. It felt good to breathe. And, she realised, she was hungry. She hastily arranged and tied the kerchief she'd stolen over her unkempt hair, then dropped the needle back into the sewing basket and kicked it into the shrubs. What did Anne care if it got returned? The tavern-keeper's wife might find it later, or maybe a beggar would, and sell the thread and needles to some other wife, and pocket the money. Anne tipped her head from side to side. The bones in her neck popped and cracked, in a pleasureful way. She ran a hand along the stitching on her neck, beneath which the severed skin puckered and came together, rejoining. How was that possible? How was any of this possible?

Anne felt secure enough now to move from her hiding place. She peered around the corner of the tavern, into the alley. She'd left the side door ajar, and she returned to it. A great thirst consumed her, and this time she didn't go up the stairs to the tavern-keeper's dwelling but rather entered the tavern itself, through a back hallway. The tavern was dingy, its floorboards sticky with spilled ale. Through the grimy windows, a wan light filtered, catching dust motes in its beams. So there was enough money to pay a glazier; the snoring tavern keeper and his wife must be doing a tidy business, he pouring out mugs of ale to labourers, tradesmen, pilgrims ready to spend any coin on drink, she birthing him heirs in the small bedroom upstairs.

The floorboards above the large trusses framing the tavern ceiling creaked and moaned. Anne could hear the footsteps of a child racing across the wooden planks, probably fresh out of bed and running for the chamber pot. The mother's heavier footsteps followed, plodding and calm. Anne needed to hurry. She fetched a dirty tankard off a nearby table, uncorked a keg of ale, filled the vessel, and gulped the ale down in a few long swallows. It tasted sweet, just a hint of bitterness, and weak. She worried that it would leak out of her neck, along the healing stitches, but it travelled swiftly down her throat, filling her empty stomach.

The footsteps on the floor above increased in number and quickened. She heard a door squeak on its hinges. She poured herself another tankard of ale and drank it. Then, spying a bowl full of water, she cupped some in her hands and rinsed the dried blood off her neck and décolletage, off her face, so that her skin was clean, before rushing out of the side door to the alley. There, she hiked her skirts, squatted, and let out a strong stream of urine. It kicked a puff of dust up when it hit the dirt below, then flowed past her feet, towards the river, like everything else.

Anne looked down at her gown. It was covered in dried brown blood. Beneath it, the skirt of her red kirtle was relatively clean, but beneath the kirtle, her smock was stiff in the front, near her crotch, with what she supposed was her own piss, released moments after decapitation. Luckily, she hadn't shat herself, as she knew people sometimes did upon dying. The gown's fur hem was caked in mud from the riverbank. Small bits of straw clung to the fabric at her knees, left there from kneeling on the scaffold.

The mess on Anne's clothing was conspicuous. What she wanted was a clean gown appropriate for her station as Queen of England, wife of the king, mother to the Princess Elizabeth, true heir to the throne. She knew that she would fare better, though, would stand out less, dressed as a commoner. That way, she could make her way back across the bridge, unnoticed; she could sneak into whatever palace Henry and Jane were holed up in, undetected. Then what? What vengeance might she enact? Did she even want vengeance? She wasn't sure yet. She needed some time to think. But she knew that she must find her way to Henry if she was to have any control, if she was to have any justice.

Anne walked back behind the tavern and carefully removed her sullied gown. This took some skill and contortion, with no lady's maids to assist. What remained was her red kirtle, over her plain white smock. Both had been protected from too much blood by the thick gown, and the kirtle's red colour hid the little bit that had soaked through. This would do for Southwark, she supposed, where many women lacked gowns. Even the tavern-keeper's wife had had just a kirtle laid out over her bedroom chair.

Anne needed something to cover the wound on her neck. She remembered that she'd asked her lady Margaret Lee to bring her one of Elizabeth's silk swaddling cloths in the Tower, from when the child was an infant, so that she could be buried with it. She'd hidden the cloth inside the bodice of her kirtle, beneath her smock, close to her skin. She felt inside her bodice. It was still there. Carefully, she retrieved it and held it to her nose. It smelled of Elizabeth as she had as a baby, sweet like bread, and lavender, from the sachet it had been stored with. Anne wrapped the silk cloth around her neck. The fabric was just long enough to encircle it. Digging in the scrubby trees, she retrieved the sewing basket, threaded a needle, and sewed the two ends of the silk cloth together to form a collar, so that the stitches holding her head in place were hidden. She crumpled the gown and kicked it into the shrubs, along with the sewing basket. There, she thought, done.

It was in this condition that Anne stepped out from the alleyway alongside the tavern and back on to the streets of the unruly borough of Southwark. What did she know about Southwark? That it was south of London. That she'd been here a handful of times on official business with Henry. That to travel south of London one must pass through Southwark, or take a barge down the river, avoiding it, which of course was more dignified. That portions of Southwark operated under the authority of the Bishop of Winchester. That it had a reputation for lawlessness.

On the street, the people were going about their morning business. The houses here were spaced further apart than those in London. Little gardens were dotted between them, adorned with chickens and geese. A few buildings down, a wooden sign in the shape of a pig standing over a large knife hung from a pole. Must be a butcher's shop. And next to that, a building with a wooden sign in the shape of a working-man's shirt. Must be a tailor's.

Further up the road Anne saw a hostel. She knew people travelling to London from the south stopped in Southwark to rest for a night before crossing London Bridge. She knew those headed south to Canterbury on a pilgrimage also stopped to rest a night before their long journey. She knew, as well, that there were prostitutes in Southwark, that men came here to visit the brothels. Within the city walls of London, prostitution was illegal, but in Southwark there were the stews, brothels that were allowed to operate. A wink and a nod to the wives of London, who wanted prostitutes out of the city, and to the husbands, who wanted a place to behave like animals. How could you tell a hostel from a brothel? How could you tell a working woman from a prostitute? Anne wondered. Outside this hostel, two women beat at a set of thick drapes with wooden bats, sending up billows of dust, while the hostel keeper sat in a wooden chair, watching them, arms folded across his belly. It wasn't even noontime, so, Anne supposed, it would be hard to spot a prostitute.

3

The Good Man of the Snow

It had been a mistake, Anne thought as she walked the streets of Southwark, heading west towards London Bridge, to steal the boat and drift across the river. She ought to have hidden and stayed in the Tower, where she'd have been closer to Jane, closer to Henry, closer to whatever she chose to do next. She'd panicked, waking up headless, and in her panic she'd erred. Now she'd need to cross the bridge back into London.

As Anne walked, her stomach grumbled with hunger. There were food vendors here, but she had nothing to pay them with. She'd stashed her remaining jewels in her pillowcase before her execution, directing Lady Margaret to ensure they were given to Elizabeth. Lady Margaret was one of the only ladies-in-waiting sent with Anne to the Tower whom she liked. The others had been chosen for her, the worst ladies, the ones with snide faces, who tittered under gloved hands, who'd eyed and maybe fucked her husband, even after his jousting accident left him limping around the palace and stinking of rotted flesh. She had wondered what gifts they'd been given to accompany her to the Tower, to spy and report on her – probably Anne's own lands, own wealth, given to her by the king, then given to the ladies, or more accurately to their husbands, as a reward for their service. By the time she'd hidden her jewels in her pillowcase, she'd been so hysterical with the impending doom of her execution that one moment she was laughing, the next crying, swings in mood that the bad ladies certainly tattled back to Thomas Cromwell, the king's loyal aide and most trusted adviser. On her way to the scaffold, Anne had been handed a small purse by one of these bad ladies, but she'd given the money to the poor gathered there to receive her final alms, and to the executioner, as a fee for his service. None remained.

When Anne passed by a baker's open stand, she waited until he turned his back, then slipped a hot bun up her sleeve. The bun heated her cold, stiff fingers, and the bites she tore from it as she strolled tasted sweet and eased her hunger. She was nibbling her stolen bun when she passed a pillory in the middle of the street, to which a man was nailed by his ear. What offence had the man committed? Maybe theft. Maybe adultery. Maybe speaking ill of the crown. The man looked exhausted, slumped to his knees on the small wooden stage, his ear crusted in dried blood where the nail had been driven through. He must have been there for some time. It was likely he'd have to tear his ear to get free. That was part of the punishment of the pillory; nobody came to remove the nail – the offender had to break free on their own. Anne wondered if this man would have the strength to do so, or if he would die of thirst and exposure on the stage first.

She knew the story of the pregnant woman who had been nailed by her ear to a pillory for insisting that Katherine was the real queen and Anne a whore, a violation of the Act of Succession, which made denouncing Anne as queen in speech or writing a crime. What had happened to that pregnant woman? Anne imagined she'd been able to free herself, eventually, tearing her ear in the process. Had she survived her labour? Had her babe? For a moment, Anne felt guilt at the poor woman's fate. Then she reversed herself. The people had to be taught lessons. It wasn't like Anne herself had ordered the woman nailed to a wooden pole. For that matter, it wasn't like Anne herself had made the woman speak treasonously.

The man nailed to the pillory looked at Anne imploringly, as though she could help him down from the wooden stage of his suffering.

'I shall pray for you,' Anne said, and the man looked away and closed his eyes.

Prayer had always comforted Anne. She knew people questioned her religious convictions, her faith, but it was true: she was a devout and faithful woman. But she had questions. She didn't believe the Eucharist really transformed into Christ's blood and body; it was clearly just wine and bread. She thought the mass should be delivered in English, not Latin, a language the common people couldn't speak or understand. She thought each person should be entrusted with their own salvation, should form their own relationship with God. She sneaked copies of English translations of biblical passages not just to other noblewomen but also to her maids, who she felt had just as much right to the word of God as the nobility.

These beliefs made Anne a reformer and a radical, and there was a time only a dozen years earlier when she'd have been accused of being a Lutheran and burned at the stake for such heresies. That was before she and Henry started courting, before Cardinal Wolsey tried and failed to secure Henry an annulment from his first wife, Katherine, inciting the king's ire and falling from favour. Before Anne and Cromwell introduced Henry to reformist ideals, pushed him from two directions – a lover's and a statesman's – to reconsider the power of the Catholic Church in England, and the stranglehold Rome had on matters as personal as whom the king married or divorced. Before they pushed Henry to reconsider his own relationship with God, which, since he was a prince, ought to be the most direct line in the nation to the Lord and His desires for England.

One of Anne's finest prayer books was the one Henry had given her as a New Year's present in 1528, two years into their courtship. At the time, Henry had Wolsey trying to negotiate an annulment from Katherine, whom everybody knew he shouldn't have been allowed to marry in the first place because she had previously been married to his elder brother, Arthur, who'd died from a fever just a few months after their wedding. When Katherine married Arthur, Henry had been a child of ten, but he'd been transfixed by the Spanish bride, and, by the time he was fifteen, was begging his father, Henry VII, to allow him to wed the dowager princess. The old man refused, and Henry had had to wait until he died to wed Katherine. Marrying Katherine was one of Henry's first acts as king. He was seventeen, Katherine twenty-three. Although Henry, Katherine and several courtiers had sworn that she and Arthur had never consummated their marriage, and so were not legally wedded – thus securing a dispensation from the pope that allowed Henry to marry her – Henry now swore all involved had lied. Katherine had slept with Arthur. Therefore, she was his sister by marriage. Therefore, their marriage had never been valid and should be nullified. It was right there in Leviticus: *If a man take his brother's wife, it is an unclean thing, he hath uncovered his brother's secrets, they shall be childless therefore.* The death of all his male children by Katherine, Henry now argued – for his one living child with her, a daughter, didn't count – was evidence that they had displeased the Lord God.

It would be another five years before Anne would marry the king, though she didn't know that on New Year of 1528. She'd been living in her own apartments in Hampton Court, right under the nose of Queen Katherine. Anne thought the old queen stodgy and swept up in superstitions. She was always cloistered away in long devotional prayer sessions and dressed in black, for she was perpetually in mourning for her many lost children. Her clothing smelled, not unpleasantly, of incense, from the daily masses she attended, and cedar, which lined her wardrobe to keep the moths from devouring her ample-waisted gowns.

That New Year's Day had been filled with festivities. Henry and Anne rode out at dawn for a hunt and returned to a lavish breakfast in the great hall, which servants had bedecked with holly boughs and twisting sprigs of ivy. Anne's brother George was there, laughing merrily with Thomas Wyatt and Henry Norris at jokes that Anne was too far away to hear. Katherine sulked with her ladies in the shadows at the far end of the hall, taking meagre bites of her food, whatever her teeth, badly decayed and always paining her, would allow. Anne had been seated brazenly next to Henry, at the top table, where Katherine should have sat, so confident were they that Anne would soon be queen.

Breakfast bled into cards and luncheon, and games in the courtyard. The grass shimmered with frost and the courtiers could see their breath in vapoury clouds as they talked and jested, drunk by the afternoon, in high spirits.

Henry had given her his New Year's gift after the courtyard games but before the evening feast. The two slunk off, tipsy on wine, to Anne's chambers, where Henry kissed her passionately, untied her bodice and fondled her breasts, untied his own codpiece and placed his penis in her hand to stroke, whispered in her ear, 'I want to put a royal prince in you,' humped and moaned until he came in her hand, until she came, too, for he also had a hand up her skirts.

When they'd finished, he pulled out the present. Where had he been hiding it? For it had seemed, when they'd come into the room, that he'd had nothing in his hands. Perhaps he'd had it tucked in the back of his hose, beneath his doublet? He presented it to her as the two lay snuggling in bed. 'For my Anne,' he said, and she marvelled at its splendour, this book of hours, printed in Paris – not a handwritten manuscript but exquisite nonetheless for the beauty of its printed font and its hand-painted illuminations, for its blue velvet cover, framed in silver gilt, studded with three glimmering jacinths. 'I shall treasure it always,' she told him, gushing over the gift as the two dressed themselves, so that nobody would know what they'd been up to, though surely everybody could guess what they'd done when they'd both disappeared from the afternoon games. And yet, they hadn't had sex. Anne was, and remained, a virgin.

It wasn't until the evening, on her way to the feast in the great hall, that Anne realised Henry's gift to her hadn't been as special as she'd thought. She was walking past Katherine and her ladies when she overheard the queen showing something off to the small circle of women. 'So beautiful!' one declared. And another, 'The lovely silver gilt on the cover! And those gems!'

''Tis true the king loves me dearly,' Katherine replied, making pointed eye contact with Anne as she passed. 'He gave me this prayer book as a New Year's gift this morning, when we shared a special moment with our daughter, the Princess Mary, after breakfast.'

Anne did remember Henry dipping out of the card games after breakfast, though because Katherine never stayed around for cards or games any more, she didn't think to observe where the queen had gone, or to put together that the two might be with their child, sharing a family moment. Now it was all Anne could do not to imagine the threesome laughing happily and embracing before a warming fire, the king and queen showering their daughter with affections Anne would have preferred to have for herself. Anne kept her head down as she walked past, to hide the tears that were rising.

George pulled her aside as she entered the great hall.

'My sister,' he said, 'what troubles you?'

Anne shook her head, embarrassed to admit to the duplicate gifts, to the possibility that Henry was not as committed to ending his marriage as he professed, to the way his behaviour could at times seem thoughtless and cold, as though he were mimicking social expectations, like gift giving, without actually understanding the spirit of such activities.

From his pocket, George pulled out a sprig of winter holly and stuck it behind his ear. "Tis I, the Green Man!' he declared, dancing playfully from foot to foot, in imitation of the May King. 'Or perhaps the Winter Man, garlanded in icicles.' He waggled his fingers to imitate spears of ice.

'The French would say *le bonhomme de neige*,' Anne replied, smiling slyly and wiping a tear from the corner of her eye.

' "The good man of the snow"?' replied George, incredulously. 'Well, I suppose I must be, for I am a good man, and it has started to snow.' Indeed, outside the windows of the great hall, large snowflakes fell, sticking to the glass and sliding in wet clumps to the bottom of each pane.

George squeezed her hand. 'Take heart, sister,' he said. 'For whatever *she* may say or boast' – he nodded to Katherine, gathered with her group of ladies – 'the king only has affections for you, and soon she will be out of the palace, a dowager princess again, and you sitting on the throne.'

It was two days later when Anne observed Thomas Cromwell hurrying down a corridor to a meeting with the king with a third copy of the prayer book. 'God be with you,' he'd said to her, nodding, as he rushed past, holding his stack of papers and the silver-gilt, jacinth-studded prayer book to his chest. So, one for his wife, one for his mistress, one for his lackey, Anne thought, and just for a moment, she wondered if she might in fact be interchangeable with Katherine, her competition in the bedchamber, as well as with Cromwell, her competition in the council room.

Even so, Anne enjoyed the prayer book and read it faithfully, keeping it with her as the court moved from palace to palace. She wondered where it might be now. She'd wanted Elizabeth to have it, but as with many other possessions she'd left directions for her daughter to receive, she doubted it would make it to the child's hands.

As Anne walked down the street, dodging pilgrims and Southwarkers, she imagined herself strung like a marionette and George holding the strings with his icicle fingers, the *bonhomme de neige*, a sprig of holly behind each ear, dancing her into the king's bed, into her marriage with the king, into the seat of influence — not just for herself but for her father, keen on advancing the family's name and wealth, and for her Uncle Norfolk, patriarch of her mother's family, a powerful man determined to acquire even more power, and, of course, for George.

No. She shook her head, gazing down the row of shops. That wasn't fair. George loved her. He hadn't controlled her like a puppet master, hadn't forced her to do anything she didn't want to. She'd walked into Henry's embrace willingly, one foot in front of the other, convinced she'd always be treasured, that she could show the king a better way, convinced, most of all, that she'd come out alive.

4

The Bear

It was evening when Anne reached Long Southwark, the road that led to London Bridge's south gate, when she remembered the fee she'd need to pay to cross, and recalled again that she didn't have any money. She averted her gaze from the bridge's gate, not wanting to see what she knew was there: the heads of Henry Norris, William Brereton, Francis Weston, Mark Smeaton, and her own George.

West of the bridge, past the stalls of Borough Market – closed for the day – Anne could see a crowd gathering. Ale was already flowing as labourers ended their days, as wives left babes in cradles to go and make merry, to follow the buzz of the crowd towards excitement. Surely Anne could find some money among the tightly packed Southwarkers, loose in someone's pocket or dropped along the street.

No sooner had she stepped into the crowd than she was pushed along, the chill she'd felt in the evening air replaced by the warm heat of many bodies. In her red kirtle she was indistinguishable from a common woman, her undergarment mistaken for a peasant's best dress. She hurried to keep pace with the throng. Down the road they travelled, past the church with its hidden nuns, past the Bishop of Winchester's palace, past the notorious Clink Street Prison, whose stench of disease and defecation made Anne gag and recall her own imprisonment. Though it had been more comfortable than the wretched Clink – she'd been offered three meals a day, ladies to wait on her, pen and paper, her almoner John Skip – such comforts hadn't kept her from death.

The king was a mercurial man. Anne knew his advisers thought they could control his wild-dog mind, train it to attack what they wanted, guard jealously what they loved, but Anne had never felt that way about Henry. She knew any power she had over him rested in his passion for her, which was plentiful at first but waned over time, and her ability to bear a son.

'Of course,' Anne had assured Henry during their long courtship, 'I am very fertile. Look at my elder sister, Mary, your former mistress, who has already borne you a fine son.' For it was true, both Mary's children were rumoured to be the king's, though Mary's late husband, William Carey, had claimed them as his own. The boy, just a babe when the king began pursuing Anne, was sometimes introduced as the son of the king, his parentage an open secret among the aristocracy.

Obviously it made Anne uncomfortable that before Henry courted her, he'd had an affair with Mary. Mary, her fine, pretty elder sister, discreet, quiet, golden-haired, pleasantly plump, who had been mistress first to the King of France, François, when she and Anne were ladies-in-waiting to Queen Claude at the French court, and then to his English counterpart, Henry. Unlike Anne, Mary hadn't made Henry wait. She hadn't refused the king's carnal advances. She'd lain with him, taken pleasure in his touch, played the part of the mistress, known her place. And she'd done it in plain sight of her first husband, a marriage arranged for her by the king so that any children Mary bore as a result of their affair would not be bastards. The compliant William Carey, who looked the other way, who appreciated the lavish gifts bestowed upon his wife by the king, who consented to raise another man's children as his own, to allow them to inherit his family's wealth and land, who would cede all – his wife, his land, his money, his dignity – to the king he loved. William Carey, a good fellow, a good man, a fine friend, a solid husband and partner, obedient, a docile subject, a pleasure to have at court, a man who knew his own best interests, who would not lose his head on the scaffold for indiscretion, for raising a fuss, for protesting, who would never.

When the king pursued his annulment from Katherine on the grounds that she was his legal sister, having first married and bedded his brother, the matter of Mary's children came into stark relief. The king couldn't be seen having fathered children with the sister of the woman he professed to want to marry. That would be hypocrisy. That would call into the minds of the people, the pope, the clergy, Henry's own black conscience, that he had done the very thing he accused Katherine of doing: he had fucked, or aimed to fuck, two siblings. He had fathered children with, or aimed to father children with, two siblings. No, Henry wouldn't let such a thought enter his consciousness, the deep, labyrinthine trap of his mind, where all winding paths led to a lightless centre in which he stood alone, naked and huffing, raking his foot like a hoof through the dirt of his memories, a bull unbound, always right. And so, it became even more pressing that William claim Mary's children, that they be Careys, that, although they bore a striking resemblance to Henry, they not be linked to him, so that he could get his annulment with a clean conscience, so that he could marry Anne with a clean conscience, so that, one day, when Anne's own daughter would play with her beautiful older cousin Catherine, she wouldn't know the girl was also her half-sister.

In fact, Mary's affair with the king was ongoing when Anne initially caught Henry's attention, at the Château Vert pageant thrown by Cardinal Wolsey at Whitehall Palace. Though it was not the first time Anne had met the king – they'd met twice before, once when she was a child, sent by her father to live and be educated in the Low Countries with the Archduchess Margaret of Austria, and once when she was a teenager in France, serving as a lady-in-waiting to Queen Claude – it was the first time he remembered meeting her, and after he started courting her a few years later, this was the story he'd tell of their first meeting. Since Henry's narratives were always right, she never contradicted him.

At the time of Wolsey's pageant, Anne had been back from France for a few years, serving as one of Katherine's ladies-in-waiting, but mostly existing outside the king's notice: one of many women wearing expensive gowns who orbited his wife. At the pageant, seven women, including Anne, dressed up as feminine virtues – Mary, Anne's sister, as Kindness; Mary Tudor, the king's sister, as Beauty; Jane Parker, who would later marry George, as Constancy. Wolsey had had a wooden tower built for the occasion, draped in green cloth – the Château Vert – and in the pageant, the beauties were kidnapped and chased up the tower by a set of chorus boys dressed up like women, playing the feminine vices: Disdain, Jealousy, Danger, Scorn, Unkindness, a Sharp Tongue, and Strangeness. At the end of the pageant, the feminine virtues were rescued from the feminine vices by a gang of young men dressed as masculine virtues: Nobleness, Youth, Attendance, Loyalty, Pleasure, Gentleness, Amorousness, and Liberty. Henry led the men, dressed himself in cloth of gold, with tinsel woven into his hat.

Anne had played the part of the virtue Perseverance. She wore a white gown, on to which she'd needlepointed a golden thistle to represent the perseverant plant, and a golden pitcher to represent perseverance of service. In her hair she wore a bird's nest woven from golden ribbons, with three small gold-plated eggs perched in it to represent the perseverant starling, that modest, industrious bird. After she and the other virtuous women were rescued by the king's brigade, all of them – the virtuous women, the chorus boys dressed as the feminine vices, the virtuous men, the king, the observers – moved on to a series of court dances, and when the king asked Anne to partner with him for a canario, she couldn't say no. The two held hands briefly, squaring off, facing each other, shuffling and stomping their feet in intricate Spanish patterns, circling each other, glancing back over their shoulders while doing so, as scripted, as part of the dance, eyes meeting, and yes, Anne held his gaze too long, longer than proper, long enough to kindle a spark of interest in him.

In her periphery, Mary, her sister, dressed as Kindness, bobbed dutifully around William Carey. Mary, who later that night would surely go to bed with the king. Mary, whose silky hair glistened in the candlelight, for it was Shrove Tuesday, late winter, the days still short. The night had come early, the candelabras and chandeliers had already been lit, though they hadn't yet eaten the evening meal. Outside, the snow swirled and swirled, like the sins of Christ, if he had any, like the sins of them all, swirling in a blustery confessional just outside the walls. Tonight they would feast, and tomorrow Wolsey would paint an ashen cross on each of their foreheads and the long fast of Lent would begin.

In the middle of their canario, as they stomped and circled around each other, the ribbon nest in Anne's hair loosened, and one gold-plated egg slipped from her head and fell to the floor. Henry noticed, knelt down to retrieve the little egg, and, on bended knee, said, 'You dropped this, my lady.' As he returned it to her, he ran a finger on the inside of her wrist, sending a pleasant shiver up her arm. 'I wouldn't want Perseverance to lose one of her treasures so easily.'

Later, she'd spied Henry whispering to Wolsey and casting glances her way. To persevere: to persist in doing, to persist despite obstacles, to focus on the good, on the goal, on the desired ends, despite impediments. Anne had been good at that once. She'd persevered while the great matter of Henry's annulment from Katherine was settled. She'd persevered through England's split with Rome, necessary to achieve Henry's annulment. She'd persevered through the names she was called at court and on the streets: the concubine, the goggle-eyed whore, the woman king, the witch. 'What I don't understand,' Mary had drawled at her more than once during her long, chaste engagement to the king, 'is why you don't just do as I did and bed the poor man – put him out of his misery, enjoy his virility while he still has it, wed someone else and have a couple of gorgeous, fat babies the king will endow with lands and titles – it's really very simple, Anne.' But Anne didn't want the life that Mary had, the cast-off mistress, powerless – or was she really? – Anne had thought. Anne had kept her eye on the prize: Henry, and the love that she felt for him; the throne, and the power that came with it; the prince she hoped to birth and mother. She'd persevered.

The crowd jostled away from the bridge, towards what Anne now saw was an open-air arena, into which the rowdy Southwarkers began to funnel. A drunk young man, perhaps twenty-six or twenty-seven years of age, with a group of his friends, bumped into Anne, and she clutched his elbow, saying, to the barker collecting money at the arena gate, 'I'm with him, sir,' and curtsying.

The young man, blond and broad with a red beard, raised his eyebrows in amusement and paid her fee. When he turned to her and said, 'You're a fine wench, aren't you?' she laughed and replied, 'Yes, sir, and might I sit with you to take in this spectacle?' Her voice rasped in a way that it hadn't before her execution, like a sickle was stuck in her throat.

The arena housed an octagonal dirt ring, surrounded by a wooden barrier about the height of a man, around which benches on risers had been placed so that the crowd could see whatever was about to take place: a fight, or perhaps a play. Anne staked out her place in the first row of seating, beside the man. After a day of wandering the streets of Southwark, it felt good to sit.

The barker opened a gate on one side of the octagon, carried his stool into the arena's centre, and spoke. 'Good Christians!' he began, raising his arms to the crowd, who fell silent. 'You are gathered here to behold a fearsome spectacle, on this auspicious day, the whore queen dead!' The crowd cheered, and Anne winced — surprised, even after her own execution for treason, at how much the commoners detested her. Surprised, as well, that no one here, that no one all day, had recognised her, though she supposed she had rarely set foot in Southwark, and never on the streets among the commoners. The only likeness of hers they'd have seen might have been a crude drawing. 'On this very day,' the barker continued, 'the king hath announced his betrothal to the goodly Englishwoman, Jane Seymour, most modest of maidens, who has taken as her motto "bound to obey and serve".' Anne had expected Henry to betroth himself to Jane quickly, but the news of his engagement, belted out to an arena of drunken commoners, made her furious. So he really had had her executed and then, not even observing a decent mourning period, immediately become betrothed to his mistress. Had she meant nothing to him? Anne saw around her many women in the crowd nod approvingly at the barker's announcement, pleased, she supposed, with Jane's submissiveness, bound to obey and serve, the role a woman ought to play, the role Anne had never been able to. 'May she birth many princes!' the barker concluded. At this the crowd cheered again.

 Then, before Anne had much time for further thought, the barker exited, taking his stool with him. Through the gate a large, huffing bear ambled into the ring. Its hide was slashed with scars, and half a dozen new wounds oozed blood. From the way the bear stumbled, head turning sightlessly towards every sound, pupils large and black, Anne could tell it was blind. Through her anger, she pitied the beast.

 Next came the dogs, shooed in by men in long leather gloves. The rough gang of mastiffs stalked about the dirt ring, growling first at the crowd, then at the bear. The dogs circled the bear, closing in tighter and tighter. At each corner of the octagon, safely behind the wooden partition, a man stood on a stool, with a long wooden rod, shouting 'Yah! Yah!' and smacking the beast every time it ambled past, on its flank, its hind, its greying head. The bear rose on to its back legs, let out a cry that shook the benches the audience sat on, and slashed its claws through the air.

Anne reached for the young man's hand, suddenly afraid of the old blind bear, of the dogs, of the men with rods. The dogs leaped up at the bear's neck, trying to lick the blood that oozed from its fresh wounds. They must be starved, Anne thought, and the wounds cut on the beast by the barker to attract them. Then, one by one, the bear, though blind, caught the dogs in its powerful jaws, shook them violently until their necks snapped or their backs broke, and left them to die on the ground. The bear paced, but rather than look triumphant, it panted, exhausted, head down.

The side gate opened again, and this time the barker ushered in a donkey with a monkey strapped to its back. The monkey screeched and wailed, flailing its arms, trying to undo the straps that held it to the donkey's back with its human-looking hands. It knows its fate, Anne thought. She remembered her own terror, her trembling execution speech, the way her voice had wavered in fear as she stood on the scaffold, the executioner behind her with his sharp sword, how she'd looked and looked around Tower Green up until the moment that the blindfold was slipped over her eyes, hoping for Henry to appear and save her. He hadn't.

The donkey brayed and bucked. One of the men in the corners produced a whip and snapped the donkey's haunch so that it charged full speed at the bear, ramming its side. The bear turned, teeth bared. The monkey slapped the bear's face, trying to stop the bite it knew was coming. It shrieked in fear. Anne closed her eyes. She couldn't stand to look. The bear made quick work of the monkey, and of the donkey too.

Bleeding, limping, the bear paced the circle of the arena. It roared at the crowd, who booed and hissed and threw rotten cabbages at it. Where had they got the rotten cabbages? Anne wondered. They must have smuggled them in under their cloaks. Or had the barker been handing them out at the door? Now a team of musicians weaved their way down the steps between the sets of risers: a lute player, a flautist, and a man shaking a tambourine. Their merry music enlivened the crowd to dance and cheer. A performer dressed as a jester threw bread to the people, who dived for it, hungry. When was the last good meal they'd had? 'In honour of Jane, the obedient!' he called as he moved along the risers.

'Watch now, miss. I'll get us some,' said the young man, whose hand Anne realised she was still holding. He rose to his feet, full of vigour, and leaped up the risers blithely, reaching a stout arm out to catch a hunk of the warm, fresh bread. Grinning, he returned, holding his treasure to his chest. He ripped it in half and gave the larger chunk to Anne, who shoved it in her mouth, for she too was hungry. The bread was yeasty and delicious.

During all of this, the bear paced and snarled in the arena, turning its head to the sounds of the musicians, to the cheers of the crowd scrambling for the bread, every now and then getting whipped by the men standing in the corners. This bear is a terror, thought Anne, though it is blind and lame. In its injuries and age it is more dangerous, more reckless, ready to bite anything that crosses its path, untamable, though the men may think they've tamed it.

For a moment, the bear turned its head towards Anne, and its sightless black eyes looked both at and past her. Then it swung its head at the lash of a whip from one of the corners, seized hold of the whip in its jaw, and pulled. The man wielding the whip must have wound it around his arm, because when the bear pulled the whip, the man flew off his stool, over the wooden partition, and into the arena. The bear flung its head from side to side, whip clamped firmly in its jaws, and the man, whip wound round his arm, flew side to side too. At first, the man screamed in agony, as his arm dislocated from his shoulder, then broke, and his head hit the dirt floor again and again. Then his screams stopped, and he went limp, his eyes half-closed.

The gate on the wall of the octagon swung open and the barker rushed out with a sword, followed by the other seven whipping men who'd stood in the corners, who now held ropes and daggers. The whipping men swung the ropes around the bear's neck to try to hold it back, to try to save the eighth man, who lay limp at the feet of the bear, still tethered to his whip, which by now the beast had dropped.

With determination, the barker came upon the bear and drove his sword into the beast's chest. The bear howled in pain and blood poured from its mouth. The seven whipping men in turns jabbed their daggers into the bear's sides, and the barker withdrew his sword, with much effort, and drove it into the bear's soft flank, twisted and turned it, and then the bear stopped moving, and collapsed.

The crowd roared its approval, and Anne roared too, rising to her feet with the rest of the spectators, arms held above her head, hands in fists, cheering. The voice that came out of her throat was a bellow, low and caked with dust.

She knew then that she must kill Henry, that he was wild and wounded, like the bear, that he was untamable, that he would hurt others, including Elizabeth, that though others might think they could control him, they could not. She must kill Henry, and she must do it before he hurried to marry Jane, before he could father another heir, who would stand in competition to Elizabeth and threaten her safety. This was the only way to protect Elizabeth, who would be safest if she sat on the throne, the king's legal heir, and the only way to protect England, for Elizabeth could make a better country – a country not beholden to Rome, not ministered to by a corrupt and decadent church, not governed by men only interested in fattening their own coffers. Elizabeth could carry on where Anne had been forced to leave off.

Anne cheered the bloodied men who'd slain the bear. And when the young man next to her embraced her and kissed her on the mouth, she kissed him back, for she was alive, and powerful, and filled with purpose.

5

John and the River

John, that was the name of the young man whose hand Anne had held during the bearbaiting, whose arm she clutched gleefully when the dead bear was shoved to the side of the arena and the wounded whipping man – maybe he was dead, Anne couldn't tell – was carried out on a litter. He'd whispered in her ear, 'I'm John,' after they kissed, but before the musicians flooded the arena floor, dancing and playing joyful songs, joined by acrobats who contorted into crescent-moon backbends and walked on their hands, and the same jester who'd thrown bread to the crowd, now dressed in a ruffled shirt covered with bells that jangled as he juggled two, then three, then four brightly painted wooden pins.

The seven whipping men brought out a large, rose-shaped firework, which they lit on numerous wicks that sparked and burned down to shoot a cluster of rockets into the open air above the audience, where they exploded and rained down real apples. Anne herself caught one and took a large bite, letting the juice run down her chin before licking it away. Then she put the apple to John, who took a bite and, eyes gleaming, licked the juice from Anne's hand, pausing longer than needed on the tip of her pinky. Next four peacocks trotted into the arena, tail feathers shimmying and shaking as they strutted around in the dirt, sounding dragonish cries. How Elizabeth would have loved that, Anne thought.

How she would have held out her chubby toddler arm to try to nab a fistful of bright feathers.

When the performance concluded, John ushered Anne out of the arena. It was twilight, and the first stars shone faintly in the darkening sky. She clasped John's hand. 'I know a place where we can be alone,' he said, pulling her towards him and leading her past the hostels and brothels, down a short series of streets, to the bank of the Thames.

The tide was in now, the muddy flatlands she'd crashed into upriver surely covered in water, the little boat she'd stolen probably washed back into the river's current, bobbing along passengerless past London Bridge, past Westminster, past Whitehall Palace, past the countryside, past Hampton Court Palace, where Anne had reigned, radiant, living up to her motto, 'the most happy', over dozens of parties more splendid and expensive than the spectacle she'd just witnessed, though none as exhilaratingly bloody. Unless of course, her boat had been found and pulled in, returned to the Tower dock, or pilfered by wherrymen eager for an extra vessel to take Londoners across the river, to earn a few more pence. And who wouldn't be inclined to do so, who wouldn't see an opportunity floating past, there for the taking, and pounce? 'What a peculiar thing,' Anne imagined a wherryman thinking, or, maybe just, 'Mine.'

The thrill of the bearbaiting shivered through Anne's body, how the beast had been brought low after it imperilled others, after its true nature had shown through. How its blood had mingled with the dust and soaked into the ground, and the people hadn't cared or noticed because everyone was rejoicing, because the threat had been subdued, because food had been shot into the air, because they were hungry and wanted something to eat.

John, standing beside her on the bank of the Thames, was going on about his ma and her tailor shop, about his work as a blacksmith, which explained his strong arms and the coin in his pocket that he'd been all too eager to spend. What Anne needed to do was keep quiet. She knew she looked dishevelled, and smelled faintly of blood and piss. She didn't suppose it mattered to him, drunk as he was. She was cold and he gave her his jacket, warm from his body, and smelling of sweat, wood fire, and ale. How could he not see that she was dead? A whore, a witch, a concubine, a traitor to crown and country? She smiled and nodded along as he talked and talked, and when he went to kiss her again, she opened to it. His mouth tasted of bread and apples; his beard rubbed gently against her chin.

'You are a virtuous woman, I can tell,' he whispered in her ear.

'Yes,' she croaked back. That was what he wanted, then, a woman to pet and play with, not to bed, not right now. A woman he could introduce to his mother, a fine wench in a red kirtle with a peculiar silk collar that he could make his wife. It surprised Anne that he might mistake her for such a woman, though of course he did not know she wasn't a maiden, had already borne a child. Perhaps in this light he couldn't see that she was past her thirty-fifth year.

The darkness had settled along the river so no one could see them, and they sank into the damp grass. Anne let him loosen the strings of her kirtle's bodice and kiss her breasts, as he rubbed his hand between her legs, over her skirts, then under, then sank beneath them, placing his mouth against her. She leaned into it, grinding her pelvis until she came, hard and fast, a relief, a pleasure. And didn't she deserve to enjoy her body, to feel good, when she had only ever lain with Henry, but he had lain with so many other women, and would soon, once he wed her, lie with Jane? – though Anne would put a stop to that, she hoped – didn't Anne deserve a little pleasure? At the same time, John slipped a hand inside his trousers, which he'd loosened hastily. He worked furiously there for a moment, before moaning. Anne felt a stickiness on the inside of her ankle.

How many times had she done this very thing with Henry? As the annulment proved more and more difficult to obtain, there had been many occasions like this, where they'd crossed almost every line. Anne had wanted him, too, and not just for his body and power. She'd loved Henry. In Henry, she thought, she'd found her intellectual equal, a man she could talk to about the important ideas of the day, about reform and the human condition, who spoke Latin, French. Here was a man who'd educated his daughter, who found Anne, a smart woman, witty and entertaining, who pulled her to his side at parties when she talked politics and shared her opinions, who called her 'my Nan', proudly. Here was a man who never told her that her voice was shrill, though she knew that when she was passionate it hit a certain timbre that drove others to walk away from her, on to happier women and happier topics. 'Your eyes are black onyx,' Henry had told her in the private room of her London house when he came to visit her. 'Your eyes are black pearls, black opals, obsidian stones.' He'd loved her dark eyes, which she knew others had compared to mud, to dung, to the grave. Henry could see her beauty. And he'd adorned her neck with jewels, sparkling collars she mistook for tokens of affection.

In the dark of the riverbank, John had fallen asleep. Anne retightened her kirtle, adjusted John's jacket around her shoulders. She lay back, put her hands behind her head, and gazed up at the starry sky, searching for constellations. She could see Hercules, the strongman, and Lyra, the small lyre of Orpheus, the poet who followed Eurydice to the underworld to bring her back from the dead because he loved her so dearly. Not like Henry, who might as well have swung the sword himself, so hastily did he send Anne to the scaffold. Near Hercules, Corona Borealis, the crown. If she could have plucked it from the sky and placed it on her head, she would have; she would have held a second coronation here, on the bank of the Thames, leg sticky with a blacksmith's semen. In her night crown, she imagined, she'd grow to the size of the heavens, a giantess. She'd step across the river and its sleeping swans, easy, find Henry, and crush him under her foot. Fa. Fe. Fi. Fo. Fum. She'd stomp in the blood of that Englishman. She'd stomp on each of his betrayals.

Anne searched the night sky for Taurus, the bull, but didn't find him. On the Boleyn crest were three bulls. Boleyn. Bullen. Bull. Anne knew her surname was from Boulogne, in France, from where some great-great-grandfather had issued forth and done heroic deeds during the Norman Conquest. She'd seen this ancestor depicted on a tapestry, a large moustache extending beyond his face, which turned towards the viewer, while the rest of his body, in profile, rode a horse forward into the battle scene that covered the fabric. Someone had liked the play on words, Bol for *bull*. Bulls were strong, angry, righteous, manly.

Bullheaded was a word that had been used to describe Anne, by her father, by her husband, by the women who whispered behind her back at court, by her own sister Mary, by Thomas Cromwell, who she'd once thought was her ally. When Anne knew she was right about something, she couldn't let it go. She couldn't let it go that Katherine was actually Henry's sister by marriage, that their marriage was incestuous, heretical, illegal, and in need of rapid annulment. She couldn't let it go that Henry's first daughter, Mary, was a bastard who should not be in the line of succession. She couldn't let her copy of Tyndale's English-language Bible go, though it was forbidden in England and a punishable offence to be in possession of it. She couldn't let it go that the pope had too much power, that the church was a second government extending out from Rome and undercutting the authority of Europe's kings and queens, who ought to be the final link to God, ordained by God as they were. She pushed and pushed for Henry to declare himself head of the churches of England. She pushed for reformation. She was bullheaded. It was her nature. She didn't know when to shut up.

And why should she keep quiet when she was right? When she knew better? When she was smarter and better read and more thoughtful and able to connect ideas more quickly and spit out beautiful sentences and arguments like the great orators of ancient Rome? Why should she hide the light of her intelligence? Perhaps Henry's greatest betrayal had been when he stopped loving her for her intellect and started hating her for it, when he started telling her to hold her tongue, not to speak out of turn, when he told her that she had one job, to make him a male heir, and until she did that she should shut her mouth, when he stopped visiting her in her chambers, stopped talking to her, stopped laughing at her witticisms, when he said to her, upon her anger over his affairs, 'You must shut your eyes and endure as well as more worthy persons, and you ought to know that it is in my power to humble you again in a moment more than I have exalted you.' She had thought he was a different sort of man, a man who could recognise and receive her for her mind and spirit, not just for her body and the heirs it could produce. But she could see that she was wrong.

Anne had been eleven when her father sent her across the Channel to live and be educated in the Archduchess Margaret's palace at Mechelen, in the Low Countries, which Margaret ruled as regent for her young nephew Charles. There, Anne learned about the ancient queen Boudicca, and her mind wandered to her now, as she lay by the Thames, the site of Boudicca's bloody victory. Latin came easily to Anne, and she remembered reading the Roman histories of ancient England. Boudicca's husband had been king of the Iceni, though under the thumb of the Roman invaders, to whom he supplicated himself for security. He prospered and lived a long life, but when he died, leaving his kingdom to his daughters, the Romans, assuming a weakness, assuming women couldn't lead, charged in. His household was looted. His wife, Boudicca, was lashed. His daughters were raped.

Boudicca did not take kindly to being lashed. She did not take kindly to her daughters being raped. The Roman historians described her as a tall woman with long red hair and a shrill voice. Wasn't that always how powerful women's voices were described – shrill, shrieking, annoying, loud, grating? The message being that it was better for women to shut up, to keep their shrill voices quiet. But not Boudicca. The army Boudicca raised was over a hundred thousand strong, populated heavily by women. Where were the men? Hiding away. Afraid. Before she conquered London, Rome's stronghold, and burned it to the ground, Boudicca delivered a speech. 'It is not as a queen but as a citizen I fight, avenging my lost liberty, my lashed body, the defiled honour of my daughters,' Boudicca's speech began. 'The Romans come for your liberty, your bodies, your way of life. The Romans hide their women away, rape them, devalue their power. If you value your liberty, you will fight with me. The gods are on our side and we will have our revenge. This is what I, a woman, will do; as for men, they can live as slaves if they choose.'

Anne had recited this speech in Latin, in French, in her own ad hoc English translation, running through the halls of the Mechelen palace draped in an old cloak, shrieking, 'I am Boudicca! As for men, they can live as slaves!' Of course, Anne had been a girl then, and nobody took her childhood play seriously. The archduchess herself had laughed at the sloppy costume, at Anne's speeches. Anne remembered Margaret's stern face breaking into giggles. Once, she'd even chased Anne down a long hall, pretending to be a Roman general, then pretending to die in agony when Anne turned and stabbed her with an imagined spear. Judicious, wise and calculating, Margaret, like Boudicca, was a woman ruling singularly where men could not. And shouldn't that have been my fate? Anne thought, mulling the story over. Shouldn't it be Elizabeth's? My daughter, my dearest love? Shouldn't I make that fate Elizabeth's, put my daughter, my smart, precocious daughter, on the throne?

When Elizabeth was born, Anne had tried to nurse her. Noblewomen in France, where Anne had spent her teenage years, were nursing their own babes, and Anne wanted that closeness with Elizabeth. She had persuaded Elizabeth to take some milk before Henry found out and put a stop to it. It just wasn't done in England, he'd said, not by royalty. He'd been gentle enough about it – this being early in their marriage, when he was still infatuated with her – but firm. His decision was final. So off to a wet nurse Elizabeth went every time she squawked, and Anne had to watch, jealously, as another woman fed her daughter, as another woman got to snuggle with and coo to her Elizabeth, her princess. She could add this to the list of things Henry had taken from her: her reputation, her virginity, her freedom, her brother, and, finally, her life. The man was like a whirlpool, sucking anything that came too close down into the obliterating, icy depths of the sea.

Failing to find Taurus in the stars, Anne searched for a leopard, she searched for a white falcon, both her emblems. She searched for an *A* and an *H* carved together in the dark wood of the night sky, two initials intertwined in the heavens – her love, her failure. It wasn't there. She needed money to cross the bridge. The bridge, which she could see upriver from where she lay next to John, asleep still in the grass – the windows of its shops and houses lighted and reflecting into the black water below. She needed to hurry. She had already lost a day, and she knew Henry would wed Jane quickly. He was an impatient man on a quest for a son, eager to put a baby in the belly of that quiet, pale-eyed virgin.

She knew John had money in his coat pocket, a few coins that he'd saved up for a big night out. She'd given him that, hadn't she? She reached into the pocket, pulled the coins out, and held them in her fist. Then she slid his jacket off and laid it over his sleeping chest, before kissing him on the forehead, gently, as a mother would kiss a child, and slipping away.

6

The Stews

The dirt road Anne found herself on was dark and mostly silent. A light breeze blew across the bankside street, chilling her. She wished she'd kept John's jacket, though it would have made her stand out, an unaccompanied woman in a man's coat. It was the middle of the night by now. A few men sang drunkenly, arms around each other's shoulders, stumbling by her. Anne hurried along, stuffing the coins she'd stolen into her bodice.

As she walked, Anne thought again of Elizabeth, barely three months old when she was swept away with Lady Bryan to the palace at Hatfield, where a household was established for the infant princess. How could a baby have her own household? And yet Elizabeth did. She had servants and maids and ladies and a wet nurse, and Anne and Henry got letters updating them, and occasional visits. The Princess Elizabeth was having terrible trouble with teething. The Princess Elizabeth required new garments. The Princess Elizabeth pulled the hair of her sister, the Lady Mary, so hard that Mary wailed and hid in her room. For Anne had arranged for the bastard Mary to serve her half-sister, so she would learn her place, so she would accept her new role, her new title, her removal from the line of succession.

Elizabeth had Anne's dark eyes. All her life, people had called Anne calculating, and though she could never see it in herself, she saw it in Elizabeth, in the way the babe wailed for

Lady Bryan when someone she didn't like tried to hold her, then smiled at the offender slyly once she was safe in Lady Bryan's arms. The way she would giggle and bat her baby eyes at those she adored and those she wanted to adore her. Elizabeth, with her crown of red hair, with her fiery intelligence. Not quite three now, she spoke in full sentences, knew all her colours, could carry a sweet tune. At Christmas, when she'd visited Anne and Henry at Hampton Court, Anne, walking with her mother, had come upon the child on the floor of her nursery. Elizabeth had removed her stockings and sat counting her toes, first in English, then in Latin, then in French. 'You were the same way as a child,' said her mother, who was also named Elizabeth, but was called Bess. 'Always so clever.'

Of course, all contact with the child Elizabeth ceased once Anne had been falsely accused and locked in the Tower. She knew a visit would seal the girl's fate as a pariah, an excommunicated daughter of the king. Among the reasons she hadn't fought the annulment of her marriage to Henry, granted to him the day before her execution, among the reasons Anne had gone peaceably to the scaffold, was to protect Elizabeth from Henry's wrath. She'd been party to the terrible way he treated Mary, who'd been his long-loved princess for ten years when Anne and Henry began their courtship. It hadn't taken much persuading on Anne's part to convince Henry to reduce Mary's allowance, to decree her a bastard, to send her as a servant to her younger sister's house. Anne knew how easily the same fate could befall Elizabeth. Even so, Anne longed for Elizabeth during her imprisonment. Just one more touch, one more snuggle, one more game of peek-a-boo.

After Anne had spent some time wandering alone and cold through the streets of Southwark, a commotion in the distance caught her attention. A man's voice, firm and chiding, and the melody of women's laughter. The swing of a door on unoiled hinges. The racket was coming from a street or two away. Anne turned down an alley, then hooked a right. There she saw again the large and imposing Clink Street Prison, an establishment she'd heard the Bishop of Winchester, Stephen Gardiner, boast about over stuffed pheasant and spiced wine when he'd dined at Hampton Court. That had been a big feast, and Anne had reigned over it, laughing as Henry told bawdy jokes about corrupt priests taking liberties with daft peasant women in the confessionals.

Gardiner was a staunch Catholic, but had helped Henry argue for his annulment from Katherine. He'd nodded along solemnly as Henry told a long joke about a priest with a secret wife who he fucked every night on a feather mattress and who bore him seven bastard sons, who each became a priest in their own right, and each fathered seven bastard sons, who became priests and fathered seven bastard sons apiece. 'How many bastard priests were there, then?' the joke went but the answer was 'Who can count, for aren't all Catholic priests bastards?' Anne could tell Gardiner found the joke distasteful, vulgar, offensive, but he didn't say so. He was playing his cards right. He knew that the church's sway in England was ending, that the Liberty of the Clink, the seventy-acre territory surrounding Winchester Palace and the Clink Street Prison, would remain his to govern if he came over to Henry's side, if he denounced the pope and served the king as his true sovereign and prince of the churches of England. And it had worked. She imagined Gardiner sleeping soundly that very night in Winchester Palace, whose imposing outline she could see above the roofs of the houses she walked past.

Anne hid around the corner from the Clink Street Prison and watched a finely dressed man – he must be the jailer – and three women spill out of the opened gate and gather in a half-circle in the street.

'Now, I don't want to see any of you lasses back here again,' the man said in a falsely self-important voice, as if he were in on some joke, as if he recognised the need to pretend to an authority he didn't want or know how to wield. The women laughed.

'Sure thing, love,' a large brunette, who appeared to be the leader of the three, said, blowing him a kiss and waving over her shoulder as the women walked off into the night. She looked to be in her thirties, near Anne's age. The two younger women trailed behind her, giggling at her irreverence to the jailer.

They must be prostitutes, Anne thought, for why else would three women be arrested, then released in the night? Anne could make some guesses about what they might have done to secure their freedom, although it also crossed her mind that the Liberty of the Clink, that Stephen Gardiner, that all of Southwark, had a vested interest in keeping prostitutes in the brothels, and a regular clientele of men catching wherries across the Thames to patronise them, to spend their coin on drink at the public houses, on lodging at the hostels, and on whores in the brothels. The bishop had discussed this himself, over the dinner where Henry had joked about bastard priests, how men had wants that must be met, how all men needed to release some pressure from time to time, and some more frequently than others. 'I suppose it must be true if you declare it so, Bishop Gardiner,' Anne had replied, 'but tell me, is there a time and place for women to release some pressure?' She remembered how the bishop had looked at her and stammered, scandalised, about how a woman's duty was to serve her husband, and not have wants of her own. 'Well, I want another cup of wine,' Anne had said, laughing, as a servant rushed over to pour her one, and the bishop sat red-faced, embarrassed. She remembered how Henry had looked at her with amusement in that moment, how he'd arched an eyebrow flirtatiously at her, and how later that night they had indeed released some pressure as he'd pretended to be the bastard priest from his joke and she'd pretended to be the priest's secret wife. Such games were a strategic move to keep the king happy, but Anne enjoyed them as well.

Lagging a short distance behind, Anne followed the women, who were merrily chatting their way down the road, and when they peeled off from each other, Anne trailed the youngest of them, a woman with copper-coloured hair. A few minutes later, the woman turned in her tracks.

'Who comes there?' the woman exclaimed into the darkness.

Something metal glinted in the woman's hand. Anne supposed it must be a knife, which she'd had hidden in her belt or garter, though it unsettled Anne that she'd missed the woman reaching for it.

''Tis only I,' Anne spoke back, stepping into the woman's view. 'Lower your dagger.'

'No,' said the woman. 'Not you. Who lurks behind you?'

Anne turned and looked behind herself, confused, for she saw nobody there. She opened her mouth to speak, to explain to this woman that she had nothing to fear, but before she could utter a word, a man stepped out of the shadows. John. How had Anne not heard him following her? She shot her fingers to her silk collar, nervously.

'Why are you following me?' the woman spoke. She held the dagger firmly in her hand, pointed at John.

'I've come to take my money from this whore,' John said, nodding at Anne, 'who robbed me while I lay sleeping by the river.'

Anne thought about the coins she'd shoved in her bodice. Her money for the bridge toll. 'I did no such thing,' she replied. 'And I'm no whore.'

''Tis no shame if you are,' said the woman. She lunged at John, who inched back, towards the shadows. 'This woman said she did not rob you. Now go, leave us.'

John spat on the dusty road. 'First she did things with me that only a wife should do, then she stole my money while I slept afterwards. I ask you, what would you call that? Where did she learn to do those things? From you, perchance? I want my money.'

'I did no such—' began Anne, but the woman cut her off.

'Get out of here,' the woman said, lunging forward again. John looked down at her dagger. 'Don't think I won't use it,' she said through clenched teeth.

John looked from one to the other of them, as though calculating his chances of overpowering them both: a prostitute with a knife, and a woman in a funny silk collar who had got him off and stolen his last few coins.

'Fine,' he said, backing away. 'Just like a whore to defend another whore.'

'Get out of here, river trash,' the dagger-wielding woman replied.

'I doubt you'll be chasing me away when I come to your brothel with money, goose!'

'As if I'd be so desperate, dog!'

John shook his fist but didn't turn back. Instead, he walked down the street, disappearing around the corner.

Anne trembled with fright. After all she had been through, that a silly commoner could rattle her like this. She must have looked half-crazed, in her dishevelled kirtle, with her odd silk collar, her hair a mess beneath the kerchief she'd stolen from the tavern-keeper's wife. She was thirsty and hungry.

The woman moved towards her and put a hand on her shoulder. ''Tis all right, love, he's gone now,' she said.

'How can I repay you?' Anne asked. 'That man was deranged. Please, I have money. Can I give you some, as a reward?'

'I bet you have money,' the woman replied, and Anne realised the woman believed John's story that she was a prostitute.

'No,' said Anne, 'I'm not a prostitute.'

'So what if you were? Would it be the worst thing?'

'I have money,' Anne repeated, not wanting to engage her question. 'I can pay you. Please, I need a place to spend the night, and something to eat and drink. I can pay you for those things.' The woman looked at Anne warily. Anne supposed this woman had been paid money for a great many things, and probably by women as well as men. 'I don't want your body,' she added. 'I just want a place to stay. I can pay.'

The woman snorted, her expression hard to read. 'Lower your voice,' she spoke, 'or we'll wake the good people sleeping here.' She looked around at the darkened windows of the dwellings surrounding them. 'Your young lover has already made enough commotion.' She stepped closer to Anne. 'Show me your money.'

Anne pulled a penny from her bodice and held it out in her palm. The woman took it and held it up, examining it, checking that it was real.

'Come with me,' the woman said, turning and walking away with some haste, the coin still in her hand. Anne was quick to follow.

The entrance to the brothel where the woman led Anne was non-descript: a plain wooden door behind which sat an old man, feet propped on a desk, snoring, a drained tankard tipped over at the base of his chair. In the hearth, a fire smouldered down to embers.

'Slip off your shoes,' the woman whispered to Anne, keeping her voice low so as not to wake the sleeping man. Anne removed her slippers one by one, holding them in her right hand. It occurred to her that the day before, she'd held her own head in that hand, braced against her body, as she fled the Tower. Could that have been real? She ran the fingers of her left hand below her collar. Yes, the rough stitches she'd sewn were still there, the skin between them puckered and swollen, but healing. Anne caught the woman watching her and pulled her fingers quickly out.

'Come,' the woman mouthed, her eyebrows knitted together

with consternation, and Anne followed her up a set of stairs, down a short corridor, and into a room filled with many beds and many women. All appeared to be asleep, some in the beds, some sprawled on the floor. 'You can lie here,' the woman said, nodding to a narrow space between one of the beds and the wall. Though three women slept on the bed already, the woman sat and nudged them over, then lay down on the bed's edge nearest the gap. A person could catch their death sleeping on a cold, hard floor like this, Anne thought, and she wondered what fevers burned through the bodies of these loose women, sleeping one atop another like new kittens. Not that it would matter to her, Anne supposed, being already dead.

'Well?' said the woman. Anne lowered herself to the floor, wedged into the gap between the bed and wall, and folded an arm under her head.

As Anne lay on the cold, hard floor, she thought about comfort, about the comforts of her life as queen, about the comforts of her life before she became queen. When the king decided he would leave Katherine, annul their marriage, and marry Anne, he bestowed many treasures on her and her family. First came the gifts of land. For a brief period, right after Anne returned from France, there had been talk of arranging her marriage to James Butler, a distant cousin, to settle a dispute between her father and his over who was rightful heir to an Irish earldom, who should get the lands associated there, and the income they provided. A marriage between Anne and her cousin James Butler would keep the land and title in both branches of the family, pleasing the Boleyns and the Butlers. Cardinal Wolsey had been hot to arrange the marriage and settle the argument. The arrangements fell through, though – the first of two potential engagements for Anne that Henry scuttled, his eye already on her, unbeknownst to her at the time. Initially, the lands seemed like they'd stay with the Butlers, but these were some of the earliest parcels to be given to

Anne after she agreed to marry Henry. More followed, sweeping tracts of the English countryside she added to her accounting books.

Then came the titles. She pushed for her brother, George, just twenty-five at the time, to be named ambassador to France, just as her father had been, and wrote letters to French King François's court insisting that he be treated with the same regard as an elder statesman. She knew there was gossip about this, snark and backbiting, that people in both courts, English and French, started calling George Boleyn *le petit prince*. The little prince, spoiled baby brother of the *putain*, a man barely old enough to shave being given the responsibilities and privileges that should have fallen to a man older, wiser, more experienced, more politically connected, someone who had worked for it. By 1530, Henry made George Viscount Rochford, and his wife, Jane, Viscountess Rochford, a great rise in station.

A year later, a comet streaked across the night skies above England, dazzling nobility and commoners alike: a sign from God, a good omen, that the Lord was pleased that Henry was ending his sinful marriage to Katherine, was righting the wrongs of incest, hallelujah, see God's bright eye pressed into the sky, staring down at them all. Comet blazing in the background during an evening proclamation, Henry made Anne a marquess.

And, of course, there were the smaller presents, the tokens and objects accruing over seven years of chaste engagement, of want and unfulfilled lust: twenty-one sparkling diamonds Anne had set into necklaces and rings; a golden girdle she wore over her finest gowns; golden tablets on to which were engraved her favourite Bible verses, in English and French; gold buttons her seamstresses sewed as decorations on to the sleeves of her gowns, that jangled when she walked; a rose made of rubies that she set atop her writing desk to remind herself she'd soon be a Tudor; a cameo brooch of Our Lady of Boulogne; and a golden whistle, small enough to fit in her palm, that she wore around her neck on a thin gold chain and used to call Henry. In those years, in the years of their long engagement, he always came when she whistled.

She thought, as well, about barbs. Every rose has thorns; even the ruby rose Henry gave her had blunted barbs that encircled the green glass stem it was set upon. The quince trees the gardeners grew in the Boleyn orchard at Hever Castle had long thorns that had kept the child Anne and her siblings from reaching into their low boughs, really child height, perfect for filching and absconding with the sour fruit. Sea urchins had poison prickles to keep away hungry fishes, so too some squids had barbed tentacles to catch and tear their prey. And Anne had her barbed tongue, which, as the engagement dragged on, struck and struck again. In private, she accused Henry of wasting her youth, of squandering her chances at a successful match (see her dashed engagements to James Butler, and, later, Henry Percy), of leading her on, of dithering intentionally, of not loving her enough, of not working hard enough for the annulment, of being complacent to live in the sin of his incestuous marriage to his first wife because maybe he enjoyed fucking his own sister? 'Well, did he?' she demanded in one spectacular argument, the king shamefaced. 'For if he didst not enjoy incestuously fucking his sister, why couldn't he get the annulment already, for Christ's holy fucking sake?'

But her barbs were not just for Henry. When Katherine, seeking to cling to her illegal, incestuous queenship, arrived at Greenwich Palace in 1530 to celebrate Christmas, Anne said, within that lady's earshot, 'I wish all Spaniards were at the bottom of the sea. I care not for the queen or any of her family. I would rather be hanged than have to confess that she was my queen and mistress.' Henry, embarrassed that he couldn't control his estranged wife, frantic that he was displeasing his betrothed, his Nan, sent Anne one hundred pounds for a New Year's gift as recompense. Unhappy with courtiers who continued to support the displaced queen Katherine, Anne had the phrase *Ainsi sera, groigne qui groigne — Let them grumble, this is how it will be —* embroidered on the livery of her servants, who she paraded around haughtily, like living signs. Courtiers be damned.

She was never subtle. When a papal nuncio arrived from Rome ordering Henry to return to his lawful wife Katherine, Anne told the man to his face, 'The people care neither for popes nor for popes in England, not even if St Peter should come alive again.' When the Duke of Suffolk crossed her, she accused him of molesting his daughter. When Bishop Fisher dared to disagree with the petition of annulment, she ordered his cook to lace his food with laxatives. She was pushy: abruptly cancelling meetings with cardinals and ambassadors to suit her hunting schedule; placing a wooden chair beneath a window at Hampton Court so she could look through and spy on a meeting Henry had set with Eustace Chapuys from which she'd been excluded. Wolsey took to calling her *the night crow*, the unnatural woman who stayed up late filling Henry's head with ideas.

Once she and Henry had finally exchanged vows, had finally wedded, she ordered that Katherine give her all her jewels, which after all were the property of the crown, pushing and pushing when Katherine refused, until Anne brought her to heel, until Anne had the jewels around her neck, around her wrists, upon her head, in her own closed fists. Anne even demanded that Katherine give her the christening gown she'd brought with her from Spain, a gift from her royal parents, in which the Princess Mary had been baptised, so that Anne could use it for her own daughter, Elizabeth. And though she did not win that battle, her audacity in demanding the gown, her cold-heartedness in attempting to prise from an estranged, dethroned mother the baptismal gown worn by her only surviving child stunned the court, who added the slight to their tally of Anne's wrongs.

This sharp tongue, these barbs, always the sharpest in the room, her quickness to cut someone down, her irreverence, her lack of concern with whom she displeased or offended, followed her to the end. When she got off the barge at the Tower of London after her arrest, she asked Constable Kingston if she'd die without justice, meaning without a fair trial. 'Even the poorest man in England has justice, madam,' he'd replied, and, to that, she'd tipped her head back and laughed, because she, of all people, knew that wasn't true. Of course, this was reported back to Henry. And there is nothing any man, kings included, hates more than being laughed at by a woman.

Eventually, Anne, cold and sorrowful on the brothel floor, fell into a deep sleep in which she dreamed of a leopardess, teats swollen with milk, swishing her tail between the stiff trunks of the night forest, holding a deer's hind leg in her jaw, searching for a cub she'd left in the care of others and now could not find. In the dream, the trees jeered at the leopardess, called her names when her back was turned: *Putain. Concubine. Wishes she had a prick*, one whispered in a bark-filled voice. *Has taken the king's prick*, said another. High above, the leopardess's cub was passed between the branches of the jeering trees, scared, unreachable. The dream was so vivid, Anne could almost feel the leopardess's whiskers brush against her cheek.

7

A Bargain

In the morning, sleet plinked against the window of the many-bedded room, which was now deserted, except for Anne and the woman. Sleet in May, only a month from midsummer, Anne thought. She shuddered to think of George's head, slicked with ice on a pike on London Bridge. She didn't suppose her father would pay to get it down. He had his own reputation to protect, and her sister Mary's. Anne hoped he'd also be thinking of Elizabeth. She didn't think her Uncle Norfolk would pay either, since he'd presided over the jury that convicted George. Both men, her father and her uncle, were busy trying to stay in an impetuous king's good graces. Even so, she hated to think of George's head out there, alone and cold. Anne stretched. Her body ached from sleeping on the hard floor.

The woman sat on the edge of the bed, looking down at her. Anne could see, in the daylight, that she was quite comely, slender and pale, a dash of freckles across her nose and cheeks. She looked younger than Anne, but not by as many years as Anne had assumed last night. Her hair was pinned neatly atop her head beneath a white wool cap. She must have been awake long enough to tidy herself. How long had Anne slept?

The woman was staring at her. 'Your collar,' she said. ''Tis odd. I saw you fidgeting with it last night. Why are you wearing it?'

Anne remained silent, not wanting to reveal more than was necessary. She moved her fingers to the collar, checking that it remained in place. It did.

'I can tell you're a lady,' the woman went on. 'Your shoes. They are too fine. Even with the muck covering half their beauty, I can tell they were expensive.'

What did the woman want? She'd been kind to take Anne in last night, brave to defend her from John in the dark street, but now she looked at Anne appraisingly, as though taking inventory. The woman shifted off the bed and stood over her, extending a hand to help her up. Anne took it and shimmied out of the gap. A fire flamed in the hearth.

The woman motioned to a wooden plate with a dry-looking slab of cheese and two hunks of bread, set on a table beside the hearth. She must have brought these up. 'Would you like some?'

Anne nodded. She was famished. She grabbed a hunk of the bread, broke off half the cheese in her hand, and shoved the food into her mouth, chewing hungrily.

'You don't talk much,' the woman said. And after a pause, 'Have you left your husband?'

Anne thought about the story she might tell this woman. She couldn't tell her the truth, but she wanted to tell a lie that would be near the truth, a story that would be easy to tell and to remember. The woman sat on the bed, and Anne joined her.

'Yes,' she said. 'I have left my husband.' True, for how much more could you leave a husband than to die?

'Did he hurt you?' The woman eyed Anne's collar.

'Yes,' Anne replied again. True, for hadn't Henry ordered her beheading? 'My good husband loved me. When we met, he was married to another, but then she died. Upon his wife's death we wedded.' Sort of true – Katherine had waited until three years after Anne's marriage to Henry to finally die. 'He had already bedded my sister, but I stayed pure for him.' True. The woman raised an eyebrow. Everyone loved a scandalous story.

'I thought he loved me. I loved him. I bore him one child, a daughter, who I must find and keep safe.' Here, her story ebbed further into lies, for though Anne missed Elizabeth terribly, she had no intention of trying to retrieve the child, who was off at Hatfield Palace, guarded and secure. Better to leave her where she was. Once Anne killed Henry, Elizabeth would be queen, and well taken care of. Still, a story like this, of a beaten and cast-aside mother trying to rescue her daughter, might curry this woman's sympathies. The woman looked at Anne expectantly. She wants to know what happens next, Anne thought, pleased with herself. I've intrigued her.

'Though he loved me passionately, he believed malicious rumours that I'd taken a lover, though I had not.' That was all true. Anne had only ever lain with Henry; she'd had no other lovers. Anne gestured towards the silk collar around her neck. 'He tried to kill me.' True.

The woman touched Anne's arm. The touch was warm and gentle, pleasant. She felt herself relax. How many stories like this had the woman heard before? Anne wondered. How many of the women sleeping in this room last night had turned to prostitution after mistreatment at the hands of their husbands?

'The collar is covering up bruises, then,' the woman said. 'Did he strangle you?'

'Yes,' Anne replied, letting the woman fill in the blanks in the fabricated story.

The woman let out a long breath, sat back, and gazed into the fire. ''Tis a sad tale, my lady. You've been woefully mistreated.'

'I need to cross the bridge,' Anne said. 'To find my daughter' – she hurried to fill in the lie – 'before he does her harm. She's just a babe. My husband, lecher that he is, has found a new mistress.

I'm sure he plans to wed her and cast my daughter aside, a bastard orphan. I must retrieve her.'

Anne looked at the woman. Like many Englanders, her eyes were an airy blue, as though she'd been stitched together from the sky itself. Her gown was clean. Her shoes were clean. She wore a cloak tied neatly at her neck. Though she worked in a brothel, she was well kept and well spoken. She was cunning, sympathetic, quick with a knife, of sound body. She'd be useful to have as a companion.

'I never should have crossed the river in the first place, but I was taken in by a deceptive wherryman, who saw me running through the streets, alone, and offered to ferry me to safety. He took the little bit of money I had on me and abandoned me on this side of the river.' This new lie spun out of Anne so easily, a reason for her to be on this side of the river, a story that made her sound vulnerable, in need of protection, that it surprised even her. 'Can you help me?'

The woman's gaze stayed on the fire. She was quiet, contemplating.

'No,' she said at last. 'I have my own troubles to attend to.'

'Last night, you were so adept with your blade,' Anne said, seeking to flatter the woman. 'I do not know these parts. I'm an easy mark.'

'Had you lain with that man?'

'The man from the river?'

'Yes.'

Anne thought about her answer. 'No. In a moment of weakness, I did let him touch me, and I touched him.'

'And did you steal his money, as he accused?'

'Yes,' Anne replied. 'I did.'

The woman scoffed and shook her head.

'I needed it to pay the bridge toll,' Anne explained. 'So I can save my daughter.'

'How much did you take?'

'Two shillings and a few pence.'

'Two shillings and a few pence! You can't do that sort of thing to men like him,' the woman replied. 'You stole a month's wages from that man. Did you really think he wouldn't come after you?'

Anne shrugged. She hadn't really given the man much thought at all. She'd taken what she wanted from him and left him behind.

'You're a bit foolish, I think,' the woman said, brushing the breadcrumbs off the bed as she spoke, 'though you are a woman of high position. But I suppose that's how your kind are.'

'My kind?' Anne asked. She didn't like the woman's tone. In other times, she'd have slapped a commoner for speaking to her with such impudence.

'The nobility,' the woman replied. And to clarify, as if she thought Anne too dense to understand, 'Lords and ladies, with your fine clothes and shoes and carriages. With your hot meals and servants. Everything is done for you, so you don't learn to survive on your own.'

'I can pay you to help me cross,' Anne said, not liking the direction in which this conversation was going. The woman's comments stung; Anne prided herself on her independence. The woman was probably jealous of her wealth and station. Perhaps a richer reward would entice her. 'In my husband's house, there are many jewels. I can pilfer one,' Anne lied, 'give it to you, then you could sell it. You wouldn't have to work here any more. You could afford a servant, hot meals, rent a fine house.'

'Ha!' the woman said. 'What good would a jewel do me? When your murderous husband discovers its absence, he'll send men looking for it, and I'll be arrested trying to sell it, and have my hand lopped off for theft. I've no interest in bleeding to death on the pillory stage, nor in dying from a festering wound should I survive the axe's swing.'

Anne winced.

'I see my words upset you, my lady. Do I speak too plainly? After all, what do fine people like yourself know of working women's struggles, of punishments, or pain?' The woman paused. 'Though I suppose the queen was beheaded. Did you witness the execution?'

Anne shook her head. 'No,' she said. 'I fled the night before.' That was a lie that Anne wished were true. 'My master slept beside his mistress in our bed, mistaking me for dead upon the floor where I lay, pretending. 'Twas then that I roused myself and fled. I did not see the queen perish.'

'Nasty business,' the woman continued. 'Though I heard she'd lain with a hundred men. The king's own friends, a common musician.' She lowered her voice. 'Even her own brother. Can you imagine bedding your own brother? Mine's hairy and stinks of eels and rancid tallow. Spends all day walking on stilts through the fens to empty his eel traps. I wouldn't bed him if he paid me a hundred pounds.'

'I wouldn't know anything about that,' Anne said. This woman was from the fenlands, then. A prostitute and a fenlander, and yet she was composed, well dressed, and clean, and had treated Anne with some kindness. Anne reached out a hand to touch the woman's, to try, again, to sway her sympathies. 'I'm Anne,' she said.

'Ah!' the woman exclaimed. 'An omen! She shares a name with the monstrous queen but escaped her jealous husband instead. Oh! And just like your rogue husband, the king has a new mistress too! Truly there are many parallels in your stories, my lady, for have you heard the king is now betrothed to be wedded to . . . well, her name escapes me. Some noblewoman. Katherine. Or another Anne? No, no, wait, Jane! He's betrothed to an Englishwoman named Jane. Jane the obedient, she is called. Don't know that I'd like to be called "the obedient". Seems a woman might want a bit more wilfulness to survive in this world, but then I suppose I'm not engaged to the king.'

Anne fought to keep her face impassive, though the reminder of Henry's hasty betrothal to Jane rekindled her anger. And, the woman was right, 'the obedient' was a pathetic moniker. Even so, she shouldn't let on. 'The world is full of scoundrel men, I suppose,' she said, 'but I wouldn't presume to criticise the king.'

'Wise,' the woman said. 'I still cannot help you.'

'Forget about the jewel as payment,' Anne said, scrambling for a way to entice the woman into helping her. She wanted – no, she needed – a protector, someone to look out for her, someone strong and savvy to help her navigate Southwark and the bridge crossing, to help her get back to London. 'I can pay you in coins. All the money I have, less what it costs to cross the bridge. And more, when we get to my husband's manor,' she added, digging herself deeper into her lie. 'Nobody can trace coins. Nobody would know I'd stolen them from him to give to you.'

'It isn't the issue of payment,' the woman continued. 'I'm leaving Southwark today. I have other obligations.'

'But don't you live here?' Anne asked, gesturing around the cramped room.

'Oh good Christ, no!' the woman said, laughing. 'Neither do the others.' She nodded towards the empty beds. 'I suppose a woman as fine as yourself wouldn't know about these things.' The way the woman said *fine* made Anne understand she meant anything but.

Anne looked at her, confused.

'We're not whores, we just work as whores from time to time,' the woman explained. 'When money is low. When taxes are due. When rent is due, or the crops fail, or a husband's business is slow. When the beer she brews at home moulds and spoils instead of turning into sellable drink. That's when a woman comes here, or to another house like it in the stews, to make a crown or two to bring home. We don't live here, we just visit.'

'Oh,' said Anne, embarrassed by her lack of knowledge. 'Please pardon me. I did not know.'

''Tis fine,' the woman replied. 'Why would you? 'Tis why I'm here myself, to earn enough to clear some debts and buy a stock of flour for the coming year. My young ones are back home, where I pay a woman to keep them while I come to the city to earn some money. I have to return home, pay her, and retrieve them. For she has her own food to buy and debts to pay.'

'Can't you send the money in a letter? Then you could help me.' The woman stood, and so did Anne, keen to hold her interest, to persuade her. 'For more money, of course,' she added.

'Listen to her! "Can't you send the money in a letter?" As if I don't want to see my own babes! As if the money wouldn't go missing before it arrived.' A meanness flashed across the woman's face. 'Can't you send someone else to fetch *your* daughter?' She turned and walked towards the door.

'Wait,' Anne called after her. 'I can make it worth your time. I can pay you five pounds.'

The woman stopped, her hand on the doorknob.

'Just think of the security that sum would buy you, would buy your children. You only have to take me over the bridge and to my husband's home. He'll be gone on business for three days,' Anne lied, 'so I can sneak in easily and get your payment. From there, you can catch a fine carriage north to the fens with the money you'll earn. You can help me get my daughter. Then I can help you. We can help each other.'

'I don't need your help,' the woman replied. 'To be clear, I'd be helping you. You'd be paying me. And there's a difference between the two.'

'Yes,' Anne replied quickly. 'Yes, of course.'

'The bridge crossing takes but a few hours, and you'll need to pay your toll and mine too. You should have enough for that with what you stole,' the woman said. 'That'll be for starters. When we get to the other side, we'll go right to your husband's manor, for my payment. You get me for one day only.' Anne nodded. The woman looked outside – the sleet had turned to rain, but a thin sheen of ice clung to the window – then back at Anne. 'You're badly dressed for this weather. I don't suppose you've got any warmer clothes stashed away somewhere?'

Anne pulled on the sleeves of her red kirtle. Even in this fire-warmed room, she was cold. She thought of her gown, soaked in blood and shoved under the bushes behind the tavern where she'd sewn her head back on. 'No,' she replied.

'Right,' said the woman, 'of course not. Late May and the weather is as fierce as November. "Autumn in spring", as my dear mother used to say. And why you're here in nothing but your kirtle. Though I suppose you ran in the night. Perhaps you didn't have time to grab proper clothing?'

'Yes,' Anne said. 'That's it exactly.'

'I suppose you can borrow one of my gowns,' the woman said, 'and a cloak.' She pulled open the door. 'Though I'll expect payment for the use of both. You can add that to your bill.'

'Thank you,' Anne said.

'Well, are you coming?' the woman asked, impatiently.

Anne followed the woman down the hall, to a cramped dressing room with half a dozen trunks. 'Many of these girls are Southwark girls,' the woman said. 'They come for a night and don't bring any possessions.' She drew a key from a small purse at her wrist and slid it into a lock on one of the trunks. 'But those of us that journey from further away have to keep provisions here.' The lock popped open and the woman raised the lid of the trunk, pulling out a grey wool gown. 'It may not be as fine as you're used to,' she said, holding it up to Anne, 'and 'twill be a bit large on you, as you're awfully thin and a bit shorter than I, but 'twill do.' Anne nodded and reached for the gown. The woman pulled it back. 'My lady,' she said, 'not to be indelicate, but would you first like to bathe?'

'Why?' Anne asked.

The woman cocked her head. 'You have a certain odour.' She paused. 'My lady, you smell like piss.'

Anne stared at her. What she said was true. Anne knew it. She could feel her cheeks begin to flush.

'Perhaps when your lord husband was strangling you, you may have wetted yourself?' the woman added, trying, Anne imagined, to provide an explanation for the stench that laid the blame for it on someone else's actions. 'The bathing tub is downstairs. Women who need it bathe in the mornings. 'Tis likely being filled now. Shall we make use of it?'

Anne considered, then nodded. Though she didn't want to take a bath in a tub shared by many prostitutes, the woman was right; she stank and the stink made her stand out. Better to bathe, so she could move among the living unnoticed.

Downstairs, in a small room, the woman shooed away another prostitute who was pouring a pot of hot water into a wooden tub lined with bedsheets.

'Here,' she said to Anne when the room was empty. 'You may undress and bathe. You're lucky. You get first use of the tub, while the water is warm and clean.'

Anne looked at the tub. It was not as fine as what she was used to. At Hampton Court, she had bathed in a copper tub supplied with running hot water, filled with herbs and oils, attended by her ladies and maids. At the other palaces, servants filled bronze tubs with steaming water. In France, she had bathed with the other ladies-in-waiting, in a large open bath scented with lavender into which they all climbed once a week, so as not to offend Queen Claude with their smell. She remembered her friend, Étiennette, whose back she helped scrub, who scrubbed her back in return, as they splashed playfully in the large French bath.

No, it was not what Anne was used to. But it would have to do. The woman helped her unlace her kirtle, then turned her back as Anne slipped off her smock, garters and red stockings and lowered herself into the tub. The water felt good; its warmth drove the chill from her. 'Is there any soap?' she asked the woman. And, remembering her French baths, continued, 'Perhaps some lavender to crush into the water?'

'Lavender?' the woman said, amused. 'My lady, you are in a brothel. We have one bar of soap that we share. We haven't herbs to scent our baths.' She handed Anne a bar of soap that Anne guessed was made from animal fat. It smelled a bit like sheep, but when Anne rubbed it between her hands, it lathered. She used it to wash her body.

'Will you not take off your collar?' the woman asked.

'No,' Anne replied, taking care to keep her neck above the water, away from the delicate silk, away from her stitched wound.

'I've seen bruises before. You needn't be ashamed,' she persisted. 'You might be more comfortable.'

'I said no,' Anne replied forcefully.

'Suit yourself,' the woman said, and left Anne alone to finish her bathing.

When Anne was done, she dried herself with a linen cloth set beside the tub. The woman had gone upstairs to fetch a new smock for Anne to wear, having discovered the smock she had been wearing was the source of the piss smell, and Anne slipped into it, then into her red kirtle, which the woman helped tighten after determining it was clean enough for Anne to keep wearing. Anne took a moment to slide back on her garters and red stockings, also deemed clean enough for further wear. 'My, so fine,' the woman had said, impressed with the delicate weave of the wool stockings.

Then the woman helped Anne into the gown, tightening the

laces to fit her slight frame. It was hard to believe that only four months earlier Anne's belly had been round enough for her to loosen her bodice, to show off the baby growing there. It was never too soon for a queen to flaunt her fertility. When Anne missed three menstrual cycles and her belly rounded out, she'd been fast to do so. How quickly the bodies of women expand and contract, Anne thought, how very changeable we are. The woman pulled the laces of the gown one last time, knocking the breath out of Anne, then tied them.

'Let me tidy your hair,' the woman said, and before Anne could stop her, she'd pushed her to sit on a stool. She removed the kerchief Anne had stolen from the tavern-keeper's wife, brushed and pinned her hair into place, then covered it with a clean white cap that matched her own, which she must have procured when she went upstairs to fetch the clean smock. 'Here,' she said, handing Anne a summer cloak. ''Tisn't as warm as mine, but 'tis better than nothing, and 'twill have to do.' She stood back for a moment, giving Anne the same appraising look she'd given her when she woke. 'You are a beauty, in your own way,' she said, nodding, pleased with the outcome of her labours. ''Tis more visible now that you've cleaned yourself. Right, then, let us be on our way.' She turned, exited the little bathing room, and began walking towards the brothel door.

'Wait! I don't know your name,' Anne said, hurrying after her.

The woman glanced back over her shoulder, her eyes like the good blue of the sky. 'I'm Alice,' she said.

8

Mr Fox

Alice walked quickly, and Anne struggled to keep up, skipping around wide puddles in the street, hoisting the borrowed gown up with one hand so as not to muddy its hem, though she supposed this was pointless. The hem would get soiled eventually, and really, what did Anne care if she ruined this prostitute's middling gown? And yet, Anne felt Alice's eyes upon her, critical, and found she wanted to please her. The two walked at a brisk pace up one street and down another, around this corner and that, passing shops and children who played in the muddy street, pilgrims and travellers, good wives strolling in pairs with baskets, doing their household shopping. Or were those servants? Anne didn't suppose she could tell the difference.

The air was cold and cut through the thin cloak and wool fabric of the gown. Anne shivered and pulled the cloak tightly around herself, careful to keep it from snagging the silk collar. She kept her head down and eyes on the ground, avoiding the gazes of the citizens of Southwark.

By the time the two neared the bridge, the gown's hem was caked in mud. When Alice turned to scold her for not walking fast enough, Anne noticed her eyes drop and narrow. She's probably adding it to my tab, Anne thought.

'I don't know why you're dragging your feet,' Alice snapped.

'I am weak; I can go no faster,' Anne replied. But it wasn't true. She didn't want to confront the bridge gate, decorated with five heads, one of them her brother's, though she knew she needed to, to cross the bridge. Her fears were well founded. As she and Alice approached the bridge, the pikes and their heads came into view, and when the women were close enough to see them clearly, Anne stopped and let the skirt of the borrowed gown fall from her hand. 'Oh,' she said, and could say no more.

The heads were indistinguishable from one another. As was customary, each had been boiled and tarred before being impaled on a guard's spear, and Anne knew that in another week they'd be thrown in the current of the Thames below. Anne didn't know which heads belonged to the king's friends and groomsmen, Henry Norris, Francis Weston and William Brereton, which to the musician Mark Smeaton, who'd brightened her chambers and parties with his light and airy lute songs, and which to George, her dear brother.

George. Anne's heart. Her second self. Her playmate and confidant. She remembered chasing George through the corridors and gardens at Hever Castle, her beloved little brother, as he skidded around corners in his stockings, throwing his head back, giggling, his golden curls flouncing up and down, gorgeous as Ganymede.

She remembered George's clingy hug when she left Hever Castle for Mechelen to stay with the archduchess, how he whispered 'Don't go' imploringly in her ear before she stepped in the carriage her father had arranged to take her away. And how her mother had stood to the side, dabbing her tears with a kerchief, for what could that woman do, what could any woman do, to stop their children from being sent away by husbands who hoped to place them in powerful houses, into powerful marriages, to use them for connections and upward advancement?

When Anne returned from the continent a decade later, more French than English, both she and George had grown from children to adults. George was taller than her, a young man, the king's cupbearer at court, handsome and rakish. A mischievous smile dressed his face as he cracked jokes to her about the other courtiers, spilled gossip about who was having an affair with whom, about whom the always aloof Mary was flirting with, about Mary's affair with the king, about Mary's dull, though attractive, husband, William Carey. So tall was George that he had to duck down to talk to Anne, to whisper the secrets of court into her ear.

And she remembered George's bad marriage. She remembered his wife, Jane Parker, who always seemed jealous of the intimacy she and her brother shared, who had the air of a woman perpetually shut out. She remembered George counselling her through her life at court, first as Henry's fiancé, then as his wife. And, in the weeks before her arrest, George warning her that the tables were turning, that she was falling out of favour with the king. Anne realised, staring at the heads impaled before her, that she had hoped that whatever magic had worked on her had also worked on George – that he, too, had awoken after his execution, still living, and was wandering around London searching for her. It hadn't.

'My lady, have you never seen a head upon the gate?' asked Alice, seeming annoyed that Anne had stopped walking, that she was standing there gawping at the boiled and tarred heads.

Anne paused, searching for her voice. 'No,' she managed to reply.

''Tis a good reminder of what happens to traitors,' Alice chided. Then, perhaps noticing Anne's distress, she added, 'Though 'tis a bit barbaric if you ask me.'

Anne nodded. Her hands shook. In fear, in anger. She noticed and tried to calm them.

'I don't know why the queen's head isn't up there,' Alice continued. 'Though I suppose 'tis a last kindness from the king. They say he loved her passionately. Must've if he was willing to part with the good Queen Katherine to have her.'

A trio of well-dressed women pushed past Anne and Alice, paid the gate guard their toll, and walked through the stone archway, on to the bridge, glancing up at the heads and tittering.

Alice nudged Anne. 'There was a time when I could have been whipped in the street for calling Katherine queen,' she added. 'Though now that the great whore is dead, I suppose we're free to say what we please.'

Anne sighed. Though she had no reason to expect the common people of England would side with her over their much-loved Katherine, she felt disappointed that Alice was so quick to dismiss her, to insult her memory with that tired epithet, 'the great whore' – how boring, what low-hanging fruit. And who was Alice, an actual prostitute, to proffer such an insult?

'Are you a Catholic?' asked Anne, moving out of the way of a crowd of pilgrims exiting the gate. Perhaps Alice's religious beliefs inspired her hatred, Anne thought; perhaps the woman was a devout papist and despised her for her religious reforms.

'Well, I suppose so,' Alice replied. 'In the fens, we pay dues to the monastery that oversees the land. The good brothers there baptise our babes when they can make it down into the marshes to do so, and they bless our weddings and our dead. But,' she continued, putting her hand to Anne's elbow to guide her gently towards the gate, ''tis a difficult thing to reach the chapel from the marshes, so we do not go to mass often, or have to do much praying, and that suits us. Now, make quick with your money,' said Alice, as they approached the guard.

Anne reached into her bodice and pulled out a penny – more than enough to cover both their tolls. She handed it to the bridge guard, who was dressed in a red wool coat and scowled as the cold rain lashed his face.

'You may pass,' he said.

Anne took one last look up at the five tarred heads.

'Gruesome sight, ain't it, miss?' the guard asked.

'Yes,' Anne mumbled, aware that she was staring, holding up the flow of traffic. She looked down and pushed through the bridge gate with Alice.

The cold of the day sank into Anne's bones, and she remembered a fever she'd had when she was ten. The fever, which began with a sore throat and blossomed into a deep red rash, had stretched for days. Her mother, on counsel of the physician, had sent her to bed. Was there worry that she wouldn't survive? Perhaps, for weren't all children at near constant risk of mortal peril, from illness or accident? She remembered one night, when she'd been moaning and tossing in her sickbed, George had sneaked into her chamber and crawled in beside her.

'Shall I tell you a story?' he asked. He was a canny child, and though he was three years younger than her, only seven, he loved to dote on and baby her. He was a voracious reader and could bring any tale to life.

Anne nodded. George snuggled in beneath the covers, propped up on a few pillows.

'Once,' he began, 'there was a young lady named Anne who was of marriageable age. Her father was a wealthy lord, and she had a brother named George who loved her very much.'

Anne remembered liking this part, that George had named the heroine after her, and the brother after himself.

'Lady Anne had many suitors, but of all of them, she liked Mr Fox best. She'd met Mr Fox at her father's country house. Anne, listen!' he barked, for she was falling asleep. She forced her eyes open, though her head pounded. 'Nobody knew much about him, but he must have been very rich, for he boasted about owning a big castle, though nobody had seen it.'

Anne shifted under the covers, her legs restless and aching.

Heat radiated off her. Her sweat soaked the linens on the bed. George continued, pretending not to notice.

'It was decided that Lady Anne and Mr Fox should marry. When Lady Anne asked Mr Fox where they ought to live, he said, "Why, in my castle, of course!" and he described it to her and told her where to find it. But he didn't invite her or her brother to come and see it.'

George brushed Anne's hair from her forehead and gently blew on it to cool her down.

'A few days before their wedding, Mr Fox was called away on urgent business, but he promised to return. Temptation got the better of Lady Anne, and she went traipsing through the woods and countryside, until she found a castle that must have been Mr Fox's, for it was just as he'd described it, and just where he'd said it would be.

'Engraved upon the gate to his castle were the words "Be bold, be bold". Lady Anne liked this, for she'd always been a bold girl. She pushed the gate open but found no one there. So she went to the doorway, and engraved upon the archway above it were the words "Be bold, be bold, but not too bold". How odd, thought Lady Anne. But she pushed the door open and went inside. After wandering the spacious castle, admiring the many fine tapestries and paintings, Lady Anne came upon the great hall. Engraved upon the archway above its door were the words "Be bold, be bold, but not too bold, lest your heart's blood should run cold". How odd, thought Anne, but being the bold and curious girl that she was, she opened the door to the great hall, and what do you think she saw?'

'I'm sure I couldn't imagine what,' Anne mumbled. Her mouth was dry, and she smacked her lips together. 'George,' she said, 'I'm thirsty.'

'Just wait, this is the best part,' George replied, grinning devilishly. 'The bodies and skeletons of many a pretty young lady, all stained with blood!'

'No!' Anne scolded, appalled. 'George, wherever did you hear such a barbaric story?'

'I'll never tell.' George shot her a mischievous look before continuing. 'Lady Anne thought it was time to get out of that wicked place, so she closed the door, went back down the stairs, and was just about to leave the castle when she saw Mr Fox through a window, dragging a young woman through his garden. Lady Anne hid behind a large vase, just in time, as Mr Fox dragged the young woman, who seemed to have fainted, through the door and into the very corridor where Lady Anne hid. Just then, Mr Fox spied on the young woman's hand a diamond ring. He tried to pull it off, but it was stuck. Mr Fox drew his sword, raised it high above his head, and sliced the young woman's hand right off. It flew through the air and landed in Lady Anne's lap.'

'George!' Anne exclaimed.

'Let me finish, Anne, it gets even better.' He was obviously enjoying scandalising her. 'Mr Fox looked around for the hand, but failing to find it, he dragged the woman up the stairs, and Lady Anne heard the door of the great hall open, then close. Seeing her opportunity to flee, Lady Anne made haste to leave that cruel place, taking the young woman's hand with her.'

Anne was very drowsy by now, her fever pulsing in her head, but she tried hard to stay awake for the end of the story.

'The next morning, Mr Fox showed up at Lady Anne's house for their wedding breakfast. Lady Anne sulked at the table and would not look at him. "Is something wrong, my lady?" asked Mr Fox. "Why, yes," replied Lady Anne. "I had the strangest dream last night. I dreamed I went to your castle, and in it was a room full of women you had dishonoured and killed, and then you came into the castle, dragging another woman, whose hand you cut off to steal her diamond ring." "Foolish woman," replied Mr Fox, "'twas just a dream." Lady Anne rose to her feet. "No!" she cried. "The dream was real, and I have proof!" Anne held up the young woman's severed hand and pointed it at Mr Fox accusingly. At once, her brother George and her father and her uncle and all her friends drew their swords and cut Mr Fox to a thousand pieces.'

Anne was almost asleep. 'George, you're terrible,' she muttered through her fever and drowse, playfully hitting him on the arm. 'Just awful.' He giggled and slipped out of her room, quiet-footed, so as not to wake Mary, asleep in the other bed, who'd certainly be cross with them, would tell them to quit telling fairy stories, quit being such babies, start acting their ages, threaten to tell their parents of their misbehaviour. In a few months Mary would be gone to France to serve at court, and in a year Anne would be in the Low Countries with the archduchess. Evenings like this, which had once seemed plentiful – with George sneaking into the girls' room to gossip and play with Anne while Mary, ever the eldest child, kept herself aside and apart, always more grown up, always too old for their play and laughter, her eye on the distant prize of adulthood – would soon come to an end. That night, in her fever, Anne dreamed of the bodies of the young women, dancing bloody and mutilated into Mr Fox's great hall, and one by one collapsing into a large pile, on which perched a white falcon. And she dreamed of her brother, George, who would surely save her from such a fate, were she ever to be married to a licentious killer.

That was George, she thought now as she walked with Alice on to London Bridge and away from George's severed head. Always dear, always mischievous, always comforting. How she wished he could have protected her at the end, like the brother in the story he'd told her all those years ago. How she wished that George, her father, even her proud, mean Uncle Norfolk, would have drawn swords and cut Henry into a thousand pieces, or that she might've.

9

The Trial

George had been at his best the last time he and Anne were together, after their arrests and imprisonment. They sat together at a big wooden table in the king's hall at the Tower, as first she was tried, convicted and sentenced to death, then he. Under the table, she held George's hand. Two thousand spectators packed in to witness the great whore's trial – adulteress and brother fucker, liar and traitor, dirty little homewrecker getting her come-uppance. The air crackled with spite.

In the audience was half the court, ladies-in-waiting who'd always hated her, a smattering of clerks, ambassadors and diplomats, dukes and duchesses, viscounts and viscountesses, including George's own wife, Jane, whom Cromwell called as a witness against George and Anne. She'd always resented Anne for her closeness to George, always resented George for the way he stood too close to other men, laughed too loudly in their company, flirtatiously touched their arms when bantering, neglected Jane in the wedding bed. Not present was the king. Not present was her father. Not present was her mother, who had been sick with a fever at her arrest, whose health Anne had worried over in the Tower, who Anne had been eager to see. No, the good woman was not there, either from ill health, or self-preservation.

Not present was Mary, who by then had been banished from court for remarrying, in secret and below her station, after her first husband died. Anne regretted going along with Mary's banishment now. What a silly thing to banish your sister for, even if she had shown up to court giddy with having married behind your back, visibly pregnant, flaunting her goddess-like fecundity in your face. She wished Mary were at the trial, but then again she was safer away, living on the purse of money Anne had sent her when nobody else at court would answer her pleading letters, not their parents, not Cromwell, not even her former lover, the king.

Under the table, Anne gave George's hand a squeeze. A pulse to say *I love you*. A pulse to say *I'm scared*. He looked at her, the same sea-grey eyes from her childhood. The same rakish looks. The same blond curls. My Ganymede, Anne thought, my golden cupbearer. George, her brilliant brother, her better half. He squeezed her hand back. A pulse to say *We've had a good run, Sissy*. A pulse to say *I love you too*.

And what about Cromwell's accusations? Cromwell, sweating at the front of the hall, a social climber, the king's man through and through, talking piously about incest and all Anne's supposed affairs, talking about her sexual appetites, the insatiable and disgusting queen, absolutely animalistic, would hump anything, even a bedpost, even the corner of a table. What kind of woman, what kind of ungrateful woman, what kind of queen. Though Anne knew that Cromwell knew she was no harlot. She was no horned-up bitch in heat. Anne knew Cromwell knew she was barely recovered from her last miscarriage, and the one before that, and the one before that. Cromwell, the liar, the persuader, the tactician.

Making his case easier was Anne's habit, picked up from her time in France, of allowing men into her private apartments. This was de rigueur in France, where French queens entertained noblemen and advisers in their chambers. It was not customary in England, where the only men who were supposed to be allowed in the queen's chambers were the king or male relatives.

But of course she had to have noblemen and councillors in her private apartments – she was busy working, appointing abbots and abbesses, weighing in on who should be a groom of the king's privy chamber, lobbying for her allies to rise in prominence in land and title, securing strategic wardships for children like her nephew, Henry Carey, who stood to inherit a great fortune after the death of his father.

She'd been as busy as a king, and needed to be able to conduct the business of state in her apartments, just as Queen Claude had done in France, just as Margaret of Austria had done in the Low Countries. But in England, strict land of manners, a nation that was European but not continental, such things were not done. Why, she had all those men in her rooms because she was fucking them! it was easy to argue. And Cromwell did, though he knew better, though he had been one of the men in her apartments, doing the work of governing England with her. But, he could now argue, and did, why else would a woman entertain men in her chambers if not to fuck them? For certainly it could not have been for reasons of governance or intellectual exchange. Everyone knows a woman's only use is what's between her legs, which might be an insatiable cunny, if she is bad, like Anne Boleyn. Or might be the head of a baby crowning, if she is good, like the sainted, obedient and quiet Virgin Mary, to whom all women should aspire, on whom Anne should have modelled herself more closely. Here, Cromwell nodded sanctimoniously.

Never mind that there was also always a surplus of ladies and maids in Anne's rooms. Of course it was not lost on Cromwell, he did not hesitate to remind, that these maids were oft as nought flirting with the men in Anne's chambers, that, in the French style, these ladies and men of court were playing cards and dancing in the queen's chambers and, worst of all, writing love poetry to one another in a bound book he held up as evidence of the general licentiousness of all present in the queen's chambers. What kind of horny bacchanal was going on in there? Never mind that the bacchanal was mostly chaste, that there was flirtation and fun, but not more, not under Anne's eye. Never mind that Anne sat aside, not dancing with men, not writing love poetry. No, Anne was constantly being watched, constantly monitored, for half the ladies were those appointed for her, whom she had not chosen, who were effectively spies. Anne was never alone; she had no time to slink off into the bedchamber or a quiet room and fornicate with Henry Norris, or William Brereton, or Francis Weston, or the lowly musician Mark Smeaton, or, most outlandishly spun falsehood, most ridiculously fabricated accusation, most odious lie, her own fucking brother.

At the trial, Cromwell could barely make eye contact with her, that bloated carp of a man; Anne could taste her hate for him, coppery, like blood in her mouth. What did he want? The king to himself and Anne out of the way. But he didn't actually want to *see* her die, he didn't actually want to *see* his lies play out – he wasn't a complete monster. He didn't want to stand before the scaffold and witness the swordsman slice her head off and feel the spatter of blood upon his pale, creased cheek. Maybe he didn't think Henry would actually kill her?

Anne was convicted quickly, her discussions with Kingston, the Tower constable, used against her, though they had not been confessions at all but rather justifications: explanations of how she had been misperceived, how she had been slandered and lied about though she had never stepped outside the bounds of courtly flirtations. Everyone knew Anne would be found guilty. Everyone knew she would be sentenced to death. Leading the jury was her Uncle Norfolk, her mother's domineering brother, who had been so keen to shove her into Henry's bedchamber. When Anne was arrested, he'd said, 'Tsk, tsk, tsk,' shaking his head disapprovingly, barely containing a self-satisfied grin, for hadn't she outshone him, as she outshone many men, hadn't the flower of her success outgrown his?

Nobody was surprised at Anne's conviction. The world loves to put a woman in her place. But when George was convicted, an audible rumble moved through the spectators. So eloquent he'd been in speaking in his own defence that it seemed truly possible he'd be acquitted. When the jury returned George's guilty verdict, he'd squeezed Anne's hand under the table and mouthed 'Be bold' to her. Be bold, be bold. Boldly, his head now decorated London Bridge. Boldly, Anne had seen it, one of five, tarred and indistinguishable, her beloved brother, desecrated.

Of course, there had been rumours about George, that he'd had a secret lover, or a string of secret lovers. That those lovers, all or some of them, had been men. Anne didn't know anything about that. She loved George, and she didn't pester into his personal matters, though of course, like all the men in her life – her father, her uncle, the king – she couldn't say the same of George, who constantly advised her on who she should court, who she should marry, how quickly she should try to conceive another child, on who was flirting with her at court and to what end and when she should reciprocate and when she shouldn't. The two spent hours discussing Anne's personal life, her love life, the way her love life could be used for her own self-promotion, for the family's.

Had George had lovers? Maybe. Had some, or all, of those lovers been men? It was certainly possible. Did Anne know, definitively, the answers to these questions? No. She didn't think that Jane, George's wife, knew the answers to these questions, either, though the spite with which she testified against him suggested her suspicions. George was enigmatic, good at making others feel like they shared a special intimacy with him, when, in fact, he rarely revealed anything personal about himself.

*

'Dead men's shoes' had been the refrain of Anne's trial. 'You look for dead men's shoes,' she'd said to Henry Norris, teasingly, when he'd dragged his feet proposing to her cousin, 'for if aught came to the king but good, you would look to have me.' You won't marry my cousin because you're waiting for the king to die so you can step into his shoes and marry me, the woman you truly lust after. That had been her meaning: a joke badly told, a joke that landed poorly, a joke misunderstood, misconstrued. Of course she didn't mean she wanted to marry Norris, or fuck him, or that she had fucked him.

'Dead men's shoes,' Cromwell trumpeted around the great hall, to the jury, to the two thousand attendees, all the while refusing to meet Anne's eyes. He couldn't even show her that common decency. He couldn't face what he'd done. It didn't matter, after all, if Anne had fucked Norris. In conjuring up the dead men's shoes that she'd joked that Norris wanted to fill, she'd imagined the king's death, and that in itself was a crime, under the very laws she'd helped Henry write. She was getting her just deserts. She was getting her due. She was reaping what she'd sowed. She was a hussy and a slut, Cromwell argued, and her crimes didn't stop with tawdry fantasies and hidden affairs; she'd actively imagined the king's death, wanted it, waited for it, spoken of it, could perhaps even have spoken it into being, into a real plot to take the king's life, if she hadn't been arrested, if she hadn't been stopped, for the good of the king, for the good of the whole damp and musty country.

The sun in the king's hall that day had blinded her, shining through the high-arched windows, making her squint. 'If you keep making that face, it'll stay that way,' Anne's mother used to say to her when she rolled or crossed her eyes as a child or sneered or snarled. 'Look happier, little raincloud, little bull,' her mother used to urge. Mistaking the squint for a scowl, Cromwell crowed, 'Look, the lady cannot even make it through the proceedings without mocking us with her expressions. She knows not her place!' And at that, Anne had given up and actually glared at the man. Who cared? He was going to kill her no matter what she did. Let this shadow man know how she really felt about him. She glared, but it was no different from the squint, and she wasn't sure if Cromwell noticed the change.

Even Anne's defence, her courtroom speech, couldn't save her. She'd capitulated. She'd admitted to her sin, her one sin, which was nagging Henry, telling him what to do, not showing humility, not being humble, pussy whipping him into submission, bossing him, bossing him, bossing him. She'd risen from the table and declared, 'I do not say I have always shown him that humility that his goodness to me, and the honours to which he raised me, merited.' She'd admitted to that. Squinting into the sun, she'd admitted it, Cromwell in his stuffy velvet robes refusing to look at her, Uncle Norfolk on the jury rolling his eyes, George's wife somewhere in the audience yawning, bored, eager to be a widow, eager to be done with George, her flamboyant, effusive husband. George, seated beside her, had watched her admiringly. Even in their demise they were allies. Even then their love for each other shone with a lustre that others envied. 'I have been ever a faithful wife to the king,' she'd proclaimed, standing to address the jury, and it was true. George, looking up at her with such affection.

Though as always, she had gone too far. In her defence, in her speech, she had raised the king's infidelities. She couldn't help herself. 'I confess,' she'd added, defiant, 'I have had jealous fancies and suspicions of him, which I had not discretion enough, and wisdom, to conceal at all times.' What a foolish thing to do, to raise the spectre of the king's adulteries at her own trial for adultery. Only Anne would do something so daft, so hard-headed, so stubborn. Yet there, still, was George, looking up at her admiringly.

When they pulled George away from her, after the trial, after they'd both been convicted, he mouthed again, 'Be bold. Be bold.' Her George.

The next time Anne saw him, two days before her own execution, he was being marched past her chamber window at the Tower with the other four doomed men, on his way to the scaffold on the hill outside the Tower walls. She preferred to think of him that way, forever walking away from her, after one last smile and wave as he passed, head squarely on his shoulders, not as she'd just seen him, defiled and displayed, mutilated, defeated, a barbaric trophy hung up by a barbarous band of men, by a barbarous government, by a barbarous court and council, in a barbarous country, headed by her barbarous husband, who, no matter how many ribbons he tied above his codpiece, on his shoulders, no matter how many refined portraits he had painted of himself, no matter what good works he thought he'd done, would always be the barbarous man who killed her beautiful, kind, smart gem of a brother, would always be Mr Fox, dragging another dead body through a finely appointed castle, after he'd extracted all he could from it.

10

Like a Swan-Man, He Dived

London Bridge felt more like a busy street than a bridge, Anne thought as she followed Alice on to London's great architectural feat, its great connector of north and south, pumping people and commerce into and out of the city. Buildings lined both sides of the bridge, each sharing a wall with its neighbour, so that no gaps existed between them. Shops populated the ground floors, and living quarters the first and second storeys, which cantilevered towards the centre of the bridge's thoroughfare, so that the sky, in places, was scarcely visible. In this way, walking across the bridge felt very much like walking through a crowded tunnel. Merchants, tradesmen, pilgrims, the servants of nobility, middling wives, all moved in and out of the crowds, in and out of the shops – a mix of haberdasheries, glovers, other makers of refined goods, and grocers.

'Let's stop here and get something to eat,' Alice said, looking back over her shoulder at Anne, who perpetually lagged behind her in the crowd, and gesturing towards a pie shop. 'Catch up with me, will you?'

Anne hurried to match Alice's stride.

'I don't know why you're trailing me like a duckling,' Alice said, sounding bemused. 'You're the lady, after all, aren't you? Shouldn't I be walking five paces behind you?'

Anne smiled. It was a good question. She didn't know what it was about Alice that made her seem worth following, but there was something – the way she carried herself, her slender build and the wisps of hair peeking out beneath her plain cap, the smile that came so quickly to her face when she was amused. She was magnetic. A shyness, unusual for Anne, crept over her.

'Come,' said Alice, and the two ducked into the pie shop, where they ordered meat pies. Anne pulled two pence from her bodice to pay the pieman, a squat, balding, middle-aged man missing half his teeth. Near the counter sat a basket of fresh strawberries. Under their feet, under the floorboards, under the stonework of the bridge, the Thames flowed past, but Anne didn't notice.

'Can we have a handful of those fresh berries, as well?' Anne enquired.

'Yes, madam,' replied the pieman.

'Odd to see strawberries so early in the season, isn't it?' Anne asked.

'Yes, madam,' said the pieman, looking up now and catching her eye. One of his eyes, Anne noticed, was blue and the other brown. 'They've been driven up by cart from Brighton, though even there 'tis an early season. There's a gardener there who grows the berries in a glasshouse. 'Tis how he gets the fruit so early.'

Anne took a handful of the berries, which she split with Alice, who bit into one immediately, holding the green stem between her fingers. 'Delicious,' she said, licking a bit of juice off her lip.

'They say the queen herself asked for strawberries for her last meal,' the pieman added, smiling at Anne coyly. ''Tis the food of royalty.' Was he flirting with her?

'I don't believe that,' said Anne. Her last meal had been communion bread and wine, delivered to her by Thomas Cranmer, Archbishop of Canterbury, shortly after her last confession, which did not include a confession to any of the misdeeds for which she was convicted and executed, but did include a confession to thinking hateful thoughts about the king, about Cromwell, and about simple Jane Seymour. The pieman cocked his head and narrowed his eyes at her.

'Wonderful,' said Alice, taking another bite of her strawberry. 'You don't get food like this in the fens.'

'Aye, 'tis true, you won't find berries like this in the north,' said the pieman, chuckling and at ease again, and he and Alice continued chatting. Anne made her way to the back of the shop to look out of the window. She'd almost forgotten they were on the bridge, but water rushed below in white-capped tumults. Anne put her hand against the wall to steady herself.

''Tis because we're near a starling, madam,' said the pieman, suddenly beside her, his voice too close.

'What?' asked Anne.

The pieman leaned against the wall. 'One of the bulwarks of the bridge. The shop's built over it. That's why the water breaks and rushes so. Its current is broken by the stone leg.' He looked her up and down, scratched the side of his nose with a dirty finger. 'Are you well, madam? Do you need to sit down?'

Anne smiled at him warily. Something about his demeanour, the familiarity he assumed, unsettled her. 'No,' she replied.

'That's a peculiar collar you're wearing,' said the man, pointing to Anne's neck. In this light, the difference in colour between his two eyes was more pronounced. The blue eye caught the light off the water, making it paler, colder, and the brown eye looked yellowish, almost vulpine. Anne imagined, for a moment, the man as a fox, badgering a mouse into a corner of the night forest.

'Come, Anne, let's go,' said Alice, forcefully, from the front of the shop, breaking Anne's focus on the rushing water, on the pieman's animal eyes. Anne looked at her and saw an urgency in the set of her jaw, in the arch of her right eyebrow.

'Yes,' Anne replied, 'we really must.' She smiled again at the pieman, whose hand, she saw, now rested on the window ledge, inches from her own. 'Good day, sir.'

Outside the shop, the two women ate their pies and berries as they kept pace with the slow-moving crowd. Anne was used to sitting at a fine table to eat. Even in the Tower she'd had plates and cutlery, a warm fire, a pitcher of wine. Did Alice often eat like this, on the move, no time to sit down and savour or enjoy? Anne's mind stayed on the pieman, his unnerving closeness, the greediness in his eyes, and on the churning water.

'It must be wearying to live on the bridge,' she said.

'I suppose you get used to it,' Alice replied, her mouth half-full of pie.

'I don't know if I could,' said Anne. A cross woman pushed past them, holding a child by his ear while she muttered under her breath, parting the crowd momentarily, before it closed back in on itself.

'Bridge people become bridge people,' Alice said. 'They spend most of their lives here. These people, like the pieman, rarely leave. Their children are born here, some die here.' Alice nodded to the cantilevered living quarters that arched above them. Most had their shutters closed. ''Tis a lonely life, defined by water. They make their living from fear of the river, from those too scared to cross by boat. As they say, "Wise men go over London Bridge, only fools go under."' Alice paused and gave Anne a wily look. 'Even their privies empty into the river.'

Anne chuckled. 'You can't be serious.' Though Anne knew she must be, for hadn't the garderobes at the Tower, even at Hever Castle, emptied into the moats? The moat at the Tower was flushed out by the tides of the Thames, to which it was connected, twice a day. The moat at Hever was cleaned only by the rainwater, and all knew not to touch the moat water, which in the drier months stank. Anne also knew that the water between the bridge's last set of starlings, nearest to London, was placid and calm, and that no buildings had been constructed over that portion of the bridge, so that it could be used for royal barges to pass through, riding the currents up- or downriver as the tides turned. She'd done it herself many times. And yet, she played along, pretending to be surprised.

'I am!' insisted Alice. 'They build their privies off the backs of their houses, and any business you do there travels through a pipe and falls directly into the river.'

'Well, I shall be glad we're not taking a boat under the bridge, then,' said Anne, 'for I would not want to be tossed through the currents and covered in shit.'

Alice laughed. 'Ah! So the lady has a sense of humour!'

'Yes,' replied Anne, glad that she'd pleased Alice, 'I strive for happiness and delight.' And that was true, and had been true. Anne, the most happy, up late playing cards with courtiers, up early for a ride or a hunt with Henry, always up for one of his quick rough fucks. Anne, up for anything. Anne, there to amuse. Anne, the humorous. Anne, the bold. Anne, the brazen-tongued. Anne, up for merriment, even as she suffered miscarriage after miscarriage, even as she was filled with sorrow from the losses. She'd worn herself down doing this, pretending to be joyful through her misery, going and going. She'd grown exhausted, thin. Not that Henry had noticed, or if he had, he'd been annoyed, not concerned. Still, it felt good to make Alice laugh. It felt good to be happy.

The women walked on, settling in behind a man coaxing a hog with a long rod. Their pace was halting, hardly more than a shuffle. The narrowness of the bridge caused the crowd to walk shoulder to shoulder, prevented the two women from quickening their pace and walking around those moving slower than they'd like to. They couldn't be more than a third of the way across.

Anne was glad she had her money hidden in her bodice and not loose in a purse. It would be easy to pick someone's pocket in this crowd. She noticed that Alice had wound the strings of her small purse twice around her wrist and clutched the purse itself in her tight fist, to prevent its theft.

'There's a story,' Alice said, 'of a bridge-dwelling man whose young daughter fell from a window of his house into the river last summer.'

'Really?' Anne thought of the terror the child must have felt.

'A servant left a window open, and the babe, who couldn't have been but two or three, toddled over to it and toppled out, right into the moving water.'

'What happened?' asked Anne, her concern for the imagined child rising. What if Elizabeth had such a fall? Who was there to watch Elizabeth now, to make sure she didn't fall from a window? She wished she could write to Lady Bryan and tell her to instruct Elizabeth's tutor, nurse and ladies to watch the child around windows, not to open low windows in her nursery, even if the weather grew hot this summer.

'Well,' Alice continued, drawing out the details of the story, seeming to enjoy Anne's interest in the tale, perhaps – or was Anne imagining this? – to enjoy Anne's interest in her. 'The father was in the room, and he dived out of the window after her, like a swan-man, caught her by the back of her smock in the rapids, and pulled her to the river shore. Saved her life.'

'She lived?' Anne asked in disbelief.

'Yes,' Alice replied, smiling, for who didn't like to tell a story with a happy ending? Then a sadness passed over her face. 'You know, sometimes I wonder what men are worth. In my line of work, I meet a lot of unkind men, rogues and knaves, violent sorts, liars, and I hear stories like yours, of your tyrant lord. But then I hear a story like that, and I suppose there can be some good in them.'

'Why did you ask me to leave the pie shop so urgently?' Anne asked.

'I didn't like the way that man was looking at you, like you were something to consume. You really must be careful, Anne. That man saw you had money, and that you were weak, leaning against the wall, barely able to stand, transfixed by the water. He noted the oddity of your collar. He was sizing you up, looking for your vulnerabilities, places he could push to take advantage of you, part you with your money, maybe more.' Alice's brows knitted together. 'I don't know what he planned to do, but I didn't want to stay and find out.'

'Thank you,' said Anne. She was embarrassed to admit that she'd never given much thought to the interior lives of shopkeepers and workers, common folk. Haberdashers were there to make hats. Wool merchants to sell wool. She rarely interacted with skilled labourers or tradesmen, let alone cooks or street vendors, and when she had, they knew their station and addressed her with deference. It had never occurred to her that the same duplicitous behaviours that existed at court, the same cunning and plotting and taking advantage, might exist among the lower classes. Perhaps there was a whole world of knowledge about commoners that she hadn't been privy to, hadn't been offered the chance to learn, or hadn't bothered to.

She put an arm through Alice's so the two were linked at the elbows, a gesture of intimacy. She was glad to have Alice with her. Alice responded warmly, pulling Anne closer to herself. Maybe I've found a friend, Anne thought.

Friendship had been difficult for Anne in England. At the French court, she'd been well liked, someone people wanted to invite to parties, to spend time in deep discussions with. In England, she'd struggled to fit in. She thought of her English ladies-in-waiting, daughters of nobility, some whom she loved well, who were her cousins or childhood friends. But there were more who disliked her, like her aunt Lady Shelton, her father's sister. She'd always resented Anne for rising in station, and resented her even more when Anne arranged for her daughter, Mary Shelton, to be the king's mistress during Anne's pregnancy with Elizabeth. Choosing the king's mistress for him, a cousin of hers no less, would keep the king satisfied, but more importantly would keep him under Anne's control, under Anne's watch. 'Thou hast ruined my girl's virtue,' Lady Shelton had said to her, furious, when she'd discovered the affair. Anne had shot back, 'Remember your place, you daft cow,' for Lady Shelton had the droopy face of a heifer, and wide, bovine hips from birthing no fewer than ten children, an astonishing number, a barnyard number.

Other ladies disliked Anne because of her dress, because, of all things, she wore a swooping French hood that showed off the front and mid-scalp of her dark, thick hair, instead of a conservative gable hood that covered it up, as God intended. Apparently, according to these half-wit ladies, God could not tolerate a woman's natural, parted hair. Anne always seemed to be saying the wrong thing, speaking too loudly, getting a cold look for talking over someone's mediocre husband. But wasn't she queen, after all? Shouldn't she have been able to speak over whomever she chose? 'She wants to be the king. She wants a prick and all,' she'd overheard one of her ladies whisper to another as she thrusted suggestively, after Anne had cancelled a meeting between the imperial ambassador, Eustace Chapuys, and the king because she wanted to go hunting with Henry instead. And though she'd sent that lady away, disgraced, as punishment for her insubordination, the comment stung.

She didn't want to be a man at all; she just wanted to be treated with the same respect a man would be. She wanted choices, the option to cancel a meeting with a spying ambassador she knew was sending nasty letters about her back to the continent if she so chose, the option to tell her husband not to associate with such a man either, the control to stop him from doing so. She wanted to be in charge, to have dominion, to decide. And wasn't she queen? Shouldn't she have had those choices? But perhaps this intensity, this sense of purpose, this sense of her rightful place at the top of the hierarchy — after all, she'd earned it, by marrying the king, by being smart enough to hold his eye, once she'd drawn it, with her intelligence, wit and good planning — was why so few ladies in England wanted to be her friend.

She felt Alice's strong, slender body shift next to her as she walked, and thought again of her friend Étiennette, with whom she often walked arm in arm in France, who she had sometimes held hands with, shared a bed with, who she had sometimes even kissed — '*Juste practiquer*,' Étiennette had said, *just practice* — who was then eventually married to a duke, and left court, as Anne knew she would, such things were common. 'De rigueur,' Étiennette had said when her engagement was announced. Of course she would be married off, of course. Already Anne's head had swum with visions of the husbands she imagined waiting for her in England, of her cousin, James Butler, with his Irish castle and earldom, who she knew her parents were eyeing for a match, or perhaps some other love, yet to be found out, maybe a duke, maybe a member of the king's council, a man of politics. She'd held these imagined husbands like a clutch of trump cards dealt to her in an amusing game. 'Oh, Anne,' Étiennette had said, the night before she left court to marry her duke, '*fais-le comme ça*,' before running her fingers through Anne's, showing her how to tease a man, or a woman.

Yes, Alice might be a friend, Anne thought. She felt it so keenly that she almost started speaking to her in French, the language, for her, of familiarity, kindredness, and affection.

11

Thomas Becket

The bridge was so crowded and slow-moving that it took almost an hour, nearly to midday, for the two women to reach the Chapel of St Thomas, the halfway point of the crossing. The building next to the chapel, on the ground floor a glover's, was under renovation. Carpenters pushed through the crowd with beams, masons with large stones. The tradesmen and their materials and tools compressed the crowd of bridge crossers into an even narrower lane, and a woman knocked into Anne, loosening her arm from Alice's and throwing her off-balance. Alice reached out to catch and steady her, then rejoined arms with Anne.

'Would you like to visit the chapel and say a prayer?' Alice asked. ''Tis the chapel where the pilgrims start their journeys to Canterbury.'

'That would be nice,' Anne said, eager for an escape from the crushing crowd, for a place to sit and rest her tired legs, having walked more in the past two days than she was used to doing. 'Do you know the story of Thomas Becket?' she asked, referring to the saint the chapel was named for. As a reformer, Anne had the impression that most commoners participated in a religion they scarcely understood, something she'd been trying to remedy.

'Yes, of course,' said Alice. Then, as though she were a child reciting for a tutor: 'He was a priest who ran afoul of an old king, and who the king's men slayed. They say the top of his head was cut clean off, so that his brains showed, and yet he kept praying.' Alice looked at her, perplexed. 'Do you not know the history, my lady?' The two pushed through the crowd, cutting across the flow of bridge crossers towards the chapel.

'I do,' Anne said, feeling sheepish for assuming Alice's ignorance. ''Twas King Henry II. Thomas Becket was his chancellor, and then the Archbishop of Canterbury. They were friends and confidants, until the two feuded over the rights of the church. Becket wanted the church to have more power, and King Henry less. Their conflict spilled into the public eye, and some of the king's devotees attacked Becket, murdering him. They say the king was so aggrieved at his murder that he mourned for him until his own death, years later.' The two found themselves in front of the big wooden doors to the chapel, which had been propped open. Pilgrims streamed in and out, dropping a coin or two in the collection box, kneeling and crossing themselves as they entered or exited.

'An odd story, that,' replied Alice as she and Anne stepped into the chapel. Alice lowered her voice to a whisper, matching the quiet inside. 'First you love a person, then despise them, so much so that they are killed at your behest, and then you regret it? But I'm surprised you adhere to the story; aren't you a reformer?'

'Why would you think that?' Anne asked. She and Alice chose a pew in the middle of the chapel, halfway to the altar, and seated themselves.

'Well, you're a noblewoman from London, and most noble families are on the side of reform, probably because they're lining their own pockets with the treasures of the church.'

'You believe that?' Anne realised they were still arm in arm, and hastily withdrew hers, then regretted it, missing immediately the warmth of Alice's body.

'Why wouldn't I, my lady? All I've ever seen the rich do is get richer, and at any cost.' Alice settled her gaze reverently ahead to the altar.

Anne tried not to take offence at this comment, that the nobility was inherently greedy, feeding off the demise of the monasteries, motivated only by the increase of their own wealth. Was this what commoners thought of her and her kind?

'That story,' Alice continued, 'reminds me of the dead whore queen herself. That the king could love her so much, he'd leave his first lawful wife for her. Then come to hate her so, that he not only sentenced her to death, but couldn't even bother to come to the execution. All of London heard the cannon fire that blasted out that morning, to let the city know, to let the king know, that the queen his lover was dead.'

'I wish you'd stop calling the late queen a whore,' Anne said, keeping her voice low, so as not to disturb the prayerful around them.

'What do you care?' Alice replied. 'I'd have thought you wouldn't mind. Isn't the dead Queen Anne the same as the mistress your husband took, and aren't you the same as old Queen Katherine, ousted from her marriage bed, just as you were, by a mistress eager to slip into her husband's arms?'

Anne could see the point that Alice was making. In both the fabricated story she'd told Alice, and the real story of her life, she had indeed been supplanted by a younger mistress, just as she'd supplanted Katherine. But Alice misunderstood the legality of her situation with Henry and Katherine. 'I don't think it's that simple,' Anne said. 'Katherine was the king's sister by marriage. Their wedding was unlawful, and so Queen Anne did not oust her from her marriage bed, as there was no marriage bed to begin with. And Queen Anne was no whore. She was a virgin until their wedding night. And even if she'd been unfaithful, which she wasn't, does that mean she deserved to be beheaded?'

'How do you know Anne was a virgin until their wedding

night, or that she wasn't unfaithful? And, who says Katherine was the king's sister? The very church the dead Queen Anne pushed the king to take over? Not a big surprise that they ruled in his favour. But if you ask around London, ask the common folk, Katherine was the rightful queen, until her death some few months ago, God rest her soul.' Alice crossed herself. 'And as for Anne Boleyn's beheading, that's the law, not my own judgement. I agree 'twas harsh.'

'Don't you think it's a little hypocritical, though, for you to call the dead Queen Anne – God rest *her* soul – a whore,' Anne paused to dramatically cross herself in turn, 'given your own occupation?'

Alice shot her an annoyed look. ''Tis low of you to bring that up. I do what I do because I need to. What need did the dead Queen Anne have to steal another man's wife?'

'It wasn't theft if the marriage wasn't legal. Besides, perhaps instead of being angry at this woman or that, we ought to be angry with the men who leave their wives to begin with.'

Alice held Anne's gaze, lingering a few moments longer than seemed necessary. 'Fair point, my lady. Now shush, I want to make my prayers.' Alice knelt on the stone floor and bowed her head over her clasped hands. Anne did the same.

The chapel was bigger than the one Anne had woken up in two days before. The stained-glass windows behind its altar created the illusion that the church was on land, but Anne knew that the same river water that churned below the pie shop also ran below the church. The thought was dizzying. For a moment, she imagined George's head being thrown into the river, as she knew it would be in a week's time, as all traitors' heads were once they'd spent their allotted time adorning the bridge gate. She imagined George's head knocking against the stone pilings, turning around in the underwater currents, perhaps opening its eyes, revived in the ancient water of the Thames, and mouthing

'Help'. No. Her brother was dead. He'd stay dead. Whatever business he'd had in this world was finished. He would meet her again on Resurrection Day. Would she wander the earth until then, a living ghost? Would she recognise him, his body, without his head? Or would his head, wherever it rested on the silty river bottom, next to old Roman coins and pagan statuettes, awake and find its way back to his body?

Next to her, Alice was mouthing her prayers, eyes closed. She must be atoning for her sins, Anne thought. Perhaps she was praying for her children. Anne knew she shouldn't feel affection for Alice, that her work as a prostitute was wicked, but hadn't Christ shown affection to Mary Magdalene? Hadn't she washed his feet with her tears? He'd kept her close and holy, not an apostle, because she was a woman, but almost.

Anne had her own prayers to make. Lord Almighty, she thought, I do not know your purpose, or why you have seen fit to raise me, like Lazarus, from the dead. I pray that I can do good with the extra time you have given me, that I can secure Elizabeth as the true sovereign of this great nation, as the true head of the English churches, as the true protector of the faith. Lord Almighty, give me strength.

As Anne prayed, she felt the cold floor of the chapel rumble under her knees. She could hear the rush of the water beneath the chapel, the rhythm of it, shaking the cold floor, shaking her. She could hear her own heart beating, faster, faster. Beneath her forearms, the wooden back of the pew in front of her rumbled too. Her body flushed. A soft sweat broke out in her armpits, on her legs, her lower back, the skin above her upper lip. In her head, a buzzing, as though a swarm of bees had slipped its hive and gathered there. She imagined the water churning, the head of her brother tossed in the froth. She took in one breath, and another, faster, faster. She needed to breathe, yet could not draw a deep breath. She could feel Alice looking at her.

'Alice,' she whispered to the strong woman beside her, who had saved her from John by the river, who had fed her, whose dress she wore. She could barely make her voice come through. 'Alice.' She felt Alice reach for her, grab her upper arm to steady her, but the buzzing was stronger than Alice's grip. Anne slumped to the ground, unconscious.

When she came to, a man stood looking down at her. Nausea filled her belly, low and unrelenting.

'Here she comes,' the man said. To his left stood Alice. Alice, thank God.

'What happened?' Anne said. Her voice was hoarse and caught in her throat. 'Where am I?' She looked around. She was in a large room, hung with tapestries. Through the window, she could see daylight, the blue sky. The man, she realised now, wore priestly vestments. A father, then. She must still be in the chapel. She lay on a large wooden table.

'Here,' the priest said, coaxing her head up to slide a pillow beneath it.

'You fainted, love,' Alice said. She turned to the priest. 'Perhaps she was overcome by the Holy Spirit, Father. Do you think she may have been visited by the Lord himself?'

Anne rubbed her head gently. It was sore, and she wondered if she'd bumped it when she fell.

'No,' replied the priest. 'I don't think the Holy Spirit visited her. I think her bodice is tied too tightly.' He turned Anne on her side. 'Do you mind, miss?' he asked. He was about her age, she thought, balding a little, but otherwise in good physical form.

'No,' Anne replied. 'Go ahead.' As the man loosened the gown, she felt the relief of her lower ribs and belly no longer confined, able to expand fully with each breath.

'She's awfully pale,' the priest said. 'Has she been ill? Suffered a loss of appetite? Vomiting? Had heavy courses?'

Why was he talking to Alice about her and not to her directly?

Alice shrugged. 'I dunno, Father. But she's had a good fright, and rough treatment at the hand of her husband, if you understand my meaning.'

The priest nodded. 'Miss.' He spoke to Anne, raising the volume of his voice as though she were hard of hearing. 'Have you been ill? How are your courses? Have you lost a babe? Do you lose large quantities of blood during your monthly cycle?'

Anne looked at him, puzzled. She pulled her mind through the ache in her head, her voice through the catch in her throat. She had lost a lot of blood, of course, during her execution, but certainly couldn't tell that to this priest, or to Alice. 'Yes,' she lied. 'I suffer from heavy courses.' She paused, caught her breath. ''Tis Eve's curse,' she threw in for good measure, for didn't clergy love to link the bodily suffering of women to original sin?

'This good lady needs to eat,' the priest said to Alice. 'She needs to regain her strength.'

'We ate some meat pies just this morning,' Alice replied.

'She needs to eat again,' he said.

Outside the window, clouds dawdled past, ever so slowly, a barely perceptible change, transfixing Anne. Their slow movement, the gentleness, stood in pleasant contrast to the breaking waters below, which, from this height – they must be on an upper storey of the chapel – she could no longer hear or feel.

'I thought that if a woman fainted, she needed blood let,' Alice said.

'Well,' replied the priest, 'have you ever seen a person made better by bloodletting?'

Alice shook her head, confused.

The priest continued. 'I'm not a physician, but I've often seen a hearty meal, a moment to rest and pause, to pray, do more good than a bleeding ever has.'

Anne could see another woman moving in the corner of the

room, a servant. A chambermaid? A cook? The woman hunched into herself.

'Sister Judith,' said the priest, 'go to the butcher and fetch a kidney. Come back and cook it up for this good woman.'

Sister Judith, that must be the woman in the corner. Judith looked over furtively, then nodded.

'And fetch an onion and some turnips too.'

Sister Judith was gone for some time. Anne closed her eyes and tried to rest, but found the Lord's Prayer running through her mind. As a child, Anne had learned the prayer in Latin. *Pater noster, qui es in caelis, sanctificetur nomen tuum.* But English translations of the prayer were becoming more numerous. *O our Father which art in heaven, hallowed be thy name. Let thy kingdom come. Thy will be fulfilled as well in earth as it is in heaven. Give us this day our daily bread, and forgive us our debts, as we also forgive our debtors.* Here, Anne paused, thinking of debts, which abounded in England. One man might owe another for rent, for a mule, for a bet, for money to buy his wife a new gown, for a physician's bill. A subject could be in debt for taxes, and the nobility were often in debt to maintain their opulent lifestyles. These debts, unlike the debts in the Lord's Prayer, were rarely forgiven.

When a subject was executed in England, so too, their debts remained. Anne's last purchases, her final debts, had been clothing for Elizabeth. In the days between her arrest and trial, uncertain of her fate, she'd tended with a mother's focus to her daughter's wardrobe. She hadn't been at all confident of Elizabeth's position were she to be found guilty and executed. She'd imagined Henry would declare her a bastard and remove her from the line of succession. She didn't think Henry would cast Elizabeth out completely – he hadn't done so with Mary after his marriage to Katherine was annulled – but she imagined she'd no longer be a princess, and that her clothing allowance would be cut. Her daughter would need a full summer wardrobe, as well as warmer clothing for autumn. She was growing so fast, last year's dresses and gowns would never fit her, and Anne didn't want the child to be cold or unfashionable. From her chamber in the Tower, Anne had ordered dress after dress, nightshirts, smocks, shoes, bonnets. She ordered ribbons to trim her gowns, and silks to sew them out of. Finally, she ordered a beautiful green velvet gown for Elizabeth to wear at Christmas, trimmed with cloth of gold. It had pained her to think that she might not be there to see the child in the special gown, to hear her laugh with delight at the Christmas pantomime, to cradle her in her arms when she fell asleep mid-banquet at the end of the busy day.

Anne didn't know, or care, what would happen to these final debts. Let Henry, who had so easily condemned to death the mother of his child, pay them. If not, let Anne's parents, who'd done nothing to save her. Or let them go to her sister, Mary, the only surviving Boleyn child. Better still, let the debts stand on the accounting book, a record of her love for her daughter, a record of Henry's cruelty in killing her, in taking that love away, in leaving his own daughter motherless. Let Elizabeth see them when she became queen and know that her mother, in her final days, had been thinking solely of her, had been worrying over her bonnets and cloaks, over whether she'd have enough shoes for autumn, had been loving her, though she could not touch or see her. Let Elizabeth know how much, how very much, her mother loved her.

Eventually, Anne fell asleep. Alice and the priest chatted in the background of her dreams, in which they became a nicer Cardinal Wolsey and Uncle Norfolk, concerned about her fate, instead of hostile towards it. By the time Sister Judith returned and cooked the kidney and vegetables into a meal for the three of them, several hours had passed.

When Anne woke, the priest offered her wine, and she took some sips, sat up, and joined Alice before the fire, while Sister

Judith set the table and brought out their supper. This priest was gentle enough, Anne thought, as the three of them ate their portions of kidney and bitter roots. 'Eat, miss,' he encouraged her. And then he asked, 'What is your name?' When she replied Anne, he said, jokingly, 'A fainting Anne with a mysterious neck wrap arriving in my chapel two days after the queen's execution? You aren't a ghost, are you?' and Anne laughed, because of course such a story was absurd.

'No, Father,' she replied, 'for I am not the only mistreated Anne in England.'

'Careful, lass.' The priest shot her a warning look. 'Such words might now be treason. Who can say what this king will decide one day or another that we can say, or must pledge?' He looked at Anne and Alice conspiratorially. 'Though I assume I'm among friends here. No spies of the king in this room.'

The priest was a kindly man, indeed, and kept them for a while, chatting before the fire, so that Anne and Alice both lost track of time. When pressed for an explanation of who the women were and how they came to be in the chapel, Alice said merely that she was a fenlander, in London to visit her good cousin Anne, who'd taken her for a day of shopping along the bridge, and the two had happened into the chapel for a moment of prayer. Anne marvelled at Alice's adeptness at thinking up falsehoods on the spot.

'Ah,' the priest said, 'the fenlanders are loyal Catholics, devoted to the church, hardworking, with joy in their hearts.' This was not how Anne had ever heard the people of the fens described. More often, they were called layabouts and cretins. This was what Anne had always been told, when the topic of the fens came up, and whether they ought to be drained, turned into farmland, taken from the monasteries, and given out to lords for profit and rents.

Anne had wanted the proceeds from the dissolution of the

monasteries to go to education. Turn them into universities, she'd urged, interjecting herself into council meetings, interrupting Cromwell, or one of the king's other councillors, to bang her fist on the king's round council table and make her points. More colleges for young scholars, a way to strengthen the intellectual fervour of England, to bring the nation into the modern era. She'd envisioned pupils reading Erasmus and other humanist thinkers, and artists and philosophers visiting from the continent, as they had at the French court. It was her right to tell these men what they ought to do, as their queen. She'd missed the way they met eyes with each other behind her back, cast their gazes to the table in shame that a woman was monopolising the Privy Council meetings, was in the meeting at all.

Anne had championed her ideas for the betterment of England in the council room. But Cromwell had other ideas, ways to line the royal coffers with the riches of the church he'd been so eager to dissolve. At first, she'd thought Henry was being manipulated into Cromwell's plans, as when the topic came up in her presence, he professed to support her. But over time it became apparent that Henry was complicit in directing the church's wealth into his own purse and his friends' pockets, that perhaps it was even his idea, that perhaps he was never even very interested in reform, but more so in the increased wealth and power that it brought.

When Anne and Alice left the chapel, the sun was low in the sky. They must have passed more time there than Anne had realised. Alice held her arm to steady her, her touch pleasant and caring, and they rejoined the crowd of bridge crossers, now starting to thin as London's curfew neared.

'We'll have to hurry to your lord's house,' Alice said.

Anne nodded. She needed to find out where Henry and Jane were. Alice had been so kind to her, she wasn't sure how to resolve the lies she'd told her, and she wanted to get Alice the money she'd promised her, for hadn't she always been a woman of honour, a woman who kept her word? Being dead should not change that.

She knew that the Tower was a short walk from the bridge's north gate. She knew, as well, that it would soon be time for the guards who had been off duty in London to return home to the Tower for the evening. She had a brief opportunity, when they were distracted by greeting their peers and changing posts, to sneak across the Tower drawbridge, over the Tower moat, through the double gates, which would be opened for the returning guards to enter, and into the Tower grounds. Once inside, Anne could find her way around the compound easily. She could creep into the Tower mint and pilfer some pounds, and perhaps even locate her jewels, to ensure they made it to Elizabeth. She could take a moment to gather herself, maybe ask Alice to continue with her, for extra payment, of course. For what if Anne fainted again? She needed someone she could depend on, someone strong and savvy. Of course, she also enjoyed Alice's company.

It's not a bad plan, she thought, as she leaned against Alice and walked the rest of the length of the bridge, as the sky continued to darken, as they neared the bridge's north gate.

12

The Ghost in the Room

The City of London's nine o'clock curfew was mostly for noise control. In a city this large, with blacksmiths and carpenters and coopers and stoneworkers and all manner of others engaged in noisy occupations, there needed to be some hours of quiet, when a person could reliably sleep or have a moment of peaceful prayer. Even the city's church bells ceased to toll after nine, not commencing again until morning. There were also the inns and taverns to think of, and the way poor and middling people alike would drink to excess if given the chance, would stay up carousing and fighting and gambling. Never mind that the nobility did these very same things, and at any hour they pleased. Anne herself had thrown many a party that extended deep into the evening hours, even into the early-morning hours, drunken guests bellowing in the courtyards, shouting oaths at the stars. But nobody would call the constable to Hampton Court Palace, or Whitehall Palace, or the Tower of London. Anne had hosted loud, frolicking parties at each of these royal residencies. In fact, Anne had invited Kingston to many a rowdy evening, a few of which he'd attended. This familiarity no doubt led to the ease with which she spoke to him during her imprisonment, the defensive explanations she gave to him for the accusations against her, her professions of innocence, the demands she made to be allowed to speak directly to Henry – surely, she could talk sense into him – all of which were used as evidence against her at trial.

Even so, the City of London and its lord mayor, with whom Anne had also attended festive gatherings lasting late into the night, could countenance no noise or activity past nine from its common people, so Anne and Alice had perhaps half an hour to be off the street.

It was as the two exited the bridge's north gate that a woman in a silk gown, busy scolding her lady's maid for almost dropping a parcel containing a porcelain bowl, walked right into Anne.

'*Merde!*' the woman exclaimed. She eyed Anne and Alice, in their commoner's gowns. 'Watch where you are going!' The woman spoke with a French accent. Maybe a diplomat's wife, maybe a French lord's, though nobody Anne recognised, so she must not be that important. Haughty enough to expect the right of way on a public street, to expect others to clear a path for her.

Before she could remember herself, that she was not the living queen but rather the dead queen pretending to be a commoner, Anne replied, 'You watch where *you're* going, and how *you* speak to me.' Alice tugged at her sleeve, her look imploring Anne to quiet down and walk away, for wasn't she hiding from her husband, didn't she want to remain hidden?

'Watch how I speak to you?' the woman asked, stepping back as though she'd been slapped. Her lady's maid behind her shook her head in dismay. 'You forget your place. What are you, a shopkeeper's wife?' She paused, looking at the two bedraggled women who had wandered off London Bridge just before curfew, no parcels in hand, no evidence of having been on the bridge to shop, or for any other discernible purpose. 'Or perhaps you have other wares to sell?'

'Excuse me?' Anne replied. 'What did you say to me?'

'*Putain?*' the woman asked. 'Prostitution is illegal in London. Shall I call the guard?'

Anne took a step closer. 'Go ahead,' she said, her dead breath in the woman's face, 'and see how it ends. For you are in a fine enough gown' – she pinched the gown's silk fabric between her fingers – 'but you wear it poorly, as though it is not yours but someone else's. Who's to say you didn't borrow it from an older sister, or a better-off cousin, who will surely be upset to find it missing. And you stroll off the bridge at a late hour too, imperilling the honour of your lady's maid. *Peut-être que vous êtes des putains? Peut-être que vous la vendez?*'

The woman looked around herself, unsure, then grabbed her maid's hand and hurried away.

Anne and Alice stood for a moment, watching the woman go. 'What did you say to her?' Alice asked. 'How did you make her leave? I thought she'd get us arrested.'

'I accused her of being a prostitute, and moreover of selling her maid into prostitution.'

Alice grinned. 'You are a sly one, Lady Anne, and clever.'

Anne felt a blush rise in her face. She was glad to have impressed Alice, but she needed to watch herself.

'Where did you learn to speak French?' Alice continued.

'I lived in France for ten years,' she said, then caught herself and finished, 'raised and educated in the house of an aunt.' She had almost said that she'd been a demoiselle at the French court. Careful, be careful.

'Hm,' Alice said, and Anne couldn't tell whether the 'hm' was approving or disapproving, yet she felt Alice reappraising her, changing her calculation of who she was. 'Mysterious woman, you are,' Alice added, tilting her head to the side, considering. Behind her, the sun dipped below the western horizon, slashing the sky in garnet and gold. 'Now, let us make haste. Which way to your lord's manor?'

Anne placed her hand on Alice's arm, the lie she was about to tell building. 'The thing is,' Anne began, 'I've remembered my lord has some pounds locked away for safekeeping at the Tower mint.' Alice's look changed from contemplative to suspicious. Anne could feel a distance wedging between them, her and this clever, kind woman she'd been so happy to win over only moments ago. She continued, hurrying to try to fill the lie in with details, to make it more believable. 'For he is friends with the king, and the king has allowed him to keep some of his riches at the Tower.'

'Your husband is friends with the king?' Alice asked. 'Why did you not say so before, when I asked if you'd been to the execution of the queen?'

'I didn't think it was necessary information,' Anne replied.

Alice huffed. 'Necessary information,' she mumbled. 'What is your lord husband's name, Lady Anne?'

Anne thought for a moment, panicked, then blurted out the first name that came to mind. 'Charles Brandon.'

'Charles Brandon!' exclaimed Alice, for even she recognised the name of the King of England's best friend. 'Your lord is Charles Brandon?'

Anne nodded.

What an odious lie. Anne had detested Charles Brandon since she was a child, when he had come with Henry to visit the archduchess at Mechelen. Henry and Brandon, young men in their twenties then, had stayed up into the early morning playing cards with Margaret. All three had been terribly drunk, Anne knew, because she had stayed up late too, hiding in the shadows of the great hall. After much carousing, Brandon had proposed to Margaret, and she'd jokingly accepted. Brandon had demanded a ring to seal the betrothal, and Margaret had given one, not imagining that not only would Brandon not give it back the next day when the night's revelry had worn off, but that he'd parade it all over London, besmirching Margaret's good name, until she had to send armed men to threaten him and get it back.

When Anne encountered Brandon again at the English court a decade later, he had scandalised everyone by running off with the king's own sister, Mary Tudor, and marrying her in secret. Only Charles Brandon could get away with this level of deception, and he did; Henry forgave him after a short while and welcomed him back to court. Henry's sister passed away a few years ago, and Brandon, nearly fifty, married his ward, a fourteen-year-old girl who had been engaged to his son, a fact Anne found repugnant. But she didn't expect Alice would know these latter details, and so, she thought, she could be safe in this lie, repulsive though it was. Anne couldn't imagine being married to a scoundrel like Brandon, and could never understand why Henry had been so partial to him. Didn't he know that a person was defined by the company they kept? Although, perhaps, in the case of Charles Brandon, that was the point. Perhaps, like Charles Brandon, Henry was a self-serving womaniser, which was why he liked Brandon's company. Perhaps Anne had simply failed to see Henry clearly, completely.

'No,' replied Alice, shaking her head. 'You're not being truthful with me. That cannot be.'

'I am,' Anne insisted.

'You're telling me,' Alice said, 'that this whole time, I've been cavorting with the runaway wife of one of the most powerful men in England?'

'Cavorting? I'd hardly say we've been cavorting.'

A man pulling a cart loaded with produce looked over his shoulder at them.

Alice lowered her voice. 'I will be punished, my lady,' she hissed. 'I will be jailed.'

'Weren't you just in jail?' Anne asked.

''Tis low of you to bring that up, my lady. Every working woman in Southwark ends up in the Clink from time to time. We pay the jailer's bribe and are released. 'Tis of no consequence.'

'You shall not be arrested,' Anne whispered, pulling Alice's arm to lead her down Thames Street. A few red-coated guards stumbled in front of them, drunk and returning to the Tower for the evening. Anne and Alice followed them, though at a far enough distance that they couldn't be overheard.

'How are you going to get in?' Alice asked. 'Surely the Tower is well defended and closed to runaway wives.'

'Lower your voice,' Anne replied. 'I can hear you are sceptical, but you need to trust me.'

Anne ushered Alice, stubborn in her reluctance, down the street, shushing her and exhorting her to hurry. The two strode past Billingsgate Harbour, which was in the process of closing down for the evening. Dockworkers loaded and unloaded a final few crates of goods from the large ships that kept London's import and export market humming. The ground floors of the timber-framed buildings that lined Thames Street, which mostly housed shipping-related businesses – rope merchants, coopers, carpenters, blacksmiths who beat out the many iron parts that held the towering ships together – were darkened. The upper floors, residences, were lit with candles, and through the windows Anne could see families finishing their suppers, laughing, playing games. She wished that she could float up off the street and settle into one of the cosy merchant homes, perhaps play the role of a long-lost cousin come to visit from the countryside, gather a few rosy-cheeked children on her lap, and snuggle in beside a crackling fire.

The two walked on, into Tower Street Ward, where, the Tower now in sight, Anne spied a dirt alley that ran between several crowded buildings, down to the riverbank. Surefooted, Anne scampered through the narrow alley, pulling Alice behind her. She knew all the roads and alleys around the Tower, from her time here before her coronation, when she'd been heavily pregnant with Elizabeth and eager to leave her apartments and walk around the grounds and the streets surrounding them. Of course, a team of ladies had trailed her wherever she went, reminding her to be careful of the prince in her belly.

'Stay here,' Anne instructed when the two reached the paved walkway that ran the length of the river. Here, past Billingsgate and the quays, the riverside was quiet, dark. The walkway dropped off steeply, a stone retaining wall separating the higher ground they stood on from the riverbank. Anne gestured towards a ladder that led to the riverbank. 'Climb down and hide against the wall. The guards are changing. I'm sure you saw the red-coated men in front of us, heading for the Tower.'

Alice nodded, warily.

''Tis dusk. The light is dim. I'll sneak in behind them while they're distracted with the change,' Anne explained. 'I'll be in and out quickly.'

'My lady,' Alice said, her voice low and full of warning, 'you are mad.'

But Anne was already walking away from her. 'Get down by the river and hide,' she urged. 'I'll be back shortly.' Anne retraced her steps, back up the alley, turning for a moment to see Alice's head disappearing below the stone wall as she descended the ladder. Good. Alice would be safe there, hidden. Back on Thames Street, Anne settled her pace a few yards behind the guards returning to the Tower. She followed the men as they neared the bridge over the Tower moat.

The bridge to the Tower of London consisted of two portions, joined together at a right angle, so it looked like a backwards *7*, if one were standing at the Tower side, having already crossed the moat, or a backwards *L*, if one were standing at the bridge's beginning, on land, waiting to cross. What starts with *L*? Anne thought, to occupy her mind as she slunk through the shadows behind the tipsy guards, down the first line of the backwards *L*. *Lion*, two of which lived in the menagerie by Byward

Tower, which she would pass through shortly. *Lady*, which she had been once. *Loyalty*, which she hadn't been shown. *Lazarus*, who rose from the dead. Beneath the bridge the water of the moat lapped gently. Anne stepped softly. *Licentious*, like her womanising husband. She ran her hand along the railing, drew her cloak tightly around herself so the grey fabric enveloped her, so she became more like a shadow. *Larder*, keep a full one to have ample food for the long winter. *Larks*, which would trill here in the morning. *Lanterns*, which she hoped no one would light and spy her. She rounded the corner of the *L* and passed beneath the arches of the Middle Tower.

Limestone, from which the outer and inner walls of the Tower were constructed. *Liberty*, as in a territory, like the Liberty of the Clink, but also as in freedom, which she now had, the liberty of the resurrected to traipse through the Liberty of the Tower. *Love*, as she loved her daughter. She trailed the guards up the long upstroke of the backwards *L*, keeping a dozen paces behind. *Lilies*, which would bloom soon. *Lack*, there were so many things that she was missing. *Lust*, as Henry had felt for her, and others. Anne kept a fast pace, kept to the stone wall of the bridge. *Lemons*, and other citrus, which arrive in winter on ships from Spain. *Life*, which she seemed to have more of than she deserved. *Luck*, which she hoped she'd have, glancing at the arrow slits in the Tower wall. She hoped they weren't manned by archers. They must not have been. No arrows flew. *Lilibet*, the name she sometimes called her daughter. *Land*, which she could see in dark silhouette on the side of the moat she'd just left. Alice waited for her there.

The guards in front of her chattered merrily. At Byward Tower they greeted their comrades, exchanged news of the day, swapped pleasantries, stories and ribbings. They didn't see the slight woman lurking behind them, hidden by the shadows of the angles and pitches of the Tower wall. She slipped through the double-arched gates behind the men, beneath the double iron portcullises, which were suspended by metal chains that could be released to send them crashing down, to bar the way. No one saw her, no one noticed. The guards gathered outside Byward Tower, chatting, waiting for the Ceremony of the Keys, which would commence in about an hour, near ten o'clock, when the gates would be locked. Anne needed to hurry. From the menagerie pit, she heard the lion and lioness prowl and roar. *Late*, do not be late.

Anne had often thought that the Tower of London was shaped like an uneven pentagon, a pentagon drawn by a child, a drunkard, or a fool. Though she supposed all kings a bit foolish, puffed up as they were by their councils, chancellors, courtiers, wives, children, by all around them assuring them of their valour and righteousness, of their brilliance. The Tower was surrounded by two walls, the outer and inner curtains, and a horseshoe-shaped moat that sat abreast the Thames and rose and fell with the tides of the river. A dozen individual towers dotted the inner curtain. The Beauchamp Tower. The Flint Tower. The Salt Tower. The Bloody Tower – Anne shuddered to think of it. Within the perimeter of the inner curtain: the inner ward and the Tower buildings. The White Tower sat in the centre of the inner ward, that old stone fortress William the Conqueror built, which attracted ravens, who nested on its roof. In life, Anne had found the birds ominous, their bald caws and intelligent eyes. Hungry for death, they'd seemed.

Off the White Tower, in the south-east corner of the Tower grounds, the much newer royal apartments and queen's lodgings stretched, and the king's hall, where feasts were hosted and trials held, including Anne's. These newer buildings were large, bold structures, with finely decorated rooms, constructed in the inmost ward, the private courtyard where the king and queen could gather with their favoured courtiers. St Peter ad Vincula, the chapel from which she'd risen two days ago, stood in the north-west corner of the inner ward, before a series of timber buildings Henry and his father had constructed that housed the vast number of courtiers and visitors that frequented the Tower, as well as their many servants, and sometimes soldiers.

The mint, however, was in the outer ward, the wide lane that ran between the outer and inner curtains, where the guards and other service workers lived and made their lives in houses built between the walls. The mint wasn't far north of Byward Tower, in an area of the outer ward known as Mint Street, which also housed the various workshops associated with the mint as well as houses for the minters and their families.

Avoiding the guards gathered at Byward Gate, Anne kept to the shadows, concealed, heading north. Soon she came upon Mint Street, which at this hour was quiet. By now the sky was dark. The windows of the minters' houses, too, were dark, the minters asleep for the night, recovering from long shifts stamping coins, the heat of the mint furnace, and the exhaustion of all the jobs of the mint: smelting metal, pouring the smelted metal into moulds to form the disc-shape of a coin, sliding the hot metal discs between two iron dies, holding the iron dies steady, swinging the hammer against the dies to strike the face of the king on each coin. Anne had visited the mint early in her queenship and been fascinated with the process. She'd imagined her own son's face being stamped on to the coins of England one day. Now she imagined Elizabeth's.

Anne crept on until she was crouched in the shadowed front porch of one of the minters' houses. A few yards away, two guards sat at a small table before the mint door, playing cards. Anne looked around for something to throw, to misdirect the men's attention. At her feet, she spied a toy wooden horse on wheels, no bigger than her hand, probably left there by a minter's careless child. She picked it up and threw it past the guards. It clattered along the paving stones.

'Did you hear that?' said one of the guards, a middle-aged man with a trim beard, turning his head to follow the noise.

'Probably just a rat,' said the other, a younger man who dismissed his counterpart without looking up from his cards.

'We best go and check to make certain, though,' said the first. He rose from his seat, and when the second man reluctantly followed, taking the torch from beside the door with him to illuminate the darkness, Anne slipped into the mint unnoticed.

It took a moment for her eyes to adjust to the absence of light in the building, for at least in the outer ward, the stars provided some illumination. But there was the hearth where the large furnace fire burned all day long, and there were the workmen's tables, the dies set atop them, the big hammers leaned against the wall. Anne knew there were several chests of coins in the back room and was surprised, when she found her way to them, to discover that one was unlocked. Likely some minter in a hurry to get home, neglecting his duties. Anne tsked. But his mistake was her good fortune. She opened the chest lid and counted out ten pounds. She didn't want to take more than she could carry, or so much that it would be noticed, but she wanted enough to complete her journey and pay Alice the five pounds she owed her. She shoved the coins in the bodice of her dress, where the shillings and pence left over from robbing John already sat.

The guards hadn't yet returned when Anne peeked out of the mint door, so she dashed quickly out. The lioness roared from the menagerie, as though reminding her to hurry back to Byward Tower before the guards closed the gates. *Late, don't be late.* 'Quiet down,' she whispered, as though the beast could hear her.

Anne desperately wanted to know what had happened to the jewels she'd hidden for Elizabeth. She knew she should leave now, before the gates were closed, but her trip to the mint had been faster than she'd expected. Surely she could make it to the royal apartments, to see if the jewels were still there. Anne knew no royalty was present – none had been here for her execution, and they'd stay away from the site of violence for at least a few weeks – and so, the apartments wouldn't be guarded. She couldn't resist.

Keeping to the dark wall of the Tower, she sneaked back past Byward Tower – which stood empty, the guards must have gone inside – around the corner, then made haste through the Bloody Tower to the inner ward, saying a quick prayer for the two ghostly princes, Henry's child uncles who'd been murdered there by their own uncle, Richard III, usurper of the throne. She hurried past the perimeter of the White Tower, into the private courtyard of the inmost ward, then, stealthily, into Lanthorn Tower, which housed the queen's apartments, where she'd spent the days leading up to her coronation three years earlier. At the top of the turning stone staircase, she found the wooden door, unlocked, behind which were the rooms where she'd spent her last weeks. She cracked the door a few inches, enough to enter.

The rooms were just how she'd left them. Her shawl was draped across the back of an upholstered chair pushed under a round wooden table before the hearth, which still held the ashes from her last fire. A partially emptied pitcher of wine and one dirtied goblet sat on the table, from her last evening in the dwelling. Her book of hours, the one Henry had given her all those years ago as a New Year's gift, lay beside the pitcher and goblet, flipped open to a prayer about the Resurrection, with an illumination of Christ rising above the graves of the dead, whose faces poked through the earth like fresh loaves of bread. It was as though Anne had just stepped out for a walk and would be right back, not as though she had walked away to her own execution.

Anne walked into the next room, the bedchamber, over to the four-poster bed, and reached inside the pillowcase, where she'd hidden her jewels with the instruction to Lady Margaret

Lee, Thomas Wyatt's sister, to deliver them to Elizabeth. How she'd loved Lady Margaret, who'd been like a sister to her when they were children growing up in Kent, she in Hever Castle, the Wyatts in Allington Castle, their nearest neighbours. It was into Margaret's hands that she'd pressed a small prayer book before she was taken to the scaffold, in which she'd inscribed, 'Remember me when you do pray, that hope doth lead from day to day,' and she knew Margaret would remember her, would pray for her, would keep her memory.

The jewels were still there; Margaret must not have been able to return for them yet. One ruby, set in a ring. One black onyx pendant on a string of pearls. One gold diadem, studded with small sapphires. Anne slipped the jewels down her bodice, next to the coins. The metal of their settings scraped the flesh of her ribcage. Perhaps this is how the monks feel, she thought, wearing their penitent hair shirts. Though instead of hair, some of the most expensive jewellery in Europe sat against her chest. Maybe she'd be able to deliver the jewels to Elizabeth herself. Anne put the pillow back where she'd found it. She backed slowly out of the bedchamber and through the antechamber with its hearth and table, careful not to upset the tableau of the rooms as she'd found them. The last thing she needed was ghost stories floating around.

As she turned to go, she thought of her last terror-filled night in the queen's apartments, of the wild tears she'd cried for herself and Elizabeth, of the lady's maid she'd slapped across the face when the woman tried to comfort her, of the way she'd called out for her mother, begged her ladies to tell her if the good woman was still ill – had she recovered from her fever? She thought of the way she'd placed her hand over her breast to feel the rampant beating of her heart, to feel its refusal to give up, to feel, one last time, the thumping evidence of herself, that she existed, that she lived, that she was a real person. She had cried herself to sleep, eventually, and her dreams had been of escape. In one, her mother arrived and swept her riding cloak wide to cover them both, then muttered some enchanted words that changed them into ravens and they flew out of the window. In one, Henry broke down the locked apartment door to rescue her. In another, her brother George emerged from a secret doorway with Elizabeth held in one arm and a candle to light the way through a tunnel that twisted and turned back to Hever Castle, where the three could live happily together. She'd woken at dawn, puffy-eyed and exhausted, to face her fate.

She thought as well of the nights she'd spent here with Henry, when these rooms had been not a prison but her coronation suite, and of all the ways he'd loved and touched her, of the promises he'd made, then broken. There, by the bed, she could almost see him, knelt down in prayer as she pretended to sleep, worn out by pregnancy and two days of entertaining, readying herself for the ceremony that lay before her, for the long, spectacle-laden coronation procession she would make through London, to the hallowed sanctum of Westminster Abbey, to be crowned Queen of England, to the fate of love and fortune she thought awaited her in her marriage. That fairy-tale past was the real ghost in the room, not Anne.

With a cold hand, she shut the door behind her.

13

Thomas Wyatt

Anne intended to proceed directly to Byward Tower, to exit before the Ceremony of the Keys, which surely couldn't be more than half an hour from now, maybe less – she should hurry, hurry. But as she tiptoed through the inmost ward, she heard the voices of two men from a low window in one of the long timber buildings that housed favoured courtiers. Crouching down, she crept closer, her ear trained on the voices, until she was right below the opened window.

'I wouldn't say no to a suckling pig and a pitcher of good wine,' spoke the first man. 'Something to restore my strength after the bloody performance that's just played out on these grounds.' Anne recognised the voice immediately: dear Thomas Wyatt, her childhood neighbour and lifelong friend, who'd been accused of lying with her and imprisoned along with the others, though not executed.

'Sir,' spoke the second man, 'you are the king's prisoner, and not in a position to be making complaints about the food.' The second man chuckled. He was being coy. Anne recognised his voice as well: kind and good-humoured. William Kingston, her jailer and confessor.

Anne wasn't sure how Thomas Wyatt had escaped the axe's swing. Given his courtly advances towards her, and their long friendship, it had seemed certain he'd be tried and executed.

Wyatt had always been smitten with her, giving her ribbons and hand-picked bouquets when they were children, writing poetry to her when she returned to England a sought-after lady at court. He was sweet, in his own way, if not a bit entitled. The son of a powerful man, already married, though miserably, he'd propositioned her to be his mistress shortly after her return to England. This type of man felt they were owed a woman's affections, that they deserved not one wife but two. She supposed Henry had been the same way, except he had more to offer her, and the power to extricate himself from his unhappy marriage, which Thomas Wyatt lacked. Yet for a moment Anne wondered what her life would have been like if she'd taken Wyatt up on his offer. Would he have set her up in a country house replete with servants, where she'd have had time to think and write, only visited by him on occasion for playful lovemaking? She wouldn't have married Henry, then, wouldn't have got herself into such a mess. She shook her head. No, in that path there'd be no passionate love affair, for she'd never really been attracted to Tom, only attracted to his attraction to her. There'd have been no shining sun of Henry's affections, no coronation, no queenship, and, most devastatingly, no Elizabeth.

The two men prattled on about the food and the day's mundanity at the Tower, whatever book Wyatt was reading, his request for some paper and ink so he could write. Anne stayed, crouched below the window, listening. She knew she should leave but couldn't pull herself away from the familiar voices of these men who were so recently her companions but now seemed to exist in a different realm of being. Then the mood between Wyatt and Kingston shifted.

'I never saw such a bloodthirsty misuse of the law,' Wyatt said. 'I never saw such a good lady treated so poorly.'

'Sir,' Kingston cautioned, 'I am the king's servant. Be mindful what you say.'

'Tell Cromwell I have my complaints,' Wyatt snapped. Cromwell, Anne thought. Of course, a friend of Wyatt's father and his protector at court. That's why Wyatt had been spared; Cromwell was backing him. Good, thought Anne, Wyatt didn't deserve to die. None of them did.

'She was found guilty, sir,' Kingston went on. 'They all were.'

'Guilty,' scoffed Wyatt. 'By a false jury if ever there were one, full of sycophants and petty men, those seeking to flatter and control the king.'

'In my opinion, sir, nobody controls the king,' Kingston replied. 'And those who think they do end up here, with me.'

Below the windowsill, Anne shifted on her feet. How odd, she thought, that after death she could still get sore legs. As if instinctively, she felt under her collar at the gash on her neck. Still there, the ridged scar and the hastily sewn thread. She pulled her fingers back out and smelled them. The smell was pungent and cheesy, like the lint from inside a bellybutton, or the skin behind a child's ear. She shifted on her feet again, and a pebble kicked loose beneath her right slipper and rolled away from her, bouncing a few times on the courtyard stones.

'What was that?' asked Kingston, and Anne ducked lower as he stuck his head out of the window and searched the darkness of the inmost ward for whatever had caused the noise. She was glad he didn't look down. She was so close, she could have reached up and touched him. She pressed her thin frame tighter against the wall, hoping the shadows would continue to cover her.

'I'm sure 'twas nothing,' Wyatt replied, dismissively. 'And what of her grave?'

Kingston pulled his head back into the prisoner's chamber and mumbled something inaudible.

'Don't think I haven't heard the Tower gossip, Kingston. Your guards are as loose-lipped as a gaggle of old women. Her grave robbed, the body missing? Poorly guarded, was it? Who knows where her corpse lies now, in what criminal's hands.' Wyatt paused. 'Though one guard told me he thought perhaps her own family arranged to have it robbed, to have the body carried to Hever, buried on family ground.' How Anne wished that were true, that her family had cared enough, or had had the means enough to steal her back, to secret her home. She also regretted leaving the empty chest in the chapel, instead of filling it with something else or hiding it away, though what would she have filled it with, and where would she have hidden it, and how, her head at the time being unattached to her body? And wouldn't a hidden chest, missing entirely, have been just as suspicious as an empty one?

'I would not speak of those rumours any further, Wyatt,' Kingston urged. 'For the arrow chest in which she was laid to rest has been buried, and even the king does not know 'twas empty, and if the people find out – you know how superstitious they are. Ghost stories will abound. And if those rumours are traced back to you. Well.'

Wyatt persisted. 'And now I hear Henry and Jane are betrothed?' Was he looking for a fight? He'd always been a contrarian, loud-mouthed. He and Anne had had that in common.

'Yes, sir,' Kingston replied.

'What kind of a fool,' Wyatt continued, 'would give up the great Anna Bullen for plain Jane Seymour, mopey and chaste, never saying a word to cross anyone. Never saying a word, full stop. I wonder, good Kingston, if she can speak at all?'

'I rather think that is the point, sir,' replied Kingston. 'A nation can only have one sovereign at a time, and Anne sought to rule from the king's side. Jane knows her place.'

Anne almost laughed out loud, a madwoman's response, then caught herself and quieted. What he said was true. She had tried, at times, to usurp Henry's power, to direct him, when she felt he needed directing. What kind of woman tries to boss around the King of England? What type of woman can't keep her opinions to herself? What type of woman accuses a king of adultery at her own trial for being adulterous against the king? Anna Bullen, that's who, the woman who doesn't know when to shut her mouth. Anne de Boulogne who doesn't know her place. Anne who can't shut up. Just shut up. Just shut up. Anne realised she was hitting herself on the forehead with the palm of her hand. Just shut up. Just shut up, she thought, hitting herself again, again. Just shut up, you dumb whore. One more hit. And then she stopped.

'How long do you suppose it will be before he weds her? Ten days? A dozen? Maybe a fortnight? He won't wait long, for surely he desires to know her better, to explore her hidden countries, if you understand my meaning. I suppose he's brought her right back to Hampton Court and installed her in Anne's chambers,' Wyatt said, 'as if she could ever take Anne's place.'

'Sir,' cautioned Kingston again, 'watch yourself.'

'Go tell it to Cromwell,' Wyatt snapped. 'He knows how I feel. Let him come here himself and drag me to the scaffold.'

'Sir,' replied Kingston, and Anne imagined him lowering his head, deferentially. Ever the gentleman jailer.

'We both know Cromwell's not going to kill me. He'd have done it already if he intended to,' Wyatt said. A chorus of starlings began chirruping on the riverbank, their high-pitched song loud enough to reach the Tower courtyard. They sound unsettled, Anne thought, all singing the same song of dissatisfaction.

''Tis likely that is true, sir,' Kingston replied. 'At any rate, the king has taken his betrothed to Whitehall Palace. No doubt, as you surmise, the two will be wed soon, and she will be your new queen. I suggest, sir, that you alter your tone towards her. There are some sins from which even Cromwell cannot save you.'

Anne felt her anger rise again, hot and hungry, for Whitehall was the palace she and Henry had renovated during their long courtship. It was there that Henry had taken her when they were first married, after Thomas Cranmer, newly appointed by the king as Archbishop of Canterbury, had finally issued Henry his annulment. Henry and Anne had travelled to Calais to get King François's blessing, so that they had continental backing for their marriage, then exchanged private vows and consummated their relationship in Dover, before settling back in at Whitehall. She had never felt happier than she had in those early, heady days of their marriage, when Henry was content to have finally got what he wanted, and Anne was content to give it to him. And it was there, at Whitehall, two months later, Elizabeth already growing inside her, that Henry had more officially married her, in a second ceremony, ordained by a priest, with actual witnesses. How could he bring Jane there? Did the man have no remorse, no sentimentalities, no sense of place or memory? Was one woman the same as another to him, one wife the same as the next, a vessel to be bred and bred until the king at last had his male heir?

No, thought Anne, Henry had loved her. Something had turned him astray. Jane. Or the fall from his steed on the tilting yard, the wound to his head. When he had fallen, his men said, he had held his hands up, fingers splayed, as though reaching for help, then gone limp and lost consciousness. Was he reaching for Anne in that moment, for the son she carried in her last pregnancy? Perhaps he was reaching for Katherine, his first wife, who had, after much delay, died just a fortnight before? No, thought Anne. No. Henry had loved her. He had loved her and only her. He had told her so. The intensity of his love had overwhelmed her. She had never been desired so fiercely, loved so jealously, guarded so covetously. 'You are mine and only mine,' he'd whispered in her ear, on the night of their private wedding in Dover, when she gave herself to him. Mine and only mine. Wasn't that proof of love?

Anne shifted on her feet, and another pebble slid beneath her slipper.

'That noise again,' said Kingston, walking over to the window. 'Is somebody out here?' Once more he stuck his head out and searched the darkness. Anne's heart beat hard with fear. What if she were caught? Would she be jailed? Beheaded a second time? Or burned as a witch? She wasn't sure if she could die twice but knew she didn't want to experience the pain of a fire.

'Let me see,' said Wyatt, pushing Kingston aside and looking out of the window himself, first left, then right, then up, then down, directly into Anne's face. He went pale. 'Anne?' he asked, his voice barely above a whisper.

Anne looked up at him, mouth agape, unable to speak. 'Thomas,' she croaked out, after a moment.

'What is it?' asked Kingston from inside the room.

Thomas stood, silent, looking down at her. Anne remembered all the games of hide-and-seek they'd played as children. She'd been so good at hiding, and Thomas so easy to surprise. She'd delighted in it. When he'd come upon her behind a tree or inside an empty room, she'd jump out at him, shouting *Boo!* and he'd scream and startle. He had the same look on his face now.

She smiled. 'Boo,' she said, then stood and ran across the courtyard.

'Anne!' called Thomas. 'Anne Boleyn!'

She turned and put a finger to her lips. 'Shhh.'

Thomas looked so very happy to see her in that moment, as though, if he could, he would leap through the window, chase her through the courtyard, catch her in his embrace, and never let her go. He wiped a tear from his cheek, though he was smiling. She turned again and ran.

'What is it?' Kingston asked once more, this time more loudly, and looking behind herself, Anne saw him shove Wyatt aside and take his place at the window, his face slack with disbelief.

''Tis a ghost!' Kingston exclaimed. ''Tis that good lady's ghost!' He crossed himself. 'Please, good lady,' he shouted after her, 'forgive us!'

Anne ran on, across the private courtyard, through Coldharbour Gate, into the open yard of the inner ward. She didn't look to Tower Green to see if her scaffold remained. She didn't want to see it. She rounded the corner of the wall enclosing the inmost ward and ran towards the Bloody Tower's open gate. What time was it? Had she beaten the guards, who must certainly be about to gather for the Ceremony of the Keys? She paused inside the arch of the Bloody Tower's gate, cloaked in the structure's shadows, and peeked her head around the edge.

'Halt! Who comes there?' the sentry shouted, and her heart sank, for she recognised the first call in the Keys Ceremony and saw at Byward Tower a half-dozen guards gathered for the official locking of the gates.

'The keys!' replied the chief warder.

'Whose keys?' asked the sentry. Anne knew this script by heart, so often had she heard it. There was no escaping through Byward Tower Gate now. She could hide in the Tower overnight, or flee as she had two nights ago, through River Gate, which was directly across the gap between the two walls, a short run; she'd be visible to the guards for only a moment. She decided to take her chance.

'King Henry's keys!' she heard the chief warder call as she dashed from the Bloody Tower to River Gate.

'Pass King Henry's keys. All is well,' the sentry responded.

Anne reached River Gate and ran below its raised portcullis, out on to the dock. This time, no barge or boat waited for her.

'All's not well!' she heard a guard call. 'I saw a woman running between the curtains!'

And then she heard the scuffle of boots, and men running. Before her, the Thames, and surrounding the dock, the thin strip of wharf, lined with unmanned cannons, that connected back to the riverbank on which she'd left Alice. She had no choice. She turned and ran down the wharf, as fast as she could go, under cover of night, she hoped, under cover of enough darkness that she wouldn't be taken down by an arrow shot from an arrow slit. She ran as fast as she could go, her gown tangling between her legs. She hoisted it up and pumped her legs. The guards ran out on the dock, shouting after her.

"Tis her!' she heard Kingston's voice bellow, for he must have joined the guards on the dock. "Tis Anne Boleyn!'

Fearing that she would be captured, without further thought, Anne leaped into the water of the Thames.

14

The Women Ran Still

The river water was cold and moved fast. It seeped through Anne's clothing, her gown and kirtle, her smock, reaching all her most sensitive parts, groin and navel, breasts and armpits, cold against her skin. It soaked her hair, which slipped out from beneath her cap and whipped around her face, around her head and neck, tugged against her silk collar, and tangled in her cloak, for she'd been pulled all the way under the water by the current. She knew how to swim, a little, having learned in France at Queen Claude's insistence – that forward-thinking lady – but the current overtook her and carried her quickly downstream. Flapping her arms wildly, she pushed her head above water and gasped for air. She could see the Tower wharf receding from view in the darkness, and moving quickly by her – or, rather, she was moving quickly by it – the riverbank. It wasn't more than a few yards away. She swam as hard as she could towards it, pulling her arms in big strokes and kicking her legs.

She needed to reach land before she travelled too far downriver and passed Billingsgate Harbour, after which point it would be impossible to extricate herself and she'd be swept into the currents of London Bridge, churned and tousled under the water, maybe meet her second death, if such a thing were possible. Anne kicked her legs more furiously and, feeling her slippers sliding from her feet and curling her toes to try to hold them in place, took long, hard strokes with her arms and moved towards shore, towards the riverbank. She pushed and pushed. In her mouth, the taste of copper. Her airways constricted with the cold of the water, with the force of her breathing, so that she wheezed with each short breath.

She began to lose strength. She was pulled, again, under the water, the weight of her wet smock and kirtle and gown tugging her down. Suddenly, there was Alice, like an archangel, storming into the river, swimming in quick strokes out to her, grabbing the back of her gown, and with a strong arm, dragging her towards the riverbank. Where had this woman learned to swim so well? Perhaps in her swampy homeland. Alice hauled Anne to shore, where the two collapsed, sopping wet, on the stony bank. Anne coughed out a mouthful of dirty river water and adjusted her cap, which had come loose and hung by just a few pins.

'You saved me,' she managed to utter, looking astonishedly at Alice, amazed that this woman she had met only yesterday had now thrice come to her rescue, had now thrice saved her from danger – from John, from the pieman, now from the river – had shown her such care.

Alice, in turn, gave Anne a bitter look.

'Why, my lady,' she said, 'are there armed guards chasing after you from the Tower wharf?' For both women could hear the guards shouting indistinctly to each other in the night and see the lights of their lanterns as they searched the ribbon of land upriver, from which Anne had dived into the water. 'You said that this would be easy. You said to trust you. Clearly you have been spied. What danger are we in?'

Anne tried to hold her voice steady. 'We need to run,' she said, ignoring Alice's questions. 'Now. We need to leave before they come after us.' She imagined the guards completing their search of the Tower wharf, then returning to Wyatt's chambers to get his report on the mysterious woman who had run through the Tower and disappeared in the Thames. No doubt Kingston would be directing them on what to do next. Would he send the guards after her, assuming her a look-alike to the queen, not the queen but a different woman bearing an uncanny resemblance to her, who must be caught for trespassing on the Tower grounds? Or would he believe what his eyes had seen, what his mouth had spoken, that she was the ghost of the recently beheaded queen, who could neither, and should neither, be captured nor punished? Or, believing his eyes that she was a ghost, would he decide anyway that she needed to be pursued and captured? Anne couldn't know what he would do and didn't want to wait around to find out.

'Quickly,' she said. From the ground, Alice grabbed her cloak and purse, which she must have taken off before diving into the river. She tied the cloak at her neck, slid the purse on her wrist, and the two drenched women scrambled up a nearby set of stone stairs, leading from the riverbank to Watergate Street. The river water squished in Anne's slippers with each step she took. The women ran, holding hands, dripping water behind them, sometimes slipping and sliding through the streets and alleyways of London, to Bishopsgate Street, then through Bishops Gate, and beyond the city wall to the little village of Shoreditch, a good mile and a half from where they'd begun. In this hamlet, the women ran still, breathless now from exertion, neither woman being used to running this far, over low fences and into the chickenyards of modest houses, between hedges, which caught and cut their skin, until they came to the edge of the borough, where they collapsed in a copse of trees, and looked at each other, panicked.

'I thought you said nobody would see you,' Alice said, when she had caught her breath, the anger she'd expressed on the riverbank flaring back up. 'I thought you would be in and out. Did you get the money?'

'I didn't think I'd be seen, but a man I used to know recognised me.' Anne tried to brush the dirt and bits of twig from the skirt of her gown. Though the run had dried the fabric a little, the night air chilled her mercilessly, and she shivered. So did Alice, pulling her cloak, which had been dry but was now damp from the wetness of her clothes, tighter around herself, as if it would make a difference. 'We need to leave,' Anne said, 'before we are caught.' Anne thought again of Kingston and the Tower guards, who might be chasing them, or who might be sending an urgent message to the king that the ghost of his late wife had been spotted at the Tower. As much as she hated to delay finding and killing Henry, she knew she needed to leave London, at least for a couple of days, until things settled down, until the Tower guards searched and found no one and returned to their posts.

'What do you mean, before *we* are caught?' demanded Alice. 'I've done nothing wrong. I think you mean before *you* are caught.'

'You think these men won't arrest you too?' Anne shot back. 'A common prostitute accompanying a lady with money stolen from the mint? You think whatever judge is assigned your trial wouldn't have you whipped in public? Wouldn't have your hand cut off? You think these men, who know me personally, wouldn't believe me if I told them you'd kidnapped me and forced me into this theft? That they'd take your word over mine?'

Anne couldn't believe the words she'd just spoken, threatening to turn Alice in, threatening to have her punished – Alice, who had shown her such care, who had saved her life more than once – and yet Anne had always done what she needed to survive. Of course, if Kingston or his guards actually caught up with them, they'd recognise her as Anne Boleyn, come back from the dead, and whatever awaited her would be terrible indeed.

'You'd do that to me?' Alice asked, a look of disbelief visible on her face even in the darkness.

'What do you think?' Anne replied.

For several moments, Alice was silent. Then, she stammered, 'Th-there's a carriage stop not far up the road from here. We can catch it in the morning. It heads north, to Bishop's Lynn. From there we can take a boat downriver to my home in the fens.'

'The fenlands?' Anne said. It was the last place she wanted to go.

'Nobody will come looking for you there,' Alice said. 'There's good people there. Trustworthy people.' Anne wondered if that was a dig at her. 'People who won't bat an eye at hiding a stranger.' She paused. 'Besides, I can see my babes.'

'Ah, there it is,' said Anne.

'There what is?' replied Alice. 'That I want to see my children? Just like you? Aren't we on this whole journey so you can rescue your daughter? Do you think I don't want to see my children too? Do you think I don't pine for them, just because I'm not a gentle lady?'

'Ha! "Not a gentle lady" is an understatement.'

Alice glared at her. 'Take off my gown,' she demanded.

'What?' Anne said, disbelieving that Alice would speak to her this way. 'What did you say to me?'

'Take it off. I'll leave you here in your undergarments,' Alice said. 'See what I care. If they catch me, let them come with their punishments. Take off my gown right now and see how far you get without me.'

'No,' said Anne, panicking. Alice was right; she'd be helpless without her. 'No, don't leave me. I'm sorry. I should have considered your desires, your safety.' She reached into her damp bodice and pulled out five pounds; the money and jewels had held securely there, by some miracle, even in the river. 'Here is the money I owe you,' she said, holding it out to Alice. 'And I have more that I can pay you. I will accompany you to the fens. Please. You can hide me there.'

Alice took the coins from her and examined them, letting out a low whistle. 'Five pounds,' she said. 'I thought you were deceiving me. I didn't think I'd see a farthing from you.' She slid the coins into the purse at her wrist.

'Well,' said Anne. The trees cast long shadows in the moonlight, and Anne wished she could slink into them, hide herself, always self-serving, always putting herself first, ruthlessly ambitious, so quick to disregard the kindness of a stranger. What was wrong with her?

Alice sighed. 'Well, indeed,' she said. 'All right, we can sleep here for a few hours, then catch the morning carriage.'

Alice turned away from her and settled into a soft spot on the grass. Anne lay down beside her, badly wanting to apologise for her deception, for her harsh words. She held out a hand and touched Alice's back.

'Don't,' Alice said, swatting Anne's hand away.

15

Goodnight, Dear Heart

Anne thought, as she lay shivering by Alice's side, hoping for sleep to descend and ease her suffering for a few hours, of how she'd got herself into this mess. Not of how she'd got herself into the mess of breaking into the Tower of London as an undead woman, committing theft, and being spied escaping, nor of how she'd got herself into the mess of her own execution, but how she'd got herself into the original mess, of knowing Henry to begin with, of opening the door of his affections, his interests, and of hers. Henry liked to tell people that their first meeting was during Wolsey's pageant at Whitehall, when Anne was dressed as the virtue Perseverance. It was a romantic story, and one Anne loved to hear, as it involved both her captivating beauty and the king's passion for her. She never corrected him that this was not, in fact, the first time they met. That had happened almost a decade before the pageant, when Anne was a girl of twelve, staying with the Archduchess Margaret.

Henry and his man, Charles Brandon, the very same Anne had just lied to Alice that she was married to, had come to the Low Countries on the invitation of Margaret to celebrate a military victory in France and discuss the particulars of Henry's newly acquired French territory, which bordered Margaret's protectorate. Their dealings done for the day, they joined the archduchess and her court at cards. The night was rowdy and raucous. Wine flowed freely. The king, Brandon and the archduchess were all quite drunk. This was the same night when Brandon jokingly proposed to the archduchess, talked her into giving him her ring as a token, then later went about London showing it off, telling everyone they were engaged.

That night, Anne had stayed up late. She'd crept into the gallery where the card tables were set up and mooned about on the edge of the room, watching the adults at play, imagining herself as one of them. 'Why, hello, Your Majesty,' she imagined herself saying to the king, as he drunkenly banged his hands on the table, shouting about how he'd been fleeced by the archduchess, who was surely hiding cards up the sleeves of her gown. Margaret threw her head back in laughter at this accusation from the young king, just twenty-one years old, seated across from her. '*Bonjour*, Your Majesty,' Anne imagined saying as she curtsied to no one, lost in her play.

She was just a girl, a smart girl, but just a girl. She had not yet had her first period, did not yet have breasts. She had just lost the last of her baby teeth, had only just grown the last of her molars. Margaret had commented that she could see the woman in her, the woman who was about to arrive, but Anne couldn't see it, and wasn't sure she wanted to become a woman, not yet. Anne, looking in the mirror, saw a thin girl, fast of foot, who loved to ride and hunt, as smart as any boy, who had a habit of blurting out whatever thought crossed her mind.

And yet, looking at the king, Anne had felt herself grow shy. He was so handsome. Athletic, with a full head of hair, tall, all his teeth in place, none half-decayed. She could see this when he smiled, when he opened his mouth to laugh. She was drawn to him. She didn't think he would notice her, standing there, but he must have, because she fell asleep, and when she woke, she was in the king's arms.

The gallery was dark. The king was carrying her through

it, into the corridor, towards her bedchamber. Margaret walked beside him, chattering away, thanking him for carrying the child to bed, saying that Anne must have sneaked out to see the grown-ups at play and fallen asleep from all the excitement, and goodness knew the archduchess couldn't carry a girl of almost thirteen years. ''Tis no bother, Margaret,' Henry had said, ''tis no trouble at all.' Anne, half-asleep, had closed her eyes in his arms. He'd carried her into her room, alone – the archduchess stood outside in the corridor humming a melody Anne couldn't quite remember – and tucked her into bed, kissing her on the cheek, letting his hand rest on her shoulder, which was bare, her gown having slipped down off it. 'Goodnight, dear heart,' he'd said, and she'd rolled over, grabbed the rag doll she'd insisted on bringing with her from England, snuggled into it, and fallen asleep.

The next morning, the king was gone, and Margaret was all abuzz about her missing ring, and what a scoundrel Brandon was. Anne wondered if the whole encounter had been a dream, though she was sure it had not. There had been a tenderness in the kiss he'd given her, in the way he'd called her 'dear heart'. When they met again at the Château Vert pageant a decade later, it was clear he didn't remember this long-ago meeting, where she'd been just one more adoring courtier, one more girl on the edge of womanhood, lining up to fawn over the handsome young king, there for the taking.

Henry didn't remember their second meeting, seven years after the first, either. By then, Anne was an attendant to Queen Claude, living with her at the French court. Like any court, it moved from palace to palace, three weeks at one, three weeks at another. Claude and François, the French king, lived separately, meeting often enough to keep Claude almost continually pregnant, then parting ways. François would go back to Blois or Chambord or

Fontainebleau, while Claude preferred to stay in Amboise. It was to Amboise that François brought Leonardo da Vinci, just a year after Anne had joined Claude's retinue. François set the old master up in the Château du Clos Lucé, just four hundred yards from the Château Royal d'Amboise, the royal residence. The two châteaux were joined by an underground corridor that the young François used to discreetly visit Leonardo for long hours of conversation, even calling the old man Papa.

Claude was no stranger to the old man either. He visited her during her confinements, when she lay suffering in bed, telling her jokes and sketching her ribald charcoal drawings that made her blush and laugh. Anne, by then a teenager, remembered fetching the queen cool water and wine, mopping her brow with a damp cloth, holding her hand as she suffered the final weeks of one pregnancy after another, catching eyes with the wizened Leonardo, whose long white beard hung to his chest, and who called her *la dame des yeux noirs*, 'the lady with black eyes', or *la belle fille*, 'the beautiful girl'. And though he was not there to educate Claude and her women, Anne watched the man carefully, noticing his love of art and progress, his willingness to propose ideas others thought grandiose or unachievable, and his sense of humour, which put those around him at ease.

When the old man died, François was at his bedside and wept openly. The whole court mourned. François framed and hung the paintings Leonardo had brought with him to France: his dark-eyed *Mona Lisa*; a pastoral, glowing painting of the Virgin Mary pulling a cherubic toddler Jesus off the back of a lamb and on to her lap, the Virgin herself seated on the lap of Saint Anne, her mother, Christ's grandmother, who looks on amusedly; and his wild-haired, seductive portrait of John the Baptist, head still attached. This was Leonardo's legacy, an oil-on-wood world of lush colour, voluptuousness, coy smiles, a sense of peace amid chaos, where even those who would succumb to gruesome deaths of crucifixion and beheading were shown bemused and serene, enjoying better moments.

Anne was nineteen when the Field of the Cloth of Gold was held – a drunken, riotous two-and-a-half-week summit between France and England to celebrate the signing of a peace accord between François and Henry. Cardinal Wolsey had worked tirelessly to orchestrate the midsummer festival in Calais, liaising with Anne's father, Thomas Boleyn, English ambassador to France, about pertinent details. Twelve thousand people converged on the improvised tent city, draped everywhere in shimmering cloth of gold, to celebrate the accord, to witness the two young kings uniting in peace. François arranged for fountains in the encampment to flow with wine, which attendants drank gluttonously, vomiting in the grass when they'd overindulged, slipping off to make love in richly decorated, multichambered tents. Anne attended with Claude, who was heavily pregnant with her fifth child.

As queen, Claude hosted a banquet for Henry, on the same evening that Katherine hosted a banquet for François, one of many shows of unity among the royal families, whose allegiance had been further strengthened by the betrothal of the two-year-old French heir, also named François, to Henry and Katherine's only surviving child, the sickly four-year-old Princess Mary. Claude's banquet had been a stunning affair, with roasted peafowl, voluminous amounts of wine, and revelry by candlelight late into the evening. As the musicians struck up their melodies, the courtiers danced galliards, hopping and leaping to the fast five-step dance, faces red with drink and exertion. Anne had stayed at the periphery, bringing Claude a stool to prop her swollen feet on, some bread to keep down the nausea that had plagued the queen throughout her entire pregnancy, rubbing her swollen legs. In this way, she had shown Claude care. She had loved Claude, who, although sidelined by her frequent pregnancies, had pushed for reforms within the French church, had championed the arts, had ideas of her own that she advanced steadily with François, her position of power strengthened with each child she bore.

Late in the evening, Henry approached Queen Claude and asked if he might steal away the dark-eyed beauty so dutifully serving her for a dance. Anne blushed at the invitation. Claude nodded her approval and off she went, hand in hand with the King of England. The musicians began a new song, and Henry and Anne stepped and hopped quickly. Every five steps Henry leaped and landed astride Anne, one leg lunging forward, one stepped back. Anne was transfixed by his beauty: his tall, muscular frame; his sharp, intelligent eyes that looked deeply into hers; the pink of his fair cheeks; his thick auburn hair. When the lavolta arrived, Henry grasped Anne by the waist, lifted her into the air, and spun her three-quarters of the way around, their eyes locked, her pulse quickening in her exhilaration, before setting her back down. For a moment, she thought he might lean down and kiss her, so intensely was he gazing at her, but then, just as quickly as he'd plucked her away from Claude's feet, his eyes shifted to something behind her and he stalked off, not even saying goodbye.

Anne turned and saw her sister Mary standing at the edge of the dance floor. Mary had already left France to serve as one of Queen Katherine's ladies-in-waiting in England and to wed William Carey, a marriage their mother had crowed about in letters to Anne. What was she doing in the French tent, Anne wondered, and not with Katherine at her banquet? Henry went to Mary and took her hand, bending low to whisper in her ear. Mary smiled and nodded to Anne, and Anne realised Mary must have asked the king to pull her poor sister out of servitude and dance with her, and now, obligation finished, he could return to Mary, the true Boleyn beauty. She realised, as well, that the rumours she'd heard were true: Mary was Henry's mistress and her marriage to William Carey a convenient cover-up for any pregnancies that might arise. Henry and Mary danced the rest of the evening, and, when the festival ended, she accompanied him and the rest of the English court back to London. Less than two years later, Anne followed, to serve Queen Katherine as a lady-in-waiting alongside her sister. By the time Mary's affair with Henry ended and Anne's long engagement to him began, Queen Claude, still only in her twenties, but mother to seven children, had died from complications of a miscarriage.

The second-to-last day of the Field of the Cloth of Gold, Cardinal Wolsey delivered a mass in a grand tent cathedral, to the courts of both kings. When the mass ended, a dragon flew through the sky, with fiery eyes, shooting sparks from its open mouth. The people gathered there gasped and clapped in awe and terror. Only later did Anne learn that the dragon was an elaborate kite, made of canvas and hoops and filled with pyrotechnics, pulled across the large field by a cart. This dragon was an illusion of magic, of predestination, a harking back to an earlier, mythical time of fairies and giants, when kings were chivalrous and ladies were chaste. It was a false promise to restore the fabled greatness of the past, to bring England back to a golden yesteryear that had probably never really existed in the first place.

Though she didn't believe in sanctification, Anne, cold on the ground beside Alice, wished she could, like Saint George, slice the head off the dragon kite that had flown over the Field of the Cloth of Gold all those years ago in France, and watch the pyrotechnics inside it set ablaze the many fine tents below, including the one where she imagined Henry had fucked her sister. She wished that she could slice the head off Henry himself, and return his brutal favour.

16

The King May Perish. Hide

In the morning, Anne groggily roused herself from the forest floor. Forest? Could you call this spit of trees a forest? Nearby, a brook trickled past. Lark song filled the air. The long grass where the two women had slept was bent over, as though two deer had slumbered there. That's what anybody who saw this spot would conclude, Anne thought. Of course, if the Tower guards had the hounds out, they wouldn't be fooled. They'd pick Anne's scent up on the grass, dead or not.

Alice grumbled under her breath as she tried to pin her hair and cap back in place, scowling at Anne.

'If you have something to say to me, say it,' Anne said.

Alice remained silent.

'Well?' Anne demanded.

'Do you know what I dreamed of last night?' Alice asked.

'What?' Anne replied. She hated hearing about the dreams of others, which always bored her. Other people's dreams were about predictable things: flying, losing their teeth, a strange man in the woods. Worst had been Lady Worcester, one of her ladies-in-waiting, whose dreams centred on her bungling husband's debts, and involved his selling off her jewels to pay them. How awful to dream so literally. Lord Worcester had indeed been in debt, due to his lack of skill at cards, and had indeed sold off Lady Worcester's jewels. Lady Worcester had begged Anne for loans so often that she'd lost count of how much she lent her. Five hundred pounds? A thousand? More? Even with all those loans, all that assistance, Lady Worcester had testified against Anne at her trial, a series of lies spewing from her duplicitous, indebted mouth.

'I dreamed a wounded dog turned up at my door,' began Alice.

Good lord, thought Anne, this dream is starting off dull indeed; if a wounded dog showed up at my door, I would kick it away.

'Not that I need another mouth to feed,' Alice continued, 'but the dog was so sorrowful-looking that I took it in, and fed it, and bathed it. The dog spoke to me. It said, "I am a bitch who has been wronged, help me find my pup." It wore an odd silk collar. But when I left the dog alone to fetch wood for my fire, I returned to find not a dog but a wolf, and not a silk collar but a diamond one. I said, "Who are you?" and the wolf growled and bit my arm, and ran off in the night, and where the wolf bit me, thorns grew that wept pus.'

''Tis a strange dream,' said Anne, a bit nervous now at how intently Alice was looking at her.

'Who are you?' demanded Alice.

'I've already told you. I'm Lady Anne Brandon, the wife of Charles Brandon, friend of the king,' replied Anne, her voice barely above a whisper.

'I don't believe you,' said Alice. 'I think you're the animal in my dream, pretending at being a wounded dog, when you're actually a wolf.'

''Twas just a dream, Alice,' said Anne. A breeze blew through the new leaves in the trees above, rattling them, sending a shiver down Anne's spine.

'I heard the men calling after you from the Tower,' Alice said. 'They were calling "Anne Boleyn", the name of the dead queen.'

Anne paused, thinking quickly of how to cover her lie. 'That's because I knew the queen, and she has just been beheaded. They were calling out to me with the news.'

'Do you even hear yourself? Do you think me stupid? That makes no sense,' Alice said. She pointed at Anne's neck. 'Why do you wear that silk collar? What's under it?'

Anne put a hand to her throat. 'Nothing,' she insisted.

'What are you hiding?' pressed Alice. The morning was growing brighter now, the sun rising in the sky like a shiny coin.

'What are you suggesting?' Anne replied. 'That I'm the dead queen come back to life? That I reattached my own head and am fleeing across the country with a mouthy whore?'

Anne regretted the words the moment they were out of her mouth. Alice looked at her with such spite. I have done it again, thought Anne. I have driven another person I care for to hate me. Alice drew back her hand and slapped Anne, hard, across the face. 'You watch your mouth,' she spat.

Anne held a hand to her cheek. Tears slid down her face, from the pain of the slap, from the pain of Alice's disdain. Then she remembered who she was. She was the rightful Queen of England, dead or not. And Alice was a common prostitute, who had no right to speak to her like that, no right to strike her.

'No, you watch yours,' Anne said. 'Are you simple, woman? Nobody can rise from the dead, except the good Lord Christ. Not me. Not you. Not even the king himself will be able to do so.' Anne took a step closer to Alice. 'And you should watch how you speak to your betters. After all, you are a woman of inferior status.'

In the distance, the clop of horses' hooves, the turn of wheels on the packed-dirt road. A carriage was nearing.

'Something is off with you, with your story,' Alice said, looking at her sceptically. 'But I'll help you because I'm a good Christian woman.'

Anne laughed.

'Is something funny about that?' Alice demanded. 'You think it's so easy to live a pious life when you don't have two pence to rub together? When you're born into poverty, and the monastery or some landlord owns the land your people have lived on for generations? I'm no different than you, except that chance made you the daughter of a lord, and me the daughter of a fisherman. I'd like to put you in my position and see what choices you'd have made. And,' Alice continued, 'for one so high and mighty, you certainly don't mind wearing the clothes I paid for on my back, or eating my food, or seeking the protection I've learned to provide myself with thanks to many working nights. The world is not all pageants and parties and church and charity, my lady.'

Anne tried to interject but Alice pushed forward.

'Some of us,' Alice said, her voice rising in volume and pitch, 'have had to work for our suppers. Something you noble folk know nothing about. I've done nothing but help you, and in return, you've done nothing but take advantage of me. Insult me. Lie to me. I'll help you get to the fens, but when we arrive, you're on your own.' Alice shook her head. ' "Inferior". I'm not inferior. If anything, you and your ilk, dining in your castles while the common folk suffer and starve, are inferior, because you lack the wits to see how your wealth, how your ease, is prised from the hands of the very "inferior" people you disdain.'

The sound of the carriage drew closer.

'Alice,' Anne started. 'I—'

'Come,' Alice interrupted, 'we need to catch the carriage. Make haste, and keep your ignorant head down.'

Anne followed Alice out of the stand of trees and up the road, her face still stinging from the slap. What a woeful wretch, Anne thought, talking to her betters like that. But at the same time, she wondered if Alice was right. Was she a wolf pretending to be a dog? Was she the noble lady throwing parties while the peasants suffered? Surely she had earned her status, or some ancestor had. She was entitled to it. It was hers, like the jewels that pressed against her breasts inside her bodice, which she had earned by marrying the king, by bearing his child, by visiting upon him her womanly affections, by being his wife. And she had been a good woman, had given to charity, had tried to direct the funds from the suppressed monasteries into universities and hospitals. She had given alms. She had pushed England out of the arms of the Catholic Church, so its people could be free of the greedy priests. So they would not have to pay for pardons, pay to get into heaven, give their money to debauched monks who spent it on wine and women. She had done all this for the common people, like Alice. Was it not what they wanted?

The carriage ride to Bishop's Lynn was bumpy and long. Anne sat between Alice and an old woman, who kept her needlework on her lap for the entirety of the journey, even when her head slumped forward against her chest in sleep. Across from them sat a mother with two girls, busy playing with rag dolls. When Anne and Alice climbed into the carriage, the younger one said, 'Mama, she looks mean. Is she a witch?' and Anne realised the scowl she wore, from her fight with Alice, and tried to force a smile for the child, but it must have looked more like a grimace, for the girl hid behind her mother's arm. Beside her, Alice mumbled, 'Indeed, wouldn't I like to know?' and Anne longed to be back at court, a team of servants who knew better than to talk back to her helping her don a fine gown, draping her with jewellery, pinning her French hood in place just so. Adorned thusly, Anne, the most happy, would be ready to entertain. Instead, she rode in a cramped carriage in a borrowed gown next to the angry prostitute who'd lent it to her.

Anne recognised the woods they rode through. The land belonged to the Earl of Essex, Henry's second cousin and a former counsellor to his father – an old man she and Henry had dined with once, while his wife gave her insufferable looks and crossed herself heavily before the meal, uttering her Catholic blessing in Latin, a papist devoted to the old queen, who wasn't a queen at all. Not like Anne, the true queen.

The carriage jerked and the old woman next to her farted in her sleep. Anne wrinkled her nose in disgust. They moved slowly now as the road narrowed through a dense forest passage. For a moment, Anne thought she saw, through the open window on the carriage door, a leopard's spotted tail disappearing between the trees. She remembered the large menagerie of wild cats at the French court. There'd been a lion, of course, like the ones at the Tower of London, but also a cheetah, a leopard, and even a panther, brought from the East by ship, black as night with startling chartreuse eyes. She'd liked the panther so much, she'd had a silk gown made in the same deep-black colour, then spent a drunken evening stalking around the palace halls, leaping out at the French courtiers, growling. *Putain! Merde!* they'd exclaimed, laughing, and Anne had laughed too.

Alice sighed loudly and crossed her arms, leaning against the carriage wall, as if she couldn't bear to touch shoulders with Anne. The nerve. Anne scooted herself closer to the old lady on her other side. The carriage bumped and jostled.

Anne couldn't stop thinking of Henry and Jane holed up at Whitehall: Anne's palace, Anne's chambers, Anne's territory. Jane had always seemed to Anne to be a simple woman. As a lady-in-waiting she'd been dull and subservient, usually silent, quick to follow directions, quick to submit, quick to say 'Yes, madam', no matter whom she was speaking to, quick to obey.

Two years ago, Anne had found Jane playing with a litter of kittens by the rosebushes in Hampton Court's large garden, an odd activity for a woman well into her twenties. 'You're Caroline,' Anne heard Jane say as she walked closer to her, curious about the woman's behaviour. 'And you're Esmerelda.' One by one she named them: Mary, Anne, Catherine. 'And you're Aethelred,' she said, holding up a black-and-white runt. Then she held up a larger cat, the mother, and placed her tenderly on her side, teats showing. Anne walked closer still, then paused a few feet away, beside a shrub. Jane didn't seem to hear or notice her. 'Now 'tis time to nurse,' Jane said, and moved each kitten to its mother's tummy, encouraging it, Anne supposed, to suckle. 'Now 'tis time to play,' she said, removing them, too quickly Anne thought, for surely they wouldn't have had time to feed, and holding up two at a time, making them dance around each other, like lifeless dolls.

It wasn't until Anne took a few steps closer to Jane that she realised the cats were dead. All of them. The kittens were stiff and breathless, the mother's eyes rimmed with flies. Anne retched at the sight. Jane turned and looked at her. Had she heard her coming all along? 'Your Majesty,' Jane said, standing and curtsying, a dead kitten in each hand.

'Jane,' Anne had asked, 'what are you doing?'

'I'm playing, my lady,' Jane had said. 'Do you not see my kittens? Do you wish to cuddle with one?' She held out the black-and-white runt.

'Jane, do you not realise the kittens are dead?' Anne had asked. What had happened to the kittens and their mother, to strike them all down? Some disease? An animal? A cruel-handed child? Had Jane herself killed them? More to the point, what had happened to Jane? Had she been struck in the head? She'd always been daft, but had never seemed unable to discern reality before. Had some lecherous courtier groped and violated her? Anne had seen such behaviour once, at the French court, from a thirteen-year-old lady-in-waiting who was raped by a viscount, and then spent the next week talking to her own shadow, going so far as to carry on an elaborate debate with it during a banquet, while others dined and danced, trying to ignore the child and her ravings. At the end of the week, the girl had been sent home to convalesce. Anne didn't know what happened to her after that, only that she didn't return to court.

'Are they?' Jane had asked. Then she'd looked down, and, as though she'd been smacked into wakefulness, dropped the kittens. 'Oh! I'm sorry, my lady. I'm not sure what came over me.'

'Let's get you inside,' Anne had said, and taken her back to the palace to be cleaned up and cared for. By dinner, Jane had returned to her faculties.

Imagine Anne's surprise, then, when she discovered Henry's affair with Jane, just before New Year, five short months ago. Anne had been pregnant, with the last lost baby. Katherine lay dying in a castle in the north, languishing, taking her time. It was the necklace that caught Anne's eye, a locket with an *H* engraved on it. Anne saw it around Jane's neck over dinner in the great hall at Hampton Court. She'd marched to Jane's side, enraged, picked it up from between her collarbones, and prised it open. Inside, a portrait of the king. And Jane, sitting there with a serene expression on her face, contented, not even averting her eyes, not even apologising. 'You harlot!' Anne had shouted, ripping the locket from Jane's neck. The room went silent. The court, the lords, the ladies. The gold thread in the rich tapestries hanging from the walls glittered in the candlelight. Above her, carved wooden heads – the eavesdroppers, they were called – hung impassively from the rafters, a reminder to all courtiers that they were always being listened to. From the head table, Henry looked at her with a stony expression and shook his head.

Although he apologised to her that night, profusely, caressing her pregnant belly, it was only a week later that Anne came upon Henry kissing the tops of Jane's breasts in his chambers, her bodice half-undone, just as he used to do with Anne, when they were playing chaste, when they were waiting for Katherine to be deposed, fooling around but not crossing the line of taking

Anne's virginity. Even so, even with this treachery, even though it pained her heart, she told herself the affair was just a phase. Jane was just a mistress. She was a toy, an amusement. Anne forced herself to ignore her own precarity, that if Henry had been able to discard the mighty Katherine, royal by birth, beloved princess of Spain, aunt to the Holy Roman Emperor, he could even more easily cast her aside, Anna Bullen, a countryman's daughter, a subject with no blood ties to powerful European monarchs. Anne should have taken the threat more seriously, but who would have thought the dead-kitten woman – the woman who said yes, who obeyed, who couldn't raise her voice to protect herself, to say no, to ask for what she wanted, who, rumour had it, could barely read – would so successfully usurp Anne?

And Henry, her Henry, cavorting with that thoughtless wench in Anne's palace, in Anne's rooms, planning to wed her while Anne's body was fresh in its grave, or would be, if Anne's body hadn't refused to die, wasn't currently being jostled in a carriage on its way to the godforsaken fenlands.

After Elizabeth was born, Henry had said, 'The next one will be a boy,' and Anne did try. She'd been pregnant three times in those two and a half years, and it wasn't unusual, she'd told Henry, for women to lose pregnancies, to lose one, or two, or even three. It wasn't a bad sign. It wasn't God's curse. And yet, she'd grieved each lost pregnancy, and none more than the last. Her body still ached for that baby, that boy. She'd been past the quickening, enchanted with his small kicks and flutters. The baby, a prince she was sure, would be the tie that bound Henry to her, would make him forget about meek Jane Seymour and guarantee Anne's power as mother to the prince while Henry lived, perhaps as Queen Regent if Henry died before the boy was of age, and as Queen Mother once the child had taken the throne. Her power would be lasting. She could make real change in England, could usher in the renaissance of thought and music and art and poetry that had swept the continent, could reform religion for the people, could do good.

And then Henry had his fall in the tiltyard at Greenwich Palace. His accident. His injury. A page rushed a message to her. *The King may perish. Hide.* The message, scrawled on a piece of parchment, was from her father, who was at the king's side. And she had hidden. Her position was tenuous. She had tried to endear herself to the English nobility, to the stodgy English court, with their draughty buildings and old ideas, but she could not stop herself from telling them about a better way, about the better ways of France, of the continent, where a revolution of ideas was brewing. She'd looked French, to begin with, with her dark hair and eyes, and, after so many years there, had taken on their customs, their habits of dress and speech, their mannerisms. Englishwomen accused her of being aloof, uncaring towards those around her. But she simply couldn't be bothered with those who chose to remain ignorant. She was not well liked by the court, many of whom had supported Katherine, many of whom supported the king's daughter, the bastard Lady Mary. She was vulnerable. She knew it. Her father knew it too.

So, as Henry lay near death in a tent next to the jousting yard, she had hidden in the little private chapel at the back of her chambers, where she prayed and wept. Henry, her king, her love, her lover. She had wept in grief for him, and also for herself, and where she would stand if he died. What if this baby, too, was a girl? What if the bastard Lady Mary rose up an army? She was of age, after all, nearly twenty – she could rule. Elizabeth was only two years old, off at Hatfield, under the very same roof as the Lady Mary. What if Mary suffocated Elizabeth in her bed in an attempt to grab power? Or, what if Elizabeth became queen but Uncle Norfolk manoeuvred to become regent and shoved Anne aside, so that she couldn't see her own daughter? What if

Anne died in childbirth and couldn't protect Elizabeth, or this new baby? What if the baby was born healthy but then died? The catastrophes Anne imagined swelled around her, stealing her breath. She wept at each imagined doom. But most of all, she wept for Henry. She wept so many, many tears for Henry. When he didn't die, when he came to, when he limped back into the palace, bandaged at the head and leg, supported by Henry Norris and Charles Brandon, her brother George trailing behind them, a caring hand on the king's back, she'd covered the king with kisses, helped tuck him into his bed, collapsed beside him in relief.

The bleeding started five days later, on the day of Katherine's burial, which none of them attended. Just a drop or two, but her ladies noticed it, and Henry was informed and summoned his physicians. Anne was sent to her bed, to lie as motionless as possible, with the hopes that the bleeding would stop. When the contractions started, the midwife was called, and the little babe slipped from her so fast. After, the midwife had said, "'Twas a boy,' and tipped his small body towards her, so she could behold her dead child, her failure and lost hope.

Anne wept for hours. When Henry finally limped in, for the leg wound he'd received on the tiltyard was severe, he was angry. 'I see God will not give me male children,' he'd said, and the look on his face was murderous. She'd struggled out of bed then, and taken his hand, and kissed it. She'd fallen to her knees and kissed his bandaged leg, which had already begun to smell rank, kissed his slippered feet. 'Please, my lord, please,' she'd begged. 'We will try again. My love, please, there is a boy inside me, there is a king, waiting to arrive. I know it, I know it.' His expression softened, and she saw the grief in his eyes, his love for her, and knew she could keep him. They would try again. They would take a trip to France, after Anne recovered, and she would whip him into a frenzy of desire and conceive another son. This time, there would be no accident. She'd guard Henry jealously. There'd be no Jane, flitting on to Henry's lap with her bosoms shoved up in front of him. This time, Anne would be the centre, a force to hold Henry's attention, like she used to. This time, she wouldn't lose the baby.

What a fantasy, she thought now. When they'd pulled her on to the scaffold four months later, she was still weak from the miscarriage. They never made it to France. Cromwell had begun building the case against her, perhaps with Henry's consent, perhaps with his direction, even as she bled in her birthing bed. It didn't help that she'd miscarried on the day Katherine was laid to rest. The superstitious in the court whispered that Katherine had cursed her. Part of her believed them. She spent her nights weeping for the lost prince, whose face haunted her dreams.

In one dream, he floated just above the Thames in a ball of light, saying, 'Mother, Mother, I am here,' and as she ran to the riverbank to swim out and catch him, to save him, he dropped into the water and sank. In another dream he cried beside her, hungry, but her breasts were empty, and she couldn't feed him. A nurse swept in and said, 'Your Highness, this babe is with the Lord now,' and she'd looked down to see him wasted and dead. And in one sweet dream, he lived and toddled at her feet, as she laughed on the lawn at Hampton Court, next to Henry. Elizabeth, a young girl, played in the garden in the distance. 'Come to Papa,' Henry bellowed, and the boy tottered over to him, eyes shining with joy. But when Anne woke, there was no baby, there was no Elizabeth, there was no sunny lawn, there was no Henry. There was no one.

17

The Fens

At sundown, they arrived at Bishop's Lynn, and the coachman hustled them out of the carriage. 'We'll stay the night at yon inn,' said Alice, who hadn't spoken to Anne for the entire journey, and still seemed upset, 'then hire a boat to take us upriver to the fens in the morning.'

The two had a hearty supper at the inn, fish soup and ale, before retiring to their room, where they slumbered side by side in one bed. Alice was chatty throughout dinner, gossiping away to the innkeeper's wife about customers she'd had in Southwark, this man who belched at the moment of release, that man who cried for his mother when they were done, another who just wanted to recite Ecclesiastes in Latin to her. That must be a priest, Anne thought, further evidence of the debauchery of the clergy, though she didn't know why she continued to tally such behaviours; nobody here cared, and she'd never again be in a position of power to do anything about them.

Anne didn't talk much, but fidgeted with her silk collar, thinking of Elizabeth, wondering if the silk swaddling cloth still smelled like her, then deciding it must not, probably the river had washed her smell out. What a pity, for wouldn't Anne like to inhale her daughter's sweet scent one more time? All the more reason to hurry, she thought, thinking of the jewels in her bodice, of her hope to see Elizabeth again. Yet here she was, waylaid far off course, where all she could do was pray that Henry would fuss over enough wedding details to delay the date of his marriage to Jane and allow her adequate time to return to London and complete her task. By the end of the meal, she was tired and annoyed.

In the morning, she woke in Alice's embrace, soft and gentle, and for a moment she thought she must be back with the Archduchess Margaret, in whose bed she sometimes slept as a child. She thought as well of all the times she'd shared a bed with Étiennette, in France, at Claude's court. Just two demoiselles in a bed together, nothing more, though Étiennette held her gently, stroked the backs of Anne's arms to help her fall asleep. Though Anne would wake up with an arm under Étiennette's head, with Étiennette's leg atop hers. Though the two slept pleasantly intertwined, young body against young body, intimacy a pleasure that lay where skin touched skin, until the sun rose, and the two maidens hastened out of bed to play their courtly roles. But now it was Alice who held her.

'You were crying in your sleep,' Alice explained, in a quiet voice, a voice just for Anne. "Tisn't my first time comforting a crier.' Anne thought she was about to talk about comforting a customer, but instead Alice said, 'My daughter was colicky as a babe, and I had to rock her for hours, and even after she stopped crying, she'd only sleep if I held her.' Anne relaxed into Alice's arms, closing her eyes. It was nice, she thought, to be hugged and held by a mother, to be cradled and cared for. She hated that Alice was upset with her, and felt regret at the words she'd spoken.

'Alice,' she began, opening her eyes. They lay so close to one another that she could see every freckle on the good woman's face. 'I am sorry for how I spoke to you in Shoreditch. You did not deserve to be chastised so harshly. My temper got the best of me.'

Alice stiffened, perhaps remembering she was angry with

Anne. 'It isn't just your words.' She put a hand to Anne's neck, atop the silk collar. 'What lies here, my lady? What falsehood are you telling me? I have helped and helped you, and yet you deceive me. I do not know the purpose of your flight, your rash behaviour. Is it,' Alice paused, 'that you are not who you say you are?'

The women lay there, warm in the little bed. Anne searched for words she could say to Alice. She could not say 'I am the dead queen resurrected', nor 'I am Anne Boleyn, who you and others call the whore, the concubine', not even 'I am bewitched and have lived beyond the swordsman's true swing', though all would be true. Alice's face was open, inviting. 'Share,' her expression said, 'tell me.' Anne shook her head. She couldn't.

'I have seen how you are,' Alice said. 'You push through the world, sharp-tongued. An anger burns in you, sets you on your toes in the morning, sends you running through your day. There's a beauty in it, but also a terror.' She held the silk of Anne's collar between two fingers, feeling its smoothness. 'It does not have to be so. You could set your struggle down. You could share it with me.'

'I can't,' Anne said, though she wanted to. 'I can't.'

Alice held her gaze a moment longer. Her face close enough that Anne could have kissed her on the tip of her nose if she wanted to, if she leaned forward a few inches, or on her lips.

'Well,' Alice said, at last, 'we'll need to be getting up now.' And the two women hastened out of bed, just two women travelling together, nothing more, to catch their boat.

The boatsman, who met them just outside the village on the River Great Ouse, was a fenlander, like Alice. In the early morning, a low fog hung over the river and its banks. Anne supposed this was because they were just upland of the fens, and its poor air was rising, afflicting the village. The boatsman didn't seem to care, probably because he was from the fens and used to it. Anne had once heard of a fenlander who bragged of having twenty wives. He'd marry women from upland and bring them down to the fen to care for the children his previous wives had birthed before dying, and, within a year or two, having been forced into stepmotherhood over an unruly brood of children and fucked night after night by a dirty swamp man, the new wife would contract swamp fever and die, maybe having added one more motherless child to the clutch of half-siblings before her departure.

Motherless children existed in all walks of life, as did stepmothers – Anne had been one herself, to the Lady Mary – but for a man to take more than one or two wives over his lifetime was unseemly and spoke to a disregard on his part for the lives of the women he wedded. Some men were like that, wedding and breeding one wife after another. Anne had thought Henry was not one of those men, although here he was, having disposed of two wives, hurrying off to a younger, more breedable third.

The fenlander was named George, and he and Alice knew each other, and bantered merrily. The three followed the river into the fen, where a strong sulphur smell hung in the air, and a thick fog covered water and land alike, as if a cloud had descended from the sky and lowered itself upon them. Or as if they were rowing to the afterlife, as if George were not a common boatsman but Charon, that ancient ferryman shuttling the dead to Hades, or a kinder angel, Gabriel perhaps, taking Anne to her eternal reward. But her eternal reward was apparently not heaven. It was to sit in this rickety boat, rowing into a disease-filled swamp so that she could hide until it was safe for her return to London, where she imagined Henry would be, planning his wedding to the simpleton Jane, so she could sneak into Whitehall and kill him. Just thinking of killing the king, just mentioning his death, was a form of treason for the living, as Anne well knew, but Anne was not the living.

As George rowed the boat through the fen, the river forked and twisted. They followed its curves and meanders until it emptied into a wide, open marsh. Tufts of land, small islands, broke the dark water's surface here and there; reeds and rushes poked out of it in watery fields. Every so often, an eel's back brushed the side of the boat.

'Get into my traps, devil eels!' George exclaimed, laughing.

Alice laughed too. 'George traps eels,' she explained to Anne.

''Tis how a fenlander makes his money, miss,' George added, swatting a mosquito away from his jaw. 'And pays his rent to the landlord.'

'And who is your landlord, sir?' Anne enquired, out of politeness, though she already knew the answer.

'The fenland is common land,' George replied, 'and always has been, and rightfully should be. But we pay some rent in eels to the monks in the monastery, and they keep the noblemen out of our marsh, with their talk of draining and drying it. The monks get fat on eels, and are happy, and offer us their blessings.'

Anne nodded. She had tried eel once and hadn't cared for it, but she supposed one ate what one had to.

'Anne is a proper lady, George, whose husband is supposedly a nobleman,' Alice said, and as she did so, she dipped a cupped hand into the swamp water and splashed some on Anne. 'There, my lady,' she continued with a laugh, 'is a splash of holy water, to cleanse you of whatever ails you, to absolve you of whatever secret sin you cannot reveal. There is your baptism and blessing.'

Anne wiped the water off herself. This water was certainly not blessed, she thought, though the further they got into the fen, the less it stank. The sulphurous smell was replaced by the pleasant scent of water lilies and damp rushes. Garishly coloured orchids hung from the branches of the trees that grew on strips of land dotting the swamp or in the shallows of the water. At every turn, some new surprise of plant or animal awaited them. Anne gasped when a huge grey bird fluttered up out of the water on impossibly long wings, tucking its thin legs into itself.

"Tis a crane,' Alice explained to her.

The fen teemed with animals, fish, fowl. Bumps Anne thought were rocks revealed themselves to be turtles, sticking blue- or yellow-striped heads out of their shells to gaze with beady eyes before receding into the water. Flying insects hovered on bright wings, leaving behind rings of ripples where they touched the water's surface. If Anne believed in magic, in fairies and bewitchings, she would wonder what sorcery lived here.

Around one bend, to Anne's astonishment, leafless boughs shot up through the water, as though the marsh and river were flowing through the tops of a dead forest. 'Witch Finger Woods,' Alice said. "Twas a forest once, many years ago, before our time, or our parents' or grandparents'. And then it flooded, and the fen waters took it. At high tide, the branches are completely underwater, and at low they poke up, like witches' fingers.' Alice hooked her hand into the shape of a claw to demonstrate. Anne shivered, imagining the forest floor, the paths and mossy boulders and hearts carved by lovers into tree trunks, all covered by the icy water.

On the other side of the witchy forest was a small island with a floating wooden dock. A round hut, with a roof that appeared to be thatched from the same reeds that rose ubiquitously through the fen waters, stood near its shore. 'Here you are, Alice,' George said, rounding the boat up to the dock and tying it to the wooden piling. When he stepped on to the dock it sank a little with his weight, and for a moment his feet dipped below the water, before the dock buoyed back up. Anne noticed that his boots were coated in thick grease, to keep them dry in the swamp. She was not so lucky, for when she took his hand and joined him, her slippers soaked through with swamp water.

'Holy water, my foot,' Anne said, and Alice and George

chuckled at her, enjoying the sight of an uplander struggling in their swamp. When George grabbed her by the waist and lifted her off the dock on to dry land, she could smell eels on him.

Alice, fleet of foot, stepped one foot on to the dock and sprang, before it had a moment to sink, on to the drier ground of the island, skirts clutched firmly in her hand to keep them dry. ''Tis simple,' she said to Anne, who stared in amazement at her balance and skill.

'I'll be back tomorrow at first light,' George said. He nodded to Alice, got back into his boat, and rowed away.

'Your man is a strong rower, and gentle,' Anne said to Alice, hoping to smooth over their disagreement with a compliment.

Alice laughed. 'George is not my man,' she replied. 'He's my brother. Not all of us have a team of servants, my *superior* lady.'

Anne couldn't help but think of her own brother George, of how much she wished he'd row up in a modest boat, stinking of eels, and carry her away.

The door to the hut flew open, and a stout woman emerged and stood in the dirt yard looking at them. 'Alice, is it you?' the woman called, and at the woman's words, a half-dozen children ran out around her. Two of them, a boy and girl, darted forward, shouting, 'Mama! Mama!' They flung their arms around Alice, pressing themselves into her skirts.

'My babes,' Alice said. She bent down and embraced them, smelled their hair, kissed their cheeks, and cried with joy. 'My loves.' Alice hoisted the children up into her arms and carried them into the little hut.

18

Parsnips

The inside of the hut was cosy and warm. A bed stood against one wall, a pile of rolled-up mats stacked next to it. Those must be where the children sleep, thought Anne. On the opposite wall was a hearth, with a low fire burning, and something delicious-smelling bubbling in a pot over the open flames. There was also a small table, with two large chairs and four little ones, still cluttered with wooden plates from breakfast.

'I've got rabbit stew on for supper,' said the woman. Seeing Anne's gaze settle on the cluttered table, she added, 'Constance, go and fetch some water from the rain barrel as I told you to, and wash these dishes.'

A tall girl scampered outside to fetch the water for her chore.

'Alice, 'tis good to see you,' the woman said, turning her attention back to the two women. 'And Robert and Martha'll be glad to have a visit from their mother. Who's this you've got with you?'

'Ah,' said Alice, gesturing towards Anne, who stood awkwardly beside her. ''Tis my new friend, the Lady Anne.' She leaned forward and whispered mischievously, 'She's on the run from her husband.'

'Oooh, Anne, like the dead queen?' the woman asked. Anne was surprised that the news of her execution had reached even this forgotten corner of England.

'Yes,' said Alice. 'Isn't that a *coincidence*?' She shot Anne a loaded look.

'Well, madam,' the woman spoke to Anne, 'you're welcome here. I'm Ethel, and this is my brood.' The woman swept her arms out, motioning to the children who played around her.

'Ethel is a child minder,' Alice explained. 'She watches babes for three or four mothers who must leave for work.' Anne wondered what *work* meant. Were they all prostitutes, like Alice?

'That I do,' said Ethel. 'Love 'em all like my own too.' As if on cue, a tow-headed boy came up and threw his arms around Ethel's ample waist, smiling contentedly and closing his eyes.

'Ethel, I have your payment.' Alice rummaged in her purse, pulling out two crowns and handing them to Ethel, who walked over to a wooden box on the table and placed them inside it. 'We'll stay the night here, if you don't mind, and then take the children back to my father's house in the morning. I shouldn't need to leave again for work for a while.'

'Will we get to see Uncle George?' Robert asked, pulling at Alice's skirts to get her attention.

'Ah, you've just missed him, love, but he'll be back again to fetch us in the morning.'

'Hooray!' shouted Martha, jumping in a circle around Alice's legs. 'Hooray! Hooray! Hooray!'

'Mama,' asked Robert, grinning, 'did you bring us anything?'

'Ah yes, of course,' Alice said. She reached into her purse and pulled out a small wooden fox, which she handed to Robert, and a small wooden winged horse, for Martha. 'This is a Pegasus,' Alice said, kneeling down by her daughter. 'That's a horse that has wings to carry it wherever it wants to go.' Anne hadn't realised Alice had gifts for the children; she must have bought them before Anne joined her.

Martha threw her arms around her mother's neck and covered her face with kisses. Then she took the winged horse in her hands and zoomed around the little hut, pretending to make it fly from table to chair, chair to bed, bed to hearthside.

'Well then,' said Ethel, 'why don't you take your dark-eyed beauty out and gather some parsnips for the stew.'

Anne looked around herself, wondering for a moment if Ethel meant another dark-eyed woman.

'Don't call her a beauty,' Alice responded, chuckling, 'or she'll get an even higher opinion of herself.' Turning to go, she looked at Anne and said, 'Come on, then.' Anne blushed and followed Alice out of the hut.

The island the hut sat on was bigger than Anne had realised, and heavily wooded. 'This is where Ethel snares rabbits,' Alice said as they traipsed through the woods. Anne ran her hands along the rough-barked tree trunks they passed, noticing the ferns that sprang up along the forest floor, between rocks, and the moss that covered one side of everything. 'That's how you can tell which way is north,' Alice explained. 'Moss grows on the north side of the trees.' Here and there, downed trees decomposed into richly coloured crumbles. The whole place had a dank, earthy smell that pleased Anne, who'd always been comfortable out of doors, on a hunt or a ride. The two women walked in silence. Alice led the way, and Anne followed, grateful for the quiet.

Near one fallen pine, Anne spotted a cluster of pale-stemmed mushrooms with amber caps. 'Look at those,' she said. Alice turned. 'Aren't they lovely?'

'Yes,' said Alice, 'they're jewel mushrooms.'

'Jewel mushrooms! Shall we pick some and eat them?' Anne asked. This was as close as she was likely to get to jewels in the fens.

Alice laughed. 'Not if you value your life, my lady. They're poisonous.' Alice looked around. A few feet away, a patch of orange fungi grew, each mushroom fringing out like a veil. Alice bounded over to them. Anne followed. 'Now these,' Alice said, 'are chanterelles. These are delicious, and not a bit deadly. Here, use your skirt to make a pocket, and let's fill it up. Ethel will be pleased with these.' Alice picked five or six and deposited them in Anne's skirt.

'Why not pick them all?' Anne asked. 'Surely more would be better.'

'My, you noble folk are greedy,' replied Alice. 'If we pick them all, there'll be none left for later. Ethel doesn't have another island to pick mushrooms on, another patch of land to annex and call her own. She must live off what's here.'

'Oh,' said Anne, embarrassed, again, by her lack of awareness. 'I suppose I hadn't thought about it that way.'

'I suppose you hadn't,' said Alice, standing and dusting her hands off, then continuing down the path.

The two walked a short while before they got to a marshy shore on the opposite side of the island. The same reeds Anne had seen throughout the fens grew bountifully here, interspersed with tall, leafy stalks.

'Where are the parsnips?' Anne asked. She'd only ever seen parsnips cooked, on her plate, peeled, buttered and dusted with herbs. She had no idea what a parsnip looked like before it passed through the hands of a cook and then a servant and was placed before her on a table set with fine linens, plates and cutlery, but she was pretty sure they grew in gardens, and no garden was in sight.

'The parsnips are right here,' said Alice, who seemed confused, and pointed to the reedy area, as though their location were obvious.

'Are the reeds a different breed of parsnip?' asked Anne, realising that her knowledge of the world, so specific to a life of intellectual study and court politics, was relatively useless in the fens. Even her knowledge of the outdoors, gained mostly through hunting expeditions, was paltry, as those events were organised for her, by someone else. She just needed to show up, and a horse would be saddled, a basket packed and transported for lunch, a bow strung, ample arrows provided and ready to use, a guide there to lead her through the woods, and servants to carry home her kill.

'Oh, my lady.' Alice chuckled. 'What do you learn about with your tutors and books?'

'Well,' Anne replied, 'philosophy, theology, mathematics, theories of governance. Of course, Latin and French. And I've been reading Tyndale's English translations of the scripture. Have you read them, Alice?'

'Anne,' Alice said, looking her straight in the eye, her expression amused but also tender, 'my question was one asked for effect, and did not necessitate an answer, though your learnedness is impressive, and something I wish I'd had access to, smart as my father always said I was. But, no, I haven't read "Tyndale's English translations of the scripture". I don't know who that is, for one. And, though I have learned my letters some, enough to read and sign a contract or read and write a letter, I do not possess any books, nor can I imagine having the wealth to do so. Besides, I rather enjoy having the scripture read to me, in Latin, at mass. Preserves the mystery.'

Anne thought, a bit embarrassed, of the large volume of books she owned. What would it be like to be so poor as to own no books? Anne owned forty volumes by the French theologian Jacques Lefèvre alone. Nevertheless, she persisted. 'I could recite some of the scripture for you in English, if you'd like,' Anne said. 'For example, listen to the beginning of Genesis: "In the beginning God created heaven and earth. The earth was void and empty and darkness was upon the deep and the spirit of God moved upon the water. Then God said: Let there be light, and there was light." Isn't that lovely?'

Alice pondered Anne's recitation, asked her to repeat it, then went silent, thinking. "'Tis strange, my lady, and makes me a little sad. "The earth was void and empty and darkness was upon the deep." I think of the sea beyond the fens, deep and wide and terrible. On a calm day it seems like a person could walk across it, 'tis so smooth, but on a stormy day it can crush a ship like that, and where do the men go who were on the ship? I imagine the icy deep they sink to being, as you say, void and empty and dark. Sends a shiver down my spine.'

'Yes,' said Anne, 'but 'tis also our salvation. The Lord God's spirit moves upon the water and brings light. We do not have to live in darkness, scared. We can find His glory. 'Tis there for all of us, equally.'

'You are an odd one, Anne,' Alice said. 'You sound like a Lutheran, and I'm afraid you will be hanged for heresy. In the company of others, you should keep such thoughts to yourself.' Some of Anne's hair had slid out from her cap, and Alice reached out and tucked it back in place. 'Though I won't tell a soul you've spoken them,' she added mischievously.

'A change is coming,' Anne said. She caught Alice's hand in hers and held it for a moment. Alice let her. 'The true religion. You shall see, Alice. Even here to the fens it will come.'

'You may be right, and I suppose if it does, I can thank you for better preparing me, but, at this moment, we need to pick some parsnips. Come.'

She let go Anne's hand, nodding playfully to the reedy marsh, to which she walked. There, she grabbed one of the tall, leafy stalks, and, with two fists, pulled. Out came the lumpy root of the plant. She held it up, like a prize. 'Now I shall teach *you* something, Lady Anne. This is a water parsnip,' she explained proudly. 'The root here is the edible part.' She snapped the root off its stalk. 'Come, hold out your skirt and I'll add it to your bounty.'

Alice added one after another of the parsnips to Anne's skirts, joining them with the small pile of mushrooms that dwelled there. As she worked, she whistled calls back to the birds that sang in the trees and marshy waters. Here and there, she cracked a joke, as when she held a hairy parsnip root up to her chin and exclaimed, 'Look! I'm the old lady in the woods growing whiskers from my chin!' What a delightful woman, Anne thought. Here was Alice in her element, finding food, making merry, chattering with birds, not at all concerned with what anybody might think of her.

When Anne's skirt was full, the two women headed back. Alice again led the way. Anne trailed behind. The more they walked, however, the wearier Anne grew. Eventually, she had to stop and lean her hand against an oak to try to catch her breath.

'Are you well, my lady?' asked Alice. 'You're flushed and sweaty.' Alice walked over and placed a hand on Anne's forehead. 'And hot. Here, give me the vegetables.' Alice moved the mushrooms and parsnips from Anne's skirt into her own.

'I'm fine,' Anne replied. But she worked hard to pull in a full breath and shivered, as though chilled. 'I'm just a bit lightheaded. Perhaps 'tis all the exertion?'

Ahead of her on the path, she thought she saw a man, dressed in black velvet, walking away. Could it be Cromwell? She rubbed her eyes and looked again. No, it was just a tree; there was no man there. She felt dizzy. In her ears, the same buzzing that had overtaken her in the chapel on London Bridge.

'Let's get you back to Ethel's,' said Alice, and Anne could hear the worry in her voice. 'You do not look well at all.'

When the two returned, Alice emptied her skirt of the mushrooms and parsnips and then she and Ethel helped Anne into the dwelling's sole bed.

'Here, madam,' said Ethel, fluffing the single pillow and placing it below Anne's head, 'you lie down and rest. The fenlands can overwhelm an uplander. There's so much nature here, so much splendour. For some, 'tis too much.' She tucked the blanket up to Anne's chin and told her to close her eyes. Anne obeyed, and the sleep that overtook her was dark and dreamless.

Anne woke, some hours later, to the sound of children screaming. Was there a crisis? A fire? No, Anne realised, the children were screaming for joy. She rolled to her side, still tucked into the warm blankets of the bed, and watched them. They were playing charades. One by one, each child got up and mimed an action or pretended to be an animal. The other children shouted their guesses. The child up now, a girl about the same age as Alice's daughter, squatted low and strutted about the room, shaking her bottom and flapping her arms like wings. She darted her head forward in a pecking motion.

'Goose!' Martha guessed.

'Duck!' said Constance.

'Loon!' called the tow-headed boy.

'No!' replied the girl. 'I'm not a waterfowl. Do I look like I'm swimming?'

Anne propped herself up on an elbow. 'She's a chicken,' she croaked.

Startled, the children turned and looked at her, letting out another round of screams.

'The dead lady is awake!' Robert shouted.

'The witch has risen!' shrieked Constance.

The girl who'd been pretending to be the bird said, 'You're all bad at this game. I was pretending to be a woodpecker.'

'Now, now,' said Ethel, 'she's not a witch or a dead lady. Are you feeling better, Anne?'

'I'm thirsty,' Anne replied. Sweat beaded on her brow and dampened her undergarments.

'Drink this,' Alice said, offering her a cup of water.

Anne hesitated. 'Is it from the fen?'

''Tis from the rain barrel outside,' Alice explained, rolling her eyes. 'I wouldn't give you swamp water to drink.' She felt Anne's forehead, her touch cool, pleasant. 'She's still hot,' she said to Ethel. 'Do you think it could be swamp fever?'

'Maybe,' Ethel said back quietly, so that only Anne and Alice could hear her. 'Though it doesn't usually come on this fast. Didn't you just arrive in the fens this morning and come straight here?'

Alice nodded.

'I don't know what this is,' Ethel said. 'Likely 'tis something she contracted before coming here. Has she been acting strangely? Has she had dizzy spells? Vomiting?'

'This lady does nothing but act strangely,' Alice replied.

Ethel gave her a vexed look. 'I'm not here to get in the middle of whatever lies between you and she. You'll have to sort that out yourselves.'

Alice blushed. 'Sorry. Yes, she fainted two days ago, when we stopped in the church on London Bridge to pray. The priest had to carry her upstairs to his quarters. He loosened her bodice a bit and that seemed to help. Then he fed us a good supper, and she recovered some. She mentioned having heavy courses, and he seemed to think she was weak from losing blood.'

'Maybe,' replied Ethel. 'Though this fever concerns me.' She looked over at the children, who were clustered around the table, pushing and shoving each other and laughing. 'Constance,' she called, 'fetch me the dried feverfew from beside the hearth so I can make this woman a tea.' Constance untangled herself from the bevy of children and brought her minder the herb. 'Now go outside and pick some brookweed,' Ethel instructed the girl. 'She can have that with her supper.'

'Isn't brookweed for scurvy?' asked Alice with some scepticism.

''Tis, but who knows what this lady's got. We'll treat for all and hope that something shall take effect.'

Alice nodded. 'I'll go and wet a cloth to cool her head.'

By the time Alice came back with a wet rag and Ethel had brewed the feverfew into a rather bitter tea, Anne had sat up in bed, propped against the wall. The girl from the charades game and the tow-headed boy climbed into the bed with her, snuggling up at her sides as she drank from the steaming mug. Anne realised how much she had missed the feel of a child beside her, cuddled into her, relaxed, as though just the presence of her body, the body of a mother, of any mother, was a powerful sedative. A third child, the youngest of Ethel's brood, tried to climb on to the bed, but her little legs were too short. She looked about the same age as Elizabeth – two, maybe three. Anne extended a hand and pulled her into the cosy nest.

'I'm Martha too,' said the child, smiling sweetly at Anne.

'Well, that must get confusing, having two girls named Martha in one home,' said Anne.

'We had three Marthas,' said Ethel, 'but one died of fever in April.' Ethel crossed herself and looked down at the floor, wiping away a tear. Alice drew her own Martha to her side and kissed the girl.

'Oh,' said Anne. 'I'm so sorry. To lose a child. 'Tis a loss too big to bear.'

'So it is,' replied Ethel. 'I hope it is a loss you've not had to bear, yourself.'

'No, I haven't lost a child,' Anne said, then found herself continuing, to her own surprise. Something about the cabin, these women, put her at ease. 'But I lost a pregnancy in winter – I was far enough along to tell the baby was a boy, and to be able to make out a bit of what he might have looked like, had he lived.'

'The loss of a pregnancy is still a loss, my lady,' Ethel said.

'I imagine giving your husband a son might have prevented some of his violence towards you,' Alice added, looking at Anne sympathetically.

Anne nodded, for certainly that was true.

'And you, Alice? I hope you've not had to suffer the pain of a lost child,' Anne said.

'No,' replied Alice. 'I've been lucky. I've had two babes and two is all I want, and two is what I've kept.' She pulled Robert towards her as well, hugging both children.

'Well,' added Ethel, 'you're from strong stock. Just look at your brother, strapping lad, never one to take sick for more than a day or two here or there, and your good father, still active at his age, tending his little garden and shooting enough geese to keep his family and the next family over flush with meat. Has a keen eye for an older gentleman.'

'Ethel,' said Alice, slyly, 'if you want me to ask old Nathanial if he fancies you, or tell him that he ought to, you know you can just say the word.'

Ethel laughed, shooting Alice an embarrassed look. 'Alice, you troublemaker! Always have been, even when I was wiping your bottom for your ma, God rest her soul, while she was off to work.'

'Oh, Alice, I'm sorry to hear that your mother has passed,' Anne said, and she was.

'Thank you,' said Alice. ''Twas a few years ago. She went peacefully in her sleep. And what of your mother, my lady?'

Anne thought carefully about her answer to this question. 'My mother and I were close for many years. She lived with me and my husband.' This was all true. Anne's mother had lived with her at court. She'd carried Anne's train at her coronation and cradled the babe Elizabeth in her arms after her birth, cooing at her lovingly. 'But as the marriage soured, my mother and my father cowered in fear to my cruel husband, refusing to take my side over his. I think they thought to do so to protect my daughter. They both live still.'

Alice looked at Anne intently. 'That's an awful story, my lady. A mother should love her daughter to the end, as you do yours.'

Suddenly, the children perked up and ran to the doorway of the little home. Anne could hear a paddle breaking the water outside and a man whistling. 'George! George!' the children shouted.

'George?' said Alice, getting up from the table. 'Now that's a surprise.' She headed out the door. From the bed, Anne could hear her greeting, then chatting with George. Anne wanted to go out too, but a deep fatigue had settled in her bones. She waited where she lay.

When the two returned, Anne could see George had brought a fiddle with him. 'I thought I'd come back,' George said, shrugging, 'for a little feast and festivities, and to better know the pretty lady you brought with you.' He winked at Anne, a playful grin on his face.

'George, you're a scamp,' said Alice. But she hugged him warmly.

19

The Golden Bird

It was evening when George began to play his fiddle, slowly at first, and then with such joy that the children sprang up and danced around him in twirling circles, crashing to the floor when they'd spun themselves dizzy. Ethel had already served her rabbit stew, complete with the parsnips and mushrooms Anne and Alice had gathered. Anne pretended it was a healing elixir as she swallowed spoonfuls of the hearty soup. She remembered, as a child at Hever Castle, making 'potions' with Mary and George by gathering mushrooms and grasses in the gardens, maybe the spiky leaves of a holly or last season's rosehips, and stirring them together in a pot filled with water from the little lake. 'I'm a witch!' Mary would cackle, chasing her younger siblings around with the inedible mixture. Anne and George would hide together in the large garden, tittering excitedly, hoping to get caught. That was ages ago now. Here before Anne, another brother named George, though not her George.

As Anne ate, she felt the strength return to her, so that when evening came, she was sitting up on the edge of the bed, swinging her feet in time to George's music, clapping her hands and smiling. The happiness of the fenlanders was contagious. These did not seem to be the same people she'd heard disparaged whenever they were mentioned. No, here, she saw a people who were merry and quick-witted, hardy and healthy, intent on enjoying their lives.

'Your brother is an excellent musician,' Anne said to Alice, who sat beside her on the bed, clapping along to the beat of the music.

Alice nodded. 'Yes, he is.'

'I didn't know fenlanders studied music,' Anne continued, 'and yet he is so skilled.'

'"I didn't know fenlanders studied music,"' repeated Alice in a lilting tone, as a child might mock another who has said something stupid. 'My lady, are you so convinced of the superiority of nobles that you think no one else in the world can be moved to song?'

'I didn't mean—' began Anne.

'Surely you have noticed,' Alice interrupted, 'that folks everywhere can whistle, can hum, can praise creation through melodies sung. Surely you have noticed that the nobles themselves get their music lessons from their more musical lessers. My lady, do you not think before you speak?'

'I'm sorry,' Anne said. 'I'm trying. This is all new to me.' She thought of Mark Smeaton – poor Mark Smeaton, whose head now sat on a pike on London Bridge. Smeaton, the gifted lutist. He'd been Cardinal Wolsey's musician before he was Anne's. But where had he come from before that? Where was he born? Who were his people? How had he learned to make such gorgeous music? She knew he was not from noble birth. How many times had she reminded him that he was her inferior when he'd become overfamiliar, mistaking his place in her apartments as one of companionship rather than entertainment? And yet he played more beautifully than any lord or lady, for whom music lessons were a necessary chore – another thing to become proficient at, an accomplishment to tick off a list, like needlework, Latin or jousting. Of all the nobles she knew, perhaps the only one truly gifted with artistic talent was Thomas Wyatt, whose poems were wild and bewitching, but even so Anne now wondered if there weren't common folk who, given the chance, might compose verse just as lovely, or lovelier, or wilder.

'George has always been a talent at music,' said Alice, relaxing from her defensiveness into pride for her brother. 'When we were small, he would gather up our cups and plates, flip them upside down, and arrange them in order according to the sound they made when struck with a spoon. He'd spend hours playing on the dishes the melodies he'd heard our father and uncles whistling. 'Twas truly impressive.' Alice shifted on the bed, smiling. 'I never had that in me; 'twas something he was born with. We had an uncle who was the same way, our mother's brother. 'Tis his fiddle George plays now – he passed it on to George when his hands became too bent with age to play.'

'And is this how you pass your evenings in the fens?' Anne asked. 'At play and dance? 'Tis lovely.'

Alice nodded again. 'The fens are special. We don't have landlords here. We don't have to farm. I've been out in the world enough to know how other commoners live, toiling morn till night to grow the grains they cannot eat themselves, that they must sell to turn to flour, to make other men's bread, all so they can pay the lord the rent.' Alice narrowed her eyes. '*Rent*. Rent for the land where they were born, where their parents were born, and their parents. How is that fair?'

Anne sat quietly. What Alice described was the order of things, and Anne had never thought to question it, as she'd been told of her family's right to property and governance over their lessers her whole life.

'Those people work themselves into the grave,' Alice continued. 'The menfolk toil all day. The womenfolk birth babe after babe, cannot feed them all properly, waste away from exhaustion. No.' Alice shook her head. 'That's no life. We may not have it perfect here in the fens, but 'tis our land. We take what we need. We use what we take. Our men sell some eels to make a bit of money upland, and we pay our tax to the crown, but once we've worked to feed ourselves for the day, to fix our shelters, to keep our children warm and dry, we have time to relax, to make merry, to sing and dance and fiddle, to play games. In my estimation, there aren't many other commoners in this good country who can say the same.'

Alice rose to her feet, and, changing the subject, held out a hand to Anne. 'Surely you know how to dance?'

Anne smiled shyly. 'Well, yes, but—'

Before she could finish, Alice grabbed her hand and pulled her off the bed and out among the dancing children. There, Alice led quite as well as a man, whisking Anne around the hut in a fast country dance she wasn't familiar with, but quickly picked up. Alice smiled and pulled Anne closer, whispering in her ear, 'You dance well, my lady, for a noblewoman,' then winking at her coyly as she spun her out with one arm, and drew her back in. When George finished his song, the two fell apart, laughing, as the children collapsed around them, dizzy and heavy-headed, grinning. They look like little fairy children, Anne thought, and she wished she could spirit Elizabeth here, to frolic with these spritely woodland babes, to sing and dance and love, to be safe. She could almost feel Elizabeth's weight in her arms as she collapsed into them after a good spin.

'All right, all right,' said Ethel, rising from the seat where she'd been resting her weary knees, ''tis time to light the rushes.' She nodded towards the tow-headed boy, who, knowing his job, rose and used a dried stick to fetch a flame from the fire, then walked to each of four reed torches placed about the cosy room and lit them, one by one. The torches stank a bit, of burning reed and tallow, but lit the little home up nicely.

'Gather round,' Ethel said. ''Tis time for a story and for the young ones to go to sleep. Children, fetch your mats.'

The children retrieved their mats and unrolled them in a haphazard cluster around the hearth and table. The younger Martha placed hers right next to Ethel's bed. She must like to sleep near her minder, Anne thought. Perhaps the girl had nightmares. Even George took a seat on the floor among the children, leaning his back against the wall, placing his fiddle at rest by his feet. Anne settled back on the bed, and Alice joined her, putting her arm through Anne's elbow and covering both their laps with a blanket. Anne nestled close, warm and familiar.

'Now,' said Ethel, 'for a story.'

'Oh, Ethel tells the best stories,' Alice said quietly to Anne.

'What shall I tell?' asked Ethel.

'"Tom Tit Tot"!' called Constance, seated at Ethel's feet.

The boy who'd lit the torches called out, '"Mr Vinegar"!'

'"The Golden Bird"!' cried Alice.

'Ah,' Ethel said, nodding at Alice, '"The Golden Bird". Right, then. Let us begin at the beginning.' Ethel motioned for Constance to fetch her a blanket from the bed, and the child rose, wove her way through the mats, retrieved a blanket from beside Alice, and returned it to Ethel. The good woman draped the blanket theatrically over her legs as she resettled herself in her seat. Her child audience waited, with rapt attention. Ethel grinned, enjoying, it seemed to Anne, having them in her thrall. 'Now then,' Ethel continued, 'in the old times, there was a king who had a fine castle with a fine garden. The king had spent his life growing and admiring an enchanted tree, which fruited golden apples. When harvest time came, the king noticed that each night, a golden apple went missing from the tree. He ordered his gardener to find out who was stealing the apples from the tree, or, the king threatened, the gardener would lose his head.

'The gardener had three daughters. On the first night, he ordered the eldest daughter to sit up and guard the tree. But she fell asleep, and didn't see the culprit make off with the missing apple. On the second night, the middle daughter stayed up to watch the tree, but she too fell asleep, and in the morning, another golden apple was gone. Finally on the third night, the youngest daughter sat out to watch the tree. Though she was the youngest and the smallest, she worked hard to stay awake all night, and, near break of day, she spied a golden bird swoop out of the sky, clutch a golden apple in its talons, and fly off into the forest, leaving in its wake one golden feather. She picked up the feather and brought it to her father, who brought it to the king.

'Seeing the golden feather, the king ordered the bird captured, for if one of its feathers was made of gold, imagine how valuable the whole bird would be. The gardener bid his eldest daughter to go after the bird, into the forest, and catch it. So the oldest girl, who was stubborn, walked off into the woods. Before long, she came upon a talking fox. "Take heed," said the fox. "Further up this path, you shall come to a town with two inns. One shall look warm and inviting, and one shabby and poor. No matter how tempting the warm inn looks, do not stay there, as you will forget who you are and where you are going, and will never want to leave." The oldest sister was annoyed at the fox and kicked him away with her foot. When she came to the town, she went into the warm and inviting inn without a second thought. Right away, she forgot who she was and where she was going.'

'Tsk, tsk,' said the elder Martha from her mat. Ah, thought Anne, a smart girl, who can spy foolishness, much like her mother.

Ethel continued. 'After some time had passed, the gardener sent his second daughter, who was selfish, after the first. "Find your sister," he commanded, "and the golden bird. And don't come back without them." The second daughter came upon the same talking fox as well. "Take heed," said he. "Further up this path, you shall come to a town with two inns. One shall look warm and inviting, and one shabby and poor. No matter how tempting the warm inn looks, do not stay there, as you will forget who you are and where you are going, and will never want to leave." The second sister, annoyed, kicked the fox away with her foot, and threw a rock at him. When she came to the town, she spied the warm and inviting inn, and, looking through its window, saw her sister there, dancing and making merry. "I want that good cheer for myself," said the second sister. "How dare my sister keep it from me." And she hurried into the warm inn. Upon crossing the threshold, she promptly forgot who she was, where she was going, and even that her sister was her sister.'

'Serves her right,' said Constance.

'The gardener had no choice then,' Ethel went on, 'but to send his youngest daughter, who was kind and obedient, into the woods after the first two. He hated to see her go, because she was his favourite. Not far down the path, the girl came upon the talking fox. "Take heed," said he. "Further up this path, you shall come to a town with two inns. One shall look warm and inviting, and one shabby and poor. No matter how tempting the warm inn looks, do not stay there, as you will forget who you are and where you are going, and will never want to leave." Instead of kicking or hitting the fox, the girl said, "Thank you, dear fox, for your kind advice." Impressed with the youngest daughter's manners, the fox offered to take her to the town. "Ride on my tail," said the fox, "for it will be faster." The girl rode the fox's tail to the town, and when they arrived, she saw her sisters through the window of the warm inn, dancing and making merry. She went, instead, to the cold inn.'

The younger children began to lie down on their mats, curling up on their sides sleepily.

'Seeing that he could trust the girl,' Ethel went on, eyeing the sleepy children with approval, 'the next morning the fox said to her, "I will tell you how to catch the golden bird, but you must listen and do exactly as I say. Deeper in the woods, you will come upon a great castle, with guards sleeping outside. Creep into the castle, and in the highest tower, you shall find the golden bird in a plain wooden cage. Beside it will be a gold cage. Do not move the bird to the finer cage, no matter how tempting it may be to do so."

'What the fox said was true. The girl came upon the castle with the sleeping guards. She crept inside and found the golden bird in his plain cage. But, as she stood there, she thought how the gold cage was certainly worth a fortune, and how her father, the poor, hardworking gardener, could use such wealth. "Surely no one will notice if I move the bird to the finer cage," thought the girl, but as she did so the bird let out a great shriek that woke the guards, and the king and the queen in the castle, and their son, the prince.

'The king arrested the girl and told her that he would kill her by morning, unless she caught a golden horse and returned it to him. If she did, the king said, she could marry his son, who would one day be the king.

'The fox came to the girl again. "Though you didn't listen to me, I will help you again," said the fox. "In the clearing, you will find the golden horse, and two saddles, one made of leather, and one made of gold. Place the leather saddle on the horse and ride him to the king's castle. Do not place the golden saddle on the horse, no matter how tempted you are to do so." The girl followed the fox's instructions and came upon the golden horse in the clearing. "What harm could it do to put the golden saddle upon the horse?" she thought, remembering her poor father and how much he could use the money from a golden saddle, which was certainly worth a fortune. No sooner had she placed the golden saddle on the golden horse's back than the beast galloped away, taking the golden saddle with it.'

'Why did she do that?' mumbled Robert.

'Well, she's quite stupid, obviously,' replied his sister, Martha.

'Shhhh,' said Ethel. 'Now is the time to be quiet.' She

continued her tale. 'Having failed to catch the golden horse for the king, the girl was locked in the castle tower to await her death at the gallows. "You shall die in the morning," said the king, "unless you can move that mountain outside the window, which blocks my view. If you do that, you shall marry my son, who will one day be king." Again, the fox came to the girl. "Twice you haven't listened to me, but I will help you once more," said the fox. While the girl slept that night, the fox used magic to move the mountain. In the morning, the king, amazed, freed the girl, and set a date for her to marry his son.

'Overjoyed, the girl asked if she could first fetch her father, so that he could be at the wedding. The king agreed, and also let her take the golden bird with her, so that she could prove what she said was true. He gave her two gold coins, so that she could pay for food and lodging along the way. In the woods, the girl thanked the fox for all that he had done to help her. "There is one thing you could do," said the fox, "to show your gratitude." "Anything," said the girl. "You must behead me," said the fox.'

Anne winced. She didn't like the turn this tale was taking.

'The girl said she could not possibly do so,' Ethel went on, 'and the fox said, "Again you do not listen to me, but I will give you one more piece of advice. Do not buy gallows meat, and do not sit at the edge of a river." What strange advice, the girl thought. How would a person buy gallows meat?'

Ethel paused for a moment, as though waiting for an answer. But the children had begun to doze off, and none came.

'The girl continued on her journey, and before long, she came upon the town with the two inns, where a crowd had gathered. A gallows was being built, and the girl learned it was for two women who had behaved wickedly at the warm and inviting inn. She learned the two women were her sisters, and she used her two gold coins to pay to have them freed.'

'That's the gallows meat,' Martha whispered, for she remained awake.

'As the three sisters walked home, the older sisters became jealous of their younger sister, who would be showered with praise when she brought the golden bird home, and would live in comfort as the prince's wife. They hatched a plan to kill her. "Come and sit by the river, sister," they said, and though the fox had warned her not to do so, the younger, obedient sister sat by the river with her stubborn sister and her selfish sister. They quickly pushed her into the river, and she drowned.

'The fox came back one more time. He pulled the youngest sister out of the river and breathed into her mouth until she came back to life. Then he took her to her father, the gardener, where she told him the whole story, about the talking fox, and the golden bird and golden horse, and the prince she was betrothed to marry, and how her wicked sisters had killed her. The gardener punished the older sisters by turning them into prickly rosebushes, because the gardener knew a bit of magic himself. How else do you think he had grown the golden apple tree?'

Again, no one answered Ethel. The younger children were all asleep by now, and the older children were close to it, too drowsy to be bothered with speaking.

'He went with the daughter to the kingdom of her betrothed, where she married the prince, and, eventually, became the queen. One day, the queen was walking in the forest when she came again upon the talking fox. "Good fox!" she said. "You helped me so. What can I do to repay you?" "There is one thing you could do," said the fox, "to show your gratitude." "Anything," said the queen. "You must behead me," said the fox.'

Anne put a hand to her silk collar. Under it, the scar, fleshy ghost of her beheading.

'This time, the queen knew that she must listen to the fox. She drew out her sword, for, in this kingdom, all women carried swords and went into battle like men, and cut off the fox's head. The fox did not die, though, but instead transformed into a powerful wizard. "Thank you, dear queen," he said. "I have been trapped in the body of the fox for many years, after a witch cursed me." The wizard became the queen's most trusted adviser and lived happily with her in the castle for the rest of her days.'

As Ethel's story drew to a close, Anne's heart quickened and her throat tightened. It was just a children's story, it was true, but hadn't Anne, like the girl, failed to take the good advice of others? Hadn't she, like the girl, like the fox wizard, risen from the dead? The mention of the fox's beheading caused her to panic. It was as though she could feel the planks of the scaffold beneath her knees, as though she could smell the straw laid out to catch her blood, as though she could hear her executioner saying, '*Je vous attends*,' I wait for you, as she finished her last prayers, as though she could hear the whistle of the sword as it sliced the air behind her head. Had it whistled? Her heart beat in her chest, faster, faster, like the fast-running feet of a fox. She had no idea why her heart beat at all. She had no idea why she was here, alive, in this fenland hut, instead of dead and buried, her suffering over.

She needed air. Rising from the bed and not paying any mind to Alice – who looked at her with confusion and asked, 'Where are you going, my lady?' – she stepped carefully over and between the mess of sleeping children, scattered on their mats, and hurried out the door of the hut.

In the yard, she drew in breath after breath of marsh air, though it smelled faintly of muck and sulphur. She gulped the air greedily. Her ribs ached from pulling it in. The fog had cleared in the night, and she could see innumerable stars above her, shimmering. Each star reflected perfectly in the water all around the island, as though someone had blown a handful of little lights across the landscape, across the heavens and the earth, and whispered to them, *Stay*, and they had listened.

20

The Most Happy

Anne heard Alice follow her out of the hut. By now she was bent at the waist, hands on her sides, breathing rapidly.

'My lady, are you well?' Alice asked, concern in her voice. ''Twas just a story.'

Anne turned towards her. Alice, with her fox-red hair, with her eyes like the good blue of the sky.

'I had to leave,' said Anne. 'To get some air.' She tried, and failed, to slow her breathing. In the woods an owl sang out mournfully.

Alice walked closer to her and took her hand. The coolness of Alice's fingers felt good. 'Breathe, my lady,' she directed. 'Take in one long breath. Now hold it for a moment. Let it go slowly.'

Anne did as Alice directed. She took in a long breath, held it, and released it. The hammering of her heart lessened. She took in another long breath, held and released it. Again. And again. Alice held both her hands now. Her breathing slowed and evened out.

'What is going on?' Alice asked. The two women's faces were inches apart. 'Who are you?'

'I told you,' Anne said. 'I'm Lady Anne Brandon, wife of Charles Brandon, friend of the king. I have been treated poorly by my husband.'

Alice moved a hand to Anne's cheek and stroked it gently. 'No,' she said. 'I saw how you started at the story Ethel told, when she spoke of the girl beheading the fox. I saw how the colour left you. Who are you?'

'I told you.' Anne looked down. Tears welled in her eyes.

Alice tipped Anne's chin up, softly, so their gazes met. 'No,' Alice said.

'I told you,' Anne whispered, scarcely audible.

'No. Something you are telling me is not true. You are no Lady Brandon.'

'I don't know what you mean.'

'What's beneath your collar?' Alice moved her fingers to Anne's neck, resting them on the silk cloth that had once swaddled the babe Elizabeth. She tugged at it.

'Don't,' said Anne. She tried to pull away, but Alice stopped her. She pulled Anne towards her, held her at the waist.

'Tell me,' Alice whispered. 'You come from nowhere, dressed oddly, with a tragic story.' She paused. 'One night after the queen's execution, you appear wearing a hastily made collar, spinning a yarn of a man who almost killed you, of the woman he's left you for, of the daughter you've left behind. These details. The match is uncanny. I'm a common woman, my lady, but I'm no fool. Who are you?'

'I'm Lady Bran—'

'No.'

'I'm La—'

'No.'

'You tell me, then,' Anne said. 'Who do you think I am?'

'You know.'

'Say it, then.'

'My lady,' said Alice, tugging again at the silk collar. 'Take this off.'

'I cannot. 'Tis sewn together.'

Alice took her hand away from the collar, hiked her skirt, and withdrew a small blade from her boot. 'May I?' she asked.

Anne nodded. Alice slid the collar around Anne's neck until its seam faced her. With her little knife, she popped each stitch, until the collar hung by just one thread. Alice put the blade in her mouth and, with both hands, pulled the collar apart. At the sight of the scar, she exclaimed, 'Oh!' and the knife fell to the ground.

'No,' Anne said, covering her face in embarrassment and turning away. She could only imagine what she looked like, what the scar looked like, the horror of her disfigurement. Gently, Alice ran a finger over the scar. What she must see, Anne thought, is a monstrosity, a thick, fleshy rope encircling my neck.

'My lady,' Alice whispered.

Anne brought her own fingers to the scar and felt its bulge, the evidence of all her failures, branded on her skin. With the collar on, she'd been able to deny the reality of her execution. She'd been able to pretend. With it off, all she could think of were her own shortcomings, her failure to endear herself to the manners-bound English courtiers, her failure to see the conspiracy against her coming until it was too late, her failure to best Thomas Cromwell, her failure to keep Henry's wandering attention, her failure to just shut up, just shut up already, to shut her own mouth for her own fucking good, her failure to prove her innocence at trial, her failure to live and keep Elizabeth safe. Anne sobbed, and the sobs were deep and guttural.

She felt Alice put a hand on her heaving back, brush the stray strands of hair from the nape of her neck. 'Shhhhh,' Alice said. Anne tried to stop her sobs, her chest and back catching as she pulled in long breaths. She felt Alice's breath against her neck, and Alice's lips against her scar, as Alice kissed the thick band of tissue, hesitantly at first, and then in a series of soft, fluttery kisses.

'My lady,' Alice whispered in Anne's ear. Then, 'My queen?' Anne turned towards Alice, her face streaked with tears, a line of snot running from her nose.

With the sleeve of her gown, Alice wiped Anne's face clean. She wiped her ruddy cheeks. She wiped her sniffling nose. 'That is who you are, isn't it?' Alice said. 'You are the dead queen, Anne Boleyn.'

Anne let out another sharp sob. 'Yes,' she said. What use was it to keep lying?

Alice pulled her closer, into a tight embrace. Their faces almost touching, Alice held Anne's gaze, then she kissed her, and in that kiss Anne, for a moment, forgot. She forgot the shame of her failures. She forgot the fear of walking to the scaffold, the way she'd had to force one foot before the other, the way the heels of her slippers had tapped across the wooden stage. She forgot the meek speech she'd made with her final living breaths – it had been necessary, for Elizabeth's sake, and yet part of her wished she could go back in time and rip those supplicating words out of her mouth, and say what she wanted, speak her rage in a barbed retort. She forgot the pain of her beheading, the pain of the sharp sword. She breathed in deeply, inhaling the scent of Alice – water lilies and the saltiness of sweat – and kissed her in return.

When the two women parted, they sat at the water's edge. 'Wait,' said Anne, giggling a little and thinking of the fairy tale Ethel had told. 'Perhaps we shouldn't sit by the water's edge; I hope no wicked sisters come and drown us.'

'You've already been brought back to life once, my lady,' Alice replied, taking Anne's hand in her own. 'I don't think you need to worry.'

Anne nodded again. She supposed Alice was right.

'How did this happen?' asked Alice. 'How are you here, living and breathing?' She touched Anne's scar. 'How did this heal?'

'I don't know,' said Anne. 'I was on the scaffold, praying, waiting for the executioner's swing. And I do remember the pain of that, of the sword – a pain like fire and ice. Then some time passed in darkness, and I woke in a wooden chest. An arrow chest, if you'd believe it. The stingy fucker didn't even have the decency to pay for a coffin. I fled, carrying my head, stole a boat, and landed across the river in Southwark. I stole a sewing basket from a tavern-keeper's wife, sewed my head back on, and fashioned this collar from my daughter's silk swaddling cloth, which I'd hidden in my bodice, so that I could be close to her, so that I might take something of her with me to the grave.' Anne held up the silken collar, dear treasure, remnant of Elizabeth, which she'd picked up from the ground where Alice had dropped it. Alice stared at her, transfixed. 'I don't know how this happened. I don't know how I lived. I don't know how a simple thread held my head back on, or how the wound healed. I don't know why I'm here.' Anne started to cry again.

''Tis a miracle,' Alice said, stroking the back of Anne's hand, pausing to trace a circle around a mole at her wrist.

'Maybe,' said Anne, shrugging. 'I wouldn't know.'

'My lady,' Alice said, shaking Anne's knee to get her attention. 'Yes. 'Tis a miracle. A miracle.'

Anne looked at Alice. 'Or I am damned. Doomed for my sins to walk the earth in living death for all eternity.'

'My lady,' said Alice, 'you can make anything glum. I thought you were supposed to be "the most happy"? That's what all the criers said when you were made queen. "Hear ye, hear ye!"' shouted Alice, in imitation of a royal crier. '"Queen Anne Boleyn is crowned! The most happy!" And they were singing that song, about a white bird?'

Anne remembered. 'The White Falcon'. Henry had the song composed in honour of her coronation. It was an atrocious song, rhyming 'gentle bird' with 'white as curd'. The falcon was one of Anne's emblems, meant to represent steadfastness. The song was clear about Anne's duty, exhorting the falcon to 'build a nest' and 'bring fruit'. Though of course a gyrfalcon could do more than breed; the large females of the species could stalk and hunt, could kill.

The two women talked for hours, sharing their lives and stories. Where was the father of Alice's children? Anne asked. Alice didn't want to talk about it, but then revealed the father had been a man she'd wedded for her family's sake, a man her father owed a debt to. The man was mean, and old enough to be Alice's father. When he'd drowned cleaning out eel traps three years ago, Alice hadn't shed a tear, hadn't even bothered to send George after his body, which, Alice supposed, was now sunk to the bottom of the fen, joining the legion of other poor souls whose remains rested there. Good riddance, thought Alice, and she set about her own business, heading into Southwark a few times a year to make some money at the brothel and spending the rest of her time at her father's house, where she lived now, with her children and George, her brother.

Had Anne loved Henry, or had their marriage been a way for her to raise her family's name, to rise to power herself? Alice asked. Yes, she had loved him intensely. When Anne had met Henry, he'd been handsome and strong, a hunter and an avid reader, someone who enjoyed the pleasures of life: a good game of cards, the chase of a beautiful woman, a glass of fine wine. True, he was already married, but illegally so, and moreover his wife was at the change of life, ageing out of her beauty and resigned to her chambers, unloving. Anne had known of Henry's reputation as a man with many mistresses – her own sister had been one – but with her Henry was different. He wrote her passionate love letters. He read the books she'd recommended. He'd waited and waited. Their first night together – Anne blushed thinking of it.

What did Alice do in the months she wasn't in Southwark? How did she occupy herself, and keep herself from slipping into the devil's hands through idleness? Alice laughed at this notion,

'The devil's hands? What nonsense,' but then spoke freely of her life in the fens, of the liberty she enjoyed here. She spoke of daydreaming by the water, of taking a boat out past the fens to the edge of the sea to watch the seals gather and play, of learning bird calls, of playing chase with her children on the islands that dotted the marsh. She spoke of happiness and pleasure, of splitting wood for a fire, of cosying up with her little ones and listening to her father spin a yarn, maybe a fairy tale, maybe a tale of the trickster Howleglas.

Had Anne noticed when she fell out of favour with the king? Had she known her arrest was coming? No; until the end, Henry had professed his love for her, even on the morning before her arrest, as she slipped a flower inside his doublet before the May Day joust. Though they'd had a terrible row the night before, the worst of their marriage, though Henry had questioned her about Henry Norris, about dead men's shoes, by morning he'd been warm and loving again. She'd slipped the flower into his doublet and kissed his cheek before heading to the May Day celebrations. He'd said he loved her. They'd been planning a trip to France. She thought they would conceive another child there, another boy. She had no idea the case he was building against her was almost complete.

How did Alice feel about working as a prostitute? How did she keep from becoming pregnant? Did lying with strange men bother her? No, Alice liked the power. She got to choose the men she bedded, and the money she made was hers to spend as she wished. She was a country girl dressed in finer gowns than she'd ever owned before she left the fens, and she got to buy her children toys and baubles, enough flour to make bread for the months she was home. It was enough money to pay taxes to the crown, enough to keep her father out of debt, enough to set some aside. She didn't love the men, but she didn't hate them either. And the work was just a thing she did with her body, as a farmer might use his strength to work the land, or a seamstress her hands to work the needle. The worst of it was spending time in the Clink Street Prison, which was dark and full of disease, and prone to flooding, and, worse still, ate away at her earnings, for a person had to pay for everything there, from the chains that bound their wrists and ankles, to their daily bread, to the cost of each night's lodging, if you could call the cells that flooded at every high tide lodging. But it was an unpleasantness that could mostly be avoided. She'd long ago learned to keep extra money on herself, so she could bribe the jailer for a quick release, and now she rarely spent even a full night there. There were herbs to take to keep from having a baby, and Alice kept track of her cycle using a technique Ethel had taught her, so she knew which days to avoid male company. 'Twas something all women should learn to do, in her opinion, for why should a woman be forced to have babe after babe? Shouldn't she have some say in her own life? If there were herbs to take to prevent a baby, to bring on the blood of menstruation, and ways to count days so a man's seed was less likely to take root, should a woman not be free to do so? Anne knew some of these methods too, but, unlike Alice, she'd counted days to try to bring on pregnancy, and, although she knew where to get herbs to end a pregnancy, she'd never done so.

Did Anne know why the king had killed her? She hadn't really lain with all those men, with her own brother, had she? No, of course not. Anne spoke a bit of Cromwell, the king's powerful adviser, but, in truth, she didn't think Cromwell had talked Henry into having her executed. Henry didn't do anything he didn't want to do. She had fallen from Henry's favour, though he'd hidden it while he built his case against her, or had Cromwell do it for him. She'd lost his son, and that was unforgivable. For the entirety of their lengthy courtship, she'd promised him, again and again, that she'd give him a prince, and then she'd let the prince slide out of her, too small to live. And Henry – already exhausted from his first marriage, from the full married life he'd lived for twenty years with Katherine, from all the babes she'd borne who'd died, or whom she'd lost before they were born – Henry was too tired, too hungry for a son, to wait, to try again with Anne. He wanted another wife, a purer wife, a younger wife. He wanted Anne's lady-in-waiting Jane, who smelled of milk and clean linen, who was well fed and compliant. Henry's problem with Anne, ultimately, was that she was herself – loud, bossy, stubborn, too smart for her own good, unable to shut her mouth for the love of God, and unable to bear a son.

Alice and Anne talked on and on. When the stars began to fade and the sky lightened at the horizon, Anne snuggled into Alice's arms, her body weary, her eyelids heavy, and both women fell asleep.

In the morning they were woken by the children running out of the little hut and dancing playfully around them. Anne sat up and straightened her clothing, putting her hands up around the scar at her neck protectively.

'That won't do,' said Alice, sitting up too and stretching into a yawn. 'Let's sew your collar back on.'

Anne followed her into the hut, where Ethel sat by the fire, stirring porridge in a large pot. When Alice asked, Ethel fetched her sewing basket from beneath the bed. Letting out a loud 'Sweet Saint Anne, mother of Mary!' at the sight of Anne's scar, Ethel nonetheless sewed the silk collar in place around Anne's neck. Perhaps she thinks he tried to slit my throat, Anne thought. Not far from the truth.

'Your husband must be a brute,' Ethel said, spitting on the floor in disgust.

'Yes, madam,' replied Anne, 'he is.' And though she'd thought she had cried all her tears the night before, even more slid down her cheeks.

Ethel went back to the porridge, and Alice went down to the

river with the children. She'd taken her boots off so she could splash in the muddy river's edge with them, and placed them just inside the door of the hut. Anne dug in her bodice for the jewels she'd stolen from the Tower, pulling out the ruby ring and onyx pendant, leaving the sapphire diadem for Elizabeth, should she reach her. Ruby for Alice, whose copper-coloured hair was fiery and splendid, and onyx for Anne, whose auburn hair was so dark it was sometimes mistaken for black. She slipped the two jewels into Alice's left boot. Something for her to remember Anne by, or something for her to sell and live off, if Anne never came back. Prostitution didn't bother Alice, but it bothered Anne that Alice had to leave her idyllic fens to do it, that she had to leave her children, and Anne suspected that, given the choice, Alice would prefer not to keep the company of strange men.

Anne walked out the door of the hut and smiled at Alice, playing happily with the children. George, who had been fishing on the other side of the island that morning, had returned and joined them in their play. Alice smiled and waved Anne over. 'Join us!' she sang out. 'Take off your slippers and have some fun, my lady.' How badly Anne wanted to do so. How badly she wanted to join Alice at play, not just now but always. How badly she wanted to stay.

She couldn't.

She walked over to Alice and took her hand, pulling her to the side of the hut, out of sight and hearing of the children. Alice kissed her, and Anne closed her eyes and gave in to her embrace, for a moment, before pulling away.

'I must go,' Anne whispered, though she didn't want to, though it pained her to say it.

'No,' said Alice. 'Stay.'

'I must go,' said Anne. 'I must find Henry. I need to protect Elizabeth. I need to help my daughter.' This was all true, but none of it eased Anne's pain at leaving.

Alice looked hurt for a moment; then her expression softened. 'I know. But how will you?' she asked. 'He is the king, and you are a dead woman walking. What can you do? Stay here with me. We could spend our days together. My father could build us a home on an island where we could live with Martha and Robert. You could learn to fish and be merry. Surely your daughter will be safe under the protection of her own father.'

'No,' said Anne. 'You don't know him. She's not safe. He'll cast her out, declare her a bastard, who knows what else.' Anne paused, wary to speak aloud the violence and treason of what she'd been planning, but then deciding to. 'I'm going to kill him. I'm going to sneak into Whitehall Palace, and I'm going to kill him.'

Alice fell silent. 'My lady,' she said at last. 'No. 'Tis a crime to even mention the king's death, let alone to try to kill him. And in your state? You'll be caught and captured. You'll be killed.'

'Alice,' Anne replied. 'Alice, I'm already dead. What else can they do to me?' Though Anne knew there was plenty that could be done to her, to this body that refused to die, or, God forbid, to Elizabeth, to her young body, if Anne were caught. She took Alice's hand. 'You do not know what strength lies inside me. My time is coming. I can feel it. Why else was I brought back from death? I must go. I must save her.'

Alice nodded, though she was crying. 'I don't want you to go,' said Alice. 'But I see how a mother's love drives you. I, of all people, can understand that.'

'You could join me,' Anne whispered, though she knew Alice couldn't, wouldn't leave her children, or her fen, and that she didn't want her to. She didn't want to pull Alice away from her home; from the hut filled with loving souls, waiting to welcome her into community; from the wild beauty of this landscape. Let one good thing stand. Let one good thing stay in this wretched world.

'No, you know I can't,' Alice spoke, softly. Then, with resolve, 'We will fetch George. We will tell him to take you out of the fens today. My lady,' Alice added, 'protect yourself.' She tore a ribbon from the sleeve of her gown and tucked it in Anne's bodice, lingering for a moment with her hand upon Anne's breast. 'To remember me by,' she whispered, before kissing Anne one last time, then marching to the river to fetch George.

PART TWO

The Hero's Return

21

The Bull

For two days, Anne wandered through the woods, staying close to the River Great Ouse, careful not to get too near to any village or monastery, castle or manor. 'Follow the Great Ouse to the River Cam, then the Cam into Essex. When the Cam ends, head south until you reach London,' George had directed her. 'Be sure to walk so the mossy sides of the trees are facing you. In the morning the sun should be on your left, and in the afternoon on your right. 'Tis no short journey. 'Twould take a fit man three, perhaps four days' time to reach London.'

Some parts of the woods she knew, owned by lords she'd known at court, used by the king for hunting grounds. Before the time of lords, she supposed these woods had been occupied by the Angles, and before that by the ancient tribes. She'd learned their names while living with the Archduchess Margaret, but couldn't recall which had occupied this territory, south of the fens but north of London. Was it the Catuvellauni? The Corieltauvi? To the east of London had lived the Trinovantes, and in Norfolk, her family's ancestral land, had lived the Iceni, and their fierce Queen Boudicca, burner of London, destroyer of Romans. Oh, Margaret! She wished she could go back now, crawl into Margaret's bed, like she'd done as a child when she'd woken from a bad dream, and have that good lady stroke her hair and tell her all was well, it was only a dream, nobody would ever execute a queen, nobody can rise from the dead.

Anne remembered her tutor in Mechelen well, a young monk who had at first been reluctant to heed Margaret's direction that 'her girls', as she called the half-dozen daughters of noble birth who'd been sent to her household for training in how to be a lady, be educated the same as any boy. Anne might have thought that a younger man would be open to new ideas of girls' education, as surely as he was open to the new ideas of science and art coming out of Florence and Venice. Something she had always admired about Thomas Cromwell was that he had educated his daughters as well as his son, though of course what she'd taken for an openness to the intelligence of women had simply been a care for his own progeny. He had not liked Anne's intelligence. How could the same man who cared so dearly for the women in his own life dislike women writ large so much? How could a man treat his own daughters with dignity and humanity, while insinuating that another man's wife, his queen no less, ought to shut her mouth and open her legs, for she was no better than breeding stock and should get to it? Cromwell was awash in such contradictions.

Eventually, the poor tutor at Mechelen had caved, persuaded by the archduchess's stern lectures and an offer of more compensation. 'You're as bright as you are pretty,' he'd said to Anne in a reptilian voice, when she'd mastered her Latin and French, when she'd read through the Roman histories, when she'd mastered mathematical equations. What had she learned about the ancient peoples of England there, in the oak-panelled room in which the pupils gathered to study, trussed up in expensive gowns, hair braided and pinned under French hoods? That the pre-Roman tribes had been barbaric, but proud. To a one they'd fought the Romans, though eventually all gave in. That some conducted ritual sacrifices.

Anne remembered years later, with Henry, stopping to visit the Earl of Shrewsbury at Sheffield Castle during one of their progresses – so far north, further north than she was now. The earl, an old favourite of Henry and his father before him, who'd stood stalwart beside Henry in the annulment proceedings, had brought out an ancient bowl, made of beaten metal. Atop it sat a lid, and on the handle of the lid, a statuette of a flat-faced, long-nosed woman riding a bull. In each hand she gripped one of the bull's curved horns. She straddled the beast, legs stuck straight out.

'This bowl,' drawled the earl, 'was used by the ancient tribes. One of my tenants unearthed it while ploughing. I had a scholar from King's College verify that 'tis a relic, likely used to catch the blood of the condemned in ancient sacrifices.' He'd eyed Anne flirtatiously. 'My lady, does not your family crest bear the emblem of a bull? A play on your surname? Perhaps the feminine rider is one of your ancient ancestresses?'

'My Anne is a champion rider, but I have never seen her ride a bull,' Henry had said, jokingly, pulling her to him with enough affection that she forgave the earl for his suggestive comment and, for once, held her tongue.

Blood sacrifice, then. Wizards too. She remembered her tales of Arthur and Merlin. Arthur, the ageing king whose wife, Guinevere, left him for his friend the good knight Lancelot, and Merlin, the wizard who tricked and magicked the world around him so the prophecies he foresaw would come true. She remembered the story of Brutus, grandson of Aeneas, sailing to English shores to found a race of peoples there. She remembered learning of fairies and witches that haunted the woods, of Druid rituals, of a race of giants who once lived in England, of a race of little people who lived in the woods with such sharp hearing that no action could be plotted against them because they could hear every word uttered near and far. 'Twas all a lot of superstition,

Anne thought, as she walked, a resurrected woman, among the oak and pine trees, following the paths trampled by deer or local children.

Anne wished she could have stayed in the fens with Alice. When George had paddled his boat away from the island the morning Anne left, Alice and the children, and even stout Ethel, stood waving by the dock, Alice wiping tears from her face.

'I have never seen my sister cry at a parting before,' George said as he and Anne rowed around a bend, out of view of the little hut. 'Certainly never at parting from her husband.' He peered into the swamp water, intently. I wonder if he's searching for eels, Anne thought. 'We know how Alice is,' he said. 'That she has sometimes loved other women.'

Anne was afraid George would scold her, that perhaps he'd seen her and Alice asleep by the water that morning, held in each other's arms, that perhaps he'd tell her that for two women to embrace like husband and wife was a sin.

'And we love her for who she is,' George said with startling directness. 'I'd be happy to see her happy with you. I'd be happy to see her happy. If that's why you're leaving, you needn't go. You could come and stay with us. You'd be welcome.'

Anne caught her breath. She'd spent the past ten years in England feeling disliked and unwanted by any number of people: first her fellow courtiers, then her subjects, at last her own husband. Yet here was this man she'd just met, this woman she'd just met, opening their arms to her, their home to her, who liked her just as she was.

'No,' Anne said. 'That is very kind of you. Thank you. But that's not why I'm leaving.' Seeing George's eyebrow arched in curiosity, she added, repeating her lie, 'I have to find my daughter.'

'Yes,' he said, 'your daughter.' He wiped the back of his hand across his brow, scratching some little itch there. 'I don't know who you are, but I can tell there's something you're keeping secret.'

''Tis no secret. She's in danger.'

George nodded at Anne sceptically. She doubted he fully believed her. But he stopped questioning her. The two rowed on for a while before they spoke again. They passed Witch Finger Woods, where the dead treetops shot through the surface of the water. They passed reed patches and islands. The flooded sprawl of rivers began to narrow and obey, to look less like a bay filled with islands and more like a few distinct rivers, one of which they rowed down. A flock of geese lifted off the water ahead of them, forming a loose V in the sky. Anne marvelled at the beauty of this place, at its untamed splendour.

'There's rich men who would like to drain these fens,' George said, noticing her admiration for the riverscape around them.

'I know,' replied Anne. 'I know those men. I know their plans. They'd like to use the land for grain fields and pastures. I've heard them discussing the matter.'

'*The law doth punish man or woman that steals the goose from off the common, but lets the greater felon loose that steals the common from the goose,*' George recited. ''Tis a poem, spoken by common folk. I assume you've heard of poetry,' he said, smiling and winking at her.

'Yes,' replied Anne, for she had heard so much poetry in her life. She fingered her silk collar. 'I am sorry,' she said to George. 'I wish I could stop it.'

'Mmm,' he replied, close-lipped. He gazed back out at the water. 'Of course.'

They'd rowed on, mostly in silence, until they came to a dock at the river. 'Take care, good lady,' he'd said, as he helped Anne out of the boat. He kissed her on the cheek. 'Know that you can always come back. We shall be here. I would treasure you like a second sister.'

She thought again of her own brother George, of how much she wished he were here. 'Thank you,' she said, squeezing this other George's arm with affection, before turning to walk away.

George had given her a bundle of food that Ethel had packed – a loaf of bread and some raw parsnips, a large slab of smoked fish – enough, Anne hoped, to tide her over for her journey.

'Remember my directions,' George had called after her, 'and remember that you can always return.' Anne nodded in understanding and waved goodbye.

By the end of the first day, Anne had eaten half the food in her bundle and still felt weak. She'd been ravenously hungry since reawakening in the arrow chest five days earlier, and yet despite eating as much as she could lay hands on, each day she felt more and more frail. She worried that she'd suffer another fainting spell or fever, and this time, there'd be no Alice to assist her. She made camp in a stand of birch trees, using what remained of her bundle of food as a pillow.

In the night she dreamed of a metal bowl overflowing with blood, and in the half-dark early dawn she awoke to a bull, standing over her, huffing into her startled, narrow face.

22

The Sweat

Anne thought of the three bulls of her family crest, black fabric silhouettes against a white-and-red field. She thought of the golden pinky ring George had worn with a bull's head sculpted on to its face. She thought of the bull she'd seen as a child, that had rampaged through the little village near Hever Castle, breaking in a peasant's front door as though it had been invited into the small cottage, and wounding a child with a swipe of its pointed horn. And though the child had lived, he'd lost an arm. The bull had been slain by the village men, for the animal, though domesticated, had gone wild and needed to be killed to protect the villagers, to protect the livestock, to protect the children. The village men had roasted the beast and Anne's family had come out of the big castle to dine with them around a campfire, while the village women danced and sang, drunk on mead and full of roasted beef, and the little boy who'd lost his arm slept off his suffering in the village church, its doors guarded by his older brothers.

Where had *this* bull come from, standing above Anne, unmoving, observing her, huffing in her face? For a moment, Anne worried he might gore her, as the buck-wild, angered bull had done to the village child so many years ago. But she saw that the bull was calm, quiet, with placid black eyes that stood in contrast to his bone-white hide. She reached a hand up to touch his muzzle, which was soft and velvety, like a horse's. Piercing his septum was a large golden ring. She put her hand to the ring and pulled. The bull took a step forward, though was careful not to step on her. 'Good boy,' Anne said. Then, 'Are you fantastical?' She propped herself up on her elbow and dug in her bundle for one of the parsnips Ethel had packed. She held it out for the bull, who lipped it off her palm and chewed it slowly. The creature lifted a hoof and stomped the ground, impatiently, as though waiting for her to rise. Over the bull's pale shoulder, she could see Earendel, the morning star, shining on the horizon.

She supposed she'd woken into odder situations, and worse, such as every morning she'd woken at the Tower, the terror of her fate recurring to her, coming into her consciousness again, after a night of forgetful sleep. The most terrible of which was the morning she'd woken early and watched her brother led to the scaffold from her chamber window, his little half-wave, his sad smile. Her George, her brother. A cry rose in her throat and hiccuped out of her. The bull nudged her gently with his muzzle, as if to say, 'Don't cry, my lady.' Or, maybe, 'Don't cry, Anne. Don't cry, little bull. Little Bullen.' How many times had George called her that?

For a while, Anne led the bull through the woods. The beast followed her wherever she went, like a puppy, and it felt important to keep him with her. The two walked along the river as the sun rose on her left, the bull stopping here and there to nibble on vegetation, Anne stopping to ladle river water to her mouth with her hand. She was so thirsty. And hot. Had the fever returned? She ate the rest of her bread as she walked. She ate the rest of the smoked fish. Her appetite was bottomless. Behind her, the bull let out weighty sigh after weighty sigh, as though wanting something from her that she could not give. What? she wanted to ask him. What do you want? But he was a bull, and she couldn't expect him to answer her.

The way the bull followed her, the way he tilted his head when he looked at her, reminded Anne of her favourite lapdog, whose habit of inquisitively tilting his head had led to his name, Purkoy, a transliteration of *pourquoi*, French for 'why'. And that was a good question. Why? Why was she, the living dead, leading an alabaster bull through the woods? Purkoy had fallen to his death from a window at Hampton Court Palace the year before. When she found out about Purkoy's death, she was sure he'd been pushed. She assumed one of her ladies had done it, jealous of a flirtation Anne had had with her husband. What a stupid thing to be jealous of. That was how it was supposed to go. The men of court wrote Anne poems, gave her trinkets. She was, after all, their queen, and this was the expectation of courtly behaviour, of courtly love. In return she flirted or gave small tokens of her affection: a kerchief embroidered with her initials, a silver-backed pocket mirror, a lock of her hair. Everyone knew the queen didn't actually sleep with her admirers. She wasn't the king, who was free to fuck any lord's wife he pleased. Different rules applied to her. Now she wondered if Henry had pushed the dog. The thought had crossed her mind, for a moment, when Henry told her the dog had fallen to his death – had he pushed the little dog? But surely, she'd thought, he couldn't be that duplicitous. He'd comforted her after Purkoy's death, he'd consoled her. He, too, had been devastated. Who could lie that well?

She'd been looking forward, in her own death, to seeing Purkoy again. She knew pets weren't supposed to have an afterlife. Even so, she imagined her dog would be there to greet and comfort her after her beheading, to lap her fingers and lips and communicate, with the unconditional love of a dog, that all was well. They were together again. Nothing could harm her now that she was, like her dog, dead. She'd dreamed of running her hands through his long fur as she slept her last anxious nights at the Tower. It would be her reward for getting through the awful business of the beheading. After death, Purkoy would run to her, and she'd pick him up, nuzzle him, whisper, '*Purkoy, mon chien, je t'adore.*' That she hadn't found him after death was one more disappointment of this odd afterlife.

Why? *Pourquoi?* she wondered again. Why did she seem to be walking in circles, with a puppyish bull at her heels, going nowhere and going everywhere? Leaving the fens and also returning to them? Heading to London and also away? Riding to kill Henry and also to love him? For in that stroke of death, she imagined a final expression of her love. The death stroke would say, 'Enough,' would put the beast out of his misery, would keep safe those around him. Like the blind bear in the arena in Southwark, like the crazed bull in the village of her childhood, Henry had grown dangerous in his injury and age. 'Enough,' her killing stroke would say, and it would be.

It had not always been this way. Anne remembered the year she'd left court, 1526, fuming over her cancelled engagement to Henry Percy. The marriage would have made her a countess, titled, with property, and a kind, doting man to husband her into her elevated status and wealth. But Percy's father wanted him to marry Mary Talbot, the daughter of an earl in her own right, a better match by rank, and Anne assumed that was why the betrothal had been called off, news she'd received in a curt letter written by Cardinal Wolsey, who had a hand in arranging the marriages of many courtiers, who no doubt had supported Percy's father, pushed Percy to break the engagement off. How she had ranted about the letter, saying that evening in the great hall, over supper, walking right up to Wolsey, pointing her finger at him, and saying, 'If it lay ever in my power, I will work you much displeasure.' He'd looked back at her, disbelieving a lady-in-waiting, the daughter of a social-climbing nobleman without title, the sister of the king's notoriously loose mistress, disbelieving any woman would speak to him that way, and had said, 'Girl, mind your place,' and raised a hand, as though to strike her, but she'd lurched forward at him, and said, 'Try it, old churl,' and he'd backed away. All present in the room had looked at them, looked, and then looked away, at this uncouth girl, this loud-mouthed woman. Didn't she know women ought to be better behaved, ought to accept what was handed to them, ought not rant and rave at supper, making a spectacle of themselves? Women ought not talk back to Cardinal Wolsey.

She'd retreated to the safety of Hever Castle, to her private rooms where she spent hours lying in bed, watching the light that reflected off the castle moat dance across her chamber ceiling. 'Is all well?' her mother had enquired, looking concerned, as she checked on her every few hours. From the opened chamber door, Anne could hear the sound of Mary's children playing, for Mary and her family visited frequently at the castle. Then the letters from the king had begun to arrive, and the tokens, and she understood that he wanted her for himself, that he was the reason her engagement had been cancelled, that he'd finished with her sister and now wanted a taste of her.

Henry's perseverance overwhelmed her. Letter after letter arrived, tokens of jewellery, gifts of venison, carried to Hever Castle by anxious footmen. 'I send you a buck killed late last night by my own hand,' read one letter, 'hoping that when you eat of it you may think of the hunter.' What an odd gesture, she thought, to send me meat, to imagine me imagining him as I put the flesh in my mouth. The innuendo seemed over the top, scandalous. For a year the letters had arrived, proclaiming his love, his fidelity, his dedication to annulling his marriage to his wife, the riches and comforts with which he'd shower her if she'd acquiesce to be his mistress. She wouldn't; she demanded a proposal, that he commit to marrying her after his annulment, that he promise that she'd be the next queen, that he accept they'd wait until marriage to consummate their relationship so that any child born would be legitimate, and he agreed.

Anne had returned to court then, the king's fiancé, but in the summer of 1528, the sweating sickness swept through England. Anne retreated back to Hever, where her mother and father, brother, sister Mary and her family, were already sequestered. More letters arrived from Henry, but in these letters were his worries. Illness was at the court. Was illness also at Anne's house? Yes, all at Hever Castle, Anne included, contracted the sweat. It killed Mary's husband, the good and kind William Carey. After his passing, Mary sat for hours in her chamber, staring out of the window at the rolling Kentish hills, at the trees that blanketed them, persistently green despite the illness and death inside the castle walls, a woman alone, no husband, no lover.

Henry was anxious about getting the illness. He was anxious about Anne getting it, and then anxious when she contracted it. Would she perish? Unwritten in his letters was his worry over an heir. Having lived through the death of his own older brother, having been the second in line who rose to the throne, Henry was fixated on having a child with Anne, on having his male heir, on having more than one male heir, on filling a bench with male children who could step in to take the throne after his death, who could save England from the chaos of uncertainty, from the political infighting over who would reign if the king left no heir at all, from the violence of civil war that might erupt in the absence of an heir as the nobility chose sides and split into factions.

Nobody wanted a return to the warring of his father's and grandfather's generations, when the Yorks fractured and clung to power with a maniacal but weak king, easily slayed on the battlefield, easily disposed of, no heirs left behind. This had been how Henry's own father ascended to the throne – after his troops had killed Richard III on the battlefield, he'd married the villainous usurper's niece, the sister of the lost princes Richard had

had murdered in the Tower, and claimed the throne. Henry was anxious not to repeat the mistakes of the previous dynastic family. Having a cavalcade of heirs was his way of ensuring stability, the longevity of the Tudor royal dynasty, and, Anne had often thought, of easing the sorrow of his own dear brother Arthur's death. She'd even suggested Arthur as a name for Elizabeth when she was pregnant, had the baby been a boy, and Henry had loved the idea.

Anne stayed at Hever over Christmas, after the sweating sickness had passed. Henry's letters continued, and he took to sending state papers for her to read and advise him on, like a member of his council, like a man. She'd send back pages of notes, scribbled in her bed by candlelight where she lay convalescing. For New Year's she sent Henry a little golden ship as a present. *My good Lord the King*, she'd written. *Find here a ship bedecked with a beauteous diamond, a North Star to guide the vessel homeward. On its bow, a maiden, trusting in God to deliver her.* For there'd been a little maiden on the ship, holding a glass lantern. Her meaning: the sweating sickness will end and I will return to you. I trust God will guide us through this plague, as through the plague of your incestuous marriage to your brother's widow, the miracle of your annulment. A symbolic toy, delivered on a velvet pillow by a servant in her absence, to Henry's great delight.

Meanwhile, at Hever, she and Mary exchanged oranges while Mary's children, redheaded and square-faced, ran about the courtyard, screaming and playing chase, until Mary's young son Henry ran inside and said, tattling on his sister, 'Catherine hath pulled my hair and slammed me to the ground,' and Mary said, 'How like his father he is, quick to complain when a woman treats him roughly, though never would he speak of what he's done to provoke her,' and Anne knew she did not mean William Carey, who'd never complained about anything, but Henry the king.

*

It was evening when Anne and the bull reached a small encampment on the bank of the river, where seven or eight men sat huddled around a campfire, drinking from leather pouches and singing shanties as a fat pike roasted on a spit over the open flame. Anne slowed to a halt and quieted the bull, then hid with him behind the broad trunk of a tall pine. Who were these men? Thieves? Monks? Perhaps a band of servant emissaries sent on the king's behalf with an urgent message? As she peered around the tree's trunk to get a closer look, the bull moved out behind her, in plain view of the men, let out a long, loud sigh, and dragged his front hoof through the dirt of the forest floor, snapping several loose sticks. The men around the fire stopped their singing and merrymaking and turned, all at once, to look at her.

23

The Encampment

Hoping to hide herself, Anne ducked back behind the tree's broad trunk. The bull, dumb stubborn animal, stood his ground, huffing and pawing his hoof through the dirt. She knew bulls took this stance when threatened, yet this bull, with his moon-white hide, had followed her so gently all day that his aggression surprised her. The bull raked the ground and bent his head down, horns pointed forward. Was he protecting her? Anne paused. She wasn't sure she wanted to be involved with a powerful creature who was kind to her but aggressive with others. After all, this was how Henry had seemed, tame initially but ultimately untamable, self-interested, head down, horns forward, ready and willing to gore friends, allies, religious counsellors, his own wife, whoever she be, if she stood in his way. There had even been a time when Anne had thought he'd execute his own daughter, Mary, for failing to sign the Act of Succession, recognising Henry as head of England's churches. Here, Anne had been a reluctant advocate – a stepmother, finally, not just in name but in deed – lobbying on that angry fist of a girl's behalf, for though she did not love Mary, though she found her impudent and entitled, though the girl reminded Anne that Henry had not always been hers, that hers was not the only or first family the king had had, still she did not wish to see the child lose her head, and she did not wish to see her Henry do the reaping.

The bull huffed again, his head down. Anne put a hand on his haunch, to calm him, perhaps, but also so she could give the beast a slap and send him charging if these river men proved treacherous.

'Who comes there?' shouted one of the encamped men.

''Tis a bull!' cried a second.

And a third added, 'He's going to charge!' The bull tensed his muscles. Anne stood, hidden by the tree, hand on the beast's buttock.

'Nay,' said the first man, 'this beast is only posturing. Look how it raises its head to look at us.' This man must be the leader, Anne thought, for he bosses the others.

'Simon, you fool,' replied the second. 'What would you know of bulls and goring? We all know you grew up in the city, scrubbing pots in a rich man's kitchen. The most you've seen of a bull is its tail, chopped off and simmering in a stew.' The men around the fire laughed.

'Don't you tell me my business,' replied the first man, Simon. 'I swore I saw a maid beside the beast.' Anne pressed her back more firmly against the tree, wishing she could, by mere pressure, urge it to absorb her.

'Aye,' added a new voice, 'I also saw her. 'Twas a thin pale woman with dark hair. 'Tis likely she's a ghost. These woods are haunted by all manner of spirits, and fairies too.'

'Oh, shush up, you superstitious fool,' replied Simon. 'What, do you think the ghost of some sad woman roams these woods looking for encampments of down-on-their-luck men? Or maybe you think 'tis the ghost of fair Guinevere, mistaking us all for Knights of the Round Table, come back to shower us in queenly affection?'

'No need to be vulgar, Simon,' replied the second man. Anne could hear men moving around the campfire, perhaps a scuffle in the works. Beside her, the bull huffed, head down, horns forward.

'I'd always thought of myself as more of an Arthur,' said the man who'd mentioned ghosts, 'kingly as I am.'

The men around the fire laughed again. Anne peeked around the side of the tree and saw the man who had just spoken taking a regal bow, pretending to be king.

'There! I spy her!' cried one of the campers. The men turned and a few took a step in her direction. There was no use hiding. Anne stepped out from behind the tree. She kept her hand on the bull's backside, ready to strike.

'Halt!' she called out, summoning up her most authoritative voice, though she feared it sounded weak and reedy, hungry and tired as she was, and thirsty, and with the hoarseness that had clung to it since her execution. 'Don't come another step closer, or I'll set my beast on you!' She raised her hand up from the bull's backside and held it in place, ready to smack.

''Tis a woman!' called out a camper.

'Whoa, whoa, my good lady,' Simon cautioned, and she saw he was the stoutest of the men, short but powerfully built. He held his hands out in front of him. 'We mean no harm.'

'How do I know that?' replied Anne. 'You come upon me in the woods, a band of men, drinking and carousing. What am I supposed to think?' She raised her hand behind the bull, the threat of her slap visible to all the encamped men. 'Don't think I won't do it,' she added, through gritted teeth. 'Stay where you are.'

'My lady,' Simon said, ''twas you who came upon us.'

'Are you lost?' called out one of the men. He was tall and thin, with a goodly smile.

'Are you a spirit?' called out the man who'd spoken of ghosts. He wore a friar's habit.

And the man nearest the fire, who was turning the large pike on the spit, asked, 'Would you like something to eat?' The fat from the fish popped and crackled as it dripped in the fire. She could smell the roasting flesh. She was famished. She set her hand down gently on the bull's backside.

'I would,' she replied.

'You can dine with us, fair lady,' said the cook. 'We won't bother you. For don't we all have mothers and sisters, and some of us daughters? We know better than to take advantage of a lost woman in the woods. We may not be gentlemen, but we are gentle in our ways.'

'Why are you camped here in the woods?' Anne demanded, her hand still resting on the bull's backside. 'These woods aren't yours to camp in. Haven't you homes to return to?'

'My lady,' replied Simon, 'have you not heard of encamped men, who wander the woods and live off the land? We have no money to pay our rent, no crops to harvest, no hearth to call home. 'Tis nature not the right of every man? We live here, off the land, and move from place to place, collecting what we can along the way.'

'You're thieves, then,' said Anne, raising her hand above the bull's backside again, ready to strike. She'd heard of bands of men who took to the woods and robbed nobles as they rode through, kidnapping their women and children, holding them for ransoms, sometimes defiling them.

'Aye, yes,' Simon answered, 'but you needn't fear us. We won't hurt you, my lady. We only take from those that can spare it, and we don't kidnap or touch a woman in a way she doesn't want. We can see that you're lost, and hungry. You can dine with us. You can tie your bull up yonder.' He nodded to a tree by their encampment.

'The bull stays with me,' Anne replied. Her stomach cramped with hunger. If she didn't eat, she wasn't sure she'd make it back to London. These men seemed scurrilous and were of low class, but how often had Anne been wrong about men in the past? How often had she credited noblemen with more gentleness than they possessed? Perhaps these men truly were charitable. 'I'll join you,' she said, stepping forward and grabbing the bull by the ring in his nose. 'But,' she added, 'if you try anything, *anything*, untoward, I shall set my beast on you all.' The men looked at each other. Anne could see the worry in their faces. 'He is powerfully strong, and has gored many,' she embellished. 'He'll do whatever I command him to.'

Simon bowed. 'As you would have it, madam. Here is a place where you can sit and dine, and your bull can stand beside you,' he said, gesturing to a flat rock next to the fire.

Anne walked towards the rock, the bull following her obediently. 'Does he have a name?' asked one of the campers. Like all the men here, he wore shabby, threadbare clothes. He clutched a small cap in his hands, which he must have doffed in deference to having a woman in his presence.

Anne considered what name she could give the beast. 'Zeus,' she replied, for hadn't that been Europa's white bull, a god disguised as a beast?

'Ah,' said the man. 'And are ye Europa?'

'What was that?' Anne asked, sure she'd misheard him.

'Like the myth,' the man continued. ''Tis a story my good mother, God rest her soul, used to tell around the hearth at night: the god who transformed himself into a beast to steal away the woman he admired from beneath her father's nose.'

'Your mother must have been an educated woman,' Anne said.

'Aye, she was,' the man said, looking away from her as he spoke. 'She served in the house of a noble lady, who taught her many a tale and legend, but then that good lady died in the birthing bed, and my mother came home to us. She wasn't able to find work again, and we grew even poorer, though she shared with us the stories she'd learned in that rich woman's house, until she died herself some years later.' The man quieted, suddenly bashful.

'Oh, my condolences,' Anne said, feeling bad for the man and his woeful tale.

She settled herself upon the flat rock. The cook cut a slab of meat off the fish, put it on a scrap of fabric, and carried it to her. She took it gratefully. 'My lady,' he said, ducking his head as he walked backwards away from her.

How odd, Anne thought, that these men approach me with courtly manners. And for a moment she thought that maybe they *were* the lost knights of Arthur's round table, of Camelot, and maybe she was Queen Guinevere, returned to rule them in glory in the absence of her husband and her courtly lover: a woman ready to take the reins of power into her own hands and lead a people into greatness.

As Anne ate, the men carried on their conversations and feasting, sometimes casting a glance her way, or asking her a question. One passed around a leather pouch filled with wine, which Anne chugged from, causing the men to shout in appreciation. After an hour, Anne found herself full, warm, and pleasantly relaxed from the wine. The bull stayed near her, though he had wandered closer to the river to graze on the weeds growing there. His white hide shone in the moonlight.

'My lady,' said Simon, when the conversation lulled and the men sat back sleepily, the light from the campfire colouring their faces devilish hues, 'who are you?'

''Tis no business of yours,' Anne replied.

'How did you come to wander in these woods, then?' Simon persisted.

'I could ask the same of you.' Anne shooed a mosquito away from her neck.

'You have, madam, and I have answered you.'

Anne contemplated what story to spin for these men. 'Tell yourselves whatever tale you want,' she said. 'Maybe I am a wife, fleeing her husband with a bull to sell at market so I can hop on a boat to France and join my lover abroad.'

'Oooooh,' said one of the men. 'Scandalous!'

'Leave it to the French to steal our women with their deviant carnal acts,' added another.

Ah yes, Anne thought, the canard of the French pervert. She'd been accused of being a French pervert herself, having spent her formative years in France. Anne of the loose tongue, the courtiers had joked, and they hadn't meant she was a gossip. Imagine what she could do with that tongue, what French tricks she'd learned, imagine where on the king's body she might lick and tease. As though the French had invented fellatio, when all knew it was an act common in every peasant's home in England.

'Maybe,' Anne continued, 'I'm a nun, forced out of home and hearth by the closing of my convent, wandering the countryside with my only companion, this bull.'

'Booooo,' the men replied, shaking their heads disapprovingly.

''Tis a right shame, the closing of the nunneries and abbeys. 'Tisn't right,' the friar said, and Anne wondered if he found himself here, encamped with this group of thieves, because his own monastery had been dissolved.

'We all know what a virgin nun would do with a bull,' said another camper, standing and thrusting his hips suggestively.

The men laughed.

'That's enough,' reprimanded Simon, looking at his men sternly.

Anne leaned forward, pleased to have these men's rapt attention. 'Maybe I *am* a ghost,' she said, 'come to haunt and bother.'

'Whose ghost?' asked the friar, across the fire.

'Whose do you think?' Anne asked. 'I'm certainly not Guinevere.'

'Maybe you're a woman who was dishonoured, found yourself

with child and drowned yourself in this river, and now you're roaming the woods searching for the lad that did you wrong,' said the friar.

'Perhaps,' said Anne. 'Though 'twould be a sad woman who wouldn't know what herbs to take to shake a babe loose from her womb, or who to ask to get them.'

The men nodded, for surely they'd heard of the knowledge that women passed among themselves, of keeping and casting off babes.

'I also don't like to get wet,' Anne added.

'I bet,' chortled one of the men. The friar shot him a scolding look.

'Maybe you're the ghost of a child bride, held by the lord of these lands, ill-used and left to die in childbirth,' said the cook.

The men grew silent. How many of them had seen girls married off before they'd had their first courses, abused by wealthier men and discarded when their little bodies could take no more?

Anne contemplated for a moment. 'Do I look like a child to you?' she asked.

'No, no,' the men grumbled.

At last Simon piped up. 'I was in London just yesterday, doing a bit of mending work to earn a few pence, and I heard a rumour of a ghost sighted at the Tower.'

Anne caught her breath.

'I see I've piqued your interest, my lady,' Simon continued. 'They say 'twas the ghost of the great whore Anne Boleyn, that incestuous lady who lay with her own brother. They say she returned to haunt the Tower, and to seek vengeance on the jailer there. My lady, could that ghost be you?'

'Do I look like the dead queen to you?' Anne asked Simon. Her voice wavered as she spoke. That the rumour of her sighting at the Tower had reached this commoner concerned her. Word of her sighting must also have reached Henry, who would be on high alert; her task would be trickier.

Simon stood. 'How would I know, madam? Do you think I keep company with royalty?'

The men around the campfire laughed, and Simon wandered into the woods to relieve himself. Anne sat back, wondering if the questioning was over. The men began other discussions among themselves, though she noticed the friar eyeing her, his gaze lingering on her silk collar. She clucked her tongue and held out her hand to the bull, who joined her by the fire, huffing a breath that warmed the side of her face.

Later, the encampment settled down to sleep, each man balling up a jacket or spare shirt beneath his head to make a pillow, some spreading thin blankets on the ground to lie on. Anne chose a grassy spot set back from the fire. She put an arm under her head and wrapped her cloak tightly around herself, pulling up the hood to shield her face from the chilly night air. Simon had lent her a rope, and she'd tied the bull to a nearby tree. As she drifted off, she thought she saw a man, dressed in green boughs, darting between the trees of the woods. Oh, she thought, a Jack o' the Green! And this brought her half-asleep mind to the May Day celebration she'd attended the day before her arrest. She drifted off, remembering that last happy day.

Hours later, in the middle of the night, she woke to a man's hand pressed over her mouth. Her hood was tangled around her face, her vision obscured, but she could smell fishiness on his fingers.

'Stay where you are and don't make a sound,' the man growled.

24

The Witch

Anne thrashed her head, attempting to dislodge the man's hand. As her hood slid to the side, she could see the man was Simon. His breath stank of alcohol and his eyes were glassy.

'Hold still, you vile whore!' he demanded, his voice barely above a whisper. Anne supposed he didn't want to wake his fellow campers, who might not look kindly on his violating the wandering woman they'd taken in with promises of safety.

Anne squirmed beneath him, but his weight was heavy. He straddled her body, pinning her arms down with his legs. 'Get off me,' she mouthed into his hand, glaring at him. Her eyes shot to the campfire, which had burned down to embers in the night. The men slept soundly around it, kept in a deep slumber by exhaustion and wine. Above them, the full moon shone through the leaves of trees, casting a pale light.

'I just want to see,' Simon said. 'I want to see if you're the great whore.' With his free hand, he began to claw at the silk collar around her neck. A few of the stitches Ethel had sewn popped. This encouraged Simon, who pulled harder, using both hands to prise at the collar.

'Get off me!' Anne shouted. Then, 'Help! Help!' She could see a few of the bodies around the campfire shift.

Where was Zeus? She wished she'd tied him up closer to her. From a few yards away, the bull snorted. Anne tipped her head back. She could see the beast tugging against his rope, head down, horns forward. She clucked her tongue, calling him to her. The bull tugged harder against his rope, straining against the trunk of the tree, which creaked and moaned. The rope rubbed against the tree's rough bark, where, Anne imagined, it must be starting to fray. Simon didn't seem to notice; he was busy pulling at her collar.

She turned her face towards the campfire. 'Help!' she called again. Simon struck her, hard, against her cheek. The metallic taste of blood filled her mouth.

'Shut your hole!' he spat. 'I must see. I must see if you're her, if you're the dead queen.' He yanked harder at her collar, which gave way, finally tearing from her neck. Simon yanked his hands away at the sight of Anne's scar. In his surprise he sat back, his weight heavy on her hips. She stared at him, her anger rising.

'Look what you did, you sodden-witted bag of guts,' she said. 'Look.'

'I—' began Simon, but he didn't finish his sentence. He reached a hand down and ran a dirty finger over the thick pink scar. She hated the feel of it, this criminal's hand on her most intimate mark.

'What did you think you were going to find?' Anne demanded. She could hear Zeus huff and strain against his tether. If she could keep Simon talking, surely the bull would break free and come to her aid.

Simon sat silent, transfixed by the scar. When he found his words, he said, 'I want a ransom.'

'Excuse me?' Anne asked. 'Do I look like I have money? I'm the living ghost of the dead queen, with only the gown on my back and a single bull as my companion. Where do you suppose I keep my purse?'

'Others will pay for you,' spoke Simon. He dug his knees harder into Anne's arms. She could feel bruises forming there.

'The king's men. They'll pay to have you arrested so they can kill you again, so they can burn you as a witch, for who else but a witch could come back from the dead?' Simon turned his attention to her bodice, pulling at its front. 'I'll check you for a witch's mark. My mother told me witches have a brand on their bellies, put there by the devil, so they can nurse their demon offspring.'

Anne panicked. The diadem she was saving for Elizabeth and the last of the coins she'd stolen from the Tower mint were in her bodice. She didn't want this greedy, drunken criminal to get them. She wished Alice were here with her dagger, fast reflexes and bravery, with her strength. Though Alice wouldn't have been foolish enough to make camp with a band of strange men in the forest.

Anne tipped her head back again, clucking to the bull, who tugged harder at his rope. Simon freely stuck his hands into Anne's bodice, his rough fingers scratching against her breasts.

'Aha!' he shouted, pulling out a pound. 'My ransom!'

By now several men had risen from the fire and were walking towards them to see what the commotion was.

'She's the dead queen!' Simon shouted to them. 'She's the dead queen and a witch and I've found money in her bosoms!'

'What?' shouted one of the men, looking on in horror at the scene before him. Anne saw the friar fall to his knees and cross himself, aghast.

'I'm telling you she's the dead queen, come back to haunt this good country!' Simon shouted.

'You're mad,' replied one of the men from the fire. 'And drunk.'

Anne clucked her tongue again and the bull strained harder against his rope.

'The bull!' another of the men from the campfire shouted. ''Tis about to break its tether!'

Simon looked over at the beast just as the rope snapped and

the bull charged towards him. He scampered off Anne and ran towards the river. The bull chased him, darting between trees with impressive agility. Anne rose and brushed the dirt off her back, tried to straighten and retighten her bodice, to tuck her treasures back into it. She grabbed her collar from the ground, shook it to dislodge the bits of dead leaf that clung to it, this swaddling cloth, this link to her daughter. Elizabeth, she thought. Elizabeth. She needed to get out of here so that she could help Elizabeth.

At the riverbank, the bull caught up to Simon and stabbed one of his long horns into the man's bowels. Simon screamed in terror and pain. The bull threw the man into the air with a flick of his powerful head. For a moment, Simon arced upward, as though he had taken flight, then he fell, landing in the river, his head smashing against a large river rock. In the moonlight, all could see his limp body, face down, bleeding from the head and stomach, lifeless. The bull huffed and pawed at the ground, turning to look at the men around the fire, who stood petrified.

Anne saw her chance. 'Don't move,' she said. 'Or he'll strike again.' The men looked at her. She could feel their eyes linger on her scar, on whatever they could see of it in the moonlight.

She clucked her tongue to call the bull back to her. He trotted over obediently. These men can see who I am, she thought. Simon had announced it, and they could see the scar on her neck. There was no use trying to lie or hide. But they were afraid, and she could use that to her advantage.

'I am the dead queen,' she proclaimed, loudly, to the men. And when they stared at her, dumbstruck, unmoving, 'Well, bow down to your queen, before I set my beast upon you too.'

The men fell to their knees, bowing their heads, a few muttering, 'Sorry, madam' or 'Your Majesty.'

Anne knew she needed to flee the camp. She had these men in her thrall at the moment, but there were more of them than her, and Simon was right that the dead queen resurrected would fetch any one of them a high price. She put a hand on the bull's withers, and as though he'd been trained to do so, he bent down. She stood on her tiptoes, hiked her skirts, threw one leg over the beast's broad back, and settled herself there. The bull rose. The rope that had tied him to the tree still hung around his neck. Anne took it up, like a rein. She clucked her tongue and the bull took a few steps forward. She took a last look at the men, bowed down before her.

'If you follow me,' she said, 'I'll curse you so your privy members shrivel and fall off.'

Then she kicked the bull in the flanks with both heels and galloped into the woods.

Anne had always been a strong rider. She'd ridden as a child at Hever Castle. All three Boleyn children had. She'd chased George around the castle grounds, each child on their own pony. Hers had been named Cinnamon, for her chestnut-coloured coat and mane. Anne's auburn hair, lighter in childhood, had been only a shade different from the pony's, so when riding her she'd looked like she was somehow related to her, like she was her human foal. George's pony was white and he'd called him George, after himself. In this way, they'd each been twinned in their small steeds. They'd galloped through woods and meadows, practising jumping over small brooks and downed trees, scaring foxes out of their dens.

In France, she'd been called *la chasseuse*, 'the huntress', for her agility on a steed and her adeptness at sport. She'd felled many a deer and could shoot her bow from the back of her mount, gripping the animal with her strong thighs to hold herself steady as she drew back the bowstring and aimed. And of course, with Henry she had hunted frequently. It had been one of their shared pastimes. He loved that she was as skilled as he at riding and hunting, though she had to be careful not to outshine him. She had to intentionally miss shots so that the king himself might pierce the chest or neck of a buck, whom his servants would then chase down through the woods and slaughter. She had to slow her pace on her steed so as not to outrun him. She had to come in second, always. All this she was willing to do because Henry was her king and her lord, because he professed to love her, because, together, they were changing the course of the history of England, prising it loose from the decadent, greedy hands of Rome. And because after a hunt, they would fall into bed, exhilarated, and give in to passion.

Anne could remember, early in their courtship, beating the king at the card game primero. The deck they'd played with had been purchased in France, and the face cards depicted kings, queens and jacks holding ornately patterned masquerade masks: bird masks for the spades, animals for the clubs, the four seasons for the diamonds, and fearsome demon masks for the hearts. Anne had won hand after hand, knocking out one opponent at their card table after another, until just she and the king remained. When she beat him, he'd risen from the table roaring in anger, but then picked her up and kissed her passionately. But when the same thing happened a year later, his annulment to Katherine stalled out, his temper shorter, he'd grabbed Anne's wrist and squeezed so forcefully that she hadn't been able to wear her favourite bracelet for a week because of the swelling. From then on, she'd let the king win, though she'd done her best to conceal that she was doing so, for it also angered him to know that others were throwing the game.

Anne couldn't shake the thought of the Jack o' the Green she'd imagined she'd seen back at the camp. It had looked just like the one at the May Day celebration. Could that really have been only a few weeks ago? It had been her last day of freedom, though she didn't know it then. Often Henry dominated the tiltyard at these festivals, but since his jousting accident in January, he'd had to abstain from competition, even from riding. His leg bothered him constantly, the wound he'd sustained in the accident refusing to heal completely, reopening after it had seemed healed, festering, weeping bloody pus. It stank and caused him to limp. Already, his waist was expanding from lack of exercise. Anne had stopped riding too, so as not to perturb him, though this didn't bother her, as she was still recovering from the strain of the last miscarriage. She was weak and needed the rest.

The two had arrived separately at the May Day celebration, but Henry sat next to her under the royal awning at the tiltyard as they watched the men of court ride at top speed towards each other, splintering their wooden lances on their opponents' armour. As a woman, Anne had never jousted, though she'd often wondered about the sensation, about the thrill of charging a friend turned combatant, of knocking him off his horse, of riding victorious about the yard, tossing a favour to a young woman who would swoon and sigh. It had been at a joust, after all, that Henry had first publicly declared his affections for Anne. Having just knocked a courtier – Anne couldn't remember who – off his horse, Henry had ridden over to her and pointed at a badge he wore on his chest of a flaming heart, encircled with the words *Declare je nos*: Declare I dare not. Anne had been seated near Queen Katherine, and the old queen had rolled her eyes at the encounter, brushing Anne off as one of Henry's many mistresses, quickly used and quickly discarded.

At the May Day celebration, Anne and Henry watched the jousting. They watched the May Day Queen, the twelve-year-old daughter of a courtier, a comely enough girl, get crowned with a wreath of flowers by last year's May Day Queen, the daughter of some other courtier, and process to the chapel yard. There, a dozen young girls had danced with ribbons around the maypole, and Anne had imagined Elizabeth joining in this tradition in a few years' time. Just as, in another ten, Elizabeth would surely be crowned the May Day Queen.

This year's Jack o' the Green had unnerved Anne. There was always a Green Man of some sort at these celebrations, usually a jester dressed in green clothes, often with green boughs woven into a crown that he wore on his head as he juggled and danced. This Green Man, this Jack, was covered in boughs. He wore them not just upon his head, but sewn to all parts of his clothing, so that he appeared to be a shaggy, moving shrub, a pine tree come to life. From his pine crown, a cascade of shaggy-needled branches hung down like a veil surrounding his head, front and back, so that only his eyes were visible. Anne could see that his face, beneath the boughs, had been painted green, with some type of paste. His hands, which extended now and then from the branches covering his arms to present a marigold or primrose to a little girl or young maid, were also painted green. Many times, Anne caught the Jack staring at her. She tried to keep an eye on him, but he'd disappear from view, then seem to reappear out of nowhere, in the corner of her vision. She'd turn to find him, and he'd jump and strike a frightful pose, arms up and hands held as claws, or spin in a circle on his toes and shimmy. Once, he simply held a finger to his evergreen mouth: *Shhhhh, be quiet.*

Anne was about to find Henry and mention the Green Man to him when she noticed the king had abruptly left, and a lady-in-waiting informed her that he'd departed for Westminster with Henry Norris. She didn't know then that Henry would spend the journey interrogating Norris about an affair with her, about dead men's shoes, trying to prise a confession out of him. She didn't know that a day earlier, Thomas Cromwell had forced a confession out of Mark Smeaton, her musician, of a supposed affair. Later, she'd wonder what Smeaton was talking about. She would never step outside her marriage to the king, and if she did, it would certainly not be with a lowly lutist, an entertainer put in her chambers to amuse her with pleasing melodies. She wondered what Cromwell had done to elicit his confession. A hot poker to the skin on the man's inner thighs, creeping ever upward, towards regions more sensitive? Or perhaps he had threatened the man's family? For surely Smeaton had a mother or sister somewhere who could be hauled out of her home and beaten. Or had he simply told Smeaton that he already had evidence of his crimes, and convinced him that he'd done something he hadn't, promised that the punishment would be less severe, less painful, if he confessed now? Cromwell was, after all, a masterful persuader, a tactician, a calculating and manipulative man. Though she'd come to loathe him during her trial, she couldn't help admiring his cunning.

Henry's departure from the May Day celebration hadn't bothered Anne because she didn't know about Mark Smeaton's confession, because she didn't know the king was interrogating Norris. She didn't know that the next day, she'd be arrested on charges of treason and adultery and brought to the Tower. She didn't know the court families who most detested her, the Courtenays, Carews and Cheneys, were already coaching Jane Seymour to take her place. She didn't know that, a month earlier, Henry had been asking about ways to annul his marriage to her, then had abandoned the idea, thinking it too time-consuming, opting for a speedier alternative. Knowing none of these things, Anne hadn't been troubled by Henry's sudden departure. But as her ladies undressed her for bed that evening, her mind wandered back to the Green Man, posing like a lion for her, shimmying and dancing aggressively, shushing her. She'd have to find out which jester had worn the costume, she thought as she climbed into her bed, and demand that he be punished for insolence.

Now, racing through the forest on the back of a bull, crouched down so as not to be whipped in the face by low-hanging branches, Anne was again unnerved by the Jack o' the Green. Why had she seen, or imagined she'd seen, him here, in the woods, just hours before she was attacked by Simon? Anne wondered if this Jack was a real man or some kind of woodland sprite, come to warn her of danger. While she'd never gone in for magic or superstition, in this new world, in this new life in which she lived past death, she wasn't sure of anything.

The bull raced faster and faster through the forest, and Anne felt herself grow weary from the ride. She hadn't eaten since her fish supper the evening before. As the sky lightened, she felt her legs wobble with hunger and fatigue. Just when she thought she'd fall from the beast, he slowed and then stopped in a clearing by a pond and knelt to let her down.

25

The Sword

'Good boy,' Anne said to the bull as she dismounted and patted his back. Then, remembering the name she'd called him at the campsite, she said, 'Good boy, Zeus.'

The creature huffed in response and bowed his head. In her hand, she clutched Elizabeth's swaddling cloth that Simon had ripped off her neck. She wished she could hold Elizabeth now, shelter her from whatever cruelties were brewing at court. She examined the cloth. There were a few threads left in the fabric – some from when she'd sewn it on by the Thames, some from when Ethel had mended it in the fens – that looked long enough to tie together. She wrapped the soft cloth around her neck – a comfort, immediately– and, with some effort, tied three sets of knots that she hoped would hold it in place.

'Are you thirsty, boy?' Anne asked. The bull turned his placid eyes on her – could this be the same wild beast that slew a man just hours before? – then wandered over to the pond and drank freely.

Anne looked around, trying to work out where she was. How far had she and the bull travelled? She wasn't sure. She was still near the river. As they'd bounded through the forest, she'd kept the river to their right side, travelling south, just as George had directed when he'd ferried her out of the fens. She wondered what Alice was doing, and whether she'd found the gems Anne had hidden in her boots, and what reaction she'd had to them. She imagined Alice shaking her head at the generous gift. 'Too much,' Alice might think. But then, Anne thought, Alice might hold the gems to her chest and whisper a word of thanks. Anne liked to think of that, of Alice happy, of Alice thinking of her. She wished Alice were with her now.

Anne was startled from her thoughts by a loud bellow. The bull had raised his head from the water, having drunk his fill, and was gazing into the middle of the pond intently. He let out a second cry, as though he were calling to something stranded there. 'Shhhhh,' she said, trying to quiet him, lest his loudness draw another gang of murderous peasants to them. She shielded her eyes from the sun and gazed into the pond. Something glinted in the water. At first, Anne thought it might be a fish, though it appeared to be unmoving. Not a fish then; probably some piece of rubbish. Even so, she was curious. The water didn't look deep. Anne thought she could wade out to the shining object and investigate it further. It could be something she could put to use.

Anne sat beside the bull and slid off her slippers. Their ornate embroidery was barely visible beneath the layers of river and fen muck, dust from the journey, and, under all that, Anne's own blood. She set the soiled slippers aside, then peeled off her red stockings, untying them from the garters she wore on her thighs. She'd chosen red, the colour of the martyr, because she knew her stockings, and the red kirtle that matched them, would be visible when she knelt on the scaffold at her execution. And hadn't she, reformer of a corrupt church, redistributor of ill-begotten church wealth to the poor, been executed as much for her religious ideals as for anything else? The very definition of martyrdom. She laid her stockings atop her slippers. Finally, she untied and removed the summer cloak. Standing, Anne hoisted her smock, kirtle and gown so that she was naked to just above the knee.

Gingerly, she stepped into the water. Though it was a bit murky, its coolness was a relief to the blisters that swelled in the arches of her feet. Anne realised, as well, her own heat, a wave of fever that had clung to her since the encampment, dampening her smock with sweat. She waded out a few feet. Behind her, the bull snorted and pawed at the ground. A pair of ducks, floating on the other side of the pond, eyed her warily. She supposed their nest was nearby, or else they'd be lifting off in flight. They must be protecting their babes, she thought. She waded out further. The sun had risen above the trees by now, and it warmed her face and neck. The pond increased in depth, but not by much. Halfway to whatever shimmered in its centre, the water was up to Anne's calves. Her feet sank into the muck on the bottom of the pond. The silt oozed between her toes, its sliminess like afterbirth. She held back the urge to vomit.

As she neared the shining object, the water rose to her knees. She could make out what she thought was a blade, though by now the sun reflected blindingly off the object so she couldn't see it clearly. Just a little further, she thought.

In the pond's centre, the water reached her thighs and soaked the bottom of her gown, kirtle and smock, still clutched in her left hand. A school of minnows shot past her, darting to the edge of the pond, chasing after a cloud of gnats that hovered above the water's surface. The pair of ducks on the other side of the pond reared up, quacked, and flew away. They won't go far, Anne thought. She was close to the object now and could see it more clearly. It did have a blade, which was partially submerged in the mucky bottom of the pond. At the top of the blade, a metal hilt, and in the middle of the hilt, a large, wine-coloured topaz. So it was a sword, then, probably tossed into the water by a knight, vanquished and dying, or having just slaughtered someone and seeking to hide the evidence. A sword would be very useful indeed, for didn't Anne want to kill the king, her husband? And even if she didn't use the sword for that, it would be useful for self-defence as she finished her journey to London.

With her free hand, Anne grabbed the hilt of the sword and pulled. It wobbled in the mucky pond bottom but didn't dislodge. She'd need two hands. Reluctantly, she let go of her skirts. They floated atop the water around her, like an airy nest. With both hands, she yanked the sword, harder this time. She needn't have. The sword came out so easily that Anne stumbled back with the force of her pull, landing on her bottom in the pond, submerging herself in the cold water up to the top of her bodice, startled from the chill and grasping the sword firmly in both hands.

When Anne got back to the shore, Zeus was waiting for her, looking impatient. She sat down next to him. She was soaking wet, her clothing drenched. The bull nudged her affectionately. 'Good boy,' she said, scratching under his chin.

She examined the sword. For having been fished out of a pond, it wasn't in bad shape. Its steel blade was sharp and clean. Its hilt was a bit tarnished, but that was only an indication that it was inlaid with silver. She turned the sword over. On the other side of its blade she saw some words inscribed, but they were written in Welsh, a language she didn't read or speak. 'I suppose the inscription says "Take me up" or "Cast me back",' she joked with Zeus, speaking to him as though he weren't a bull and could understand her. 'And I am King Arthur, finding the sword in a mucky pond instead of the misty lake surrounding Avalon?' It was a silly idea. Anne was no more King Arthur than she was the ghost of Guinevere, even if her enemies had called her the woman king, seeking to insult her. Henry had been infatuated with the tales of Arthur, as had his father before him, trying to remake Camelot at Hampton Court, paying vast sums to scholars who compiled elaborate family trees linking Henry's own lineage to the long-ago king, who, as far as Anne was concerned and contrary to

Henry's beliefs, was probably the stuff of legends and not a real person. In any case, in the tales of Arthur, a beautiful woman's hand rose out of the lake to give him the sword, and Anne had fetched this sword herself.

Anne sat at the pond for a while, drying out in the sun's warm rays. She was hungry and had nothing left to eat, and she hadn't slept more than a few hours the previous night before Simon accosted her. Eventually, hunger and fatigue combined to pull her into a deep and dreamless slumber. Curled up around the sword, Anne slept until midday. When she woke, Zeus was still there, though she hadn't tied him up before drifting off. The bull nudged her, as if to say, 'Get up, madam, you have promises to keep.' She sat and brushed herself clean. The gown she'd borrowed from Alice was mostly dry.

Anne stood and picked up the heavy sword. Would she be able to swing it at the critical moment, when she found Henry? This was a twofold question. Would she be able to physically swing the sword, and would she be able to summon the resolve to slay her own husband, her king, whom she had loved so dearly? Better to worry about physicality first. Anne lifted the sword above her head. Her arms shook with its heft.

She practised swinging the sword by the pond shore, hoisting it over her head and bringing it slashing down through the air. Where would she need to strike Henry to kill him? Obviously beheading him would be the most effective, but she wasn't sure she had the strength to do so. One decisive blow to his back or chest would be a good start. Or she could pierce him with the sharp blade, run him through. She practised lunging forward with the blade, forcing it through the imagined heart of her husband.

'Die, you pizzle-brained knave,' she said, jaw clenched, and the spite with which she spoke surprised her.

As she slashed and practised, a young rabbit hopped out of its hole just a few feet from her. She froze. So did the rabbit, realising its mistake. Anne felt her stomach growl at the sight of it. She'd never killed a creature with a sword before. With arrows, yes, and she'd slit the throats of deer to put them out of their misery when arrows had injured but not killed them. Could she even catch the rabbit? Wouldn't it flee back to its underground home once she moved towards it?

With one fluid motion, she swung the sword, closing her eyes and bringing the blade down to the ground. When she cracked her eyelids, she could see that she had hit the poor creature, splitting it in half. Well, she thought, at least it hadn't suffered long. She wiped her sword clean on her kirtle and sat by the pond with the slain rabbit, whose heat warmed her hands. Since she had no knife to clean the creature, she used her hands to pull off its skin, and to scoop out its slippery innards. It was hard work, and she didn't do it particularly well. With no fire on which to cook, she ate the rabbit raw. The meat was gamey, wet and chewy, yet she devoured every morsel she could, picking muscle and tendons off the rabbit's bones with her teeth while Zeus grazed at the pond's edge.

When she finished, the bull bowed before her, in invitation. She rinsed the rabbit's blood off her hands and face at the pond's edge, put her stockings, slippers and cloak back on, climbed atop the beast's back, and settled herself. Lacking a scabbard for her sword, she slid it against her back, in the tight space between her gown and the bodice of her kirtle, so that most of the blade lay flat against her spine, while the upper third and hilt stuck out behind her head. She kicked Zeus and clucked her tongue, and he trotted away from the pond, back into the woods along the river, heading towards London.

As Zeus trotted, Anne thought back to the events that had befallen her since waking in the arrow chest in the Tower, ticking through each day in her mind, and realised it had been seven days since she was executed, a full week. Henry was an impetuous man, and she knew he'd be busy planning his marriage to Jane Seymour, or having someone else, probably Cromwell, do it for him. Anne needed to get back to London quickly. Her detour to the fens had cost her precious time. She fingered her silk collar, and wondered where Elizabeth was. Had Henry brought her to Whitehall for the impending wedding, or chosen to keep her with Lady Bryan at Hatfield, out of sight and mind? Soon enough, he'd be attempting to sire an heir with Jane Seymour and, Anne knew, having legislation written to declare her Elizabeth a bastard.

During their trial at the Tower, George had been handed a slip of paper by Thomas Cromwell, which contained an allegation about a statement Anne had supposedly made to George while struggling to conceive a boy, and which Cromwell claimed to have prised from George's wife, Jane. Cromwell handed George the paper, on which was written Jane's supposed confession of the terrible thing Anne had said, and instructed him to review it and say 'yes' or 'no' as to the truth of the allegation, the truth of Anne's terrible words, but not to read the paper aloud.

It was such a clever trick. Cromwell knew as well as Anne that George couldn't resist being the centre of attention, sharing scandalous gossip, getting a laugh. George looked over the paper for a moment, reading it silently, then, unable to help himself, stood and read it aloud. The paper accused Anne of having said to George that the king had neither the skill nor the virility to satisfy a woman, and therefore he was unable to father a son. The paper also said that Anne and George had joked about the king's poor fashion choices and bad poetry. George read these accusations aloud with a wily grin, to many gasps and giggles among the spectators in the Tower's great hall, and Anne could see the jury harden and turn against him. Cromwell smiled, knowing he had won.

Had the king been a bad lover, impotent and lacking skill,

unable to please, let alone impregnate, Anne? When they had finally married, Henry was forty-one years old, and Anne knew that some men, at this age, lost the ability to perform. But that hadn't been an issue. His passion for her was bottomless. They made love often, seven years of chaste courting fuelling a pent-up release of pleasure that delighted and exhausted them both. She'd become pregnant quickly, and given birth to Elizabeth less than a year after they exchanged private vows in Dover. And after Elizabeth's birth, she'd been pregnant three more times, though all three times the babes were lost. So it wasn't getting Anne pregnant that was the problem; it was keeping her pregnant.

As the pregnancies came and went, Henry's lovemaking became more forceful and less joyful, more businesslike and less pleasureful. He took his duty to sire a male heir seriously, visiting her chambers with frequency, performing his husbandly role. That type of pressure might make any man, especially one nearing his mid-forties, buckle occasionally, and when Henry did, which was really only a handful of times, Anne at first tried to comfort him.

'My love,' she'd said, 'surely 'tis of no concern.' He paced furiously around her chamber, naked, his half-erect penis flopping against his thigh. 'Come back to bed. We can enjoy each other's bodies in other ways.'

At this, he'd glared at her, marched back to the bed, and smacked her across the face before storming out of the room, still naked, to the groomsmen who were undoubtedly waiting for him with a silk robe and pair of slippers. The next time Henry lost his erection Anne kept her mouth shut and eyes averted. Even so, he slapped her across her breasts and buttocks, and spat at her before leaving. This pattern continued.

Had Anne joked with George about the king's impotence? She couldn't recall. She'd certainly joked about his clothing. The king had a penchant for dressing up in odd costumes – a Turkish sultan, an Egyptian prince, Joseph with his multicoloured coat — and forcing others in his vicinity to play along that they didn't realise the ridiculously costumed king was, in fact, the king, and to feign surprise when he revealed himself — a practice that Anne found childish and exhausting. She clearly remembered mocking the king's costumes to George, bowing deeply as she pretended to be the king pretending to be a sultan.

And while the king had many talents, writing poetry was not one of them. She remembered one awful Christmas poem he'd written where he rhymed *holly* with *ivy*, *hue* with *true*, and then finished with a couple of convoluted stanzas about giving his heart for ever to his mistress. Thomas Wyatt had snidely referred to the poem, which was titled 'Green Groweth the Holly', as 'Lean Groweth the Willy', and joked that it had made him unable to perform for Lady Wyatt for a solid month. Of course that was absurd, since Thomas Wyatt hated his wife anyway, and never lay with her. Anne had repeated this joke to George, and it was entirely possible that Jane had overheard. Perhaps Jane had confessed to hearing Anne joke about the king's clothing and poetry, and Cromwell had pushed her to add the other claim. It was likely Cromwell himself knew about the king's impotence, knew it was something sharp-tongued Anne might joke about to her brother.

Or perhaps Anne *had* mocked the king's virility. After he'd struck her, and then struck her again a second, third, fourth and fifth time, she'd been indignant. This was not how a queen ought to be treated. It was not how the mother of the next heir to the throne ought to be treated. Wasn't it just like a small man to strike a woman as punishment for his own incompetence? And Henry was small, Anne realised, no matter how tall his stature, no matter how many courtiers he fucked, no matter how many wives he married, no matter how many advisers he belittled and dismissed. He was a small man, forever living in his dead brother's shadow, forever trying to please the father who'd thought him silly, impetuous and incapable of leading, who'd forbidden him from marrying his dead brother's widow, so sure was he that Henry could never step into the vaunted Arthur's shoes.

Would Henry be more successful with Jane? Would his prick get and stay hard? Would he strike her, as he had struck Anne, if it did not?

Anne rode Zeus late into the evening, following the River Cam when it branched off the Great Ouse, then, after its terminus, travelling south through the woods and meadows of Essex, keeping the sun on her right as the day drew to a close. Finally, as evening fell, she rode the bull down a deserted road she hoped was heading towards London. The beast huffed and puffed as they rode, but marched on willingly, complicit in her mission. She patted his neck, whispered praises to him, let him stop here and there to nibble grass from the ditches that lined the road, to drink water from small brooks that trickled past.

It had been dark for many hours when the two crested a hill, from the top of which, in the distance, Anne could see the lighted windows and gate lamps of northern London.

26

A Great Grief

At daybreak, early, the sun barely risen, Anne woke nestled against the bull's soft, warm chest. By the time they'd taken sight of London, it must have been nearly midnight. She and the beast were so fatigued that they'd wandered into a ditch beside the road and lay down to sleep the four or five hours that remained before sunrise. She shivered and drew closer to him, pulling the summer cloak she'd borrowed from Alice tighter around herself, not that it did much good, made as it was from some thin fabric. Anne didn't know what kind. That was Cromwell's area of expertise, she thought groggily, who seemed to know everything about textiles, having so recently been a wool merchant. A wool merchant, advising the king. She scoffed at the absurdity of it.

She covered her face with the cloak's hood and tried to go back to sleep, but her mind stayed on Cromwell. Surely he'd be at Whitehall with Henry. Her greatest enemy, she'd thought Cromwell at the end, when he'd had her arrested, when he'd argued for her guilt at trial, when he'd shown up to witness her execution, certainly at Henry's bidding. Where had Henry been? The last time she saw him was before he rode away from the May Day festival with Norris, the day before her arrest. Henry hadn't shown his face at the Tower during her two-and-a-half-week imprisonment. He hadn't come to the trial at the Tower's great hall, to hear George call him impotent in front of all his courtiers.

He hadn't come to witness the execution of Anne's alleged lovers. He'd sent Archbishop Cranmer with an annulment for her to sign the day before her execution, and, when she'd refused to do so – not wanting to illegitimise her own daughter, not believing Cranmer's promises that if she signed she'd be sent to a nunnery instead of the scaffold, not caring, even if such promises were true, as she'd rather die than see Elizabeth removed from the line of succession – when she'd refused to sign the annulment, Cranmer granted one for Henry anyway, just as he had done for Henry's marriage to Katherine.

Her mean Aunt Elizabeth Boleyn, one of the detested ladies sent with her to the Tower to spy for the king, who'd never liked Anne, had delivered the news of the annulment to her smugly, saying, when asked, that the reason had been Anne's prior pre-contracted engagement to Henry Percy. Never mind that the king himself had cancelled that precontract because he wanted to court her, never mind the king himself had just three years earlier forced Henry Percy to testify that the precontract never even existed in the first place, so that Henry and Anne could wed. ''Twas your dalliance with Henry Percy, slut,' her Aunt Elizabeth had said. 'You reap what you deserve. And if that hadn't've been the reason, 'twould've been your whoring sister Mary's bedding of the king before you, that he lay with you both.' Her aunt had spat on the stone floor. 'Consanguinity and incest,' she'd continued, ''twould've been that would've voided your marriage, and no surprise there, your sister being as big a trollop as you, a whole family of whores.'

Henry hadn't shown up at her execution, either, but Cromwell was there. She'd walked past him on her way to the scaffold. He looked miserable, guilty and, even in the chilly mid-May temperature, hot. Cromwell often looked hot. He was a large, sweaty man, with the habit of wearing black velvet, no matter the season, in which he sweltered. He didn't look satisfied, as she'd expected he might, having served up to Henry exactly what he wanted: Anne gone so he could marry Jane; Anne gone and Henry not having to bother with her big mouth, her pushy attitude, her unending ideas, her miscarriages, her grief. The shot doe's neck slit without Henry having to get his hands dirty, without having to watch the animal suffer, limping and bleeding through the forest. A servant to do it for him. And Cromwell was an excellent servant. He'd served well and true. And yet at the execution he'd looked positively miserable, mopping his brow with a kerchief – was it also made of black velvet? That couldn't be – and avoiding looking at Anne as she was marched past him. She'd hoped some of her blood would spatter on him when she was beheaded, would stain and spoil his silly velvet. For what did men know about removing blood from fabric? Nothing. They knew how to draw blood, how to spill it, but they knew nothing of the blood that came from women, of menstrual blood, of the blood of childbirth, of the blood of babies lost. They'd never scrubbed a bloody undergarment in a stream when they were out riding and menstruation came early or unexpected.

When Anne first arrived at the English court, nearly fifteen years ago, Cromwell had mistaken her flirtatious behaviour and youthful hedonism for a lack of intelligence. He'd thought her frivolous, as educated as a courtier must be but not particularly clever. Then Henry had taken an interest in her, and as she and the king exchanged books and letters and stayed up for hours debating religion and philosophy, even Cromwell recognised her intellect. They were both reformers and, for a while, allies, but as they fought over the ends of those reforms, eventually they became adversaries.

The two had moved against each other again and again, strategically one-upping each other with feats of influence over the king, sometimes feuding in public. It was a game of strategy and cunning, one Anne thought she was winning. That was, until this April. Fed up with Cromwell's repeated attempts to direct the funds from the dissolution of the monasteries into the pockets of courtiers, Anne had her almoner, John Skip, preach a sermon on Passion Sunday about Queen Esther and King Ahasuerus. The sermon focused on the scheming and sinful behaviour of King Ahasuerus's adviser Haman, who pressured Ahasuerus to kill the Jewish people camped outside his city gates. Meanwhile, Ahasuerus's wife, Queen Esther, a secret Jew herself, convinced Ahasuerus not to kill the Jews, thus saving both the king from the damnation of committing murder and her people from certain death. It was clear to any who listened that Esther was meant to represent Anne, saintly in her quest to spend the vast wealth of the religious orders on education and hospitals for the people, and that Haman was Cromwell, the crooked adviser, encouraging the king to hoard that vast wealth instead.

In retrospect, Anne knew that she'd gone too far. John Skip's sermon had publicly humiliated Cromwell, and that had caused him not to cower, as she'd hoped, but rather to lash out, to work to oust her. She knew she'd gone too far, but Cromwell was under her skin, contradicting her, edging her out. He kept company with the imperial ambassador Eustace Chapuys, spy for Katherine's nephew Charles V, who Anne knew hated her. Chapuys was Charles V's eyes and ears at the court of the king who had cast aside his beloved aunt. Chapuys wasn't an old man – like Henry and Cromwell, he was only ten or fifteen years older than Anne – but he seemed old. He smelled perpetually of herbs used to treat aching joints, went to bed at sundown, and was unbelievably pious. Anne wasn't sure if he'd ever lain with a woman. She knew what he wrote about her, that he called her the concubine and the great whore in letters. A lady-in-waiting who'd recently been a courtier at Charles V's court in Brussels had told Anne that Chapuys reported back to the emperor that she was ugly and had a sallow complexion, and that she'd learned acts of sexual perversion while in France, with which she must have ensorcelled the king, for why else would he prefer an unattractive, flat-chested whore to Katherine of Aragon? Men like Chapuys knew how to take a woman down a few notches, how to aim below the belt. How to sit smugly sipping their wine before a comfortable fire and, in solemn voices, question whether women were really people, really had souls, really ought to even be mourned when they died in childbirth.

She wasn't sure why Cromwell enjoyed Chapuys's company. Sometimes the simplest explanation is the best, and she supposed that, like Chapuys, Cromwell might just hate women. Anne wasn't sure it was that simple, though. If Cromwell was just another woman hater, how to explain the pain on his face, the way he'd nervously mopped his brow as he watched his queen being marched to the scaffold for an execution he'd orchestrated and organised. Guilt, that was the emotion she'd seen in Cromwell from the scaffold. And Cromwell certainly didn't seem to hate women when he'd educated his daughters the same as his son, or when, broken-hearted, he showed no interest in remarrying after his wife died. And he didn't seem to hate women when Anne found him weeping in the Cloister Green at Hampton Court one autumn evening a couple of months after losing both his daughters to the sweating sickness. He'd wiped his eyes, embarrassed, and apologised. 'No, no,' Anne had said, 'yours is a great grief. Your sorrow is true.' Cromwell had smiled at her, grateful, and let out a final sob before patting her arm and walking back to whatever meeting with Henry awaited at that hour.

She supposed Cromwell would be at Whitehall. She supposed he was orchestrating Henry's wedding to Jane, just as he'd orchestrated Anne's execution, and her coronation before that. Just as he'd orchestrated Henry's annulment from Katherine, in the independent English church that Anne and Cromwell, then allies, had pushed Henry to take charge of. Cromwell, plain

Cromwell, with his broad, lumpy face and his pretender's black velvet clothes, was a man who could get things done. He was stalwart, steady, a workhorse. He had hands like a labourer, and the build of one too, but he was calculating. He could wait for what he wanted. He could work and wait. Anne wondered if she ought to kill him too, or if it would be wiser to let him live. He was a man who would cling to and work for whomever had power. In the absence of Henry's power, once Anne killed him, wouldn't Cromwell cling to and work for Elizabeth, the rightful heir? Wouldn't he make sure she learned her letters and her Latin, that she had a reformer's religious upbringing? Wouldn't he teach her to eschew beauty and courtship in favour of power and respect? Wouldn't he teach her to be ruthless? If Elizabeth was to be a child queen, she would need a Cromwell at her side; someone who would never eclipse her but would work himself to the bone to ensure her success, someone who would come to late-night meetings with her despite his own unsettled grief, someone who would set himself aside for her.

The light bothered Anne, though she had her hood over her face. She had hoped to fall back to sleep but could tell she wouldn't. She crept out of the ditch and on to the deserted road. Before her, she could see the northern wall of London, and one of its gates. She couldn't be too far from the Tower, she thought, but Whitehall was a few miles further to the west, past the walled portions of the city, in Westminster.

In the ditch, Zeus stirred and rose to his feet. Anne could ride him through the farmland and small villages north of London to the western edge of the city, past the walls, and come into town on foot on the Strand, walking up to Whitehall, and then, she wasn't sure – sneaking in, she supposed. But she would be conspicuous. A woman bearing an uncanny resemblance to the dead queen, about whom there were ghost stories circulating, riding a large white bull around the outskirts of London. How long would it be before a superstitious villager or farmer chased her down and dragged her off the beast's back, strung her up from a tree, or had her jailed as a witch? How long until Henry, or, more likely, dutiful Cromwell, appeared to investigate whether she was actually Anne Boleyn? How long until she was burned at the stake, Henry still living, Elizabeth in even greater jeopardy now that her mother was discovered an undead woman?

No, Anne thought, although it would be faster to ride around London, it would be too risky. Her best bet would be to leave Zeus here and make the long walk to Whitehall. She could retrace the path of her coronation, down Cheapside, to the Strand, and then on to Westminster. She could hide her face in her cloak, keep her head down, eyes down. She was dressed as a middling woman already. Nobody would look closely at her.

There was the question, then, of what she'd do with her sword. She couldn't wander through London with a giant sword protruding from the back of her dress. She could, though, tie the sword to her waist, under her gown. She ripped a long piece of fabric from the hem of her smock, to fashion a makeshift belt, raised the skirts of her gown and kirtle, and tied the belt first around the sword's hilt, then over her smock, around her waist. That way, the sharp blade would brush only the linen fabric of her undergarment, not her flesh. She wished she had a scabbard, but this would have to do. The sword was stiff, clunky and heavy, but beneath the voluminous skirt of her gown, it was hidden. Anne took a few steps. The sword swished beside her right leg, but did not bang against it, and was not visible beneath the gown's hem.

Zeus grunted behind her. What would she do with the bull? She supposed she had no responsibility to him. He'd appeared as out of nowhere, eager to serve her, and now his service had come to an end, but even so she was sad to say goodbye to the creature, who had shown her such care. She put her hand on the beast's face and whispered, 'Goodbye, Zeus.' The bull looked at her and nodded, as though he understood. He turned and walked back down the road, away from London. Anne stood watching him until he crested a hill and vanished, out of sight.

27

The Green Man

Anne walked along the road outside London, which she eventually realised was Bishopsgate Street, for some time. By the time she reached Bishops Gate, sweat trickled down her back, the day already unseasonably warm. The church bells gonged out a call to prime, morning prayer. There weren't many people about. With her hood drawn over her head and her gaze cast down, Anne walked past the gate guard, blending in with the few servants and labourers arriving in London to begin their day's work. Under her skirts, the sword swung, its hilt tipping back and forth at her hip.

She followed Bishopsgate Street to Threadneedle Street, then on to Poultry Street, until it became Cheapside, where the shops and market stalls were busy opening for the day. Here, a wife shouted down from an open window at her husband, a tailor, about a broken stair. Here, in front of a butcher's shop, a man strung up a row of plucked chickens. Here, a tired-looking woman wrangled a hutch of live rabbits into a market stall. Anne cringed to think of the rabbit she'd killed the day before. At the same time, she felt faint with hunger. She drew a pound from her bodice, and, wishing she had something smaller to use, as a coin of this value might draw attention, went into a bakery and purchased a honeyed bun. The shopkeeper eyed her suspiciously as he counted out change. Anne kept her head down, mumbled thank you, and walked out of the shop quickly, stuffing the bun into her mouth.

She hadn't walked far when a man called out to her, spying her handful of coins, 'Oi! Madam! Place a bet?' He stood in a small crowd. Beside him a boy sat on the ground, dipping a quill in ink to record wagers on a piece of parchment laid atop a wooden crate, while the man collected pence and shillings from the men and women who surrounded him, calling out dates.

'A shilling on Sunday next!' said one woman. And a man, talking over her, 'No later than midsummer will he wed the Lady Jane, I'd wager that.' A boy in an apron, must be an apprentice, held out a crown and said, 'For my master, who wants to know if you are taking bets on the date of the birth of a prince?'

Anne hurried past. She must be in time, then. If bets were still being placed on the date of Henry's impending nuptials, he must not yet have wed Jane, but she needed to move quickly, for the wedding could be happening soon. Likely not this morning, for she would have heard the peals of the bells of Westminster honouring the occasion, but perhaps tomorrow, or the day after, or the day after that. She willed herself to walk fast, though her feet ached, though she was short of breath, though she felt the heat of fever returning. Hurry, hurry, don't be late.

When she stopped at the public fountain, the Conduit, to get a drink of water from one of the jars collected there – for she was thirsty, so thirsty – she again thought she saw the Jack o' the Green, poking his head around the corner of a spice stall, but when she blinked, he'd disappeared. Probably just exhaustion, Anne thought. She tried to ignore the dizziness she'd had since waking in the ditch this morning, the heat that now radiated over her body. Just exhaustion, she told herself. No decline. No strange illness of the living dead. No Green Man.

It had been only three years earlier, almost to the day, that Anne had travelled this very route, on her way to Westminster from the Tower, to be crowned Queen of England. It was customary for royalty to travel down Cheapside, the route of commerce, on their way to their coronations, to give the merchant class that kept London's economy vibrant a view of the living gods ordained to rule them, to keep the busy workers invested in the monarchy, to make them feel a part of it. On the day of Anne's coronation, Cheapside's fountain had flowed with wine, and the shopkeepers and merchants who gathered around it drunkenly shouted their support – yes, Anne told herself, it was support, not jeers and hisses – as she was paraded down the street, reclining on a pillow-bedecked litter, dressed in a flowing white gown, for it was Whitsun, Pentecost, and she'd wanted to capture the image of a newly baptised Christian, washed with the Holy Spirit of reformation. She'd turned to her side to wave to the drunken Londoners, cupping a hand under her pregnant belly to show it off, to flaunt the babe that had grown there for six months. Here I am, she thought, your new queen, arrived to deliver unto you a prince, as Mary delivered Christ. She'd been so sure the baby would be a boy.

But, she wondered, as she walked further down Cheapside, why were women relegated to birthing princes and saviours, to the role of the Holy Mother, but not of actor, or saviour, or sovereign? Wouldn't she have been a righteous ruler of her people, had she lived? And wouldn't Elizabeth be? She'd birthed a far greater ruler than any prince; she'd birthed a cunning girl, who would be a believer in the true religion, who, she imagined, would lead England into the light of the Renaissance that had already swept through Italy, through France, through stodgy, traditional Spain, not to mention through the northern countries, where Lutheranism held strong. Yes, her daughter, her Elizabeth, would rule, and she would be divine, just, a righter of wrongs, a queen to care for the poor and destitute, to knock the men from their seats of power.

Anne passed the corner where, during her coronation procession, a large white falcon, fashioned from wire and fabric, had sat on a plaster egg on which the word *Rex* had been painted in purple lettering. Even the false bird had been assumed to be expecting a prince. The wire and fabric falcon on Cheapside was nothing, though, compared to the large dragon that had decorated the barge that brought Anne up the Thames to the Tower, three days before her coronation. That was a fantastical construction, covered in green and purple felt, with a body that moved on a series of cranks and pulleys, and a mouth that opened to breathe out real fire. What man had stood inside the contraption, shooting flames out of the false beast's mouth, hot and sweaty? Had he, like the Jack o' the Green, been dressed in boughs? When the barges landed, she'd stayed two nights at the Tower, secreted away in the royal apartments with Henry, her days spent knighting men and receiving London's luminaries – the mayor, who gave her a purse of a thousand pounds, the lords of its wealthiest families – her nights spent making love to Henry, who ran his hands through her waist-length hair and told her he loved her, that she was his true queen, who whispered through her rounding belly to the prince he believed was nestled inside her: 'You shall be a mighty king', 'You shall be a great ruler', 'You shall be the inheritor of all that I govern.' It delighted Anne to think of him whispering those words not to a prince but to Elizabeth, who would be all those things, and sooner than anyone expected.

This is why I must kill Henry, Anne thought, no matter how he begs, no matter if, in the end, I feel a spark of love. Elizabeth, not some future son, must rule. Like many women, Anne had convinced herself that a son would be better. She'd spent three years trying to conceive one. She'd wept openly when she lost one in January. Like many women, Anne had been taught to think of men as superior, of a son as superior, when in fact she herself was superior. She, who had turned the king's head to the true religion. For hadn't it been her influence, more than Thomas Cromwell's, more than Thomas Cranmer's, hadn't it been Anne's influence on the king, on his spirit and mind, that had turned him towards the true religion? Hadn't she given him a copy of William Tyndale's English Bible? Hadn't she given him Tyndale's *The Obedience of a Christian Man*, with the passages pertaining to the independence of kings from Rome marked out to guide the king's attention?

Yes, she was superior, and Elizabeth would be too. Anne was done with submitting to the whims and poorly thought-out plans of men, so often fuelled by base emotions like greed, anger and jealousy: men, marking out their territory like dogs. Enough. Her Elizabeth would do better, be better. Just as Anne was better, willing to sacrifice herself for the good of her people. Just as Alice, secure in her fen, was better, willing to sacrifice her body for the good of her children. Anne would put Elizabeth, her brilliant, precocious daughter, on the throne of England, and England would be better for it.

Anne passed by Cheapside's gold- and silversmith shops, where jewellery was made for the wives of merchants and middling men, so that those women could experience some luxury and importance, could flaunt their wealth over the peasants. She turned on to Fleet Street, exhaustion settling into her feet, which ached in her impractical velvet slippers. The blisters she'd noticed at the pond had burst, leaving her feet raw and sore. How could a dead body get blisters? How could it do anything, she again thought – eat, piss, get aroused, thirst, have a fever? There were no answers to these questions.

By midday, she'd passed through Temple Bar, out of London proper, to the Strand, the final long road to Westminster, to Whitehall. She walked faster, though her feet ached, though her head was hot, though she was dizzy. She kept her head down, stepping carefully around ruts and potholes in the dirt road, for though the Strand was an avenue lined with mansions, it was not, like the streets of London, paved.

Ahead, she saw the Jack o' the Green, the Green Man, this time clearly, dressed in green felt, covered in pine boughs. He turned back to look at her, through the small throng of people walking westward, and his face was covered in green paste. He winked and shimmied. She quickened her pace to follow him. Where? To the palace, she hoped. To Henry. She didn't care any more who the Jack was; she wasn't even sure he was real. Could others observe him? She couldn't tell. Odder men than he walked the streets of London and its outskirts. Londoners learned not to engage with the lunatics and jesters, with the deranged.

The Green Man danced before the fine mansions of the Strand, which had until recently belonged to bishops but had been handed out to nobility as Henry divested the Catholic officials of their wealth and status. The gardeners of the large homes were out, planting red peonies in pots in front of them, readying for Whitsun, which, Anne realised, was just a week away. The Green Man stopped to shake his bottom next to a gardener busy at his work, to mime humping the man, then mime beheading him. She quickened her pace once more.

It was afternoon when Anne rounded the western bend of the Thames, from which point she could see Whitehall and, in the distance, Westminster Abbey. The Green Man was turning cartwheels in the road before her, laughing, the bells sewn to his green shoes tinkling with each revolution, with each step. Her head blazed with heat; her eyes were bleary.

She remembered her coronation in the abbey, the day after her long processional through London, the pomp and ceremony of it, the ermine-trimmed cloak she'd worn, Cranmer anointing her head with holy oil, placing the sceptre and orb in her hands, crowning her with St Edward the Confessor's crown, the gold gilt of the ancient wooden coronation chair she sat in, that so many monarchs before her had also sat in. And, from around the edge of a velvet curtain, cloistered away on a balcony, as was customary, Henry, her king, her husband, peering down at her admiringly. His Anne. His queen. Anything had seemed possible then. That she would birth many boys. That she would rule England as regent should Henry perish before her son came of age. That the floor of Westminster Abbey would crack open and an enormous dragon would issue forth, blowing flames from its mouth, ridden by the holy skeletons laid to rest there, all those dead kings and queens and princes and princesses, all those holy bones pulling her and the babe inside her belly up on to the dragon's back, welcoming her into a never-ending dynasty of leadership and duty. It was her finest moment, heavily pregnant, resplendent, ancient crown upon her head, the nation bowing before her.

It felt urgent now to keep up with the Green Man, in the heat of her fever, in the fever of her mind, in the mind of her afterlife. She ran after him as he chasséd and pranced right up to the gate of Whitehall Palace, then stopped. Anne was a dozen paces behind him, and when she caught up, he reached out his green-painted hands and cupped her hot face. His hands were cool, soft; it was not an unpleasant touch.

'My queen,' he said, his voice a whisper, 'I'll be your jolly jester.' Then he turned on his heels and skipped past the guards into the palace grounds.

28

Dead Men's Shoes

Anne knew better than to follow the Green Man, who'd been able to move confidently past Whitehall's guards, either because he was dressed as an entertainer or because he didn't actually exist. A common woman, as she appeared to be, would not be allowed to pass. Anne and Henry had worked extensively to redesign Whitehall when they'd taken it from Cardinal Wolsey after he'd failed to get Henry his annulment and fallen from favour. She knew the palace's layout well, and remembered that there was a servants' entrance on the building's north side, near the great hall. She suspected she could enter there, unnoticed. She crept around to the side of the palace, staying close to the stone wall that enclosed the grounds, and found the simple, unguarded wrought-iron gate. Through it, she spied a laundress, dressed in a red kirtle, with a white smock and bonnet, hanging the king's linens to dry in the sun.

When the laundress returned to the servants' quarters through a modest wooden door, Anne removed the cloak and gown she'd borrowed from Alice. It was a relief to have them off, to remove a layer of clothing, to let her hot body cool. How was she generating so much heat? She held the practical grey garments to her face and breathed in. Underneath the smell of her own sweat and the smell of pond water, she could still smell Alice – a sweetness and faint hint of water lilies. She steeled herself, balled up the garments, and shoved them under a rosemary bush growing near the palace wall. She wouldn't need them again.

Dressed now in her red kirtle, Anne walked through the servants' gate. Among the king's linens hanging to dry, his undergarments and bed linens, and also the linen bandages for his unhealing leg wound, Anne found a number of aprons and bonnets intended for use by the servants. She tied an apron tightly around her waist and replaced the cap Alice had given her with a bonnet. There, she thought, I'll look enough like any other scullery maid, cook, laundress or chambermaid in the building. The only thing conspicuous about her appearance was the silk collar covering her scar. Carefully, so as not to tear the fabric, Anne pulled the three threads she'd knotted at the pond so that the threads broke, then held the swaddling cloth to her nose. The faintest hint of lavender, the faintest hint of Elizabeth's baby smell – was she imagining it? – still clung there. She put the fabric back where she'd kept it at her execution, inside her bodice, against her breast, beside her heart, this keepsake, this treasured remnant and reminder of her Elizabeth. From the clothes line, she grabbed a white linen kerchief and tied it around her neck. Still a bit peculiar, but better. From here, she could enter the palace through the door the laundress had just passed through.

For all the time Anne had spent at Whitehall, a frequent residence in the courtly rotation of palaces, she'd never been in the servants' quarters. She'd sent all her needs through her ladies-in-waiting, maids of honour or lady's maids. Presumably, they communicated with the many servants required to run a palace, and Anne had never had need to set foot downstairs.

Anne entered through the kitchen. It was hot and noisy. Several cooks flitted about large wooden tables chopping and preparing ingredients, then carrying them over to big iron kettles simmering over the fires of the two massive hearths. A woman banging and kneading dough at one of the tables eyed

Anne suspiciously. She bowed her head and hurried out of the kitchen into a corridor lined with many rooms. In one, a few servants were eating a meal, chatting and laughing; many of the others were furnished with two or three beds apiece and must be sleeping quarters. She turned into one of the bedchambers and closed the door behind her, breathing deeply and hoping the woman from the kitchen would not follow.

She needed to get upstairs and make her way to the opposite end of the palace. There stood the queen's chambers – she imagined Jane Seymour in them now, attended by her ladies, perhaps choosing a gown for her wedding – and, more to her purpose, the king's chambers. That was where she'd find Henry. She knew that there was only one set of stairs connecting the servants' quarters to the main floor of the palace, and that opened into a recessed alcove outside the great hall. That would be her first task: getting up the stairs.

Cautiously, Anne opened the chamber door and scanned the corridor for anybody who might see her. Finding it empty, she dashed to the staircase. With her head down, she raced up the stairs. If anybody saw her, they'd think her just another servant. If she moved quickly and stayed in the shadows, nobody would pay her much attention. Anne knew she'd never really noticed the servants inhabiting the corners of every room she'd been in. They were there, but they weren't really *there*. She would rely on that invisibility now as protection.

At the top of the stairs, Anne ducked behind a floor-length drape, pulled to the side to allow light in from a large window, so that she was completely hidden in the thick fabric's folds. On the wall beside the drape hung a large tapestry, woven with a picture of a naked Eve biting the apple, the snake wrapped erotically around her extended calf, a reminder to all who saw it of the frailty and deception of women. From her hiding spot, Anne could hear voices in the great hall. More specifically, she could hear Henry's voice, giving commands. The man had such a booming voice, no awareness of how loudly he spoke, no inclination, ever, to lower it. 'I want grouse as the main course because the Lady Jane adores it. She'll have what she wants,' he proclaimed. A second voice, quieter and harder to discern, mumbled in assent; must be Cromwell. 'Make sure all signs of the other one are stricken from this hall,' Henry continued. More muted replies. Then Henry said, 'Three days' time. You'd better be up to the task, Cromwell.' He must be giving instructions about the wedding, Anne thought. Three days – there was time then, before he wedded Jane, time for her to do what needed to be done.

Anne's heart beat faster at the sound of Henry's voice. In her first days of imprisonment at the Tower, she'd longed to hear his voice again. She'd imagined him mounting the Tower steps to the royal apartments, throwing the door open, taking her in his arms, confessing that this had all been a terrible mistake. Hearing Henry's voice would have meant she'd have the opportunity to explain herself, to straighten the whole misunderstanding out, as she'd tried to do the night before the May Day joust. They'd been at Greenwich Palace, east of the city, and Henry had confronted her about the rumours that she'd spoken of his death to Henry Norris.

'What did you say to him?' Henry demanded, his eyes pained. 'The courtiers say you said he looks for dead men's shoes, and seeks to have you. Woman, have you been unfaithful to me?'

'No,' Anne pleaded. 'No. Listen, I beg of you. I have never been unfaithful. I have been with no man but you. 'Twas merely a playful flirtation. I was teasing him about delaying his marriage proposal to my cousin, nudging him to the altar by pointing out how ludicrously he was behaving.'

'Do you believe he wants to bed you?' Henry was shouting, his face cracked with anger.

'No, my love, *mon cher*, no.' Anne placed a hand on his shoulder, trying to calm him. 'He has simply taken courtly affections too far. What am I to do, as queen? I am expected to play along with such flirtations. I am trying to uphold the customs of the court.'

'I don't believe you,' Henry had snapped back. 'I don't believe you ever loved me.'

'Please,' Anne had begged, bouncing a fussing Elizabeth gently in her other arm, for she'd had the child brought from Hatfield to present to her father. 'Please. Believe me. I would never. You are obsessed with having a male heir, my love. It consumes you. It clouds your judgement.' Anne thrust Elizabeth towards him. 'See,' she'd pleaded, 'here is your heir! Here is your prince! She is as good as any prince – she is better.'

But the king had turned away, refused to look, refused to hold his own child. He'd retreated to his chambers, seething, and when the door had closed, she heard him punch the wall and yowl in pain. Elizabeth, in her arms, went red and wailed.

The two had fought often, though, and the next morning he was cordial and merry. Anne had no reason to believe that this rift would deepen, that this would be her last chance to plead her innocence to her husband, her king. That this was the last time she'd see her daughter, who'd returned to Hatfield the previous evening, cranky and splotchy-faced with exhaustion, rubbing her tired eyes as she settled into Lady Bryan's arms in the carriage, resting her head against Lady Bryan's bosom, and falling asleep to the sound of Lady Bryan's beating heart. How Anne had wished Elizabeth had been in her arms, cradled against her breast, soothed by her pulse. She cried to see the child go, and cried back in her chambers, recalling her argument with Henry, and her sorrow that she could not leave with Elizabeth. No, she needed to stay and mend her marriage. Stay, and entertain the court. Stay, and be the most happy. Stay, and try harder to be submissive. Stay, and try and try for a boy to sit on her husband's throne. There are so many reasons for any woman to stay. How Anne wished now that she had ignored them all and left.

When the doors to the great hall opened and Henry and Cromwell swept through them, it was all Anne could do not to run after the men, reach out, grab the king's arm, and confront him. But she stopped herself. What would she say? "Tis I, your wife and rightful queen, back from the dead to demand an apology and my child.' Or, "Tis I, your wife and rightful queen, back from the dead with the power to annihilate all who opposed me. Bow and beg for mercy.' Or maybe simply, "Tis I, you villainous whoreson,' and a slap across his face. No, it wouldn't matter what she said. Confronting the king now, during the day, in view of Cromwell, with guards at his beck and call just outside the palace, would result in her immediate arrest and, likely, burning as a witch. She needed to wait and confront Henry when he was alone.

This would be a difficult task. The king rarely had a moment of privacy. His grooms of the privy chamber, six noblemen who served him in his private rooms, were with him when he rose, dressed, entertained, and slept. His groom of the stool accompanied him to the stool chamber and kept him company when he defecated. Until recently, the groom of the stool had been Henry Norris. It was an intimate thing to witness another person shit. How many of the king's intimate moments in the stool chamber had Norris observed? How much grunting, straining? What moments of panicked diarrhoea?

Anne couldn't wait for the king in his private rooms, or in his stool chamber. She thought through his daily schedule, a schedule around which, until recently, she had designed her own, so that she could always be available to him, could always be ready to please or entertain him, to talk through a theological or political question with him, to be an ornament on his arm, to be his happy, happy wife, always available, always waiting. Anne knew that each evening, the king prayed in his private chapel. At Whitehall, that was a secluded chapel off the back of his private apartment. No man would enter the chapel with him; prayer was a time of solitude for the king, one of the only times he was completely alone. She must sneak into his chambers, sequester herself in the chapel, and wait.

Cromwell and Henry moved rapidly down the corridor towards the galleries and royal chambers. When Anne heard their footsteps turn the corner and she was at no risk of being seen, she stepped from behind the drape and walked into the great hall where the two men had just sat. Servants moved about, setting the tables for a feast. Surely each night at Whitehall leading up to Henry's wedding to Jane would be a celebration, and Anne wondered when the celebrating had begun. The night she was beheaded? The next day? Had Henry waited any time at all before launching into an extended bacchanal with his mistress and court? Had he waited, even, for Anne's body to grow cold? To be buried? Though of course Anne hadn't grown cold and hadn't been buried. Anne imagined the king feasting at Whitehall the very evening of her death, pulling Jane on to his lap, chuffing with laughter, drunk on wine and half-hard, picking meat from between his teeth. Had he mourned for her at all? Or had he surrounded himself so thoroughly with friends and women, kept himself so completely occupied with revelry, that he had no chance to do so?

Anne walked around the edge of the great hall. She kept her distance from the other servants, kept to the wall, so that she wouldn't be recognised as an interloper, pretending to straighten and beat dust from the tapestries, each filled with depictions of King Arthur and his knights. Here, one she'd never noticed before, of Gawain, head bent low and neck exposed, valorously showing up to receive his nick from the Green Knight's axe. Anne remembered the epic poem she'd read as a child about his turn at the beheading game. *Nay, by God that lent me my ghost, I shall grudge thee not a grain for the grim that falleth*, Gawain spoke to the Green Knight, prepared to receive his beheading, in turn, for the beheading he'd dealt that bewitched man a year before, then delighted when the Green Knight forgave him instead, when he simply scratched the young man's neck with his mighty axe and let him walk away, alive.

How many feasts had Anne eaten in this hall? How many dances had she attended? There, in the corner, was where she'd stood a dozen years earlier, dressed as Perseverance in the staged tower of Wolsey's Château Vert, when the king and his manly virtues stormed in to rescue her. There was where she'd sat, newly married to Henry, in their happy first days as husband and wife at Whitehall. There was where she'd chased Elizabeth, pretending to be a monster, catching and tickling her. 'Be tickle monster, Mama!' the child had joyfully cried last Christmas, in her high-pitched voice, her feet kicking against Anne's legs as she lifted the squealing girl up and blew a loud raspberry against her neck.

Whatever fever Anne had suffered on the long walk to Whitehall seemed to have passed, for she was no longer sweating, no longer shivering, could hold herself upright without trouble and see clearly. The doorways of the great hall were framed with oak trim, into which workers had carved intertwined *A*'s and *H*'s, for Anne and Henry. At the northern door, Anne observed a labourer on a ladder chiselling a set of these initials away, a pot of wood stain waiting on the ladder's platform to cover over the erasure. Henry was already removing all evidence of her, enforcing a great forgetting. She imagined he would soon burn her portraits and letters. What would be left for Elizabeth to remember her by? What stories would the child hear of her mother? Would she know how much, how deeply, Anne had loved her? Anne could feel herself tearing up. She took a deep breath, reminding herself that these were moot questions. She would kill Henry. She would put Elizabeth on the throne. She would make sure that enough of her memory remained at court, enough paintings, jewels, letters, so that the child would know her mother.

The servants were moving out of the room now, but Anne tarried beside the oaken door, hoping none would notice she had stayed behind. They didn't. She wandered over to the top table, and when she reached the king's seat, she arranged his spoon, knife and fork into the shape of an *A*. Now he'd have to think of her, his Anna Bullen, his Nan, not so easily chiselled away after all. She looked up at the ceiling of the great hall and noticed a small painting of a gyrfalcon in one corner, which the labourers must have missed in their hurry to remove all traces of her. Good. Let the white falcon with its beady eye watch over Henry at his last supper. Let it be an omen to him.

Not wanting to dally too long, Anne left the great hall, but instead of retreating downstairs as the servants had done, she headed towards the gallery, hoping she might move about unnoticed and make her way to the king's chambers and his chapel. She wanted to kill Henry as soon as possible, to get it over with, to be done. She could sneak in while he and his court were dining and hide in his chapel until he came in for his evening prayers. She kept her head down and stayed close to the walls.

Halfway through the gallery, she ducked into an alcove and busied herself at a servant's station to avoid two ladies walking past. She recognised them but could not place their names. One had been with her on the scaffold at her execution. The other was the daughter of one of Henry's third cousins, a country girl who had been low in the ranks when Anne was queen but apparently was in ascension now.

'Well, it happened during the Ceremony of the Keys, I heard,' said the lady who had stood behind Anne at her execution.

The second lady tutted. 'I don't like to think of it. When a woman, especially one who has behaved as Anne did, is dead, she ought to stay dead, not galivant around the Tower of London as a ghost.'

The women stopped at a window in the gallery, across the room from where Anne hid in the alcove. 'Ah yes,' the first lady said, 'from here you can see the tract of land my husband has been newly deeded by the king. It used to belong to a bishop. All ours now.'

'What good fortune!' exclaimed the second.

'Indeed,' replied the first. 'Well, as you know, I attended the whore on the scaffold,' she continued. Her nose was running and she sucked a wad of snot back into her throat. 'This hay fever,' she said, ''tis the death of me each May. As I was saying, I attended the whore on the scaffold, and I can assure you, she was thoroughly beheaded. I handled her head myself, as the jailer's wife wrapped it in linen. 'Twas all I could do not to spit in the whore's face. Disgusting, what she did.'

Anne rolled her eyes. She shouldn't be surprised that the court was repeating the lies Henry and Cromwell had told about her, but she was disappointed. She wondered if either of these women had lain with Henry. She wouldn't put it past him to lie with his own cousin, especially one so many times removed, even though she appeared no more than fifteen.

'Even so,' replied the second lady, the cousin, 'I don't like to think about the late queen haunting the Tower. What if she comes to haunt Hampton Court, or Whitehall? I shouldn't like to meet a ghost, or worry about meeting one. What if she slips into my bed at night and sucks the breath out of me?'

'I doubt the dead queen would visit *you*, if she came to haunt at court,' said the first lady, dismissively. 'Don't you think she'd torture Henry, or Jane?'

'Well, I heard,' said the second, 'that a group of men in the woods reported seeing the dead queen's ghost there as well, riding, of all things, a white bull. And that she used witches' magic to force the bull to gore a man to death. Then she showed the whole lot of them her bare breasts and her witch's mark, on which she suckles the devil's offspring.'

The first lady laughed. 'What a ridiculous story, Agnes. You truly will believe anything.'

The two women chatted for a few more minutes about a lord who was courting Agnes before leaving the gallery. Anne emerged from the alcove. It was alarming to hear the ghost stories circulating about her, though also thrilling, and part of her delighted in thinking about the stuffy English courtiers lying scared in their beds at night, fearing to peek out between their bed curtains, lest her ghostly form assault them. Let them worry. Let them fear. Let them contemplate their complicity in her downfall, in her bloody execution, and dwell in guilt. She wondered, as well, if Henry had heard the stories. She hoped he had. She hoped they sent a shiver down his spine and made his testicles slink into his body, frightened. She wanted him to feel the same fear she had in the Tower, awaiting her trial and execution, the same prolonged doom.

On the wall beside her hung a portrait of Henry's late mother, pious-faced Elizabeth of York, daughter of Edward IV, whose marriage to Henry's father had secured his claim on the throne. Anne had never met the woman. She'd died in the Tower of London when Henry was eleven, shortly after giving birth to her last child, a daughter who also perished. In portraits, Anne had always thought, Henry's mother had looked mournful and woebegotten. Saying a quick prayer for the deceased queen, she took a moment to lift the portrait off the wall, turn it upside down, and rehang it. Spying two more portraits within her reach, one of Margaret Beaufort, the king's Lancastrian grandmother, and one of his Yorkist mother's brothers – those poor babes murdered in the Tower – she did the same. That should rattle them all, she thought. She could feel her exhilaration building.

The queen's chambers, so recently her own, were empty when she reached them. She stepped in, just for a moment, just to see. No Jane, and none of her ladies either. Anne imagined they were walking in the gardens, it being a pleasant afternoon, enjoying some leisure before the evening's feast.

It was odd to see Jane's things unpacked in the rooms. Here, Jane's shoes. There, Jane's prayer book. Jane's collection of dowdy gable hoods, which Anne could see the woman was attempting to bring back into fashion in the English court, undoubtedly another rebuke of Anne's French style of dress. In the dressing room, Anne found Jane's gowns, a variety of silk and ermine, which, though regal, on the whole lacked flair. Among them, Anne found two of her own gowns. She could see upon inspecting them more closely that they'd already been tailored to fit Jane, who was taller than Anne, and heavier. Anne could have guessed that this would happen; she'd owned many fine gowns and Henry, always frugal with other people's possessions, hated to waste what could be reused. Even so, it angered her. She picked up one of the gowns, made from blue silk, and held it to her chest.

Next to the bed, she spied the cradle where Elizabeth had slept when she'd accompanied Anne and Henry to Whitehall. Still holding the gown, Anne walked over and rocked the cradle softly with one hand.

From the hallway, Anne heard footsteps and muffled voices. She panicked. At the back of the queen's chambers was a doorway to the gardens, and Anne rushed out of it, still carrying the blue silk gown. She knew there was a secret pathway to the king's chambers through a sprawling labyrinth of hedges that Wolsey had begun and she and Henry had finished. The king had delighted in chasing her through the garden maze. She'd let him 'catch' her just before the door to his chambers, through which he'd carry her, excited from the chase, and make love to her. They'd passed many a free hour this way in the months they'd spent here as newly-weds. Anne followed the twists and turns of the labyrinth, remembering where to turn and where to go straight, retracing those halcyon steps of better days. As she walked, meandering through the maze's twists and turns, taking her time, she ran a hand along the stiff leaves of the hedges. Was that the Green Man she saw in the distance, darting around a corner? When she reached the path she thought he'd taken, she peered down it but saw no one.

Eventually, she reached the door to Henry's chambers. The shadows of the hedges had grown long, and she imagined by now the king and court must be halfway through their feast. All she had to do was slip into the king's chambers, hide in his chapel, and wait. She put a hand to the door, pushed it open, and saw, standing not three feet away, a servant, who turned and looked right at her.

29

The Labyrinth

Anne recognised the man immediately. Lambert. He'd been a servant assigned to clean Henry's chambers since before Henry and Anne were married. More than once, before the annulment of Henry's marriage to Katherine, before Henry and Anne's private vows in Dover, before their official wedding at Whitehall, Lambert had helped sneak Anne in or out of the king's chambers so that the two could chat into the middle of the night, so that they could cuddle by the fire, trading stories of their childhoods and their dreams for a better England, so that they could passionately kiss, caress each other, fondle – but not more.

Lambert likewise recognised her immediately. He dropped the chamber pot he was holding, spilling the king's piss across the stone floor. 'Y-Your Majesty?' he stammered, disbelievingly. 'It cannot be.' He looked around frantically, resting his gaze for a moment on the chamber door. Anne supposed he was thinking of running from the room, of telling everyone who'd listen that he'd spied the dead queen standing in the king's chambers. A sweat broke out on his brow.

'Yes,' Anne said, still holding the gown she'd taken from Jane's chambers to her chest, ''tis I, your queen.'

'I don't—' he started.

'Don't speak,' interrupted Anne. 'You think you are seeing me but you are not. Leave this room now and tell no one, or I will haunt you till your last days, and then I will haunt your children, and their children also.'

'I—' Lambert began again. He looked down at his boots, splashed with the king's urine, and took a deep breath. Then he looked up, and Anne could see the spite in his eyes. 'I do not have to take orders from you any more, whore,' he said, and turned and ran from the room, shouting.

Quickly, Anne exited the chambers and ran back into the labyrinth. She knew she had only minutes to evade the guards who would come rushing into the garden. She ran through the labyrinth, twisting and turning, finding its most secret passageways, its most hidden dead ends. Twilight fell and the air grew cold. There, at the end of one path, in the dimming light, she swore again she saw the Green Man, dressed in shaggy boughs, crouched low, a finger to his lips, *Shhhhhhh*, but when she ran to the spot where he'd stood, there was nothing.

Anne turned back, dashing down paths, around corners, until she came to a wall of hedges that appeared solid but that she knew could be pushed through into a small, secret chamber at the heart of the labyrinth. The only other people who knew this hideaway existed were the master gardener, who'd created it before returning to the French court from which they'd borrowed him, and Henry. She and Henry had intentionally kept it secret. They'd hidden here together on more than one occasion, and he'd joked about how hidden it was, how round, how it was just like Anne's own hidden seat of pleasure, her own Venus mound, and then he'd put his hand up her skirts and thumbed that secret place until she came. Anne hid there now, the gown she'd stolen from Jane's room clutched in her arms.

Anne wasn't sure how long she stood, quick with fear, in the labyrinth's secret centre. Guards came and went throughout the maze, hunting for the interloper the servant had spotted.

Anne listened to their heavy footsteps, their rushing and weaving through the corridors of the labyrinth, their fumbling and turning around as they took false corners and faced dead ends, their cursing. More than once, she heard them on the other side of the hedges that hid her in the maze's secret centre. In these moments, she held her breath, kept her feet still, moved no part of her body. If she could have stopped her heart, she would have.

'There's no such thing as ghosts,' said one guard, just on the other side of the labyrinth's hedge wall. 'No doubt the fool's eyes played tricks on him. Maybe he's a traitor at heart and saw what he wanted to see, the queen he wished still reigned.'

'I doubt it,' replied his companion. 'The man ran shaking into the great hall, screaming that he'd seen the whore's ghost climbing into the king's very bed as he was clearing away the chamber piss pots. "That vile woman!" he shrieked. "She has risen from the grave, a stinking, undead succubus!" Doesn't sound like the words of a queen's man to me.'

'Well, 'tis just as likely the fool mistook a comely servant for the queen,' the first guard replied. 'As I said, there's no such thing as ghosts.'

'Comely or ugly? For surely the queen was a homely woman. When she walked in front of me, believe me, I wasn't impressed,' the second man said.

Both men laughed. On the other side of the hedges, Anne held her breath. She would not let her anger overtake her. She would not burst through the hedge wall and scare the piss out of these guards, kick them in the groin, tell them that mocking a woman's appearance was an ad hominem attack that revealed only the low intelligence of its interlocutor, and, what's more, many men at court had vied for her attentions, even before she'd become the queen, and did that speak to an unattractive woman? No, Anne held her breath. She stood, motionless.

Later, another guard, this one a bit further away, a bit harder to hear, mumbled, 'I don't believe in ghosts. I don't believe in ghosts. I don't believe in ghosts.' He sounded barely older than a boy. Unable to see him, Anne pictured a child, dressed up in a too-big uniform, pretending at being a guard.

It seemed to Anne that this went on for hours. The sky grew dark. The constellations crept out of the shadows above her, frozen in a court dance on either side of the Milky Way. In the distance, crows called. Eventually, the air grew cold enough that Anne shivered. She took the gown she'd been clutching all this while, the gown that had been hers originally, after all, that had only recently been altered to fit her usurper, Jane, and put it on.

Jane was a well-fed, well-loved, well-cared-for girl, and the gown hung loosely on Anne's thin frame. She'd been well cared for once. She'd had enough flesh to feel strong and comely. As best she could, she tightened the laces on the gown's bodice and tied them in place. The gown's sleeves extended past her wrists. The bottom few inches of its hem swept the ground. The ground. The ground looked inviting. Anne pulled her hands into the gown's sleeves and sank to the gravel-covered ground. She lay down on her side, pulled her knees up to her chest, and curled into as tight a shape as she could. The sword, still tied beside her waist, stuck out of the bottom of her skirts.

Anne sank into an uneasy sleep. She dreamed of Elizabeth, of chasing her through the labyrinth in her green Christmas gown. Anne hid behind one turn, then another, peeking out to catch Elizabeth's eyes, as dark and unreadable as her own, to smile and stick her tongue out at the child before running away again, leaving the girl giggling with delight. But then, the dream turned. Elizabeth ran faster and faster through the maze, around a corner and out of sight. When Anne caught up with her, instead of the child she saw a white falcon standing on the gravel walk, staring at her. The bird turned and flew, swooping low through the maze's passageways. Anne ran after it, following the falcon into an area of the labyrinth she didn't recognise. The hedges became walls, became the walls of Whitehall, became Whitehall's corridors. At the end of a long, turning corridor, at its dead end, which Anne arrived at panting and sweaty, tripping over the too-long hem of her gown, stood Thomas Cromwell.

The sun was high in the sky when Anne woke. It must be late morning, she thought, using her hand to shade her eyes as she squinted upward. She was sweaty. The day was warm, muggy, strange weather for May. She'd slept on her side and bits of gravel stuck to her face. She used the long sleeves of her gown to brush them away. She heard no sound, other than birds chittering. The guards must have called off their search in the night.

Cautiously, Anne squeezed through the wall of hedges to exit the secret enclosure. She did not want to risk another sighting, but she needed to get herself into the king's private chapel by nightfall. To not do so would be to increase the probability that she would be apprehended before she could kill the king. And, she wanted to kill Henry today, she needed to. She couldn't believe that she'd failed to do so yesterday. She must do it today. And yet, she supposed it was too early to head to the chapel, which might still be on a servant's list of rooms to sweep or dust. It was likely that, after the commotion last night, the door to the king's chambers would be guarded, so she'd have to be stealthy. She'd worry about that later. For now she was powerfully hungry. She followed the maze back to the entrance to the queen's chambers. As she suspected, the queen's door was unguarded. Henry, she supposed, was not as concerned with Jane's safety as with his own.

Anne opened the door and crept into the queen's apartment. She wandered among the rooms until she found a tray of leftover breakfast – the end of a loaf of bread, some half-eaten eggs.

Anne shovelled the food into her mouth with her hands. The last swallows of a tankard of ale remained beside the plate of food, and Anne drank them down. She caught her reflection in a mirror across the chamber and startled at the sight of herself: pale and thin, dark circles under her eyes, kerchief tied around her neck, gown too big. She did look ghostly.

Anne hadn't seen the scar that encircled her neck, only felt it, and she wondered what it looked like. She walked closer to the mirror and carefully untied the kerchief. The scar was more hideous than she'd imagined, and she recoiled at the sight of it. A fleshy band slithered around her neck, thick and pink, uneven in places where her sewing had faltered or misaligned. Anne had been a skilled needleworker in life, a pastime she and her ladies practised in her chambers frequently, but in the haste of sewing her own flesh, crouched behind a tavern with no mirror, no way to see her work, she'd made many errors. Behind her left ear, a flap of neck skin folded over on itself, stretched and hastily sewn in place. That had been the hardest part of her neck to reach. Now the skin was permanently buckled. Anne ran her fingers over the scar. Permanent. As permanent as she was, she supposed. Would there be an expiration to her reanimation? When she killed Henry, would she dissolve into air, or fall to the floor dead, or would she keep living, and if so, for how long? Would she need to escape the palace and find a way to live in this new, monstrous body?

Anne pushed the thought from her mind and retied the kerchief, hiding the gruesome scar. Her top priority right now needed to be her safety, and she didn't feel particularly safe in Jane's rooms. She thought she might cut through the palace – she knew just how to do so without being noticed – to take some air on the Thames. As she was leaving Jane's chambers, she spotted a bottle of Italian perfume next to Jane's dresses. She picked it up, sniffed it, then threw it to the stone floor, where it shattered, dousing the room in the smell of frangipani. 'I hope it was the daft woman's favourite,' she muttered. 'I hope she slips and twists her ankle in the mess.'

Anne darted from shadow to shadow as she moved down corridors and cut across galleries and chambers until, at last, she stepped out of a doorway on to a stony hill that sloped down to the riverbank. Cautiously, she descended. She'd pilfered a few strawberries from a tray in one of the galleries, and now she sat on a boulder at the riverbank, eating each berry down to its nub, then pitching the stems into the water. She wished she had a stone to skip, to watch skim across the surface of the water in a satisfying series of progressively smaller leaps until it sank. She hoisted her skirts and walked along the river, looking for a flat, round stone that might do the trick.

She hadn't walked far when she spied a man a few yards away, dressed in black velvet, staring pensively out at the water. Could it be? Before she could retreat and conceal herself, the man turned to face her.

Cromwell.

He opened his mouth, perhaps to shout for the guard.

'No,' said Anne, firmly, holding up her hand to silence him.

Cromwell paused. Then he walked towards her.

'I didn't believe the rumours were true, the ghost stories,' he said. She started to speak, but he shook his head and continued. 'The late queen has been spied at the Tower, flirting with Thomas Wyatt,' he began, as though reciting the calls of a crier or the gossip of a group of ladies. 'The late queen ambushed an encampment of men in the forest, castrated them, and strung their testicles on a necklace that she wore while walking up Cheapside, screeching like a banshee. The late queen possessed the body of a scullery maid and bade her walk into the river, where she tore open her bodice and exposed her breasts for all to see. The late queen broke into the king's chambers and tried to fornicate with his manservant. The late queen has risen from her grave and walks among us.' Cromwell paused, a faint grin on his lips, and met her eyes. Was he happy to see her? 'It is true, then.'

'Well,' Anne replied, casting a sceptical look at Cromwell, 'not all of that is true. I certainly didn't castrate any men in the forest, and I would never fornicate with a servant, despite your accusations.' Cromwell winced. 'And the bit about the scullery maid is absurd. But I am here. I do not know how.'

Cromwell was silent. That he didn't seem alarmed to see Anne, risen from the dead, didn't surprise her, for nothing ever seemed to alarm Cromwell. 'Why, then?' he said. 'Why are you here? Do you seek to injure, to assault?'

Small waves lapped at the riverbank. The tide was coming in. Anne thought about what she should say, how much of her plan she should reveal.

'I've come to kill the king,' she said.

'I don't—' Cromwell began.

Anne stopped him. 'No. Hear this. What you did, what the king did, was wrong.'

Cromwell opened his mouth to speak again.

'No,' Anne said, 'let me finish. You might think that I am just one loud and uncontrollable woman, that the king's loss of interest in me was my own fault, unable as I have been to keep my opinions to myself, to be a submissive wife, to birth a male heir. But what if the problem is not me, but him?'

The sun shone down brightly, reflecting off the water's surface, causing them both to squint. Cromwell shifted on his feet uncomfortably.

'I can see you have thought it,' she continued. 'You helped the king kill me, but what if I am one of many? Already you've helped him annul his marriage to one wife and murder another. What if he tires of Jane next? Will you help him kill her? And what if he then marries a Catholic, and steers England back into the arms of Rome?'

'He wouldn't,' Cromwell said.

'Are you so sure?' Anne replied. The two exchanged a look; Cromwell's expression was ringed with doubt. Yes, he had thought all this before. She could see it now. 'And what if,' she went on, 'after he has disposed of another wife, or two, or three, after he has reversed course on the religion of England a few more times, he comes for you? You might think that you are safe, sir. You might think that he won't turn on you, as he did to me, as he did to his friend Thomas More before me, and to Wolsey before that, and to Katherine before that. What makes you think you will be the exception?'

Two squawking gulls chased each other through the air above the river, each nipping in turn at the other's tail, locked in combat.

'The king is mercurial and always believes he is right,' Anne continued. 'You've been good at predicting his whims, at responding to them, catering to them, at staying in his good graces, but one of these days, you'll miss a turn of his mood, a change in his desires. He'll switch courses and you won't see it, and you'll become an obstruction to him. We both know what he does to obstructions.'

'What do you want from me?' Cromwell's fingers worried the hem of his velvet sleeve, and Anne remembered the leopard he'd kept as a pet, whose back he'd loved to stroke through the bars of its cage.

'I want you to make a different choice,' Anne answered. 'I want you to choose, instead, the princess. Choose Elizabeth. I will kill the king tonight, and she will be next in line to the throne. I want you to help her. I want you to secure her ascension, so that she, and not her Catholic sister Mary, is crowned. Sway the Privy Council. Sway the courtiers. Ride out to Hatfield at dawn and secure her safety. Be her protector. Be her instructor. She is already a child of the true religion. My chaplain, Matthew Parker, attends to her spiritual needs and will give her a proper religious education. You, sir, can educate her in the ways of politics and power, in the ways of court. You can be her regent, guide her and help shape England until she is old enough to rule.'

'What you are suggesting, Anne, is treason,' Cromwell cut in.

'How can it be treason if I've already survived my own execution for treason?' Anne snapped. 'By what miracle do I stand here before you? Is this not divine intervention? Is this not a sign that the Lord God speaks not through the king but through me? Does not the will of the Lord supersede the laws of man?'

Cromwell shook his head in disbelief but did not walk away. He stayed, considering.

Anne pressed on. 'Do you want your name to go down in history as a lackey to an unstable king? Or do you want to be known as the skilled regent who guided a great queen to the throne? Think of the opportunities for Gregory,' she added, calling up Cromwell's son, his only surviving child. 'Think of the marriage you could arrange for him, the ambassadorships you could appoint him to, the knighthood my daughter could grant him, the titles, the land. The Cromwells could become one of England's most powerful noble families.'

He looked at her, his expression softer.

She took his hand. 'Thomas,' she said, 'you know I'm right.'

30

Stalking Prey

The sword under Anne's skirts swayed to and fro as she marched through the palace confidently, her too-large gown billowing behind her. Cromwell's words stayed with her. 'I won't help you,' he'd said, 'but I won't stand in your way.' He'd gazed across the river and adjusted his velvet cap. 'And if you succeed, I will do as you ask. I will serve the Lady Elizabeth.'

'The Princess Elizabeth,' Anne had corrected.

'Yes,' Cromwell had said. 'The Princess Elizabeth. I will sway the council and court for her ascension. I will be her advocate.'

He'd told her that the courtiers would be busy with outdoor games this afternoon and the palace deserted. Just in case, he'd said, she wanted to position herself strategically somewhere inside. But, he'd added, he didn't want any details.

Anne walked to a window in the long white hall for which the palace was named and looked out on to the garden. The ladies of court, including Jane, were gathered under a canopy, sipping wine and eating cheese and fruit, while the men, including the king, played tennis in the covered court Henry had spent a fortune constructing. Were the men of court throwing their matches against the king? Certainly, Anne thought, for since his leg injury, he played poorly, and yet they would let him win, to avoid being the target of his tantrums and bad tempers.

Anne wondered what the ladies were chatting about beneath

their canopy. The paintings she'd hung upside down yesterday had been righted by this morning, and she was curious to know if the court had noticed, or if servants had corrected her work before anybody could see it. Even if her small perturbations had gone unnoticed, she knew they must be gossiping about the same ghost stories Cromwell had heard.

When hunting, it was best not to let the beast see you in advance of your shot, because the rush of fear spoiled the meat. If you had to chase a deer, you might as well let it flee, unless your only aim was to mount its antlers in a great hall, to show them off. Anne considered that a waste of meat. Think of all the people starving in the countryside – like the encampment of men she'd met. Though those men had turned out to be scoundrels, as their queen, she felt for their sorrows and struggles. Yes, when hunting, it was best not to be seen, but Anne wanted Henry to see her. She wanted him to be afraid. She wanted him to cry and beg when she stood over him with her sword, which after all the forest had given to her, as though in ordination.

Anne stood in front of the window for some time, hoping a member of the court would look over and see her; none did. But beside the queen's tent, the Green Man reappeared, shaking his bottom and leaping in the air. Jane and her ladies laughed as he shimmied about, and Anne wondered if they could see him. Perhaps he was real and not a fever-dream hallucination after all. Or were they laughing at something humorous in their conversation? She was too far away to be sure. The Green Man looked over at her in the window where she stood, traced a heart in the air, and blew her a kiss.

Thinking of hunting reminded Anne how hungry she was, how bottomless her appetite, how insatiable her need for food. She knew the kitchen downstairs would be busy with cooks and servants preparing the evening meal. In fact, the faint scents of roasting fowl wafted through the main floor of the palace. Not chicken, Anne thought. Something gamier. Maybe pheasant? She imagined they were cooking many birds to feed the two dozen or so courtiers outside – not a large group, just the king's favourites, but enough to require a dozen of whatever was being roasted. When she noticed the staff taking a break outside the servants' entrance on the north side of the palace, she sneaked down to the empty kitchen and pilfered an entire roast pheasant, which had been set on a table to cool. She wrapped the steaming bird in a kitchen cloth to protect her hands and hastily carried it back upstairs, where she sat on the floor of the gallery, eating it greedily, wiping juice and bits of cooked flesh off her face with the overlong sleeve of her gown. Bite by bite, she ate the entire bird. Satiated, finally, she left the carcass on the floor of the gallery – what did she care who cleaned it up? – and made her way to the king's chambers. Soon the gentry would be returning from their afternoon of play. Henry and his groomsmen would retreat to his chambers to dress for their evening meal. She needed to take her place now, while the palace was empty.

Anne was surprised to find the king's chambers unguarded. After last night, she'd expected to find a man or two stationed here, but she supposed those men were with the king. When she entered the king's dressing room, she was overwhelmed by a loud ruckus of chirping birds. The windows had been left open to let in the warm spring air, and over the Thames, an enormous flock of starlings swarmed together in a huge ball that turned in and over on itself hypnotically. One of Anne's childhood tutors had taught her that starlings formed these large clusters, called murmurations, to protect themselves from predators – safety in numbers. Though, normally, murmurations happened only in the colder months of winter and early spring. This swarm was out of season. These starlings should already be at their nests. Where, Anne wondered, was the predator they sought to confuse and outrun, one so fierce that it scared them from their broods? The loud chirruping of the birds – there must have been two hundred of them – drowned out all other sound, save for the resonating hum of their flapping wings. They swooped and swerved, swayed out over the river, then veered back towards the palace. Out, then in. Out, then in, their noise lessening and growing, lessening and growing. And then, all at once, they spun themselves up into a high column before bolting across the river and flying away.

It was then that Anne heard footsteps outside the king's apartment. Quickly, she hid behind the door leading to the bedchamber. Through the crack between the door and its jamb, Anne peered with one eye into the dressing room. Thomas Seymour walked into the room first, rosy-cheeked and jubilant, crowing about the king's wins on the tennis court, no doubt hoping to flatter his way into a position on the Privy Council, though of course everybody knew it was Edward Seymour, Jane's eldest brother, who was most likely to hold that position. Edward was responsible and prudent, whereas Thomas was a *bon vivant*, reckless and entitled. Thomas was, Anne knew, the kind of man Henry liked to hunt or play cards with, but not the type of solid workhorse he appointed to get things done.

Edward followed his brother, then came Cromwell, who must have joined them after he'd spoken to Anne along the river, and the king's three remaining groomsmen. Anne wondered about their morale. Until recently, William Brereton, Francis Weston and Henry Norris had all been among their company, a full half of the six grooms of the privy chamber. Their arrests and executions must have left the remaining three groomsmen rattled. The men looked tired, exhausted in the way that a person who is deeply disturbed but must pretend to be happy might look. Anne knew the look well. She had worn it often, pretending to be delighted in Henry's company when in fact she found his behaviour unsavoury, rude, domineering or arrogant. The weight of her mantle – Anne, the most happy – had often been heavy.

Henry entered the room last. Henry. Her Henry. It took her breath away to see him. He came straight into the room, facing her, as though he might walk up to the door, swing it aside, discover her hiding there, and embrace her. 'Oh Anne,' she imagined him saying in his booming voice, 'you live!' But of course, if his face was flush with love and happiness, with excitement, it was for Jane and not for Anne. It was for Jane, plain Jane, dutiful Jane, quiet Jane, Jane on whom the king was pinning his hopes of a son, Jane who waited, a patient bride, in chambers that just a week ago had been Anne's, Jane who was willing to sleep in a murdered woman's bed, fuck a murdered woman's murderous husband. Anne searched Henry's face for any signs of fear, but Henry did not look scared. He did not look perturbed by the ghost stories circulating the court, by the intruder found in his chambers yesterday evening. Anne wished he did.

The men talked of tennis and cards, of the feast tonight and the final wedding preparations for the ceremony the day after tomorrow. They talked of pheasant hunting and what jewels the king should wear this evening. They did not talk about the men missing in the room: Brereton, Weston and Norris. They did not talk about Elizabeth, or whether she'd been told of her mother's death, or whether she was scared or sad or lonely, or wanted her mother. They did not talk about the heads on pikes on London Bridge. They did not talk about George Boleyn, bright star of the court, brighter than all of them combined, or about his widow, Jane, or about Anne's mother or father or their sorrows, or of her sister, Mary. And they did not talk about Anne. Instead, they talked about sport and fashion.

Anne wanted badly to leap out from behind the door, her arms raised like claws, her face pulled into a grimace, and roar loudly, like the Green Man, to scare the king and his men, to rip the kerchief off her neck and reveal her brutal scar, to remind them all of the carnage they were so keen to forget, to carouse through and drink away.

'Here, look at me! Look at what you have done! I am the king's lawful wife, standing before you, shrieking and crazed. I have been given this sword by the land, and now I will use it to slay you all!' These were the things Anne wanted to say but couldn't.

A breeze through the window blew the door just enough to knock it into Anne, and it made a small thump. Most of the men didn't notice, lost in their discussion of hunting blinds and hound dogs, but Cromwell looked her way for a moment. She wondered if he saw her shadow through the crack.

And then the men swept out of the room as fast as they'd swept in. When she was sure they were gone, Anne stepped out from behind the door, trembling and out of breath, and steadied herself against the wall. She was shaken. There had been Henry, within arm's reach. Henry, who'd bewitched her with his love, who'd been her king and the divine head of her church, power on top of power. Henry, eyes like blue ice in a cold sea, sweeping, ready to demolish. Henry, who'd cried in her arms the night Katherine finally died. She wondered if Jane had comforted him after her death. Henry, whom she'd obeyed. If he'd told her to run naked through the halls of Hampton Court in full daylight, she would have done it. She would have done anything for him.

Anne crept to the dressing-room door and peered around it. Henry and his men receded down the corridor, heading towards the great hall. She moved into the doorway, hand at her throat, fingering the scar beneath her kerchief, its grotesqueness. It was hers now, a part of her.

Just as the men were about to round the corner, Henry turned and looked back. Anne froze. He was looking right at her. His face blanched. His mouth opened and moved to make words, but no sound came out. She held his gaze. Her Henry. Her love. Her destruction. The courtiers turned the corner, and Henry, pushed forward by the inertia of the group, turned with them.

31

The Altar

Anne needed to move quickly. She wasn't sure how fast Henry would regain his ability to speak, if he'd tell his men he'd seen Anne, his Anna Bullen, his Nan, standing there, corporeal, hand at her neck, in the doorway to his chambers. She wasn't sure if he'd send a band of guards to sweep the rooms. To look for what — a ghost? How would guards, with their swords and halberds, with their pretty livery and brass buttons, catch a ghost? He might keep quiet. He might keep the sighting to himself. He might question his sanity, or be concerned that others would, or be concerned that he'd scare off his new bride if he showed up in the great hall ranting about seeing his dead wife standing in his chamber doorway. Anne didn't know what he'd do, so she moved quickly. She needed to conceal herself within the chapel, now. She needed to hide.

She moved swiftly through Henry's rooms, fear mounting, blood rushing in her ears, the sword swaying to and fro beneath her skirts. When she reached the narrow corridor that led to Henry's private chapel, she ran. Her slippers, scuffed and worn from her nine days' journey in this odd afterlife, slid on the stone floor. She fell and landed hard, sprawled out on the cold stones.

It couldn't have been more than a moment or two that the world went dark. In those seconds, Anne thought, *Have I finally died? Where is my brother, George? Where is my dog, Purkoy?*

She thought she felt his wet nose on the palm of her hand, nudging her, his wet tongue on her face, licking her. She wiped her palm against her face, and drew back blood, coming into consciousness, realising she was on the floor of the corridor, that she'd hit her face with some force, that her mouth was bleeding, that the bleeding was coming from her lower lip, which throbbed, which she must have split in the fall. How was it that her body kept bleeding, kept staying alive? When would she be allowed, finally, to cease to exist? She stood. With her skirts, she wiped the drips of blood on the floor. Just a smudge remained. Anne hurried into the small chapel at the end of the corridor.

Henry's chapels were his sanctuaries, and every castle and palace he dwelled in had one. Anne had helped him design the privy chapel at Whitehall, though she'd entered it only once, when the construction on the entire palace was complete and Henry had taken her on a tour, showing off each room as if he'd built it with his own hands, rather than tasking Cromwell with hiring labourers to do it for him. The chapel was a small, octagonal room, connected to Henry's chambers by a single door. Each wall was adorned with a stained-glass window of various colours – none with images of the stations of the cross or the Virgin Mary or a tortured saint; those were just the kinds of iconography that the reformers, Anne included, were trying to remove from houses of worship. Before the back wall stood an altar, about four feet in height. The only other furnishings in the chapel were a couple of short wooden pews.

There weren't many places to conceal oneself here. Anne knew the altar, draped with a velvety purple cloth, had an open back. She walked around behind it, lifted its cloth covering, and assessed the space. It was small, only about three feet deep, but large enough to hold her if she curled up. She untied the sword from around her waist, held it in her hand, then climbed inside the altar and lowered the purple cloth behind her.

The smallness of the altar reminded her of the arrow chest she'd risen from, of its boxy shape, of its wooden build. Even the smell, of varnished wood, was similar. Anne's breaths grew fast and panic ran down her arms. She had the urge to crawl out, but she knew she shouldn't. She could hear guards sweeping Henry's chambers, their booted feet moving quickly from one room to the next, their grunts as they knelt down to peer under beds, the squeaky hinges of chests and cupboards opening and closing. They were being thorough. She could hear voices too, but from this distance, she couldn't discern what they were saying.

After a short while, the footsteps drew nearer, moving through the corridor and into the chapel. Anne caught her breath. Be still, she told herself, still as death. Pretend, she thought, pretend you are dead. Pretend you have been allowed to die. The guards moved around the pews, around the walls of the small chapel room, behind the altar. Anne could make out two sets of feet, pacing just on the other side of the purple cloth.

'Looks clear to me,' said one of the guards.

'Let's be sure to check beneath the pews,' said the other, and the footsteps moved away from the altar and out into the room, where the guards circled the pews, stopping before each one, and, Anne assumed, peering under it, to check for what? A woman clinging to its underside?

'A lot of fuss for a ghost, if you ask me,' said the first guard.

'I've never seen the king so panicked,' said the second. 'Running into the great hall, talking of ghosts, of his dead wife coming back to haunt him.'

'Sounds like a man with a guilty conscience,' replied the first.

'You should watch what you say,' said the second. 'The walls have ears, and you could get whipped in the street or worse for such talk. Ours is not to speculate about the king's actions, whether they were right or not, whether he's a good Christian man. Men have rights, if their wives turn them into cuckolds, and none more so than the king.'

'All I'm saying is that in the three years she was queen, and I was in the king's guard, I never saw her doing anything untoward.'

'Were you watching the queen that closely, that you'd know? Maybe I ought to report *you*? Were you one of the hundred men that she bedded behind the king's back?'

'Oh, pray you hold your tongue, William,' the first man replied, and both laughed. Anne heard their footsteps retreat from the room, heading back into the corridor, back into the king's chambers, where they rejoined the footsteps of the other guards, whose complaints sounded like mumbling from Anne's hideaway inside the altar. Then all the footsteps and voices left, and the chapel, the corridor and the king's chambers grew quiet.

So, Anne thought, she had scared Henry after all. He felt fear, enough to make a scene, enough to call the guards. Think of the scandal this would cause among the court, who would be whispering about his sanity, about his manhood, that he was seeing visions in the halls, scared of a shadow he imagined was his dead wife. A coward and a madman, not to mention a cuckold, which surely nobody at court had forgotten.

Of course, Henry hadn't been cuckolded by Anne, and he was not a madman; he had seen her. He was a coward, though, and not because he'd run scared from his dead wife's ghost. A person should run scared from the living dead, especially if the living dead was the wife they'd had beheaded. No, he was a coward for killing her without even talking to her, without giving her the chance to plead her case to him. He was a coward for not showing up to her trial to hear her speak, and he was a coward for not showing up to the Tower to see her beheaded.

But most of all, he was a coward for killing her, plain and

simple. He was a coward for being so threatened by his own wife's intelligence and ambition, for being so hungry for his male heir, for being so resistant to putting his daughter on the throne that he'd rather murder his own wife, whom he'd sworn to love and protect, than admit that he might not be right. That he might not be the most powerful, or strong, or capable or intelligent person in the room — that he might not be virile enough to sire a son. That the problem might be him.

She waited in the altar for many hours while the king and Jane and his courtiers dined in the great hall, while they drank wine and forgot about the ghostly woman the king claimed to have seen lurking in his doorway, forgot about the ghost stories circulating London about Anne's appearance at the Tower, in the forest, on Cheapside, forgot about the ghost the servant had claimed to see in Henry's room the night before. After all, the mind can play tricks on a person, can make a person believe they see things they do not. The king and Jane and his courtiers forgot about the ghost. They forgot about Anne entirely, about her death, about her supposed adultery, about her mouthiness, about her failures, about her very existence. They forgot about Elizabeth, sequestered at Hatfield, asking after her mother, crying softly into her pillow as her older half-sister tried to comfort her. They talked instead of Henry and Jane's wedding, of the sons Jane would bear. They toasted in conspiratorial tones about the wedding night, about the pleasures that awaited Jane. Jane's brothers, Thomas and Edward, toasted to the thought of the king fucking their quiet, obedient sister, they toasted to her betrothal, to the power it would bring their family.

All the while, Anne stayed crouched in the altar box. She thought about Alice, back in the fens, putting her children to bed, stepping outside the door to her father's modest home and admiring the stars, the way the breeze would brush the loose hairs from her face, would ruffle the little curls at the base of her neck.

She thought about how she'd like to kiss Alice again, about how much she'd enjoyed kissing her, about how much she'd enjoyed her touch, which was far softer than Henry's, the feeling of being held, of being admired, of being cared for, of being safe in Alice's keep. She thought, a little bit, of her need to be kept. That she felt safest when subordinate to a lover, Henry or Alice, and that she didn't fully understand why.

She thought of Zeus, the white bull, wandering back into the forest. She thought of how the forest had seemed enchanted, how Zeus had appeared when needed, how the sword had appeared when needed, how the very trees had seemed to glimmer with life and guidance, or had that been the fever that plagued her, that plagued her still, for wasn't she hot in this altar box? Wasn't she sweating and shivering? She imagined the Green Man – had he been real or an apparition? – leaving Whitehall and joining Zeus in the woods, where perhaps Zeus would deliver him into a stand of pines, and he would plant his feet in the ground and become a real tree. She thought of Mary, her sister, safe in the countryside with her children. She thought of her parents, safe at Hever Castle. May they stay that way, she prayed.

And she thought of Elizabeth. She thought of Elizabeth drumming her fingers on her face, calling her Mama, snuggling into her. Mama, Mama, I love you best. Mama, you're the best mama ever. Mama. Mama. She thought of how, even though she hadn't been able to nurse the child, even though she'd been whisked away when still a baby, Elizabeth's love for her was consuming and complete, of how the child knew her, loved her, wanted more of her, how that want was boundless. And she thought of how she loved her child, of how that love was consuming and complete, of how it was also boundless, of how she wanted to hold her daughter's little hand, just one more time. Anne adjusted herself in the altar box. Her back cramped and ached against the hard wood. Her legs went numb. She imagined

Elizabeth's hand in hers. She wrapped her hand around the hilt of the sword, and waited.

Eventually, Anne heard the doors to Henry's chambers open, and a cacophony of voices and footsteps. Henry and his men, back from the feast. The chatter of Henry's men continued for some time before, one by one, most left. She knew only one or two would remain, to help the king into bed after his prayers, to sleep on the floor beside him, keeping him company. She could hear the king's footsteps enter his bedchamber. She checked to be sure her stiff legs were concealed under the purple altar cloth. She imagined Henry disrobing, with the help of his men, getting into his loose linen nightgown, his silk robe and slippers. She could hear the slippers *shush shush* across the floor as he walked down the corridor to the chapel and entered it, closing the door behind him. The slippers *shush shushed* as he walked down the short chapel aisle to the altar, knelt before it, just on the other side of the wood she huddled against, and began whispering his prayers.

Anne froze. I daren't move a muscle, she thought. Be still, she thought. Be quiet, you wretch. But then, she thought, remembering her brother George's last words to her, Be bold. 'Be bold,' she whispered to herself, behind the curtain, inside the altar, inches from Henry's genuflected form. 'Be bold.'

She could wait no more. She lifted the purple cloth covering the back of the altar, stepped out of it, and stood over Henry, sword grasped in both hands, held aloft over her head, ready to strike.

32

Scream and I'll Kill You

Incredible, Anne thought as she stood over Henry, sword drawn. Incredible that he does not hear me, does not sense me standing here beside his kneeling form, so enraptured in his own prayers that he is dead to the world. What prayers was he saying? He spoke in such a whispered tone that his words were a murmur, indecipherable. Maybe he was reciting common prayers, Pater Nosters or Ave Marias. His Latin had always been impeccable. Anne had loved listening to the confident, evenly paced cadence of it, like a steady drum.

Maybe he was praying in English, private prayers for something more specific. Perhaps for the health of his new bride, Jane, asleep in her chambers. Perhaps he was praying for a son, the true heir he hoped Jane would deliver to him. Perhaps he was praying for enough virility to put an heir in Jane, for he was forty-four, his belly had grown soft and round, the hair at the crown of his head, Anne could see as she stood above him, was thinning, and certainly his occasional problems with impotence would only get worse. Perhaps he was praying for his foul-smelling leg wound to heal, for its stench was so great that it made Anne gag. Perhaps for a full return to his youth. Perhaps for his brother, Arthur, to never have died, to walk through the door of the privy chapel, velvet robes flowing, place a hand on Henry's shoulder, and say, 'Enough, brother, you can be done now. I am here.'

Incredible that he cannot hear me, has not sensed me, Anne thought. Remembering the silence of her own executioner, she stepped out of her dirty slippers. The stone floor beneath her stockinged feet was cool and soothing. Henry continued with his prayers. She could strike him now, she realised. She could lower the sword the countryside had given her and be done.

She gathered her strength, gripped the sword firmly with both hands, but something in her froze. And in that moment of indecision, Henry turned his head and looked at her. His face, now jowly, with faint lines around his eyes and mouth. Anne had known this face since Henry was barely twenty. She had watched its youthful lustre sharpen, then fade.

For a moment, Henry stared at her, silent. When he found his words, he uttered, 'Anne?' And if she hadn't known better, she'd have thought that she saw a flash of relief spread over his face, that he was glad to see her. He moved one foot forward, as though to rise from his kneeling position.

'No,' Anne said. 'Stay where you are.' She held the sword aloft above her head. 'Stay where you are, or I'll finish this now.'

Henry's eyes travelled to the sword. He was a smart man, calculating. He moved his leg back.

'Anne,' he said. 'How?'

Anne lowered the sword to her side. With one hand, she undid the kerchief at her neck, revealing the thick and jagged scar. Henry looked away, repulsed.

'No,' she said. She reached down and cupped his chin, turned his head to face her. 'Look. Look at what you've done. At what you've had done for you.'

'Anne,' he began, his voice sorrowful, 'please. Listen.' Did this man, who had spent the night of her execution drinking and dancing with his mistress and the half of his groomsmen that he hadn't also executed, feel remorse, regret?

'No,' Anne said. Then, 'What?'

'Anne,' Henry repeated, this time in a plaintive whisper.

'What?' she replied, her voice low. 'What?'

'Anne. My Anna.'

'I am not your Anna.' In the corridor outside the chapel she could hear footsteps. Henry turned his head towards the door. 'Scream and I'll kill you before they can open the door.'

Henry looked at her, panicked, assessing. He shut his mouth. The footsteps receded back down the corridor, into the king's chambers.

'What,' Anne said again, 'could you possibly have to say to me?'

'I want to tell you—' he began, but Anne interrupted him.

'How could you?' she asked. 'How could you make up such stories about me? How could you bring such shame to my name?'

Henry opened and closed his mouth, soundlessly.

'You know that I was never untrue,' Anne continued. 'You know that I knew no other man than you, that I was a virgin when we wed – which of course is more than I could say about you – you, who fucked every courtier's wife who'd raise her skirts for you, who fucked my own sister. I was a virgin. I knew only you. I loved only you. Only you. You. What could you possibly, possibly, have to say?'

Henry stared at her, his mouth firmly set, his expression hardening. 'You do not understand,' he spoke. 'You do not understand what it is to be king, to want, no, to need, an heir.'

'You had an heir! You had Elizabeth!' Anne's voice was a shout, but also a whisper.

'No,' he replied, and his voice had a cold edge. 'To need a son. To need a real heir. A woman cannot sit on the throne of England and govern in her own right. The people would not follow her.'

'They would!' Anne exclaimed. 'They would follow Elizabeth!'

Henry scoffed, narrowing his eyes. 'They wouldn't.'

Anne brought her other hand to the hilt of her sword, grasped it, and began to raise it. She didn't want to hear any more of what Henry had to say. Now was the time. Henry put a hand out to stop the sword from rising, perhaps to try to grasp its blade and pull it from her. She yanked the sword quickly, and it sliced his palm. He recoiled and looked down at the cut, as though he couldn't believe that his kingly body was capable of injury at her hands, as though he couldn't believe that she'd actually hurt him.

Blood dripped off his hand on to the stone floor.

'It doesn't feel good, does it?' she said, a hint of a smile on her lips. 'Imagine if that was your whole head.'

Henry moved towards her, his cut hand held forward. Like Christ's wound, Anne thought.

'Try that again and I'll cut more than your hand.' She thrust the sword towards him, threateningly.

He moved back. 'Anne,' he began again. He was silent for a moment, looking down and to the side in an expression Anne knew meant he was deep in thought. 'Anne,' he said, more confidently. He met her gaze. 'Whatever has done this, whatever magic has brought you back to life, 'tis a miracle. Drop your sword. You and I shall be reunited. We shall leave this chapel together, our union reanointed by my blood. We shall cover this deformity on your neck with fine collars, so no one shall see it. We shall tell the people that 'twas not you who was executed, but a look-alike. 'Twas not you who stood trial, but a look-alike.' Here he stopped, as though searching for words. 'We can say you were kidnapped, held for ransom, an impostor sent in your place, so canny she fooled even me, but devious. That – that –' He paused again. 'That the impostor's true nature shone in her whorish ways, in the way she bedded a hundred men at court. That upon her execution, your captors released you, their plan foiled, and you returned to me, my true queen.'

My true queen. Anne thought of the many times Henry had

called her that, whispered it in her ear. After they exchanged secret vows in Dover, at their witnessed wedding in the royal chapel of this very palace, after her coronation, when Elizabeth was born, at hundreds of small moments in between, at breakfasts and dinners, at parties and out hunting, at cards, in his council room, when she spoke over his advisers with a better plan, a better solution to whatever problem lay before him. *My true queen.* Anne marvelled at how quickly he'd spun this alternative history, this lie to explain her absence, this ploy to save himself.

'You can sit by my side,' he continued. 'We can rule together. If you cannot bear another child, we shall raise Elizabeth to be my heir. She shall rule after me. She shall be my successor.'

Anne looked at him, incredulously. He was so charming. *Charmant*, as Queen Claude used to say when François would visit her two or three months after she'd given birth, to impregnate her again, then leave to be with his mistresses. *Très, très charmant*, Claude would say sarcastically.

Anne didn't want to think about their happy times. She didn't want to think about their passionate courtship, about their wedding, about her coronation, about Henry holding Elizabeth lovingly in his arms as she called him Papa and tugged at his beard, laughing. She thought instead of the heartless look he gave her when she'd lost their son in January, of the words he'd uttered, 'I see God will not give me male children.' She thought of him gleefully following the mistress she arranged for him while pregnant to his bedchamber while she lay swollen and uncomfortable in bed, of the pleasure he took with this mistress in his bed. She thought of walking in on him in his chambers, with Jane on his lap, the bodice of her dress half-undone, his mouth on her breast, of how angry he'd looked when she shouted and threw the book she'd been carrying at him – how angry he'd looked at her for daring to be angry, for daring to show her anger.

She thought of how he'd double-crossed Katherine. How

he'd sworn to be her husband, then, enticed by Anne, a younger woman, and aware that Katherine was at the end of her child-bearing years, abandoned her. She thought of how he'd double-crossed Wolsey, his beloved adviser, who, once he could no longer do what Henry wanted, could not magick forth a papal annulment, had been arrested on Henry's command and mistreated so gravely that the old man had died of illness. She thought of how he'd had Thomas More executed, his friend and high chancellor, when More refused to betray his faith and acknowledge the king as head of the English churches. Anne didn't agree with Katherine, or Wolsey, or More. She hadn't liked any of them. She'd been relieved at their deaths. But she saw in Henry's treatment of them a pattern, of using and discarding people, of turning quickly to whoever stood before him offering the most, and quickly away from those who had outlived their usefulness.

She thought of how he'd double-crossed her, how he'd pretended to believe the lies about her infidelities, how he'd ordered her trial, ordered her execution. How he'd spent the night of her death in his mistress's arms, swilling wine and celebrating with his cronies, who, she knew, truly believed they'd be his cronies for ever, who didn't realise that they, too, were part of a movable cast of characters and would soon, like sins in a morality play, be cast out.

She thought of Henry lifting her up off the dance floor at Queen Claude's banquet at the Field of the Cloth of Gold, all those years ago, spinning her around, of how her heart had lit afire with his gaze, and of how he'd set her down and walked away to tease and fuck her sister. She thought of waking up, all those years ago, when she was twelve, in Henry's arms, as he carried her to bed at the archduchess's house, of how, when he'd looked down at her, when he'd laid her in bed and kissed her goodnight, she noticed, just for a moment, a look of lust, although she was a child.

And she thought of Elizabeth. Elizabeth. Henry's own daughter, whom he'd made an orphan. Motherless, because he'd killed her mother. Fatherless, because he'd bullied Cranmer into annulling their marriage, making Elizabeth a bastard. She saw, in all these stories of betrayal and heartbreak, that the common thread was Henry, that he would never change, that he would go forth in life destroying one thing after another, using up one person after another, taking and taking like a hungry animal, never satisfied, never still.

'Anne,' said Henry, his hands up, pleading.

She raised the sword above her head.

'Anne,' he begged, regretfully, like a child who'd been caught misbehaving.

She gripped the hilt firmly, felt the polished topaz inlaid there smooth beneath her hands.

'Anne, no.'

He looked from left to right, panicked, fear wild on his face.

'Anne, you don't have to do this.'

Be bold, she thought. She swung the sword around and down.

'Anne—' he spoke.

The sword sliced through his neck smoothly, in one swift blow, and his head fell to the floor, eyes open, shocked. His body collapsed, his neck issuing forth a torrent of blood that first gushed, then quickly dwindled to weaker and weaker bursts, until it only trickled.

The blood spread across the stone floor, reaching Anne's toes. It was warm and wet.

And then, he spoke no more.

PART THREE
Elizabeth

33

Of Body Small, of Power Regal

Did Henry's eyes blink once after his beheading? No, they fixed forward and did not move again. Anne stared at the mess before her, at the corpse she'd made, at the large pool of blood. She dropped the sword from her hand, and it clattered against the stone floor. Part of her had thought that once she'd killed Henry, she'd die too. She didn't. She grew suddenly hot, as though she stood before a blazing hearth. A window, she needed to open a window. She needed the air, and she needed to figure a way out of here, for Henry's men would soon grow concerned with the length of time he had spent in the chapel and come and discover him, and if she stood here, the dead queen resurrected, blood on her feet, murder in her eyes, she would be arrested and tortured. And Elizabeth, daughter of a verifiable monstrous woman, a man-eater who rose from the dead to murder a king — she'd likely be tortured as well, though a child, and possibly executed.

Anne walked, stocking-footed, to the easternmost wall of the octagonal chapel, where a small window overlooked the Thames. She left behind bloody footprints; her skirts left a smeary bloody trail. The window stuck a little. She had to push with her shoulder to open it. Outside, the Thames hurried by. In the corridor, she heard footsteps, more than one pair. A gentle knock at the door — the groomsmen would not want to disturb the king — a man's voice asking, 'Is everything all right in there, Your Highness?'

A pause. Two voices speaking in hushed tones.

A second saying, through the door, 'Only, we heard a clatter and wondered if you require assistance?'

Anne's heart beat quickly. She was hot, so hot. Beads of perspiration broke out on her brow, under her arms, at the backs of her knees. She clawed clumsily at the back of her gown, trying to loosen it.

Another knock. 'Your Majesty?'

An intense itchiness crawled across her skin. She had never been so itchy. She scratched at her face, her neck, the skin of her arms so ferociously that drops of blood appeared. She knew that she might scar her skin. What did she care? What did it matter if she marred this dead flesh?

'Your Majesty? Is everything all right?' More whispering outside the door.

What happened next happened quickly, and – though she had already risen from the dead, though she had already reattached her head, though she had found a white bull in the woods, though she had been delivered a sword from the land, like the old legends of Arthur's Excalibur, with which she had slain Henry – amazed even Anne. As the gentlemen whispered outside the door, the itchiness went deeper, seeming to crawl inside Anne's body. The heat felt like it would burn her up. She thought, Maybe this is it, what I have been waiting for, what the fever has been building towards, my work done, now may I perish? She looked down at the bloody scratches on her arms, and from one of them, a sleek white feather erupted, three inches long and attached to her flesh. Then another. Then another. Then a whole host of feathers covered both arms. She felt a pressure in her face and reached up to touch it. Here, too, feathers. And this was the last she had her hands, which shrank into her arms. Her feathered arms shrank too; her whole body shrank in size. Her head narrowed. Her nose and mouth hardened and curved outward into a yellow beak, her eyes widened into perfect circles and her vision sharpened, so much that she could see through the keyhole of the door, with startling clarity, the two groomsmen about to turn its handle.

Her legs shortened, pulling up towards her body, the skin growing thick and tough. Her feet split into talons that grabbed at the air as she tumbled to the ground, atop her gown and kirtle and smock, which had fallen to the floor as her body transformed. Elizabeth's silken swaddling cloth, the last of the stolen pounds from the Tower, the sapphire diadem she'd saved for her daughter, and the ribbon that Alice had given her lay nestled in the fabric. She'd have to leave them here. As her arms bent backwards, becoming wings, the song they'd sung about her at her coronation echoed in her ears:

> Of body small,
> of power regal she is
> and sharp of sight;
> of courage hault,
> no manner fault
> is in this Falcon White.

Just as the men of the privy chamber turned the handle of the door, Anne took flight, and she found that she had all the muscle and strength to use these new wings, to carry her small, feathered body out of the opened window of the privy chapel. She circled and dipped, flying over the garden and its labyrinth, over the secret centre chamber where she'd hidden, over the stone wall encircling Whitehall Palace, and out over the Thames.

Higher and higher Anne, the falcon, flew, and though it was night, she found that her vision was long and sharp, and that she could see all below her, all beyond her, all above her, in a panorama that stole her breath with its expansiveness. She soared above the river. She soared above London and Southwark, above the countryside. Perhaps this is what her insatiable appetite had been feeding, she thought, the falcon inside her. She swooped and glided in the night sky, freely.

As she flew, she imagined the scene the gentlemen of the privy chamber had encountered in the chapel. The king's body, divorced from his head, lying on the floor. The large volume of blood held in a human surrounding him, splashed across the pews, across the walls, across even the ceiling of the chapel, from the moment of decapitation. A trail of bloody footprints. An open window. Jane Seymour's gown, soaked in blood, crumpled on the floor, and inside it a red kirtle, like the one the dead queen had worn at her execution, a few pounds, a silk cloth, a ribbon, and a stolen diadem.

Would the court imagine Jane had slain the king, then escaped through the open window? Would they find her in her bed, asleep, her ladies swearing that she had not been elsewhere since returning from dinner and chastely bidding the king goodnight? What would happen to her? It did not matter to Anne, who flew higher and further, who left behind the gory scene, who left behind Henry, traitor and scoundrel, who'd held her heart once but did no more. Cromwell would be notified. He would rally support. He would do as she'd asked. He was a shrewd man, and powerful, a tactician. She would see him soon.

The wind blew through her feathers as she flew, riding the currents of air, weightless and unattached to anything at all. She dipped and turned. She opened her beak and let out a shriek, which was the shriek of herself and of many other women, too many women, calling out together, piercing the night with a mighty arrow of shrillness. *Enough! Enough! Enough!*

Her thoughts turned to Elizabeth. Elizabeth, her love, her heart. Elizabeth, at Hatfield Palace. She could fly there and see her. Yes. The excitement of the idea overwhelmed her, beat through her, uncontrollable. She turned and veered north towards Hatfield, the lyrics of her coronation song again echoing in her ears:

> And where by wrong,
> She has fleen long,
> uncertain where to light.

  Yes, she had been wronged. She had fled for a long time. But now she knew where to alight.

She flew with purpose, straight and true, over forest and field. When at last she reached Hatfield, she circled the palace. She could not recall which window was Elizabeth's, but her falcon vision was keen. She circled, peering into window after window. There, Lady Bryan, asleep in her bed, her lady's maid beside her, snoring. There, Lord Bryan, asleep in the chair in his chambers, beside the fire, head slumped into his chest. There, the Lady Mary, thin and frail, so often angry, but in slumber, peaceful. Finally, she spied the child Elizabeth asleep in her bedchamber, a little girl in a big bed, red curls spread out on the sheets around her like a beacon. Anne swooped low into the window, left open for the cool night breeze. She landed, wrapping her talons around the edge of the stone sill.

  The moonlight fell across her daughter, her beautiful daughter, her heart, her purpose, her daughter, her daughter. For a while, she perched and watched Elizabeth's chest rise and fall, rise and fall. The child turned in her sleep, wiped a hand across her eyes, shivered a bit. She must be cold, Anne thought, and she lifted one taloned foot, as though to step towards the bed and cover her daughter with a blanket, and as she did so, her talons erupted back into legs, and then her arms returned to flesh, her wingtips to hands, her head rounded back out, her feathers receded into skin, her vision returned to its human level, which now seemed dim, her beak bloomed back into a nose and mouth, and she stood there, completely naked, in her daughter's room.

Elizabeth opened her eyes. 'Mama?' she whispered, looking confused. 'Mama? Is that you?'

'Yes,' Anne replied. 'Yes, my dear, *mon coeur*, 'tis I, Mama.' Tears welled in Anne's eyes. She grabbed a linen sheet off the bed, wrapped herself in it, and went to her daughter, who held out her arms for her.

She swept the child up and cradled her, sobbing. Elizabeth reached her arms around Anne's neck, buried her head beneath the grotesque scar, breathed in deeply, and sighed.

'Yes, Mama, 'tis you,' the child said. ''Tis you.'

'Shhhhh,' Anne cooed. 'I am here. I am here.'

Elizabeth raised her head. She ran her small fingers across Anne's neck, across her scar, exploring her mother's flesh, which was her flesh. 'Mama,' she said, 'they told me you'd died, but I knew they were wrong. I knew you'd come back for me.'

'Oh, my darling girl,' Anne said. 'Of course. Of course. I love you. I love you so much. I am here for you now, but I cannot stay long.'

The child shook her head, frowning. 'No, Mama,' she said. 'Stay.'

'I cannot, my love,' Anne replied, knowing that she could not be here when Elizabeth's attendants entered in the morning, when Cromwell arrived with his allies to take the child back to London, to anoint her the next queen. She could not be seen with Elizabeth. She could not taint her reputation.

But she could stay for a little while. She carried the child back to her bed and crawled in with her. Elizabeth snuggled up next to her, thinking she had won the argument, that she had persuaded her mother not to go.

'Tell me a story, Mama,' she said, looking up at Anne, smiling.

Her eyelids were heavy, her blinks long. She'd always been a deep sleeper.

Anne held Elizabeth in her arms. Her Lilibet. She stroked her hair. Elizabeth closed her eyes.

'Once,' began Anne, 'there was a beautiful princess, named Elizabeth.'

Elizabeth nodded her approval. Like all children, she enjoyed stories in which she starred.

'And she was kind and good and smart, and everybody loved her,' Anne continued. 'But' – for now it was time to introduce the villain – 'she was held captive by an evil king, who'd banished her mother and locked Elizabeth in a tower.'

Elizabeth's eyes fluttered open. 'I do not like the evil king,' she muttered.

'Nobody did,' Anne replied. 'He kept a dungeon full of slimy toads and snakes, and when he spoke, his breath reeked, and he had many wives and treated them all badly.'

'Oh no! Did that make Elizabeth the snake princess?' Elizabeth asked, her tone worried.

'No, my dear,' Anne replied, 'for we do not have to walk in the footsteps of our parents.'

Elizabeth sighed in relief and closed her eyes again, snuggling back into her mother.

'The king declared that he would never let Elizabeth be queen, that he would marry woman after woman until one of them gave birth to a son, and he kept Elizabeth locked in her tower for safekeeping, where she was very lonely and cried all day long.'

'I do not like this king,' Elizabeth repeated into her mother's chest, half-asleep.

'But the princess's mother was resourceful and wise,' Anne continued, for now it was time for the heroine to enter. 'Though she had been banished to the swamps to the north' – Anne paused, thinking fondly of the fenlands – 'she endeared herself to the fairy folk who lived there by giving them gifts and listening to their troubles.'

'Oh, fairies!' muttered Elizabeth. 'How terrible! But good she was kind to them. Maybe they will help her.'

'Yes,' Anne said, amazed, even in this moment, at her daughter's intelligence, at her understanding of cause and effect, and of the outcomes of kindness and goodwill. 'The fairy folk showed favour to the banished queen and turned her into a mighty falcon.' At the mention of the word *falcon*, Anne's skin tingled.

Elizabeth nodded again. 'Mmm-hmmm,' she said.

'And the queen flew back to the palace, and with her mighty talons she pulled out the heart of the evil king, who died at her feet.'

Half-asleep, Elizabeth shuddered at the brutality. 'Her power is so big!' she said.

'Yes,' Anne agreed. 'The queen, as a falcon, flew to the tower and set the princess free, and the princess became queen, and ruled with kindness and wisdom and courage, keeping the welfare of her people first in her heart, and she never married, for she did not trust men, and did not want to give her power away.'

'But wasn't she lonely?' asked Elizabeth.

'No,' Anne replied, 'for she had her counsellors, and her ladies, and her maids, and also the queens of other nations to write letters to.'

'And her mother,' Elizabeth said, eyes still closed.

'No,' Anne said, holding back tears. 'Her mother could not stay, for the people would not understand how she had become a falcon, and would think her a witch, and think the princess a witch.'

Elizabeth said, 'That is very sad.' She slipped her thumb into her mouth and sucked it.

'Yes,' Anne said, wiping the tears from her face. 'It is, but the princess knew that her mother loved her, and would always love her, and would be watching over her, even if she could not be right there.'

By now the child had drifted off to sleep. Anne held her, and kissed the top of her head, which was warm and damp with child sweat and smelled like rising dough, wholesome and yeasty. 'I shall always love you, my dearest Elizabeth,' she whispered.

How much time passed? Maybe an hour, maybe two. Anne cradled the child, who slept in her arms, until the darkness began to recede with the first light of dawn, and the morning birds trilled, and she heard, in the distance, the clopping of horses' hooves and the turning of carriage wheels, which drew closer and closer to Hatfield Palace, eventually coming right up the drive to the manor and stopping outside it. She heard carriage doors opening and closing, and many voices. Cromwell's, louder than them all, boomed out, 'Good morrow, Lady Bryan.' The good lady must have been awakened, too, and come outside to greet the entourage. 'My apologies for the intrusion at this early hour, but we must collect the Princess Elizabeth.'

'Do you mean the Lady Elizabeth, good sir?' Lady Bryan asked. 'For we have been instructed to call her thus since her mother's death.'

'No, good lady,' Cromwell replied. 'The king has died.'

'Oh!' said Lady Bryan. 'Sweet Mary in heaven, what has happened?'

'He has been murdered at Whitehall. The Princess Elizabeth' – he said it again; how thrilling it was for Anne to hear her daughter properly called –'shall become the next Queen of England. I have come to bring her to Westminster, for her coronation, then to Hampton Court. You may accompany her, of course, as her matron of honour.'

'Yes, my lord,' Lady Bryan replied. Anne could hear an edge of excitement in her voice. She knew the woman loved her daughter. She felt safe leaving Elizabeth in her care, and in the guidance of Cromwell, shrewd as he was, to have already gathered support, to be already at Elizabeth's doorstep, to have already arranged for her coronation and ascension. He would usher her to power. Anne was sure of it.

She kissed the child, who slumbered still, one more time, and quietly, slowly, crept out of bed, so as not to wake her. She could not be here when Elizabeth's door was opened. Anne once again felt hot and itchy, but this time her transformation was rapid and painless. She hopped to the windowsill, the falcon once more, cast one look back at Elizabeth, her beautiful daughter, her love, her queen, her purpose – it had all been worth it – and flew out of the open window.

At first, Anne did not know where to go. She soared above Hatfield, above Cromwell and his men, above the big chests full of Elizabeth's belongings being carried out to the carriages. She soared out over the countryside, swooping and diving in the early-morning light. The sun rose over the eastern horizon, and its rise was magnificent. From her vantage point Anne could see the orange streaks it cast through the morning mist extend across the sky, over the land, and out over the North Sea, which, flying eastward as she was, she could also see, cold and sparkling and stretching out before her like a sheet of beaten silver. So many ships had crossed those waters, so many men, sailing from island to island, from peninsula to peninsula, conquering and raiding, thinking they owned the world. Anne flew out over the sea. She swooped and glided. She dived low and, with her talons, pierced a small fish she'd seen from high above – that wonderfully crisp vision! – and swallowed it whole. It felt good in her belly and so she caught and ate another. She felt satisfied, and free.

She followed the coastline north. She'd known where she was going long before she knew it. She'd always been headed here.

To a pucker in the coastline, a crooking inward, a river that broke into other rivers, that flooded the land, that bred fish and flowers and waterfowl, where a special people lived.

She was veering inland now, above an island in the fens, and she could see a small house, and in front of the house, Alice, in her nightshift running with her children — were they playing a game of chase? — and laughing, in the early-morning light. Anne swooped low. She could feel the legs that would carry her to Alice resting inside her talons. She would be safe here. She would be loved. And she would love, in return.

Author's Notes

This is a work of fiction. While I have tried to stay true to historical facts, some elements of the story (beyond the obvious speculative aspect of a beheaded Anne Boleyn rising from the dead and killing Henry VIII) have been altered for dramatic effect. It is not a biography of Anne Boleyn; other writers and historians have done better work there than I could hope to do.

Because many of Anne's writings and letters do not survive, I had to imagine a great deal about her. Most of the memories Anne has of her childhood are invented, as are the memories she has of her time in Mechelen and France, and many of her memories of personal interactions with Henry VIII during their courtship and marriage, with the exception of his words to her after her final miscarriage ('I see God will not give me male children'), the contents of his letters to her, and the argument they have the evening before May Day, 1536, although the details of that argument have been imagined. I do not know whether a young Anne Boleyn encountered Henry VIII at the Archduchess Margaret's palace in Mechelen, or at the Field of the Cloth of Gold, though she could have; those scenes are entirely invented. Likewise, the scenes with Leonardo da Vinci are imagined, though his time at the French court overlapped with Anne's.

In chapter 22, 'The Sweat', Anne sends Henry a golden ship as a New Year's gift. While that gift was really given to Henry VIII by Anne Boleyn, and was given at New Year's, it was more likely sent in 1527, not 1529, as presented here. While many aspects of Whitehall Palace described here are true, the labyrinth is entirely invented.

Although some elements of Anne Boleyn's trial are historically based, including the excerpts of speech Anne delivered to the jury, that her Uncle Norfolk sat on the jury, and the note given to George Boleyn regarding the king's impotence, others have been fictionalised for dramatic effect, including Cromwell's cross-examination. Perhaps most notably, while Anne and George were tried back to back in the Tower of London, the two were not tried together; Anne was escorted back to her apartments after being found guilty, and did not witness George's trial. I chose to combine the trials for concision as well as dramatic effect.

'Mr Fox', the story that George tells Anne when they are children, is an English folk tale. 'The Golden Bird', told by Ethel to the children of the fens, is an adaptation of the Grimm Brothers' tale; in the original, however, the protagonist is male. Howleglas, mentioned by Alice in the fens, is a trickster figure in English folk tales; several Howleglas stories are collected in Dave Tonge's *Tudor Folk Tales*. The first and final sentences that Boudicca delivers in her speech in Anne's flashback about learning about the warrior queen are Boudicca's words, as recorded by Tacitus (though it is likely he embellished for dramatic effect). The rest are my improvisation.

Anne's tallying-up of gifts bestowed upon her by the king, and of her 'barbs' in chapter 6, 'The Stews', are mostly true (or were things alleged against her, true or not, such as that she had a political enemy's food laced with laxatives), although some of those elements are invented (such as the glass and ruby rose). 'The people care neither for popes nor for popes in England, not even if St Peter should come alive again' was allegedly spoken by Thomas Boleyn, but I have put the words in Anne's mouth, because they felt true to her temperament.

There are historical disagreements about many aspects of Anne Boleyn's biography, including her year of birth (some say 1501, some 1507; I decided to use 1501), whether she is the middle or third child in her family (I made her the middle child), and how many miscarriages she had (I decided on three), and so I made the choices I thought best suited the character Anne Boleyn that I created for this story.

This novel required a large amount of research. Among the texts and resources I utilised were Eric Ives's biography, *The Life and Death of Anne Boleyn*; Tracy Borman's *Anne Boleyn & Elizabeth I: The Mother and Daughter Who Forever Changed British History*; John Guy and Julia Fox's *Hunting the Falcon: Henry VIII, Anne Boleyn, and the Marriage That Shook Europe*; John Matthews's *The Winter Solstice: The Sacred Traditions of Christmas*; Annie Proulx's *Fen, Bog and Swamp: A Short History of Peatland Destruction and Its Role in the Climate Crisis*; Natalie Grueninger's *The Final Year of Anne Boleyn*; William Tyndale's *The Obedience of a Christian Man*; *The Love Letters of Henry VIII to Anne Boleyn*; Robert Macfarlane's *Landmarks*; W. S. Merwin's translation of *Sir Gawain and the Green Knight*; guidebooks, audio tours and signage from the Clink Prison Museum, Westminster Abbey, Hampton Court Palace and Hever Castle (including Owen Emmerson and Kate McCaffrey's *Holbein's Hidden Gem: Rediscovering Thomas Cromwell's Lost Book*; Owen Emmerson, Kate McCaffrey and Alison Palmer's *Catherine and Anne*; and Jeremy Harte's *The Green Man*, all of which I purchased at the Hever Castle gift shop); as well as the Yeomen Tour, guidebooks and signage at the Tower of London; the Agas map of early modern London; and the podcasts *Not Just the Tudors*, *Talking Tudors*, *Rex Factor*, *Beheaded* and *And Also Some Women*. This novel owes a deep debt of gratitude to Hilary Mantel's Wolf Hall trilogy.

In her execution speech, Anne Boleyn proclaimed: 'And if any person will meddle of my cause, I require them to judge the best.' I hope that I have done so.

Acknowledgements

I would first of all like to thank Anne Boleyn. Although the version of Anne Boleyn in this novel is fictional, the real Anne Boleyn was a remarkable person – intelligent, full of ideas, a loving mother, ahead of her time in many ways – and she certainly deserved a better ending than the one she got. Thank you, Anna Bullen, for sitting with me while I wrote this novel.

Any novel is ultimately a collaboration, and I would like to thank my collaborators on this one: Renée Zuckerbrot, my amazing agent, who believed in this book from the beginning; Amy Einhorn, my editor extraordinaire at Crown; and the team at Crown who worked so hard to make this beautiful book, including but not limited to Lori Kusatzky, Patricia Shaw, Amani Shakrah, Christopher Andrus, Dyana Messina, Julie Cepler, Shasta Clinch, and Austin Parks. Many thanks, as well, to my UK editor Liz Foley, and the incredible team at Harvill: Rhiannon Roy, Lucy Chaudhuri, Christopher Sturtivant, Annie Rose, Susie Merry, Konrad Kirkham, Sarah-Jane Forder and Jane Howard. Thank you for your hard work on the UK edition of this book.

Thanks to my parents, Deb and Jeff Zich; and Steve and Holly Lehmann, for your ongoing love and support; and to my brothers, Jac Zich, Nick Lehmann and Keith Lehmann. Many thanks to my supportive in-laws, Chris and Paul Schuette and Phil Frye. Thank you to all of my friends, who encouraged me on the way to writing this novel, offered support, answered questions, lent a sympathetic shoulder, listened to me brainstorm, and whose friendship was a joy, including V. V. Ganeshananthan, Jo Luloff, Jennifer Corroy Porras, Andrea D'Agosto, Vanessa Hilliard, M. C. Hyland, Sandra Simonds and Marc Rahe. Thank you to Rebecca Hazelton and Melissa Ginsburg for talking with me about how poets write novels, and for their encouragement.

And, most of all, thank you to my husband Josh Frye, who took me seriously when I said I wanted to write a book about Anne Boleyn, and who loved and supported me in innumerable ways as I worked on this novel, including accompanying me to London on a research trip, and looking at way too many exhibits of early modern torture and weaponry. Lastly, thanks to my children, Asa and Zephyr, for their patience as their mother holed away at a desk to write, and for their continued inspiring and joyful presence in my life. I'd turn into a bird and fly across the countryside for either of you.

About the Author

Rebecca Lehmann is an award-winning poet and essayist. She has an MFA in poetry from the Iowa Writers' Workshop, where she was a Maytag Fellow. She is the author of three collections of poetry: *Between the Crackups*; *Ringer*, winner of the AWP Donald Hall Prize (selected by Ross Gay); and *The Sweating Sickness*. Her writing has appeared in *American Poetry Review*, *The Kenyon Review*, NPR's *The Slowdown* and the Academy of American Poets' Poem-a-Day. She lives with her family in Indiana, where she is an associate professor of English and Gender and Women's Studies at Saint Mary's College.